BY ROBERT MUCHAMORE

The Henderson's Boys series:

1. The Escape
2. Eagle Day
3. Secret Army
4. Grey Wolves
5. The Prisoner
6. One Shot Kill
7. Scorched Earth

The Rock War series:

1. Rock War
2. Boot Camp
3. Gone Wild

and coming soon ...

4. Crash Landing

The CHERUB series:

Start reading with *The Recruit*

HODDER CHILDREN'S BOOKS

First published in Great Britain in 2011 by Hodder Children's Books
This edition published in 2017 by Hodder and Stoughton

14

Text copyright © Robert Muchmore, 2011
Map copyright © David McDougall, 2011

The moral right of the author has been asserted.

A CIP catalogue record for this book
is available from the British Library.

ISBN 978 0 340 99916 5

Typeset in Goudy by Avon DataSet Ltd, Bidford-on-Avon, Warwickshire

Printed and bound in Great Britain by CPI Group (UK) Ltd, Croydon, CR0 4YY

The paper and board used in this book
are made from wood from responsible sources

Hodder Children's Books
An imprint of
Hachette Children's Group
Part of Hodder and Stoughton
Carmelite House
50 Victoria Embankment
London EC4Y 0DZ

An Hachette UK Company
www.hachette.co.uk

www.hachettechildrens.co.uk

GREY WOLVES
Robert Muchamore

*Hodder
Children's
Books*

WESTERN FRANCE, APRIL 1941

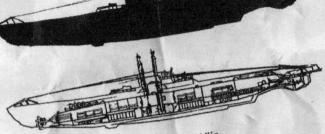

U-BOAT CLASS Viic

E-BOAT (MADELINE II)

- - -	BORDER
—	RIVER
▨	SEA / LAKE
↳	ROUTE SOUTH OF MADELINE II
⚓	E-BOAT
⊚	U-BOAT BASES AND BUNKERS

ATLANT
OCEAN

Part One

'The only thing that ever really frightened me
during the war was the U-boat peril.'
Winston Churchill (British Prime Minister 1940–1945)

In summer 1940 the German Army tore through western Europe,
conquering France, Holland, Belgium and Luxembourg in barely
two months. Britain was Hitler's next target, but the Royal Air
Force won control of the skies in the Battle of Britain, making a
cross-Channel invasion impossible.

Hitler's new strategy was slow strangulation: bombing British
cities and targeting vulnerable supply lines. With no European
allies Britain had to ship fuel, weapons and more than half of its
food across the Atlantic from Canada and the United States. But
slow-moving cargo vessels made easy prey for German
submarines, commonly known as U-boats.

By April 1941, over nine hundred British tankers and cargo
vessels lay at the bottom of the Atlantic. U-boats were sinking
ships faster than Britain could build replacements.

If the submarines weren't stopped, the British people
would starve.

CHAPTER ONE

Sunday 20 April 1941

Marc Kilgour had jumped out of aeroplanes, belted around the countryside on an old Triumph motorbike, shot a straw dummy through the heart with a sniper rifle, studied the correct procedure for attaching limpet mines to the hull of a boat, survived in the wild on berries and squirrel meat, stuffed dead rats with dynamite, swum freezing lakes and done physical jerks until he was as fast and strong as any thirteen-year-old was likely to get.

But training counts for nothing if you lose your head, and Marc felt uneasy squatting in the two-man canoe with damp trousers, an oar resting between his legs and Commander Charles Henderson seated behind.

It was near midnight on a moonless night – the only kind dark enough to infiltrate occupied France by boat.

The sea was calm, the air had bite and the blacked-out French coastline was a total mystery. They might have been fifty metres from shore, or a thousand.

They'd trained to drop into occupied France by parachute, but the RAF refused to spare prized bombers for espionage work. A fast torpedo boat for the long voyage down France's western coast would have been second best, but the Royal Navy was no more willing.

In the end they'd made the two-day journey from Porth Navas Creek in Cornwall aboard *Madeline*, an elderly French steam tug designed for harbour work rather than open sea. Their canoe was a leisure craft that had spent years hanging from the ceiling in a Cambridge junk shop, before being discovered by Henderson, who patched its cloth hull with fish-glue and pieces cut from a coal tarp.

The rest of their equipment was no better. The radio transmitter was an unreliable beast. Twice the weight of more recent sets, it left the canoe precariously low in the water and compromised the amount of equipment they could carry. Henderson had kicked up a stink, but Britain was fighting alone against a Nazi empire and CHERUB wasn't the only unit muddling through with scraps.

'Nerves holding out?' Henderson asked quietly, as his oar cut into a wave.

'Just about,' Marc said.

Henderson was the one thing that gave Marc confidence. He was a flawed human: drinker, womaniser, a short-tempered maverick who rubbed senior colleagues up the wrong way. But as some men turn genius when you give them a football, or set a maths problem, Henderson had a gift for espionage. He was completely ruthless, able to speak the five major European languages in a variety of accents, and had a magical ability to devise practical and sophisticated operations.

'Are those young eyes seeing things I can't?' Henderson asked.

Marc squinted, but could barely see beyond the end of the boat. 'What if the tide's carrying us further out?' he asked. 'I mean, are you even rowing in the right direction? Shall I take a compass bearing?'

Henderson gave a restrained laugh. 'You don't have much faith in my nautical skills, do you? Listen to the gulls. Are they getting louder or quieter?'

'Louder,' Marc said, realising that the gulls lived in colonies onshore.

Marc felt foolish: he might have been blind in the dark, but Henderson had been using his other senses to navigate.

'Clever old goat, aren't you?' Marc said cheekily.

A dark mass loomed beyond the bow. Marc thrust his oar out ahead of the canoe, then pushed hard against rocks jutting from the water. The boat tilted as its canvas side-scraped barnacles. Henderson threw himself sideways to counterbalance, but with the canoe so heavy it wasn't enough to stop water spilling over the side.

Marc threw down his oar and reached around to grab an old paint tin used for bailing out. He'd been soaked down one side when the wave came in and the pool in the hull now topped his canvas plímsolls.

Directly behind, Henderson tried pushing the boat off the rocks with his oar. The back end drifted out, but the bow was impaled on something. Marc bailed speedily, but the water kept rising. As no more had come over the side it could only mean one thing.

'Hull's torn,' Marc said, alarmed, but still having the wits to keep his voice low.

Henderson stood up. As he jumped on to the rocks the back of the boat rose up. He'd hoped taking his weight out might save the canoe, but the shift of balance set all the water running towards Marc at the front. The heavy case with the radio inside whacked Marc's back as the Atlantic engulfed his legs.

As the bow dived, a sharpened metal prong shot through the breach in the hull. Marc clambered up the tilting boat as she hit sand a metre and a half below the surface. Shallow water meant land was close, but Marc's relief didn't last. As he kicked to stay afloat his foot snared a coil of barbed wire.

Marc squeezed his face, stifling a howl. Henderson

had pulled two floating suitcases and a backpack on to the rocks before realising his companion was in trouble. He recognised the metal spearing the upright canoe as the leg of a tank trap. These criss-crossed metal tripods were designed to prevent tanks and amphibious vehicles driving up beaches.

Their presence was mystifying: Henderson had targeted a landing beach with cliffs beyond the sand. Tanks didn't do cliffs, so either the Germans had installed tank traps for no reason or they'd come ashore in the wrong spot.

But that concern was for later. Right now, Marc was stuck and kept himself afloat by locking his arms around the tank trap. In sheer frustration, he yanked his leg upwards, but the result was excruciating pain as a barb punched through his plimsoll into the top of his foot.

'For *Christ's* sake be gentle,' Henderson warned, as he knelt on the slippery rocks and leaned out. 'What if they're rigged?'

It hadn't occurred to Marc that the wire might be linked to an explosive. 'Eh?' he gasped. 'Do they do that?'

'Look on the bright side,' Henderson said. 'If you *have* snagged an anti-tank mine, neither of us will ever know much about it. Now pull your ankle up *gently*. High as you can without straining the wire.'

They'd expected wire, and Henderson had a pair of snips clipped to his belt, alongside his gun, holster and torch. As Marc pulled his knee towards his chest, Henderson felt blindly underwater, running a hand down the boy's leg until he reached the wire, and cut one side.

Marc expected the wire to peel away, but with barbs stuck in his flesh Henderson had to cut the other side and bring him up with a short length of wire still embedded. Henderson dragged Marc on to a flattish section of rock. The boy lay on his elbows and took three gulps of air, before rolling on to his back and studying the length of wire, with two barbs in his ankle and one in the top of his foot.

'You weigh enough,' Henderson said breathlessly.

Marc went up on one knee, braced for pain and ripped out the wire. As blood pooled into his sock he put some weight down on his bad foot.

'Think it's up to much?' Henderson asked.

'Hurts, but I'll manage.'

Henderson began lifting the empty canoe clear of the tank trap. Simultaneously a wave swept over the rocks, floating one of the rescued suitcases. Marc scrambled on all fours, grabbing the case handle as it teetered, but when he looked back he realised that one case was already missing.

'Where's the transmitter?'

'Six feet under,' Henderson said.

'Is it worth pulling up?'

'Not after a soaking,' Henderson said, as he threw loose rocks into the back of the canoe. 'I'll weight the boat down. The Germans will spot her when the tide goes out, but we'll be long gone, provided your leg holds out.'

The plan was to land on a lightly defended beach, bury the canoe and reclaim it for the return trip, but that wouldn't be happening now.

'Looks like these rocks form a natural jetty back to dry land,' Henderson said, as he handed Marc the snips. 'You start moving. Take one case and keep an eye out for more wires.'

Marc's wounds were excruciating, but Instructor Takada had taught techniques for managing pain. People calmly endured surgery in the days before anaesthetic and what were a few gouges compared to that?

In places the barnacled rocks dipped below the water and Marc had to paddle, though never above his knee. He held the case in front of himself, because that would hit any coils of wire before his legs did.

When the rocks ended his plimsoll squelched into mushy sand. There was a chance of buried mines, but it was too dark to deal with them, so the only strategy was to hope for the best.

'Keep low,' Henderson warned, when he stepped up behind, carrying the backpack and the other suitcase.

A shelf in the beach offered limited cover and the pair

nestled down. Henderson took a moment to find a small pair of binoculars and used them to scan the landscape.

'Anything?' Marc asked.

'Too bloody dark,' Henderson said. 'Though if we can't see them, they can't see us.'

The sea brought in a strong breeze, which rustled through reed beds beyond the sand. When the wind stopped, they heard noise coming from not far beyond. It was the sound of men in good spirits.

'Shall we move?' Marc asked impatiently.

Henderson traced the line of the horizon with his finger. 'If they've put all those tank traps on the beach, there *has* to be defensive positions along there. I'm not moving until I know where they are.'

It made sense, but Marc was cold and bloody. After four minutes of fear and pain, he broke silence with a childish whine.

'Come on, let's *go*.'

Henderson looked cross. 'It doesn't get light for six hours, but sooner or later we'll hear a door clank, or someone will step outside for a smoke. Until then . . .'

Henderson cut himself off because they'd been blessed with light. It came from a road beyond the reeds. The wavering front lamp of a bicycle was enough to make out silhouettes and, as Henderson had predicted, two pill-shaped bunkers bulged out of the reeds like frog's eyeballs.

CHAPTER TWO

Shivering and sodden, the white sand stuck to their clothes in clumps and got in all the places you don't want it to. A cautious five-minute crawl over seventy metres of beach had brought Marc and Henderson to the edge of the reeds.

Higher ground had brought the roofline of a grand house into view. The people celebrating were German men, officers judging by their accents. Apparently they'd not only landed on the wrong beach, they had found the Nazi high-ups' back garden.

This limited knowledge raised more questions. Were there men in the pill-boxes less than ten metres ahead of them? Could they walk on to the road where they saw occasional traffic, or were they behind the fences of a secure compound? And if they made it out of here alive, where the hell were they and how far from where they were supposed to land?

The squat concrete pill-box was the first problem. These circular boxes were a standard design, made from bomb-proof concrete, with an armoured door at the rear and a long open slot facing out to sea, through which mortars and machine-gun fire could be directed across the entire beach.

Henderson crept forward, while Marc stayed back with the luggage. It was impossible to move silently through reeds but the breeze and squawking gulls gave cover. Then came the first gunshot.

White birds crowed before launching into the air. Henderson assumed either he or Marc had been spotted and grabbed his pistol from its holster.

He looked up, but there was no sign of anything happening in the pill-box and no sound of men advancing through into the reeds, though Marc was spooked and crawled up frantically behind him.

'Where did that come from?' Marc asked.

Henderson gave a *don't know* gesture, then jolted again at a shotgun blast aimed high into the sky.

'Can't shoot for shit!' a German shouted drunkenly.

'In this dark,' the shooter said defensively. 'How can I see?'

With that, more pistol shots fired into the dunes, sending up plumes of sand and seabirds. This time the shotgun was more accurate and the Germans cheered as a gull fell out of the sky.

'Give me a blast,' another German shouted.

'Piss off, it's my turn!' another howled childishly. 'Do we have more shotguns?'

There were four or five men in the group. All drunk, all loud. Marc and Henderson couldn't see them because of the reeds, but the tone of the man who now took the shotgun indicated seniority.

'I'll show you proper Prussian shooting!' the officer shouted. 'Get some birds up!'

More pistol shots fired into the dunes, more frightened birds shot into the air and the muzzle of a shotgun lit up. But no birds were harmed and the officers began convulsing with laughter.

'He dropped the gun!' a youngster howled. 'He's so drunk he can't even hold the gun!'

'How dare you,' the German with the gun roared. 'I am your commanding officer. Do you want to spend next week painting decks with a toothbrush?'

To emphasise his point, the officer shot again.

Henderson and Marc buried their heads as the back door of the pill-box swung open less than three metres ahead. A fat, woolly chest staggered out. Its owner was barefoot and held up his trousers with one hand.

'Will you shit-for-brains keep your noise down? It's

getting so you can't grope a Frenchwoman in peace around here.'

A shout came back across the dunes. 'Captain Gerhardt, I had no idea your mother was in town!'

'You want me to come over there?' Gerhardt bellowed, but he turned back towards the pill-box. His heart was set on sex rather than violence.

The shooting game had run out of steam and one of the officers shouted, 'More drink!' to cheers from colleagues, who followed him to the house.

Captain Gerhardt seemed pleased with himself as he turned back towards the girl in the pill-box. 'Now, let's sort you out, eh?'

Henderson had decided to sneak up and knock Gerhardt out before he locked himself back inside the pill-box. A German uniform would be a useful disguise, even one that was too big for him.

But before Henderson made his move, a wine bottle shattered over Gerhardt's head. It had been swung by a petite French girl, who now stood in the doorway holding the neck of the shattered bottle. Unfortunately the blow had little effect on Gerhardt, who threw himself into a whale-like laugh.

'You'll get a good spanking for that,' he growled happily.

As Gerhardt forced the girl back inside. Henderson landed a knockout blow with the edge of his pistol. The girl screamed as Gerhardt toppled sideways. Henderson turned back to Marc and spoke in English. 'Get our luggage in and shut the door.'

The pill-box was lit with a single, tiny gas lantern. The floor was scattered with clothes and wine bottles. The terrified girl was a teenager, half dressed and shorter than Marc. She scooped up her dress before Henderson put a hand behind her neck and spun her body around to face the wall.

'Do *not* look at me,' Henderson warned, speaking in French now, but adding an over-the-top English accent. 'If you can identify me I'll have to kill you.'

Gerhardt was unconscious, but he was a big beast. Henderson didn't want him getting up, so he reached into a small pocket hidden behind his trouser belt and removed a deadly cyanide pill.

Pinching the nose forced Gerhardt's mouth open. Henderson caught a blast of foul breath as he crumbled the pill on to the German's tongue and clamped his jaw shut.

After a moment the hairy body began a series of violent convulsions. As Henderson stepped away, he saw the girl move slightly and shoved her face back against the wall.

'Do you *really* want to die young?' he asked.

Marc threw the backpack through the doorway before pulling the metal door shut and sliding the bolt. He could barely see his hand in front of his face.

'Not one word,' Henderson told Marc, jamming two fingers down the dying German's throat.

His gag reflex was still active and red-wine-coloured vomit shot up Henderson's arm before spattering the floor. Henderson tried not to breathe as he rolled the big German on to his chest and carefully positioned his face in the vile-smelling pool. It was an unpleasant business, but Gerhardt now looked like a man who'd passed out drunk and choked on his own sick. It was unlikely that any doctor would investigate further.

'Gather up the Captain's things and check his documents,' Henderson told Marc. 'Take his jacket and nothing else. It can't look like he's been robbed.'

'Is he dead?' the girl asked, as Henderson stepped up behind her.

'Very much so,' Henderson said, keeping his tone friendly, but deliberately breathing down her bare back. She was more likely to be honest if she was intimidated.

The girl tipped her head back and sobbed.

'I'm going to ask questions,' Henderson said, piling on the English accent. 'I'll start with a simple one, your name?'

'Delphine.'

'Delphine, that's nice. Now where am I?'

Delphine seemed confused. 'How can you not know?'

Henderson jabbed a finger between Delphine's shoulder blades as Marc read Gerhardt's identity document.

'You *don't* ask questions. You answer them, and quickly.'

'We're at Lamor Plage,' Delphine said, and then with a touch of sarcasm, 'Do you know where *that* is?'

Kapitan Maximillian Gerhardt, Kriegsmarine[1], *Underseaboat Section*, Marc read to himself. *Commissioned 1932.* There were photos, hard to make out in the gloom: a wife, a child sitting cross-legged with the family dog. The final picture was in colour and showed forty-eight men on the deck of a U-boat, with a pennant marked U27 and Gerhardt at the centre of it all.

Marc smiled. If they were shot dead now, they had at least accomplished something by blundering in and murdering a U-boat captain. Henderson was also satisfied: Lamor Plage was less than two kilometres from their intended landing beach and closer to their target. It was all good, provided they could make it out of here alive.

'What's the house?' Henderson said. 'What's it used for?'

'It was the beach house of Madame Richard. She cleared off before the invasion and now it's quarters for senior naval officers.'

'And what brings you here?'

'It's a party for the Führer's birthday.'

---

[1] Kriegsmarine – the official name of the German Navy during the Nazi era.

'Is that today?' Henderson laughed. 'Sorry, Adolf, I forgot to mail your card! So tell me, Delphine, do you enjoy sleeping with Germans?'

'My mother hates me coming here, but there's good food and they've always been very correct. At least until tonight when that great pig dragged me away and ripped my dress off.'

Marc studied Delphine as he brushed sand off his clothes. She had muddy feet and scratches up her legs where she'd been dragged through the reeds. She was clearly telling the truth, or something close to it.

'Do you know this area well?' Henderson asked.

'A little,' Delphine said. 'I live in Lorient. Twenty minutes' walk from here.'

'Is there a security perimeter around the house?'

'There's no gate,' Delphine said. 'But there's a checkpoint up where you turn off the main coast road.'

'How far away is that?'

'Two or three hundred metres.'

'And between here and Lorient, how many checkpoints?'

'On every road into the city, all around near the submarine base. Snap checkpoints can go up anywhere at any time, but not usually after curfew.'

'Thank you,' Henderson said. 'That's useful to know.'

'Are you a British agent?' Delphine asked. 'Because

you need to be careful. I don't mean to be rude, but your accent is a terrible giveaway.'

Marc stifled a laugh.

'I'll let my wife do the talking then,' Henderson said, hoping to throw Delphine even further off the scent by implying that Marc – who she'd barely seen in the darkness – was a woman rather than a boy. 'Now I'm *sure* you're trustworthy, maybe you're grateful that I saved you from that big hairy Kraut, but you *were* out here partying with the enemy. You might run back to the house screaming blue murder the second I'm out of the door. So I'm rather afraid we're going to have to give you a little pill.'

'Please,' Delphine sobbed, as she writhed desperately. 'I don't want to die. I might even be able to help you.'

Henderson laughed. 'Not one of the deadly ones, sweetie! It'll just put you under for three or four hours. Bit of a nasty headache when you come around. If the Germans ask, tell them you passed out drunk and can't remember a thing.'

CHAPTER THREE

After drugging Delphine, Marc and Henderson braved the back lawn around the grand house, cutting between partying naval officers with darkness working in their favour. Henderson wore Gerhardt's giant captain's jacket and howled a Bavarian folk song, while Marc exchanged *Heil Hitlers* with an Oberlieutenant rolling around the shrubbery with a champagne bottle wedged down his trousers.

To avoid the checkpoint by the main road, the pair climbed a stile and crossed a couple of untended fields before hitting a dirt track, aiming roughly towards the small naval town of Lorient.

Marc and Henderson had operated in occupied France the previous year, and knew that German forces were spread thin, even in high-security zones near the coast. This was unavoidable: the Germans had conquered half a continent and there weren't enough of them to go around.

But millions of French civilians had evacuated south when Hitler invaded the previous summer, and one way of reducing trouble in the northern coastal zones was to keep the population down by not letting refugees return.

The result was untended land and houses left to rot through the past winter. It was a nightmare for people who wanted to get home, but a godsend for Marc and Henderson who needed a bolthole where they could hide some of their equipment, and transform their appearance from sandy new arrivals to a respectable French father and son, down on their luck and hunting for work.

They skirted around two villages at a brisk pace before finding a suitably remote farmhouse. Its unoccupied state was obvious from the empty chicken coop and overgrown lawn. The back door didn't need forcing because thieves had already ransacked the place.

What they'd taken reflected severe shortages France had suffered that winter. Glass candlesticks and figurines stood unmolested on a window ledge, metal pans hung over the kitchen range, but there wasn't a tin of food, nor a coal in the fireplace. Anything you could chop and burn had been stripped out: curtains, doors, bedding. Only splinters and hinges remained from a kitchen dresser.

'Cold and hungry thieves,' Henderson said, as he turned the kitchen tap.

After a dead moth and some sediment came cleanish water. Marc had found the stub of a candle. He struck a match and placed the flickering light under the dining table so that it wouldn't be obvious from outside.

'How's the foot?' Henderson asked.

'Ankle's swollen up,' Marc said. 'Doesn't hurt much though.'

'Salt in seawater is a natural antiseptic,' Henderson said. 'Once you've had a wash I'll put some iodine on the wound and bandage it. Then you can get a few hours' rest.'

'What are we gonna do without the transmitter?' Marc asked, as he sat on a dining chair, unlacing his plimsoll.

'We have our fall-back rendezvous aboard *Madeline* tomorrow night,' Henderson said.

'But we lost the canoe,' Marc said, as he pulled off his plimsoll, getting a damp rubbery smell and a shot of pain up his leg. 'And that idiot Rufus dropped us off at the wrong beach, so what are the chances they'll be at the right area when it's time to pick us up?'

'We've got time to think it all through,' Henderson said. 'If we get stuck, we'll have to go south and try getting over the mountains into Spain. There are always options. In this game the only certainty is that things won't go to plan.'

Straw and a sleeping bag on the kitchen floor was paradise compared to the previous two nights aboard *Madeline*. The old tug offered a choice between a sodden rear deck, or the cramped triple bunk below deck next to the heat and racket from the steam boiler. Marc had tried both and slept in neither.

Nerves and pain made it hard to get to sleep, but once he'd won that battle, Marc was out until morning. The new day had a good feel to it, with a clear sky and warm air. He'd washed before bed, so he felt clean and cosy, and didn't want to get up as he picked sleep out of his eyes.

Henderson's sleeping bag was laid out on the opposite side of the dining table, but he was already up.

'Still alive then?' Henderson said, stepping in from the back yard where he'd been banging the sand out of his boots. 'I've made every boy's favourite breakfast.'

Marc's bandaged ankle had bled overnight. Clotting blood had glued the bandage to the sleeping bag, but the pain was tolerable as he stood up. He scratched himself, and smiled when he saw a slab of high-energy chocolate and a small tin of condensed milk.

'I've put most of our reserve equipment up in the loft,' Henderson explained. 'We'll come back if we need it.'

'What if the thieves come back?' Marc asked.

'There's plenty of wood to strip out on this floor. It'll

be all right here for a day or so.'

Marc's chocolate was rock hard and he warmed it in his hand before dipping it into the gloopy strands of thickened milk. Condensed milk was a rare luxury and he loved chocolate, but it made heavy going first thing in the morning.

'Eat up, it might be all you get today,' Henderson said. 'We've got a couple of fake ration cards but even if they're the right kind I doubt there'll be much in the shops.'

'I never get my appetite until I've been up for a bit,' Marc said. 'I checked Delphine's documents while you were interrogating her, by the way. Her ID and tobacco card looked exactly like our fakes, but her bicycle permit and ration card were different colours and she had an extra document that looked like it was specific to this area.'

'It'll be tricky getting into town to photograph the U-boats,' Henderson said, as he looked inside his boot before shaking out more sand. 'But Madame Mercier lives on the outskirts. We can get to her if she's home, and she might know a sneaky way into town.'

'That's if she's still living at the same address,' Marc said.

Henderson smiled. 'It's your bloody optimism that keeps me going, Marc. Now start getting dressed. Those plimsolls are horribly bloody and sure to raise questions. Can you walk barefoot?'

'I've lived the high life since I arrived in England, but I've been a barefoot orphan most of my life.'

They set off after Marc had dressed and taken a shit, Henderson carrying a flour sack filled with a few clothes and possessions to make it look like he was nothing but a poor peasant looking for work. Marc took a small hunting-knife, which wasn't unusual for a country boy, while Henderson had a small camera hidden in the lining of his hat and his pistol tucked into the back of his trousers.

The gun was a risk. It meant certain arrest if they were searched at a German checkpoint, but Henderson didn't want to go unarmed until he was sure they had all the correct passes and documents.

Henderson knew where they'd landed the previous night, and roughly how far and in which direction they'd walked, but it still took a while to work out exactly where they'd wandered in the dark. They moved cautiously, not wanting to blunder on to a major road, or worse, a German checkpoint.

The sun was bright and they both had a sweat up by the time they reached their target in Queven, a prosperous settlement less than two kilometres from Lorient itself. Madame Mercier lived on a curving street lined with detached villas, the kind of place you'd expect a doctor or lawyer to live with his family.

Marc and Henderson felt out of place here in their peasant corduroys and rough shirts. They noted parked cars and telephone wires going into the villas, neither being a good sign because only Germans were allowed to have them.

An agent approaching a strange house must strike a balance. You can blunder into a trap if you don't scout an area carefully, but walking around several times, peeking over hedges and looking through letterboxes, can arouse suspicions of nosy neighbours or passing cyclists.

Number eighteen sat behind high railings, with palms sprouting over the top. Alongside the villa a bare-chested man chopped firewood. At first they assumed he was a servant, but his boots had sheen, and his grey trousers were those of a shore-based Kriegsmarine rating.

Henderson gave Marc a little *keep walking* nudge, but the German had seen them peer through. He looked up and spoke bad French.

'Good morning, may I help you?'

'I'm looking for a Madame Mercier,' Henderson said, trying to make it sound unimportant. 'She used to live here, I believe.'

'She upstairs. You want?' the German said, as he stepped towards the gate to let them in while shouting, 'Madame, there is a persons here to see you.'

'Charles Hortefeux,' Henderson said, as the front door opened.

The woman who emerged on to the front doorstep was large in all directions, and looked like she'd been up late the night before. She wore a turquoise negligee, with the previous day's make-up blurred over her face and the short stubbly hair of a lady who was not usually seen without a wig.

'I don't know any Hortefeux,' the woman blasted, as she eyed the man and barefoot boy with contempt. 'And I don't need gardeners, window washers, or whatever other scheme you have to part me from my money.'

Henderson was prepared for a difficult introduction to Madame Mercier, but having the young German gawping at them from only a couple of metres away made it far worse.

'Well, Madame, if you're sure,' Henderson said, as he pulled a small photograph out of his pocket. It showed three men, with Big Ben in the background. 'Can I just leave you with this business card, in case you change your mind?'

'If it gets rid of you,' Madame Mercier said, snatching the photo, but becoming flustered when she recognised the three men. They were Polish soldiers, whom she'd helped to escape from France a few months earlier.

'Oh, Mr Horte*feux*,' she said, after a pause. She pointed accusingly at the German. 'Klaus, your accent is terrible! I thought you said Hautedeux. Well come in, how the devil have you been? Is this your son, all grown up now?'

The hallway had billowing rose curtains, china poodles, ship's bells, stuffed flamingos, a collection of cocktail shakers and the head of an ocelot. Marc choked on talc, perfume and cat.

'Is it private here?' Henderson asked quietly. 'Are any other Germans billeted in your house?'

Madame Mercier laughed, as she led them into a similarly over-the-top lounge with an evil-looking moggy skulking by the back window.

'Klaus doesn't live with me. I have an arrangement with a *very* senior officer. He's fallen for one of my best girls, but can't afford her prices. Instead he sends someone over, to mow the lawn and chop wood and suchlike, which is a good arrangement because it's impossible to get a man in for anything these days.'

'So the Germans didn't shut your business down, Madame Mercier?' Henderson asked, smiling coyly.

'Do call me Brigitte,' she said, peering through the windows to make sure that Klaus had gone back to chopping. 'The uniforms may change, but men's urges stay the same: cheap booze and easy women. Lorient has always been a navy town. The French and British shipped out and my clubs and bars were full of Germans within a fortnight. I've got places all along the main drag in town. Three upmarket ones reserved for the Krauts; the other three are for locals and the construction teams working on the U-boat bunkers.'

'Quite a little empire,' Henderson nodded. 'Would you like to know about your three former employees? Soloman was kind enough to write a letter of introduction for me; though I'm afraid it got rather soggy.'

But Madame Mercier had turned her attention to Marc, pinching his right cheek and yanking his head up.

'Is he your son, Mr Hortefeux? *Lovely* strong shoulders on him. I bet he'll break some hearts when he's older!'

Marc felt like he was being attacked by a powder puff as Henderson fought off laughter.

'And his little bare feet. Poor puffin! We'll have to find him some boots.'

'That would be useful,' Henderson said. 'Thank you.'

'So let's hear about my three young friends,' Madame Mercier said, as she gave Marc breathing space and unravelled a letter on tissue-thin paper. 'They all made it safely across?'

'They had a rough ride as I understand,' Henderson said. 'But they did well enough, especially considering that none of them are sailors. And of course, they never would have made it without your help.'

Madame Mercier looked down at herself modestly. 'I didn't do much, except put them in touch with some fishermen. Oh, and we hid them in a back room at one of my clubs while the Gestapo were out hunting. They're lovely boys. It's good to know they made it to Britain safely.'

'Of course, my son and I didn't travel from Britain to update you on your friends' safe arrival,' Henderson said. 'When the Polish gentlemen were debriefed, they told us that you're no fan of Germans and one of the best connected people in town. Lorient has the largest U-boat base in France. Those awful things are tearing British shipping apart in the Atlantic and we need to put a stop to it.'

'And how do you intend to do that?' Madame Mercier asked. 'With one man and one boy?'

'We're on an information gathering mission,' Henderson began. 'We've got until tonight to find out all we can about this area. Everything from details of bus timetables and curfew regulations, to identity documents, the layout of the U-boat pens, German supply lines and security precautions.

'When we get back to England, we'll analyse the information. If it looks promising, we'll come back for the long haul, for a full-scale sabotage operation. Frankly, Madame Mercier, you're the only intelligence contact we have within fifty kilometres of here. I doubt we can pull this off without you, especially as we've lost our canoe.'

Madame Mercier paused to think. Marc was anxious, not just because he was terrified she'd maul him again, but because they'd spent a month planning this mission and Henderson had staked his unit's reputation on a hunch that she'd be prepared to help them.

'Those Boche bastards killed my father, uncle and both of my brothers in the Great War,' Madame Mercier said finally. 'The thought of them in *my* country telling *me* what to do makes my spine crawl. So, Mr Hortefeux, tell me what you need and I'll do my best to help.'

CHAPTER FOUR

For all Henderson knew Madame Mercier might pick up a telephone, speak to a friendly German and have them manacled inside a Gestapo cell within a few hours. A spy operating behind enemy lines has to balance risks. Trusting your life to a stranger is the biggest risk you can take, but a spy who takes no risks will get nothing done.

'So why bring a boy along with you?' Madame Mercier asked, as she sat in her armchair studying Marc and Henderson's fake documents.

'Nothing more suspicious than a man operating alone,' Henderson explained.

'But a terrible risk for him if you're caught,' she noted.

'There's thousands of kids in London getting bombed every day,' Marc said. 'I'd rather be out here doing something, than huddled in some tin shelter waiting to get blasted. We've been well trained and we're all volunteers.'

'That's a fine attitude,' Madame Mercier said, as she leaned forward and spread their fake documents out across her coffee table. 'You need a Lorient zone permit and up-to-date ration and tobacco cards. If you get stopped in town with this lot, you'll be arrested.'

Marc sighed. 'So we can't go into town?'

'Go to the station first,' Madame Mercier explained. 'They issue temporary ration cards for newly arrived passengers. Then go straight across the street to the OT recruitment office. They're desperate for men to work in construction on the U-boat bunkers. If you register for work, they'll issue your zone permit. Once you have your zone permit, you can go to the main post office and register to get a permanent ration and tobacco card, plus a bicycle permit if you think you'll need one.'

'That sounds like the best part of a day spent standing in queues,' Marc said miserably.

'But we'll get original copies of all the documents we need to forge if we're sending a bigger team in,' Henderson said gratefully. 'The big question is, how do we get through security into town in the first place?'

Madame Mercier smiled. 'I'm sure Klaus would much rather drive you into the station than stand in the sun chopping wood. When you have your documents, walk over to Le Chat Botté. I'll arrange for your lunch and see if I can find someone who can help with your other requirements.'

'You're too kind,' Henderson said, as he ran his knuckles along the back of Madame Mercier's cat.

*

Lorient was well secured. All the minor roads into town were bricked off and traffic funnelled through three checkpoints on the main roads. There were two lines: a fifteen-minute line for the locals and a priority gate for German traffic.

Klaus drove a clattering Renault van that had been requisitioned from a butcher. Henderson got in the front passenger seat. Marc squatted on the floor in the rear compartment, horrified by crusts of blood and dried-out fat.

The town could have been any of a thousand small French cities, awash with grey stone and flaking paint that felt drab, even on this sunny morning. It seemed the occupiers had reduced life to a series of queues. Henderson saw queues for bread, queues for coffee and potatoes, queues at checkpoints. And because large queues bred resentment, there were small queues where you took a numbered ticket to join a bigger queue at a specified time later in the day.

The quietest place in town seemed to be the station. Lorient was the end of the line, with six platforms. But there were no trains and only one ticket window out of eight open for business. The Germans didn't want civilians in Lorient so they'd cut trains down to one every three hours. The only lively parts of the station were a barber's shop and the line for the public telephones.

Klaus led them through the station security checkpoint and took them straight to the head of a dozen-strong queue for temporary ration cards. The German's presence implied authority and the woman behind the counter took Marc and Henderson's false names and gave the briefest of glances at their ID before issuing ration cards with four days of coupons.

Klaus pointed out the offices of Organisation Todt (OT) across the square, before saying that it was time for him to return to barracks. OT was in charge of all major construction projects within Hitler's empire, from autobahns and airports in Germany, to military defences, factories, prison camps and bunkers in the occupied territories.

It was a quasi-military organisation. Officers carried pistols and Nazi daggers and wore brown uniforms with swastikas and stripes bearing their ranks. OT workers ranged from Polish and African prisoners treated like slaves, through to skilled and relatively well-paid civilian construction workers.

The recruitment office smelled of floor polish and cigarette smoke. Men lined up before three counters, where names and details were taken. Beyond that, job applicants were stripped and examined by a doctor. At the far end of the hall was an X-ray machine, where each shirtless worker was checked for tuberculosis.

Along the walls were blackboards, with available jobs and application details chalked up: *Blacksmiths, carpenters, plumbers, translators and electricians are allowed to join the priority queue. Unskilled labourers must be aged between 18 and 55. Boys 13–17 will be taken as apprentices at one-third standard pay. All workers must sign two-year contracts.*

Henderson was alarmed by what he saw, partly because he still had his gun and partly because he'd noticed that workers were being taken outside and loaded straight on to trucks to begin work.

'I think we'll have to risk doing without the zone passes,' he whispered to Marc.

As he turned for the exit a brown uniform blocked his path. By the sound of his voice, he was a native Frenchman.

'May I ask why you're leaving, sir?'

'I see the men are being shipped out straight away,' Henderson explained. 'I'd really like to go to the post office and collect my ration card first.'

'What is your address?' the man asked.

Henderson shook his head. 'I've just come in on the train from Rennes to sign up.'

'Then you and your son will be allocated

accommodation in the workers' barracks. Meals will be provided on site, and you'll receive a ration card for time spent on leave. You can stay in the queue, there's no reason to go to the post office.'

'I'd also like to make a telephone call,' Henderson said, though he knew it sounded weaselly.

'Do you already have a Lorient zone pass?'

Henderson shook his head. 'I just arrived.'

'You're not allowed to move freely in the Lorient zone without a Lorient zone pass. If you leave this building without a pass, I'll be forced to arrest you and hand you over to the Gestapo for questioning.'

The tense conversation had attracted some attention, including that of a more senior officer. This one was tall and skinny. He was German, but his French was good.

'Step away from the doors!' the German yelled, pointing his arm towards a dilapidated table. 'Spread your documents on the table.'

Marc's nerves jangled as he followed Henderson up to the desk. The German took Henderson's ID card and studied it carefully, before starting a round of rapid-fire questions designed to catch out liars.

'What was your job in Rennes?'

'Unemployed,' Henderson said, giving an answer that he'd meticulously prepared before leaving Britain.

'Your military status?'

'I have army discharge papers,' Henderson said,

pointing to them on the table.

The lanky German took the pale-blue discharge document. This was vital for any Frenchman under the age of fifty. Unless you could prove that you weren't in the military at the time France surrendered, you were regarded as a prisoner of war and could be sent to a labour camp in Germany.

'Dishonourable discharge from military duty, 1938,' the German said suspiciously. 'What was your sin?'

'Inappropriate firing of a gun in an enclosed space leading to the injury of a fellow soldier,' Henderson explained.

The German read the rest of the story from the discharge document. 'Served four months' military detention, released 13-04-39. Show me your teeth.'

Henderson opened his mouth.

'Those aren't smoker's teeth. Why have you got a tobacco card?'

The question was a trap. Everyone in France kept a tobacco card. Non-smokers gave their cigarettes away to family members or sold them, but technically your tobacco ration was only for personal use.

'Maybe I should call the Gestapo,' the German teased. 'You're clearly involved in black market tobacco trading.'

Henderson thought about offering a bribe, or pulling his gun. But both were risky options.

'Fine, I'll get back in the queue,' Henderson said,

before giving a cheeky Nazi salute. 'Heil Hitler!'

'I don't like that smart mouth,' the German said, as a few of the men in the recruiting line laughed. 'I'm going to have to ask you a few more questions in my office.'

*

Marc and Henderson ended up on a bench in the office of a man who clearly wasn't a major cog in the Nazi machine. There was a metal shelf unit and a small desk on which sat a vase containing three mini-swastika flags and some tattered silk flowers. Henderson hadn't been searched, so he had his gun ready when the brown-uniformed officer came back in the room and made a big show of opening his briefcase.

'How long have we got to sit here for?' Marc asked.

The German didn't reply. He just stared over the rims of his octagonal glasses as he took out bread and cheese wrapped in greaseproof paper. His expression said it all: *I'm messing with you because I can.* When he left, he locked the door again.

'I could pick that cheap lock with my penis,' Marc said contemptuously. 'Why are we still sitting here?'

'You need to learn patience,' Henderson replied. 'You saw where we are. There's a guard on the main door. There's a checkpoint on the station across the street. This isn't a game, you know. One mistake and we're big red splats machine-gunned up against a wall in some alleyway.'

The door opened again, but instead of the German it was a gravel-voiced Frenchwoman. She looked a bit of an old battleaxe, but she closed the door and spoke in a guilty whisper.

'Hortefeux?'

Henderson nodded and the woman threw over an envelope.

'Had to wait for old shit breath to go out for lunch. You needn't have panicked at the door. Madame Mercier called ahead; I was all set to deal with you. I get zone passes for all the girls she brings in for her clubs. Everything you need is there, including ration cards. I've put your occupation as a waiter, so you should be able to move around the centre of town without too many questions asked.'

'What happens when the beanpole gets back from lunch?'

The woman laughed. 'Thinks he's Hitler's right-hand man, but he's a jumped-up doorman. I'll tell him that we had orders to put everyone on a truck. He'll stamp his little boots, but he's too lazy to make a fuss.'

'And the other fellow on the door, the Frenchman,' Marc asked. 'Where's he?'

'I've set him straight,' the woman said. 'He takes a few francs from Madame Mercier, just like the rest of us. You need to get to Le Chat Botté. Someone will be waiting for you.'

The woman led them down a corridor towards the back of the building, and opened a door on to a wrought-iron fire escape. 'Downstairs, go left. The road narrows into an alleyway that reeks of urine. Three minutes' walk takes you to the entertainment district. You'll find Le Chat Botté in the basement beneath Café Mercier. It won't be open until this evening, so you'll have to rap on the glass.'

'Thank you *so* much,' Henderson said.

The alleyway behind the OT office was desolate. No car would ever get through because rubbish spewed out of overflowing bins. Marc trod carefully through the filth, fearing broken glass or worse. There was an overwhelming muggy heat as they passed behind a laundry, with steam shooting out of vents and the sight of women working through the tiny barred slots above the pavement.

They backed up to the wall as a Kriegsmarine officer whizzed through on a motorbike, with a girl in polka dots clutching his waist. As they choked on its exhaust fumes, the alleyway opened into a little oasis.

The small Catholic chapel had a tiny graveyard and was enveloped on all sides by taller buildings. By the main arched door was a wooden bench, spattered with pigeon crap, on which sat a lanky German eating bread and cheese.

If he'd kept his head down Marc and Henderson

might not have noticed, but the German was full of his own pomposity. He stood up, shouting an indignant, 'My god!'

They couldn't afford a noisy and protracted chase. Henderson thought about getting close and delivering a choke hold or knockout punch, but the German was going for his gun.

As Henderson reached towards his leather holster, Marc unsheathed his hunting-knife. In a single smooth movement the knife went from pocket to hand, then rotated through the air. It hit the German in the chest, puncturing his chest, just below the heart.

Henderson was stunned. The German had the gun in his shooting hand, but could raise it no higher as blood flooded his left lung and dribbled over his lower lip.

Marc closed in to finish the German off, but he'd already done enough. Henderson ran up to the chapel doors. He'd hoped to be able to drag the body inside, but three curious, smoking washerwomen turned towards him.

'Afternoon, ladies,' Henderson said smoothly. 'Sorry, I didn't mean to disturb your break.'

He closed the door before the women had a chance to see what was going on outside. The German was flat out in the gravel, giving his last twitch.

'I thought the knife would be quieter than the gun,'

Marc said, as he looked down and saw that he'd stepped in blood. 'Aww, shit.'

Henderson sensed unease in Marc's voice. 'You did what you've been trained to do,' he said. 'Who knows who'd have turned up by now if they'd heard a gunshot? Grab his legs.'

A dilapidated building alongside the chapel had a narrow gully, leading down to its basement. The German plunged down, clattering into bottles and disturbing a giant rat that bolted through the gap in a boarded-up window.

There was a small but noticeable pool of blood in the gravel. Henderson tossed the German's lunch away, then kicked the gravel about to disguise the blood. It wouldn't stand up to forensic investigation, but it wasn't obvious if you just passed by.

At the same time, Marc wiped his bloody feet on the grass. The blood was sticky and had mixed with the dirt from the alleyway to form a black tarry substance that wasn't going anywhere.

Henderson tugged Marc's shirt sleeve. 'We need to move before we're seen. We'll clean you up when we get to the club.'

Marc trembled as they started a brisk walk.

'I had no idea you were so handy with the knife,' Henderson said, as they walked fast.

'It was almost automatic,' Marc said. 'I've done knife

drill every day since December. Once hit a bunny between the eyes from twenty metres on campus.'

'The rocket will go up when they find a dead German,' Henderson said. 'So let's hope nobody looks too hard until we're back on a boat.'

They broke out into bright sunshine and saw the entrance to Le Chat Botté across a broad avenue lined with street cafés, bars and clubs.

CHAPTER FIVE

Le Chat Botté had wrought-iron tables, chessboard-tiled floor and red velvet booths. The walls were hung with photographs of famous singers and actors, but the mirrored stage only ever hosted strippers, with space for a two-piece band at the side. Out back were a dozen small bedrooms where Madame Mercier's girls plied their trade.

At night the club would heave with randy Germans, but right now it was empty. Lunch was brought down from the busy café upstairs. Soup to start, followed by smoked fish with potatoes and apple tart. Marc bolted down his first decent meal in four days while his feet soaked under the table in steaming heavily perfumed water.

Henderson ate more slowly, sipping a glass of red and

talking to a young but tired-looking waitress. He probed gently. *How many Germans come in here? Where do they work? Do they have plenty to spend? I bet you hear a few things you shouldn't when they're drunk.*

'You eating that?' Marc asked, as he eyed Henderson's untouched tart.

Henderson broke it in half with his fork, scooped one piece on to Marc's empty dessert plate and smiled at the waitress. 'Growing boy, always hungry.'

'After seeing all the food queues in town I thought we'd be getting black bread and mouldy cheese,' Marc said, with a great chunk of tart pushing out his cheek.

'Madame Mercier told us to look after you,' the waitress smiled. 'The Germans make the farmers sell everything to them at a low fixed price. So they hide as much as they dare. If you've got money, you can get all you need on the black market.'

Someone pounded the frosted glass in the basement door. As the waitress went to answer, Marc smiled at Henderson.

'We hit the jackpot,' Marc whispered. 'Madame Mercier is laying everything on for us.'

Henderson didn't agree. 'Klaus knew something was up when he brought us into town, the woman at the OT office was expecting us, that waitress didn't just know we were coming for lunch she'd been told who we were and what we were doing here. Now someone at the fishing port is trying to fix us a boat. They mean well, but they're not even taking the most *basic* of security precautions.'

The waitress came back to the table along with a kid who held three pairs of boots by their laces. There was scruffy black hair, filthy clothes and a whiff of horse manure, but no way to tell if it was a boy or girl.

'This is Edith,' the waitress explained.

'I guessed the size,' Edith said, as she dropped the boots. 'I can go back and get different ones, but it'll take about ten minutes.'

Marc took his feet out of the water and grabbed a threadbare towel off the seat behind him. As he dried between his toes, Henderson picked up one of the boots and saw that it was new.

'These look like British army boots.'

Edith nodded. 'They left millions of 'em, didn't they? Whole boatload of British boots and uniform standing on the dockside when the Germans arrived. We helped ourselves. Half the town's wearing them. Jackets and trousers too.'

To make her point, Edith raised her leg and showed her own grubby, oversized boots and cut-down khaki trousers.

Marc slid on a boot that looked about his size. 'Not bad,' he said, before looking over at Henderson. 'Got any of my socks in the bag?'

Edith keenly eyed the other half of Henderson's apple tart.

'Go on,' Henderson sighed, as he slid the plate across.

'So I can show you round the docks,' Edith said, as she pointed her thumb at Marc. 'But there's a lot less heat if I just take him.'

'Why's that?' Marc asked.

'Guards are a soft touch with kids,' Edith said, as she jabbed out her tongue and licked crumbs from the plate.

'I'll show you the route to Kerneval,' the waitress told Henderson. 'The fishermen who helped our Polish friends need to meet up and find you a boat.'

Henderson winced, hearing their departure plans voiced out loud in front of Edith. He was starting to wonder if there was anyone in town who *didn't* know what they were up to.

*

The tiny spy camera was packaged inside a French matchbox, though its weight meant the disguise wouldn't withstand serious inspection. Marc kept it in his pocket as he strolled down a cobbled alleyway two steps behind Edith.

He'd seen most of the major ports along the channel coast to the north of Lorient. Some like Dunkirk had virtually been levelled, all the others severely damaged during the invasion. But Lorient was on the Atlantic coast. It had seen little fighting the previous summer and the RAF hadn't bombed it since.

The main docks were just a few hundred metres from Le Chat Botté, but U-boats were based a kilometre west on the Keroman peninsula. This area had twin advantages: dry docks where boats could be repaired out of the water and a narrow entry point that was easy to defend against attack from the sea.

'Stop looking so worried,' Edith told Marc. 'I've been here a hundred times, stealing coal.'

Marc couldn't focus his mind. He kept seeing his knife hitting the German's chest and wondered if the man had been missed yet.

'So what's your story?' Marc asked when the silence got awkward. 'Don't you have school or anything?'

'The Krauts are talking about starting school again, because they're sick of kids causing mischief. But I'm almost thirteen. By the time they get it sorted I'll be past leaving age.'

'What do your parents say?'

'Not much, seeing as they're dead,' Edith said. 'Madame Mercier gives me a bed. I earn my keep looking after her stables and doing odd jobs.'

As Edith said this, she crossed the cobbles and deliberately mashed her boot into a puddle of oil, dirt and God knows what else.

'Duck,' Edith shouted, flicking her boot forward so that soggy clumps flew at Marc. He spun and ducked, but the dirt pelted his back.

'You're not exactly ladylike, are you?' Marc moaned.

Edith blew a kiss as she resumed their walk.

'Why would I want to be?' she asked, raising an eyebrow and baring yellow teeth. 'So that men can feel me up, and pay twenty-five francs to screw me in a smelly little room?'

'Twenty-five francs,' Marc laughed. 'You'd be lucky to get five.'

Edith jabbed her thumb into Marc's ribs. 'Pig!'

'Love you too,' Marc replied. 'How much further?'

As they walked on it became a ghost town. Doors left open, windows boarded up.

'Everyone was cleared out around here,' Edith explained. 'It's all getting flattened to make way for another U-boat bunker.'

They turned right, into a street of small houses blocked off by lengths of wire with enamel *keep out* signs. Edith cut into an alleyway, kicked a wooden gate, ran up a pile of rubble stacked against the garden wall and jumped down on the other side.

Her speed surprised Marc and she scoffed as he hesitated before jumping down into mud and broken glass. They cut through the next house and emerged back on to the street, but inside the fence.

Edith broke into a sprint. Marc followed, but it wasn't easy with stiff new boots and a dodgy ankle. You could smell sea air as they turned right again, passing a group of lads, aged between nine and eleven. They sat against a wall aiming rocks at a line of rusty cans. Marc found their presence reassuring.

'Fleabag's got herself a boyfriend,' the biggest one laughed.

Edith gave the lad an *up yours* gesture as she led Marc beside a crumbling brick wall with mounds of coal poking over the top. She stopped by a section where a couple of dozen low bricks had been knocked out.

'On this side kids get yelled at and taken back to the fence,' Edith explained. 'But the Krauts can get serious if they think you're stealing coal.'

Marc had to suck in his belly to wriggle through the hole after Edith. The coal caught the early afternoon sun as Edith clambered the mound fearlessly, her boots throwing dust into Marc's face as he moved behind her. When she neared the top, she clambered on all fours to stay out of sight.

'Good view,' Marc said, as he propped himself on his elbows beside Edith.

Little shards of coal chinked their way down the side of the heap as he nestled in the dirt and looked out. The man-made harbour was sixty metres across, and five hundred long. At the far end was a huge concrete slope, along with a ramp up which a small craft could be lifted for repairs.

Marc unbuttoned his shirt and wiped his coal-blackened fingers down his trousers before taking out the matchbox camera. It had a fold-out wire viewfinder to frame shots and an exposure dial with settings for bright, dim or medium light.

He guessed medium and snapped the shutter. He took the shots methodically, taking pictures of three sausage-shaped bunkers at the far end, one of which had the nose of a U-boat protruding from it. His next shot was of two U-boats moored side by side and covered with grey camouflage netting.

But the real spectacle lay directly across the water, where two vast bunkers were under construction. The first was built on the water, with seven U-boat-sized pens. The sides were complete and appeared to be made from concrete several metres thick.

As men hung precariously over the water dismantling a huge scaffold, other teams were building the roof. On one side only the first precast concrete blocks had been laid, but at the other end the roof was already three metres thick, with huge rectangles of armoured steel being lifted up by a steam-powered crane.

At a right angle from the first bunker, the second was at an earlier stage of construction. It had no roof and the walls just coming out of the ground. This set of pens was above the waterline and a heavy-gauge railway system linked it to the first.

'Guess they'll lift boats through the regular pens, then take 'em across on the tracks when they need major repairs,' Marc said.

Edith nodded. 'I heard that when they're finished, the biggest British bombs won't even dent that roof.'

Smaller bunkers were being built further back from the water to secure fuel, weapons and crews. Marc shot pictures until the film ran out, then took a brief moment to consider what he was seeing. The contrast between the huge new bunkers and the two U-boats moored under nets at the opposite end of the harbour showed how serious the Kriegsmarine was about protecting and expanding their U-boat fleet.

'If they build more bunkers on this side, you could have thirty U-boats docked at a time and no way to damage them until they're out at sea,' Marc said.

But Edith had more immediate concerns as she noticed two Germans jogging along the dockside towards them. They wore the distinctive dark-blue uniform of Kriegsmarine police.

'We've gotta get out of here,' she shouted, giving Marc a tug on the arm before launching herself into a dramatic head-first slide down the coal heap. 'Fat Adolf's coming.'

CHAPTER SIX

Henderson had to leave Lorient to meet the fishermen along the coast in Kerneval. The main bridge east out of Lorient had been fortified with anti-aircraft guns and had barrage balloons tethered across its width to prevent low-flying aircraft sweeping in and attacking the harbours.

He felt uneasy as the grey-uniformed guard at the Lorient end checked his paperwork. He looked about seventeen, and scratched a shaving rash under his helmet strap as he eyed Henderson with suspicion.

'I know this bar,' he said suspiciously. 'I've never seen you in there.'

If he'd had a choice, Henderson never would have picked a public place for false employment details. 'I mainly work in the back.'

Henderson felt for his gun. He wouldn't withstand a search, and looked around for an escape route as the guard eyed his ration card. There was only one guard on each end of the bridge, so he might get away if he jumped over the side and made a run along the embankment behind the bushes.

'Your zone permit says you came here a month ago, but this ration card has all its coupons intact,' the guard said. 'What have you been eating, thin air?'

Confidence and detail are the key to successful bullshitting. 'I lost my card,' Henderson explained. 'This one was issued by Mr Muller yesterday afternoon.'

The guard didn't seem happy and began unfolding the military discharge papers. As the woman queuing behind sighed, a German truck started belting across the bridge from the opposite end, blasting its horn and sending a cyclist diving for cover.

The driver squealed to a halt and leaned out of the window. He looked as young as the guard, and apparently knew him well.

'Open the gate, you homosexual!' he demanded in German. 'Hear you got back to barracks late last night. Hear you're getting busted on a charge, super-brain.'

'Who says?' the guard shouted bitterly.

'You'll get cesspit duty,' the driver teased. 'Elbow deep in shit, and a smell that doesn't wash off.'

'I'll probably meet your mother down there,' the guard

yelled, as he raised the striped wooden gate.

'Happy shovelling!' the driver shouted, as he gunned the engine, leaving guard and queue choking in exhaust fumes.

The guard was steaming. Henderson feared his wrath, but the young face told a different story. This German wanted to be home eating his mum's cooking and hanging out with his mates. He shoved the papers back in Henderson's face and waved him off, hardly able to speak. Henderson sighed with relief, but his paperwork wasn't up to scratch and the Germans might stop him again.

*

It was tough to breathe, tough to see through the coal dust. Marc's ankle hurt as he charged behind Edith. A German had blocked the easy exit through the hole, but Edith knew another way. They raced over the base of coal heaps with the huge dockside wall skimming past. Fat Adolf was in his fifties, heavy and slow, but the other officer was younger and gaining fast.

Edith was aiming for a chain-link fence, topped with barbed wire to make Marc's life even more perfect. He was older, stronger, and could have outrun Edith, but only she knew the way to their rendezvous with Henderson and the fishermen at Kerneval.

'Gotcha!' a big German shouted.

Coal crunched noisily underfoot, so they hadn't heard

the third German running on the other side of the coal heaps near the water's edge. Edith was skin and bone beneath her baggy trousers and the German plucked her up one-handed, then slammed her brutally into the wall.

Marc spun and gave the German an almighty boot in the balls. Edith's eyes rolled about in her head as the German crumpled in agony. The German who'd been chasing was now right behind. Marc launched a roundhouse kick, but his injured ankle was weak and his foot twisted in the shifting coal. The German grabbed Marc's flying leg and twisted it painfully as the boy crashed down on his back.

Edith soon had a sleeve clamped around her neck. The man Marc had kicked in the balls took pleasure in wrenching his arm painfully behind his back. Breathless and limping, Fat Adolf stumbled through the black dust clutching his chest. It wasn't his real name, just what the kids called him because of his bulk and Hitleresque moustache.

'How many times?' Adolf shouted, getting right in Edith's face, but sounding more frustrated than angry.

Edith was dazed from being slammed into the wall, but she managed to turn on the charm for an old adversary. 'Got any chocolate for me today, boss?' she asked.

'You don't understand the grief I'm getting over you

kids,' Fat Adolf shouted. 'Important men go over the other side and inspect the new bunkers. They see kids running around over here and I get it in the neck. How many times have I caught you here now? Eight, nine?'

'I'm sorry,' Edith said, as she rubbed the back of her head and felt blood. 'If you let me go, I *swear* it'll be the last time.'

'I've got new orders,' Fat Adolf said. 'Hands against the wall, legs wide apart.'

Edith did what she was told, but one of the younger Germans kicked her legs further to put her in a stress position. Then he pulled a long, wooden nightstick, swung hard and smashed her in the ribs.

Edith squeezed up her face, and tried hard not to moan. A second blow hit her across the back of her legs, knocking her down on her knees.

'You like that, little boy?' the big German said, grinning sadistically at Marc. 'Plenty more coming.'

The next blow hit Edith across the shoulder and knocked her flat. The German planted his boot on her back and hit her across the thigh. She'd been in a daze before the beating started and the big man looked like he was just warming up.

'You're teaching her a lesson, not killing her,' Fat Adolf yelled. 'That's enough.'

Now it was Marc's turn. He was stronger and managed

to stay upright, but he took four heavy blows and when it was over he was clutching his ribs and fighting for breath.

Before he had a chance to recover, they'd been dragged up to the fence and thrown through a wire gate. Edith had tears streaking down her filthy face and sobbed noisily.

The one who'd done the beating spoke to Fat Adolf in German, unaware that Marc could understand. 'We've got to teach these brats a lesson, sir.'

'Shut your idiot mouth,' Fat Adolf spat back. 'Go back inside. Look for more kids, and frighten 'em, don't kill 'em.'

As the two younger men skulked off, Edith clutched her injured thigh and scowled defiantly. 'You said your daughter's the same age as me,' she spat. 'I hope your house gets bombed and she *dies*.'

'You must stay out of here,' Fat Adolf said, clenching his fists with frustration. 'You're *only* kids. You're *only* stealing a bit of coal, but it all mounts up to a *lot* of coal. My orders are to capture or shoot anyone seen in the coal yard. There won't be any more warnings. Spread the word to all the other kids before one of you ends up with a bullet in the back.'

As Fat Adolf spoke, Marc felt around to make sure he hadn't lost anything. He felt his ID document, felt his knife and the matchbox camera. They'd got the photos, they hadn't been searched. The pain was bad but he could take it.

'Here,' Fat Adolf said, as he held out three boiled sweets wrapped in gold foil. 'I'm sorry.'

Edith didn't take them, so Fat Adolf dropped them on the cobbles and she scooped them up grudgingly the moment he was out of sight.

*

The Kriegsmarine had moved the local fishing fleet away from the U-boat dock at Keroman, to a small natural harbour at Kerneval, one and a half kilometres along the coast. Henderson found it bustling with small boats, and interrupted a boy hauling up a net of fish with a dockside pulley.

'I'm looking for Alois Clement,' Henderson said.

The boy pointed out a shabby bistro. Alois wasn't there, but the waitress told him to wait. The outdoor tables had a good view over the harbour and the afternoon sun was warm enough to sit outside. Henderson got coffee, which tasted like battery acid, and a shot of brandy to settle his nerves. The man who joined him shortly afterwards was ancient-looking with a ragged beard, leathery skin and rubber boots spattered with fish blood.

'Hortefeux?' he asked.

Henderson nodded. The man said he was Nicolas. His brother Alois was arranging a boat and would arrive shortly. Then he told the waitress to throw Henderson's coffee away and bring two cups of the good stuff.

Henderson pointed at three large boats across the harbour. They looked modern, but were rusting badly. 'Why are the big boats laid up?'

'Diesel engines with no diesel to put in 'em,' Nicolas explained. 'Not much coal either, so we're mainly back to sail-boats.'

'But you must get a decent price for your catch with so little food around.'

'It's a living, but not much of one,' Nicolas said, as two fine-smelling espressos arrived. 'Rules up to our ears: daylight fishing only, got to stay within six kilometres of the coast, which keeps us out of the best fishing grounds. Most of our young men are held prisoner. I'm seventy-three and my crew is two grandsons aged seventeen and fifteen.'

As they kept chatting, Henderson took in details, from women standing on the dockside gutting fish, to the unmanned 20mm cannons mounted on the jaws of the harbour. When the cups were dry, Nicolas glanced at his pocket watch and stood up.

'Don't know what's keeping Alois,' he said. 'We'll take a walk around to his workshop.'

Fishing had kept the old man fit and Nicolas moved briskly up a cobbled street, took a right and then ducked under an overhead door. It was a workshop, with tool racks, engine parts and the smell of shaved metal and lubricant. A man stood up by the workbench, but Henderson didn't see the one lurking behind until the shotgun barrel was being waved in his face.

CHAPTER SEVEN

A chair slammed down. Henderson got frisked before they ordered him to sit in it. They found his gun and ID papers, but missed the small knife in the lining of his jacket. Alois led the interrogation. He was thuggish and at least ten years younger than his brother, with hairy nostrils and grease-blackened hands.

'Madame Mercier is too trusting, Mr Hortefeux,' Alois began. 'If that *really* is your name.'

'My real name is Henderson.'

Alois laughed. 'You claim to have come ashore last night, but you've got no boat and no radio.'

Henderson shifted uneasily. 'If I was a German trying to catch you out, it would be easy enough to have those pieces of equipment.'

'And the boy, what is that all about?'

'Father and son is less suspicious,' Henderson said.

'The photograph of the three men in front of Big Ben looks fake,' Alois said. 'I think the three Poles were captured at sea and interrogated by the Gestapo. They spilled Madame's name under interrogation and rather than arresting her, they've sent you here to see who else you could unearth.'

Henderson tried to keep his cool as Alois picked up a large wrench.

'That's plausible,' Henderson said. 'Do you have a background in police work?'

Alois was flattered. 'I'm smart enough to know when something is fishy, Mr Henderson, or whatever your name is. You're an Englishman, yes?'

'Born and bred,' Henderson said.

'Get our man,' Alois shouted.

A door from a side room came open. The man had a ferocious-looking burn over his right cheek and the upper part of his neck. He wore a French peasant's shirt and trousers, but Henderson immediately spotted RAF flying boots and a neat moustache that was characteristically English.

'Hello, old man,' Henderson said in English. 'Shot down I suppose?'

'Ran out of fuel and ditched,' the airman said. His accent was upper crust and he seemed wary, having been told that Henderson was probably a Gestapo agent.

'We were damned lucky to get pulled out of the sea by this lot.'

'*We?*' Henderson said. 'How many others are there?'

A look from Alois stopped the airman from answering.

'They want me to ask you some questions,' the airman said. 'Things that only an Englishman should know. Are you a cricket man, by any chance?'

'More football,' Henderson said. 'Grammar school boy, you see. Rather fond of the Arsenal.'

'That's awkward,' the airman said, scratching his moustache and looking disappointed. 'I was going to ask you the names of the squad that played the last Ashes series.'

'I can tell you who won the cup last year,' Henderson said. 'Portsmouth four, Wolves one.'

'Association Football's not my cup of tea,' the airman said. 'I'm just trying to think. Could you tell me the last four University boat race winners?'

Henderson smiled. 'I'd be prepared to narrow it down to either Oxford or Cambridge.'

'National anthem, third verse?'

Henderson racked his brain. 'Not in God's land alone, but be thy mercies known?'

'That's the fourth verse,' the airman said. 'How about the rest of that verse?'

'Used to sing it on Empire Day at school twenty years

back. Can't say it's in my head now.'

Alois looked impatiently at the airman. 'Well?'

The airman's French was absolutely awful. 'Difficult,' he said warily. 'He's speaking like London. If he is German, he's a good actor.'

Henderson had two problems. First, Alois had clearly staked his credibility on the idea that he was a Gestapo spy. Second, there was no piece of information about Britain that couldn't be memorised by a German.

Alois waved the giant wrench. 'I say we tie an anvil to this bastard's ankles and throw him in the harbour.'

'If the Gestapo are on to us, it wouldn't make any difference,' Nicolas pointed out. 'He would have told people that he was coming here. They might even be watching us right now.'

'*Exactly*,' Henderson said hopefully, as he pointed at the airman. 'You've nothing to lose by taking a chance on me being who I say I am. You trusted the airman, didn't you?'

Nicolas managed a tense smile. 'We found them half drowned in the Atlantic. The Krauts would have had a hell of a job setting that up.'

Everyone looked around as the side door opened again. The three Frenchmen were half expecting a Gestapo raid and were relieved to see the waitress from the café, with Edith and Marc. Marc hurt from the beating, but sensed the tense atmosphere and felt for the knife in his pocket.

'What are you old lunatics doing?' Edith yelled, eyeballing Alois furiously. 'They're here to help us.'

'He's Gestapo,' Alois shouted. 'I'd bet my right bollock on it.'

'The Germans just beat him half to death,' Edith said, pointing at Marc. 'He took pictures of the bunkers.'

'They're cleverer than you think,' Alois said. 'It's a scheme to root out as many of us as possible.'

'In which case we're doomed anyway,' Nicolas repeated. 'We've got nothing to lose by trusting them, apart from your pride, Alois.'

While the Frenchmen bickered, Marc plotted. They didn't think he was a threat and hadn't bothered searching him. If he stabbed the man with the shotgun, Henderson ought to respond quickly and take out Alois. Nicolas didn't look too fast, so they'd probably be able to get away.

'The Englishman can't prove he's English,' Alois shouted.

'How can I *prove* it?' Henderson said. 'He said I had a perfect accent.'

Marc's hand tightened on the knife, but he was only going to move if he had to. There were too many things that could go wrong, with Edith, and the waitress, and the airman.

The airman.

Marc thought he looked familiar and spoke desperately, in his heavily accented English. 'Have you got a brother named Walters? He's also a pilot. Looks just like you, maybe a year or two younger.'

The airman shook his head, but then raised a curious eyebrow, as if he'd just worked something out.

'My name is Jarhope, but when I was training the instructor mentioned a man named Walters,' the airman said uncertainly. 'Apparently he'd been through training a few months previously and the fellow looked just like me.'

'Well I've met Walters,' Marc said jubilantly. 'He was the pilot when I did parachute training up in Scotland.'

Jarhope stepped in front of Alois. 'I'm convinced they're for real now,' he said. 'Nobody could possibly have known that.'

Marc had to translate so that Alois understood. He signalled reluctantly and the shotgun was tilted away from Henderson's head. Marc loosened his grip on his knife, Alois put the wrench down on his workbench and there were a few wary laughs.

*

While Henderson went off with Nicolas and Alois to find a boat and plan the best strategy for finding *Madeline* in pitch darkness, Marc and Edith found themselves being mothered by Alois' twenty-something daughter, Therese.

The two kids stripped and washed the worst of the dirt away in cold buckets on the back porch. For Marc, this was a day's sweat and a welcome relief from the coal dust. But Edith battled furiously, refusing to scrub several weeks of grime away until Therese threatened her with a wire brush.

Stripped of clothes and dirt, there wasn't much to Edith. Puberty hadn't kicked in and she was whip thin. Inside they got a hot bath. Marc chivalrously let Edith go first, but when she'd finished the water was so filthy that Therese tipped it away and Marc stood wrapped in a blanket for twenty minutes while more was boiled.

By this time it was early evening, with the temperature plunging as the sun vanished. After their baths the two kids drew chairs up to a wood fire and toasted their tired legs and the palms of their hands until it was time to eat.

Jarhope, the airman, was first to arrive for dinner.

'Good job you knew that Walters chap,' Marc whispered, as Edith dozed beside him. 'Otherwise I might have ended up getting chucked in the harbour.'

'To be honest, I've never heard of the fellow,' Jarhope confessed in a whisper. 'But I've been stuck here for over a month while my burns heal up. The rest of my crew have gone south already and I reckon I've got better odds shipping out with you two than trekking down to Spain with no French and this mess for a face.'

CHAPTER EIGHT

Dinner was a proper show. Madame Mercier came by car, Nicolas brought out his best brandy. Only Alois was subdued, embarrassed by his behaviour earlier on. The waitress who'd served lunch at Le Chat Botté gave Henderson a remarkable stash of original blank documents, from bicycle permits to ration cards, but she also brought bad news. The body of the OT worker had been found. Security at checkpoints around Lorient had been stepped up.

Everyone agreed it was a grave business. The Germans would clamp down. Arrests, searches, days of tightened curfews and possible revenge executions of French prisoners.

Madame Mercier stood up as gloom settled over the diners. 'To make the omelette, you break the egg,' she told them resolutely. 'This is a war and worse things will happen before we win.'

Henderson was impressed and raised a toast. 'To victory for France,' he said.

'And a safe trip home for our guests,' Madame Mercier added.

*

'It's like two pins manoeuvring blindfold through a haystack and hoping to bump into each other,' Henderson explained to Jarhope, as they sailed away from Kerneval.

Nicolas and Alois had done them proud, locating a four-metre sailing boat and safe spot to cast off outside the harbour wall well away from German eyes. Henderson was a confident sailor and reckoned the boat was good enough to reach Britain if they didn't find *Madeline*. They'd brought food and water just in case, but five days in an open boat would be no fun, and if a storm didn't get them, the Germans might.

Jarhope was no sailor and would have looked green if it hadn't been pitch dark. Marc lay at the bow, trying to ignore all the places that hurt as he cupped his ears, listening for the distinct rumble of *Madeline*'s propeller shaft. He had a flashlight and a pair of luminous wands to help attract *Madeline*, but they'd all be for it if he made the wrong call and flashed a German boat.

There wasn't even a guarantee that *Madeline* was

coming. It was a fifty-hour voyage from Porth Navas to Lorient, so the little tug had been forced to spend the day drifting seventy kilometres offshore, risking the attentions of German patrol boats and fighter planes.

Henderson sailed in a zigzag pattern. If Rufus was doing his job, *Madeline* was sweeping back and forth along a two-kilometre channel. They'd practised the technique off the Cornish coast and *Madeline* had met the canoe four times on four consecutive nights. But that didn't account for sinkings, mechanical faults, or the possibility that Rufus had navigated to completely the wrong section of coastline as he'd done the previous night.

Midnight passed by, then one, two and three a.m. Henderson decided that he'd give up at four, because if he left it any later he wouldn't be able to sail clear of the coast before sunrise. The breakthrough came with less than a quarter-hour to spare.

'I'm pretty sure it's her,' Marc said.

Henderson put up the sail and pointed the bow towards the noise. They had to be careful, because *Madeline* was expecting a canoe not a sailing boat. Marc made a V with the two luminous wands and held them up high. His eyes squeezed shut as a powerful light swept across the water. This was a huge risk so close to the French coast, but the crew aboard *Madeline* were also getting desperate.

Henderson smiled as a gust caught the sail and they finally recognised the little tug. The crew comprised Rufus, a slender Moroccan-French soldier, Troy LeConte, a thirteen-year-old from a seafaring background who'd recently completed training with Henderson's second batch of recruits, and Elizabeth DeVere, a nineteen-year-old who'd trained as an undercover radio operator, but discovered that you did a bit of everything in a small unit like CHERUB. Everyone called her Boo.

Jarhope passed up the bag of equipment and clothing as Troy gave Marc a hand on to *Madeline*'s deck.

'Any trouble?' Henderson asked Rufus.

'Nothing to speak of, Commander,' Rufus said with a smile. 'But I'm sure I'll find you some.'

'Let's winch that sailing boat up on deck, then I want full steam ahead. It'll be sunrise in under forty minutes.'

*

Madeline had been stolen by Henderson's team when they'd escaped France the previous autumn. She was now officially HMRS *Madeline* of the Royal Navy Reserve, and part of a small fleet of trawlers, tugs and passenger boats used for espionage based in Porth Navas Creek on the River Helford in Cornwall. Unofficially, nobody but Henderson was interested in a forty-year-old French tug and he'd spent most of the winter scratching together the equipment and manpower needed to get her in shape for undercover operations.

She was no warship, but she was much improved. A larger boiler for speed, a new keel fitted for stability at sea, high-powered binoculars on the bridge for navigation, an armoury of hand weapons and most importantly a 22mm machine gun that could be hauled from below and attached to a bracket on the rear deck.

The voyage from Lorient to Porth Navas would take thirty hours in peacetime, but in war this doubled because you had to stay away from the coast, out of main shipping lanes and well away from the British minefields you knew about, and the German minefields that you hoped you knew about.

So Marc faced two more sleepless days. Always noisy, wet and swaying from side to side. He sat up the back of the deck with Troy, using a coil of rope as a rock-hard pillow.

'I spy with my little eye, something beginning with D,' Marc said, as he prodded the bruises under his shirt.

'Darkness,' Troy said.

'*Shit*,' Marc laughed. 'How did you get it so fast?'

'If you're awake, one of you can go below decks and take over from Boo shovelling coal,' Rufus shouted from the bridge.

The two boys hunkered down and tried not to laugh as they faked snoring noises, but Marc was exhausted and fake sleep eventually turned real.

Henderson's boot woke him three hours later. Marc

stretched out to yawn, but Henderson yanked his arm. 'Get below decks, we need the sniper rifles. Quickly.'

It was light, but the main thing that hit Marc as he scuttled across the deck was the roar of diesel engines. A German E-boat[2] was blasting towards them, throwing up a huge bow wave. These high-speed craft were thirty-five metres long. They carried torpedoes and two heavy-calibre deck guns capable of blowing *Madeline* out of the water.

'They'll know we're up to no good if they board us,' Henderson shouted, as Troy passed guns and weapons up from below deck. 'Our only chance is to act innocent until they're right next to us. Keep calm, remember your training and be ready to shoot if they try to come aboard for an inspection.'

Marc grabbed a sniper's rifle. It came in five pieces, which he fitted together in barely twenty seconds, then he looked through the sight to check the scope was aligned properly. He slung an ammunition belt around his neck and ran up to the front of the boat, hunkering down in front of the anchor hole. Troy was down at the stern, and now nestled in the spot where Marc had been sleeping a few moments earlier. Boo had fitted the cannon on the deck and slid over a wooden frame built

---

[2] E-Boat – a small, high-speed German warship designed mainly for coastal patrol duty and mine laying.

to disguise it. Jarhope crouched in the deck hatch with a Sten machine gun.

Madeline rocked from the wash as the German patrol boat pulled alongside. Everyone kept out of sight except Henderson on the rear deck and Rufus inside the tiny bridge. They acted innocent, but both had Sten guns within reach.

Marc eyed the Germans through the anchor hole. He counted five men on deck, but none were expecting trouble from the little tug. One even sat on an upturned bucket peeling potatoes.

'A beautiful morning,' Henderson yelled across, as he shielded his eyes from the low sun.

'It is,' a bearded German sailor agreed. 'Why are you out here so far from the coast?'

'We've been out all night,' Henderson explained. 'A distress call went up from a tramp steamer. We brought out some replacement parts and an engineer. Thought we might have to tow her in, but they got her running on her own steam and now we're heading back to Brest.'

A little pantomime played out on the deck of the E-boat. Junior officer shouting to captain, captain can't hear. Junior officer walks up to bridge, arms wave, beards get scratched. Junior officer comes back looking unhappy.

'We've been patrolling this area and haven't heard any distress call,' the bearded sailor said. 'We're coming aboard, to check your documentation and search the boat.'

Henderson acted calm and shook his head. 'Knock yourselves out, I guess.'

As the German threw a rope over, Marc eyed the German captain on his bridge. The E-boat was twice as long as *Madeline*, with her superstructure lined up with their bow. The side window was open, making it the easiest shot he was ever likely to take.

There was a shudder as the two boats touched, side to side. The decks were almost level and the bearded German judged the swaying boats carefully, with two armed ratings ready to board behind him.

'Geronimo!' Henderson yelled, as he grabbed the pistol tucked into the waistband of his trousers and shot the German through the head.

Jarhope's machine gun polished off the armed men behind him. Boo sprung up, threw the lightweight awning off the 22mm gun and mowed down two men on the rear of the deck. Up front, Marc's first shot went clean through the captain's head. He hit a second man, as a third jumped out of the bridge, only to be shot from the opposite end of the boat by Troy.

Eight men had been killed before the Germans fired a shot, but the balance of power shifted when the potato peeler got himself behind the armoured flanges of a 20mm cannon at the front of the boat.

The first heavy rounds practically parted Marc's hair. The gunner aimed down, punching holes in *Madeline*'s bow, then swung across, tearing chunks out of the wooden superstructure and shattering every window in the bridge. Fortunately the two boats were too close for *Madeline* to be holed below the waterline.

As Rufus jumped clear of the flying glass, Troy shot a German coming out of the rear hatch from below deck. Marc tried to aim at the German behind the cannon, but he was shielded by the armoured flanges.

Henderson realised that the only way to stop the heavy-calibre fire was to board the E-boat, run to the front and shoot the German from behind his protective shield. As Henderson vaulted on to the E-boat, a pair of grenades came the other way.

One landed in the coiled ropes next to Troy. He batted it over the side, seconds before it would have blown his hand off. Boo watched the other grenade bounce off the deck and drop through the open hatch below decks. As Troy saw a third grenade missing the rear of the boat, he spotted the man throwing them, tucked up behind the torpedo tubes on deck, and took aim.

Jarhope jumped aboard the E-boat to back up Henderson as the grenade went off below deck, cracking *Madeline*'s cast-iron boiler and sending out a powerful blast of superheated steam. The 2cm shells continued to pound the superstructure as Rufus screamed in pain. His arms had been lacerated by the flying glass in the bridge, and Boo cut her own hands on the shards embedded in his skin as she dragged him away from the steam.

Troy had been knocked down by the grenade blast, but now took aim from a kneeling position and pumped two shots. The first missed. The second hit the German grenade thrower up the arse and left him hanging over the side.

Further up the E-boat, Henderson had climbed up into the bridge. He aimed his machine gun through the blood-spattered windows and shot the cook firing the deck cannon. With the big cannon muted and no Germans left on deck to shoot at, the only sound was the high-pitched whistle of steam escaping *Madeline*'s cracked boiler.

'Get across, all of you,' Henderson shouted. '*Madeline* could blow sky high.'

Troy vaulted easily and immediately shot a German coming out of a hatch in the rear of the boat. Boo helped Rufus, who was blinded by blood running into his eyes. But at the bow *Madeline* was more than two metres away from the E-boat, and Marc couldn't get to the rear because of the rapidly venting steam.

He shouted desperately to Henderson up in the E-boat's bridge.

Jarhope grabbed a life preserver with rope attached and threw it across. Marc caught hold, but it was heavier than expected and bent his fingers back painfully. The coal under *Madeline*'s rear deck was now ablaze, and it sounded like a shoot-out as the heat set off bullets in the ammunition store.

Marc fed his arms through the life preserver, as Jarhope knotted the rope to the E-boat's deck rail for extra safety. Marc balanced on *Madeline*'s bow ready to jump, while at the rear of the E-boat Troy hastily untied the smouldering rope linking the two boats together.

Jarhope braced against the deck rail as Marc jumped. But the boy's weight was too much to hold. As Marc plunged into the gloomy space between the two hulls, the ropes pulled through Jarhope's hands, burning off layers of skin.

Marc was strong, and started pulling himself up the rope, but *Madeline*'s hull was close and he'd be crushed if the boats came together. He could feel heat and hear crackling as the paint on *Madeline*'s hull blistered.

'I need a hand,' Marc shouted.

Jarhope was clutching his burned hands, in no condition to grab anything, so Boo had to run the length of the boat and reach over the side to grab the life preserver.

Henderson was on the bridge working out the E-boat's blood-spattered controls. He was worried that the fire would spread from *Madeline*, and the instant Marc was over the deck rail he pushed the throttle forward. The big diesel engines rumbled and the boat cruised twenty metres clear before he cut them off.

'We've got to keep our guard up,' Henderson said, as he grabbed his machine gun and jumped down out of the bridge. 'I reckon there's still half a dozen Krauts hiding below deck. Let's flush 'em out.'

CHAPTER NINE

As *Madeline*'s wooden frame burned thirty metres astern, Henderson told everyone to quiet down, hoping to hear some sign of the Germans trapped below decks. He pointed at Troy and whispered.

'Take Rufus' Sten and cover the rear hatch. Give them a couple of seconds to surrender, but don't take chances if you see a weapon. Marc, I want you covering my back down below. Only shoot if you have to. These boats are built for speed not strength, and we won't get far if we're shot full of holes.'

Henderson grabbed a docking pole off the deck. While Boo held the rear door of the bridge open, Henderson used the hooked pole to flip the deck hatch, half expecting someone to start shooting up at him.

'Looks empty,' Henderson said, as he peered down

cautiously. Then he shouted in German. 'Come out now with your hands up.'

He didn't get an answer, but Jarhope had pushed past Marc into the bridge. 'Commander, I know this is your show, but don't you think I'd be better than the boy?'

Henderson turned impatiently. 'Jarhope, you can barely hold a gun with the state your hands are in. Marc's one of the best marksmen I've ever seen. If you want a job, start searching Kraut bodies for anything interesting. Then throw 'em over the side before we're all sloshing about in blood.'

Marc joined Henderson at the edge of the hatch. Looking down beyond the ladder he saw the ship's radio, a dropped pistol and a table with a chest of nautical charts beneath.

'In for a penny,' Henderson said, as he swung over the side of the hole and dropped below.

Marc followed, thumping down on his injured ankle as Henderson tucked the German pistol into his jacket. There were metal bulkhead doors at either end of the room. The one going towards the bow was open, the one going aft was shut.

'Bet you ten shillings they're behind the locked door, but we'll check the front out first. I counted ten dead, but I've no idea how many crew these boats.'

Henderson covered as Marc ripped open the forward bulkhead. He stepped through into a corridor barely wider than his shoulders and crept up to a green curtain before swishing it back. Behind it were the captain's quarters, with a narrow bunk and a wardrobe with a flap that folded down to make a writing desk.

'Nobody home,' Marc said, as he backed out and moved forwards towards the next bunker.

'Even if you kill us you'll never get up on deck,' Henderson shouted. 'Surrender and you'll be well treated.'

Marc stepped through the next bulkhead and jumped down a metre into the crew compartment. There were three triple bunks crammed in a space that pinched in towards the ship's bow. Marc almost gagged on cigarette smoke and BO as he ripped off stained bedclothes, making sure nobody was hiding.

There was one final compartment in the bow itself. As Marc moved in its tiny door flew open. A scrawny German burst out, swinging wildly with a cleaver. Henderson shoved Marc out of the way and kicked the German in the stomach. As the cleaver hit the floor, Henderson grabbed the small man by his shirt collar and smacked him head first into a metal bunk frame, before jamming a gun against his temple.

'One lie and I'll kill you,' Henderson growled. 'How many men crew this boat? How many are left down here?'

'I don't know,' the sailor replied.

'The hell you don't,' Henderson shouted, pulling the

sailor's head back, then smashing his nose against a bedpost.

Henderson could be utterly ruthless, and Marc felt uneasy as he glanced into the compartment where the German had been hiding. The ceiling was low, with a tiny sink and toilet. This was clogged with torn paper, which the German had tried to flush, and then set on fire when it failed.

'Looks like code books and stuff,' Marc shouted. 'Bagsy I'm not the one who has to fish 'em out.'

But Henderson didn't hear because he was giving the German a good belting. 'How many in the crew?'

'Geneva convention!' the German replied. 'I am a prisoner of war, I have rights.'

'Got a complaint?' Henderson scoffed. 'Write a letter to the League of Nations. Let's walk.'

Henderson shoved the German towards the steps and led him back the way they'd come. Boo had climbed below and was looking at the damaged radio.

'Think you can get a signal out to our people?'

'Very much hope so, Commander,' Boo said, wincing as she saw the German's profusely bleeding head and flattened nose.

'Open the bulkhead,' Henderson ordered.

The German looked back nervously. 'I can't.'

'What's in there?' Henderson shouted, punching the sailor hard in the ribs.

'The crew is sixteen, but only fifteen aboard because one is sick,' the German blurted desperately. 'There's one officer in there, a real fanatic, plus a rating and two engineers. He ordered me to flush our code books and destroy the radio. He'll shoot me dead for cooperating with you.'

'What weapons do they have?' Henderson growled.

'Just a pistol I think.'

'Well hopefully he'll only shoot you once then,' Henderson said. 'Boo, open that bulkhead on three. Marc, there's gonna be engines and fuel tanks back there, so we don't want bullets flying around. How are your knife-throwing skills?

'I'll manage,' Marc said, as he slung his rifle over his shoulder and took his knife out of its sheath.

Henderson thumped on the bulkhead. 'We're coming in on three,' he shouted in German. 'This is your last chance to surrender. One . . . Two . . . Three.'

Boo opened the bulkhead door with a metal clank and jumped out of the way. Henderson shoved the bleeding sailor through the opening and gave him an almighty kick up the arse. There was a pistol blast as the sailor tripped on the ledge of the bulkhead. His body spun as the German officer shot his own man in the shoulder.

Marc glimpsed the shooter, but couldn't aim his knife before he ducked behind a huge diesel engine.

The German sailor thrashed about in agony as

Henderson peered warily through the bulkhead. Simultaneously a huge man in a greasy singlet and trousers jumped across the narrow channel that ran between two diesel engines, towards the hiding gunman. Henderson took aim at his trailing leg, but was all too aware of the fuel tank directly behind.

But the big man hadn't rushed across to help the officer, he was squashing the life out of him.

'Treason,' the officer shouted, as the other engineer and the rating emerged from behind a third engine further down the boat with hands raised in surrender.

Henderson rushed between the two engines, stepping over the sailor, as the engineer choked his superior officer.

'Don't shoot!' he shouted, raising his hands. 'A bullet in those tanks will blow us all sky high.'

'Is there anyone else apart from you lot?' Henderson shouted.

'We're all that's left,' the engineer shouted. 'You can shoot me in the head if that's not the truth.'

Henderson lowered his gun and nodded appreciatively to the big man, before waving the three surrendered Germans forwards. 'Get up on deck, no sudden moves.'

Then he shouted in English. 'Jarhope, you've got prisoners coming up. Do you hear me?'

'Ready and willing,' Jarhope shouted back.

Henderson looked at Marc. 'Tie up that officer before

he comes round, then find a medical kit and see what you can do for the bullet in the sailor's shoulder. Boo, your *absolute* priority is to get that radio working. Try and get a signal out to a Royal Navy ship. We need an escort or we'll end up being blown out of the sea by our own people.'

Marc looked down at the skinny, battered sailor. Trails of blood stretched from his head down to his boots and his right arm practically hung off at the shoulder. Marc had done basic first aid training, but this was beyond him.

'Can't you help?' Marc said, aghast.

'Whatever you can manage,' Henderson ordered. 'I'll be back as soon as I can, but if they sent off a distress signal while they were under attack, we could have half their fleet on our backs if we stick around.'

Henderson swept past Boo as she studied the controls of the German transmitter, then charged up the ladder into the bridge. Rufus had captained *Madeline*, but was laid out on deck, with blistered legs from the steam and arms embedded with glass. It wasn't pretty, but he'd live.

Jarhope had three prisoners to look after and was no sailor, so Henderson called Troy to the bridge. 'I know you can sail, but how about engines?'

'Never tried anything this big,' Troy said, as he studied the bloody controls. 'But it's a throttle and a wheel like my dad's old fishing boat.'

'Right,' Henderson nodded. 'I'm coordinating ten different things, so I want you to take the helm. Head north by north-north-west and keep an eye out for any other boats. I'll chart a proper course as soon as I can, but that's close enough for now.

'Once you've got a feel for how she handles, take her up to twenty-two knots for a quarter of an hour, then slow her down to ten. It's a long way back to Britain; I don't know our fuel status but I'll bet those big diesel engines have a thirst when you're moving fast.'

'Aye, Commander,' Troy said, proud to be in charge of a powerful thirty-five-metre boat, but a little scared too.

As Troy gently nudged the throttle, Henderson looked around for *Madeline*. 'Did the old girl go down?'

Troy nodded. 'Just after you went below deck. She was blazing – you must have been able to see the smoke over a wide area – so I told Jarhope to take the main gun and shoot her below the waterline.'

Henderson looked shocked. 'On your own initiative, without asking me?'

Troy shifted uneasily. 'Was that wrong, sir? You were below decks, I thought it was critical.'

'You were *absolutely* bloody right,' Henderson said, giving Troy a friendly slap on the back. 'Good stuff.'

Troy was getting a feel for the E-boat and pushed the throttle further forwards. 'If we get this boat back to Britain in one piece we can name her *Madeline II*.'

'Not a bad idea,' Henderson laughed as the boat picked up speed. 'Feel free to turn a little, start getting a feel for the rudder. You'll need to know what she can do if we run into trouble.'

'Right,' Troy nodded.

'Give me a shout if you need me,' Henderson said, as he moved towards the ladder. 'I'm going below to help Marc.'

'No problem,' Troy nodded. 'Oh, and congratulations on the baby, sir.'

Henderson shot back up the ladder. 'Pardon me?'

Troy gasped. 'Sir, I thought Boo already told you. I guess with everyone being so exhausted it slipped her mind.'

'Told me what?' Henderson said. 'Spit it out, boy.'

'It came through in our routine signal yesterday afternoon. McAfferty thought you'd want to know immediately. You have a son, sir; he was only five pounds two ounces, but he's in good health and so is your wife.'

'Well *bugger* me,' Henderson said.

Part Two

Four weeks later

CHAPTER TEN

Saturday 17 May 1941

Lightning flashed as a small truck crawled towards the top of a hill, getting slower and slower. The wiper blades squealed but fourteen-year-old Rosie Clarke still couldn't see more than fifty metres through the pelting rain.

'You need to change down, doll,' her boyfriend PT told her. 'You'll stall it.'

Rosie floored the clutch and put the truck in neutral, then after waiting for a second for the spinning gears to slow down she put the box into what she thought was second. The truck lurched, cogs in the gearbox sheared against one another and the engine died.

'That was first gear,' PT said. 'You need to throw the stick over for second.'

The truck started to roll backwards. Rosie hit the

brake pedal and turned the key to restart the engine, but the truck just stalled.

'You've got to put the clutch down,' PT said.

'Shut *up*,' Rosie shouted, as she pounded the steering wheel in frustration. 'I can't concentrate with you constantly babbling. Just look at the map and tell me which way to go. And stop calling me doll. I'm not your pet, your doll, your lady or any other stupid American name.'

PT smiled cheekily. 'You drive me wild when you're angry, toots.'

Rosie gritted her teeth as she started the engine again. She put the truck in first gear, let the clutch in, but stalled immediately and rolled back several metres before pulling on the handbrake.

'Well don't just sit there,' Rosie shouted. 'What am I doing wrong?'

'I thought you couldn't concentrate with my constant interference.'

Rosie let out a slow groan, then hesitated for a moment before flinging her door open and splashing down into the gravel road.

'Do you want me to drive?' PT asked.

It was raining so hard that water streaked out of Rosie's long dark hair. 'I hate you,' she said with a sob. 'I don't want anything from you or this dopey truck. Just bugger off!'

Rosie slammed the truck door and stormed uphill. PT crossed over to the driver's seat, then yelled after her.

'You'll catch pneumonia.'

Rosie spun around and gave PT the finger. 'Drop dead.'

'I'm not the one getting drowned.' PT told himself calmly, as he started the engine. He'd tried his hardest to help Rosie with her driving, but she was naturally bossy and didn't like taking instructions. Rather than try to pick her up, he decided to teach her a lesson.

'It's about a mile past the hilltop,' PT said, as he roared past Rosie, throwing up a sheet of spray. 'See you down there.'

The country lane took a few twists, passing barns and cottages, before he turned through a dark-blue gate and down a boggy path towards a dilapidated railway carriage standing on bricks.

'I'm here about a pig,' PT told the overalled farmer who came out to greet him.

'Pig, eh?' he said suspiciously. 'Who says I've got pigs? Pigs are strictly controlled and licensed. You can go to prison for illegal pigs.'

PT smiled as he jumped down from the cab. 'I heard about you from a friend,' he explained. 'She tells me you like a good whisky. Does Speyside, fifteen-year-old, sound good?'

The farmer's craggy face lit up as PT reached into the

truck and produced two bottles of Scotland's finest.

'Impossible to get hold of,' PT said. 'Whole supply goes to America to earn dollars for the war effort, but I can throw these in the deal if you *did* happen to have an unlicensed pig for sale.'

The farmer took half a step back and glowered. 'Don't like people knowing my business. Who's your friend exactly?'

'Lady by the name of Pippa. She's the cook with my unit up at the artillery range. We're having a celebration tonight, but it might go flat if all we've got is tins of corned beef.'

'Well, if Pippa sent you . . .' the farmer said, as he took one of the whisky bottles and turned it admiringly in his hand. 'Fifteen-year-old Speyside. I suppose there might be an animal I can spare.'

'Who'd have thought it?' PT smiled.

*

Charles Henderson made a dash from his cottage to CHERUB HQ, which was situated in an abandoned village school less than fifty metres away. He held a large umbrella in one hand, and clasped a tiny baby to his chest with the other. Troy's eight-year-old brother spotted him through the frosted glass and held the door open.

'Cheers, Mason,' Henderson said gratefully. 'Would you shake off the brolly and put it in the stand for me?'

'How's little Terence doing, sir?' Mason asked, as he took the umbrella.

'Not too badly,' Henderson said, as he crouched in front of a small glass case. It was home to Mavis, a large hairy spider who'd been made CHERUB's official mascot.

'This is Mavis,' Henderson told his son softly, as he stroked his tiny head. 'She's big and nasty, and if you're not careful she'll gobble you up. Very much like your mother, come to think of it.'

Terence was much too small to understand, but Mason laughed.

'I still can't believe how tiny he is,' Mason said. 'He's the smallest baby *ever*.'

'He was born two months before he was due, but he's got a good set of lungs and he's up to nearly seven pounds now.'

'So have you decided who's going over to France yet?' Mason asked.

'Well you're only eight, so we can safely rule you out.'

Mason laughed. 'I know that, sir. But it's all my brother and his mates keep talking about. It's starting to get on my nerves.'

'I'll put them all out of their misery soon enough,' Henderson said. 'Where are all the other lads?'

'Canoe training out on the lake,' Mason said. 'I wanted to go, but Superintendent McAfferty said it was best to stay warm because I only just got over my ear infection.'

'So you can hear on both sides again?' Henderson asked, as he opened the door of the office he shared with his commanding officer, Eileen McAfferty.

'Yes, sir,' Mason said.

As Henderson stepped into the office, McAfferty stood up behind her desk and broke into a big smile. Boo was also there. She looked stunning in bright-red lipstick and a well-fitted Wren's[3] uniform.

'You brought him over at last,' McAfferty said, as Henderson passed the baby across. 'Hello, Terence. Look at those tiny piggy-wigs. You know, I think he's grown since I saw him last week? But you're cuter than ever, aren't you? Yes you are, yes you arrrrrre!'

As Boo keenly awaited her turn with the baby, Henderson walked behind his desk with one eye on the pile in his in-tray and the other on Boo's slender waist and pert bottom.

'Any news on the supply situation?' Henderson asked.

Boo spun round efficiently and picked up a clipboard. 'Coming together well at the moment, sir. One of the latest radio sets has arrived at Porth Navas and been put aboard *Madeline II*. The folding canoes are due Monday

---

[3] Wren – a female member of the Royal Navy, derived from WRNS (Women's Royal Naval Service).

morning at the latest. We're still waiting on RAF confirmation, but we're expecting air support later in the operation if we need equipment dropped.'

'Took long enough, but at least they're behind us now,' Henderson said.

'I also took a call from the engineers at Porth Navas. They've located a high-speed launch built in Germany. It's fitted with sixteen-cylinder Daimler engines and the owners imported a good supply of spare parts as a precaution before war broke out.'

'That's excellent,' Henderson said. 'I was worried we'd have to cannibalise one of *Madeline II*'s engines for spare parts.'

'Oh, and your gold braid arrived from London, *Captain* Henderson.'

'Can you sew, Third Officer?' Henderson asked.

'I did needlework at Roedean,' Boo said. 'I think I can manage to add a stripe.'

McAfferty laughed. 'I thought sailors were supposed to be able to sew and mend their *own* clothes.'

'Never really got the knack,' Henderson said. 'Probably balls it up, make myself an Admiral by mistake.'

Boo smiled. 'Shall I go over to the house and collect your dress uniform?'

'Best if I go,' Henderson said. 'If my wife wakes up and sees you she might start throwing things.'

'Very good, sir,' Boo said.

Henderson looked around as the top of something streaked past the window. Then he heard a high-pitched squeal.

'Am I going mad, or did I just see a pig run by?'

McAfferty smiled as she spoke to Terence. 'I think Daddy's been on the whisky again.'

'Chance would be a fine thing,' Henderson said. 'I had a couple of bottles of Speyside put by and I can't find the damned things anywhere.'

Henderson heard someone entering the hallway outside. He stepped out of the office to find Rosie clomping up the stairs with her dress soaked through.

'What the devil's the matter with you?' Henderson asked.

'I hate my life,' Rosie shouted tearfully, before running up the rest of the stairs and slamming the door of her dorm.

Henderson briefly considered going after her, but he had as much desire to get involved with a sobbing teenage girl as he did to stick his arm in a bear trap. Instead he went outside and tracked noise and shouts to the side of the building.

PT, Rosie's twelve-year-old brother Paul and campus cook Pippa were forming a barrier to try and block in a medium-sized pig, while training instructor Khinde looked particularly fierce standing shirtless with a wooden club in one hand and a chisel in the other.

'Where the blazes did we get a pig?' Henderson asked, as he walked towards the fray.

PT smiled mischievously as the pig backed itself into a corner of the former school's playground.

'Ask me no questions, I'll tell you no lies,' PT said. 'We wanted some roast pork for the party.'

Henderson wasn't sure how to respond. As a navy officer he'd been trained to come down hard on every breach of discipline, but CHERUB wasn't drilling a crew to man a warship. Henderson wanted his agents to think for themselves, and getting hold of a black market pig had probably taught his team more about espionage than most of the training they got on campus. Besides which, he loved roast pork.

The pig suddenly took the initiative, trying to break out of the corner by swerving around Pippa, crashing into a pair of metal dustbins and running full pelt towards Henderson. He didn't fancy a collision with a sixty-kilo pig, but as he dived out of the way he slipped on the wet tarmac and his trailing leg tripped the speeding beast.

Khinde had caught up and brought down the club. The animal squealed desperately as the first blow struck the top of its head. It stumbled forwards in a daze, tripping on its own forelegs before Khinde's second blow cracked the skull and knocked it out.

As Henderson found his feet, Khinde lifted the unconscious pig's head and jammed the chisel expertly through the main artery at the throat. With its final spasms, the pig's heart squirted blood across painted hopscotch lines, narrowly missing Khinde's chest.

Pippa and Khinde had clearly dealt with slaughter before, but PT was cringing and Paul held his stomach like he was about to throw up. Henderson took the chance to reassert his authority, as Khinde dragged the bleeding pig towards the kitchen by its hind legs.

'You two boys,' he said, pointing down at the blood. 'I don't want the little ones trailing through that mess. Get brooms and water and start scrubbing.'

CHAPTER ELEVEN

It was late enough for the youngest kids on campus to start wilting, but long summer days meant that sun still hovered above the trees. A dozen boys stood around a large fire, eating pork, crackling and roast potatoes cooked in rosemary. CHERUB was part of the military, so the kids got more generous rations than civilians, but while they never went hungry, unlimited fresh meat was a rare treat.

Rosie had pulled herself together, but was still in a sulk. Her brother Paul broke away from the other boys and sat beside her in the grass.

'More pork?' he asked, offering his metal plate.

She looked away and sighed.

'I was jealous when you first got close to PT,' Paul said. 'But now I think he's a good sort.'

'I don't want to talk about him,' Rosie said. 'It's the way he spoke to me, like I was a little girl. I've driven motorbikes, and McAfferty's little Austin, but that stupid truck *hates* me.'

Paul smiled as Mason ran past, chased by a skinny girl of seven. 'Rosie, you were exactly the same when Dad tried teaching you to ride a bike. You've got no patience. Go and talk to PT.'

Rosie's lips went all thin. 'Don't tell me how to run my life,' she said. 'I had to walk down a long muddy path to reach that god-forsaken farm, and when I got to the truck, PT said he'd throw me in the back with the pig if I didn't stop moaning.'

Paul found this hilarious, but didn't dare laugh and was pleased to spot a distraction. 'Oh my god, look at Henderson!'

Rosie turned her head and saw Henderson standing close to Boo, with one hand resting on a tree and the other creeping up the back of her leg.

'Oh he's awful,' Rosie said. 'He's twice her age. He'll be flirting with me next.'

'Not to mention the wife and baby,' Paul said.

But Henderson got no more than a slight touch of Boo's buttock before she hopped away and slapped his arm. They couldn't hear what Boo said, but judging by her expression it wasn't nice. Henderson stepped away sharpish, with the careless gait of someone who'd had too much to drink.

Two more lads broke off from the main group and came over to join Paul and Rosie. Joel was fourteen, half French, half German, with shaggy blond hair. Luc was a year younger, built like a German tank and about as popular.

'So who'll get picked for the mission then?' Joel asked, as he looked at Rosie. 'I bet you do. It's only you and Boo who can send radio messages at a decent speed.'

'Odds on Marc,' Luc added with a sneer. 'Henderson's in love with him.'

'Maybe that's because Marc's *good* at everything,' Paul said.

Luc shook his head. 'Better than you maybe.'

'Luc, all you've done is train,' Rosie said. 'What do you know about working undercover? You've no experience.'

'I know if a skinny weed like Paul can hack it then I can. What were you screaming and bawling about earlier, anyway? Did PT try getting inside your knickers again?'

Rosie shot up, eyeballed Luc and poked him in the chest. 'Why don't you crawl back into the woods and join all the other bugs under a rock?'

'I know you love me really, Rosie,' Luc said. 'You can't resist me for ever.'

Luc grinned slyly as he walked away. Paul shuddered. 'I hate him *so* much! I almost don't care whether I get to go on the mission or not, as long as I'm doing the opposite of whatever Luc's doing.'

'You're not wrong,' Joel said. 'Luc's hard as nails, but I wouldn't trust him.'

Over by the fire McAfferty clapped her hands for attention. She tried to disguise her strong Glasgow accent, but it always came back when she raised her voice.

'I'd like to say a few words before it gets too late,' she began. 'We're gathered here tonight to celebrate many things. Firstly, Captain Henderson's promotion and the birth of his son Terence.'

A round of applause and a few cheers came from the thirty-strong crowd, and Henderson took a bow before McAfferty continued. 'I'd also like to mention Marc, who played such an important role in this unit's first successful operation, along with Rufus, Troy and Boo aboard poor old *Madeline*.

'I'd like to congratulate the trainees from group B, who recently completed their basic training, and welcome the new recruits who've joined us over the last few weeks who will eventually form training group C. I also believe PT will be celebrating his sixteenth birthday in a few days' time. Finally, I'd like to thank our amazing cook Pippa for the fabulous food we've eaten, and of course George the pig who gave his life to save us from another day of tinned beef.'

'Three cheers for Espionage Research Unit B,' Boo shouted when the applause died down. 'Hip-hip!'

As the third and loudest *hooray* subsided, Henderson stepped up beside McAfferty and sounded very drunk.

'Three weeks ago, me and Marc – sorry, Marc and I – spent twenty-four hours in occupied France, but that was just the beg . . . the beginning of a much, much . . . *much* larger operation. The following agents should report to classroom C tomorrow morning at ten a.m. for a mission briefing.'

Henderson felt around in his pockets for several seconds before looking up at the anxious faces of CHERUB's twelve qualified agents.

'I've lost the sodding piece of paper. Boo, can you remember who we picked?'

A few people laughed, but the eleven boys, plus Rosie, were too tense. Boo stepped up and spoke with calm authority.

'The following agents will report at ten tomorrow. Joel, Marc, Paul, PT, Rosie and Troy. The remaining agents in groups A and B should attend lessons and training as usual.'

There were no overt celebrations because the agents who'd been picked were sensitive to the feelings of those who hadn't. Only Luc spoke, making sure it was loud enough for all the staff to hear.

'This is a rip-off! Why am I the only trainee out of

group A who didn't get picked?'

'Because you're a complete tit?' PT suggested caustically.

*

At five to ten the next morning, Henderson stepped into classroom C, wearing dark glasses and with his hair standing in all directions.

'More damned rain,' he told Boo, who was already in there writing key points of the mission plan on a blackboard. 'I apologise for last night. I think we both had a lot to drink and rather made fools of ourselves.'

Boo turned away from the blackboard and spoke acidly. 'I don't recall that I drank much or did anything embarrassing, sir. But the important thing is that it *doesn't* happen again.'

'Understood, Third Officer,' Henderson said formally, as he opened up a briefcase and buried his face in his briefing papers.

He began reading from them ten minutes later, while using a pointing stick to highlight areas of Boo's chalk diagrams.

'Lorient is the largest of six U-boat bases along France's Atlantic coast. Your mission briefings contain maps of the town, details of the U-boat dock and bunkers under construction at Keroman along with aerial surveillance photographs. We've successfully established contact with a small and informally organised resistance group run by a restaurant and brothel owner named Brigitte Mercier.'

'She's one *scary* lady,' Marc added.

'So far their activities have been restricted to smuggling refugees and RAF pilots out of the country. Last week, a radio operator who has been working in France for some time arrived in the area and re-established contact with Mercier's group. We've now established daily radio contact so the locals know we're coming and are making arrangements for our arrival.

'Working with an established group like this speeds things up and has huge benefits, because nothing beats local knowledge. Madame Mercier herself is one of the best-connected people in Lorient. However, there is also a significant risk, because the group have had no proper espionage training and up to now their security has been slack.'

Paul raised his hand. 'But security should be pretty good if they all know each other, shouldn't it?'

'Security is only ever as good as your weakest link,' Henderson explained. 'Even the most outstanding person can be compromised if their loyalties are divided. For instance, Paul, if the Gestapo captured you and told you that they'd mercilessly torture Rosie unless you set up a meeting where the rest of your group would be captured and arrested, would your loyalty be to us, or to her?'

Paul looked awkwardly at Rosie. 'I'd probably let them torture her, because the Gestapo would kill us both eventually anyway.'

Rosie, along with the four boys, laughed. 'Cheers, mate!' she said.

'And what if they tortured *you*?' Henderson asked.

'Oh that's completely different,' Paul said. 'I'd sell the lot of you down the river like a shot.'

Everyone laughed it off, though in the back of their minds they all knew capture and torture was a real possibility.

'There's an old saying,' Henderson said. 'Three can keep a secret if two are dead. And the point I'm trying to make is that security is *everything*. One slip-up could get us all killed.

'To minimise risks, we'll be divided into three teams, spread over several kilometres. Marc and I will be based in Lorient, working in a bar owned by Madame Mercier and frequented by high-ranking German officers. We both speak German, so hopefully we'll be able to pick up some information when they've been on the sauce.

'PT, Joel and Troy will be based at Kerneval with Alois Clement.'

'Isn't he the one who wanted to throw you in the harbour?'

'Yes,' Henderson said. 'And as much as I didn't like his suspicious attitude when his friend was pointing a gun at my head, his cautious nature is really no bad thing.

'All plans are subject to change, but hopefully Troy will work in the port, alongside Alois, his brother Nicolas and his two great-nephews. Joel and PT are old enough to get apprentice jobs with OT, working on the bunker construction sites, or in the docks themselves. Their roles will be to learn as much as they can about U-boat operations and bunker construction, and try to spot sabotage opportunities.

'The third and final unit will be our communications team, comprising Paul, Rosie and Boo. You three will be running the radio link to Britain. You'll have to scout a suitable location when you arrive, but the aim is to find you a base a few kilometres from Lorient.

'Since we first operated in France last year, the Germans have developed an excellent radio detection service that has uncovered a large number of British radio operators. They have monitoring stations throughout France that can detect undercover transmissions to within a kilometre or two. Once the approximate location is pinpointed by the network, specially trained teams of Gestapo agents go out in the field to find the exact source of transmission. This means that the radio operators must switch locations on a regular basis.

'Our three groups will travel to France together aboard

Madeline II, but once we arrive communication will be kept to the absolute minimum. If members of one group are captured, the other two groups should be able to continue operating independently.'

Marc raised his hand. 'Sir, this may sound like a stupid question, but now we know where the submarines are, why doesn't the RAF send over a couple of hundred bombers and blow the whole place to hell?'

'It's not a stupid question, in fact many people think that's exactly what we should do, Henderson said. 'But there are two reasons why we won't. First, at present the Royal Air Force has a policy not to bomb targets in heavily populated areas of France, because it's believed large-scale civilian casualties could turn the French population against us. Secondly, there are rarely more than three or four U-boats docked at Lorient at any one time. They're small targets and the port is heavily defended.'

'What about the bunkers?' Marc asked.

Boo answered this question. 'The photographs you took of the bunkers were assessed by structural engineers and bombing experts. Attacking such heavily fortified bunkers is unlikely to do much more than delay their completion by a few weeks.'

'So this is going to be a long and hard mission,' Henderson said. 'We've got to get stuck right in, use all our training to find out what the Germans are up to, pick out their weaknesses and exploit them mercilessly. If you're captured, the dangers of a slow and painful death are all too real. So if you think it's all going to be too much for you, raise your hand now and nobody will think any worse of you for not volunteering.'

The kids glanced at one another and there was a gasp as Troy's hand shot up.

Henderson looked disappointed and aimed a hand towards the door. 'Well, I'd rather you faced up to it now than develop a bout of nerves later.'

'I'm fine about the mission, sir,' Troy said, breaking into a smile. 'But I'm absolutely busting for a wee.'

Everyone laughed until Henderson tapped his pointer on the blackboard to bring them to attention.

'All right, Troy, very funny,' Henderson said. 'But on a serious note, we've got lots to do and not much time to get through it. *Madeline II* sails from Porth Navas on Thursday, we aim to land near Lorient some time on Saturday.'

CHAPTER TWELVE

Tuesday 20 May 1941

The team were roused at five. Pippa made porridge and everyone got up to say goodbye, except Luc, who stayed in the boys' dorm sulking.

'Don't get yourself killed,' Mason told Troy, as the brothers hugged and tried not to cry.

McAfferty sobbed when she hugged Henderson, who gave in to emotion when he kissed his infant son and realised that he'd look different the next time he saw him. Soon there was a big show of hugs and sniffles, and Rufus had to hurry everyone to the canvas-sided truck because there was a train to catch.

The journey took up most of the day. Three hours to London St Pancras, Underground to Paddington, a six-and-a-half-hour ride to Falmouth and then a Royal Navy truck to Porth Navas Creek on the Helford River.

Madeline II was twice the size of any other boat in the espionage flotilla and the six young agents were excited to see her. The captured German E-boat looked utterly out of place amongst the flotilla's mainstay of French fishing boats and cabin cruisers.

'Captain on deck,' someone shouted, as Henderson led his team up the gangplank.

'Might actually be able to get some sleep aboard this thing,' Marc told Troy as a navy officer came up through the rear hatch.

He was average height, but stocky and wore thick glasses. He buttoned his jacket before saluting Henderson.

'Welcome aboard, Captain! I'm Lieutenant Commander Finch and honoured to serve with you.'

'At ease,' Henderson said, before shaking the lieutenant's hand and introducing Finch to Rufus, Boo and the six kids. 'How's the rest of our crew coming together?'

'Working up well, Captain,' Finch said. 'We've got twelve men, all volunteers from regular duties. One of the German engineers you captured has been very cooperative in terms of technical information on the boat. We had our Kriegsmarine uniforms delivered yesterday. The lads had a laugh trying them on.'

Henderson smiled. 'And the first sea trial?'

'Excellent, sir,' Finch said, as he led the party into the bridge. 'Had her up to thirty knots on the open sea before things got choppy. The boat is seven months old, which is about perfect in my opinion: long enough for the Krauts have ironed out the glitches you always get with a new vessel, but not enough time for anything major to wear out.'

'Quite a few changes,' Henderson noted, as he looked around the bridge. 'Mind you, it was a bloodbath the last time I was in here.'

'Our only problem with the sea trial was we got picked up by a Spitfire from coastal command. Damned thing shot at us, until I sent a couple of men out on deck to wave a great Union Jack around.'

Henderson smiled. 'Getting shot up by our own people is going to be a problem. We can inform major ships operating in the same area as us, but there's no way to alert the whole fleet and air command without the Germans getting wind of our operations.'

'We've made a few adaptations,' Finch said. 'British navigational gear and a radar set.'

Henderson looked surprised. 'You got hold of a radar set?'

Finch nodded proudly. 'All ocean-going navy ships are being fitted, regardless of size, but we've lost so many boats in the Atlantic and Mediterranean the navy has more radar sets than ships to put them in. The radar antenna makes us look different from a standard E-boat on the outside, but you've got to look hard and the benefits outweigh the risks.'

Finch looked concerned as Troy hovered over the controls and newly installed navigational equipment.

'Don't worry about him, Lieutenant Commander,' Henderson said. 'Troy piloted this boat back from France and even picked up my mistake when I plotted the wrong course. We nearly gave a couple of Cornish fishermen heart attacks when they saw a German torpedo boat cruising up river behind them!'

'Armaments will be our biggest problem,' Finch explained. 'There's a limited supply of German torpedoes, but without proper maintenance and crew training we're as likely to blow ourselves up if we dare to fire them. We're trying to source British replacements for the main deck guns, but that won't happen in time for this voyage, so we'll be setting off with limited supplies of German ammunition.'

Henderson nodded gravely. 'Let's try and stay clear of any shoot-outs then.' Then he turned towards Troy. 'You know the boat well enough. I've got a lot to discuss with the Lieutenant Commander, so why don't you take the others on a tour below deck, then we'll head off and try to find our quarters.'

*

Porterbrook was a mile's walk from the creek. The two-storey Georgian house was headquarters for the Helford Flotilla. Only agents and espionage officers stayed here, while the navy men who crewed many of the boats bunked at Falmouth naval base a few kilometres east.

The downstairs had been knocked together to make a large dining room and lounge. Upstairs was the bathroom and bedrooms for officers, while lower ranks and civilians had to make do with a pair of prefabricated Nissen huts in the back garden.

The house was deserted, apart from an elderly Canadian Brigadier named Ouellet and two local women who cooked and cleaned. There was a lamb hotpot waiting on arrival, which went down well after the long journey, followed by a steamed jam pudding with clotted cream.

After eating, the kids listened to the BBC Forces Programme while taking turns at a snooker table. Troy, Marc, Paul, Rosie and Joel had all grown up in France where tables were rare, and had fun competing over who was the most hopeless. PT had played a few games in bars when he'd worked aboard a steam ship, but he was annihilated by Boo, who'd grown up with a table in the family castle. She regularly rattled off breaks of fifty or sixty, while complaining that the game wasn't much of a challenge on a half-sized table.

Henderson sat in an armchair facing the Brigadier, drinking whisky and admiring Boo when she bent over the table. There was a ten o'clock curfew on campus, and the kids kept expecting him to send them to bed, but they kept on playing until eleven thirty when the BBC shut down and everyone stood for the national anthem.

The room seemed eerily quiet when the anthem ended, and Brigadier Ouellet's boots tapped the parquet floor as he stepped across to turn off the set.

'Have you all been revising your identities for the mission?' the Brigadier asked.

The kids were intimidated by his formal tone, medals and epaulettes, so their nods and *yeses* came stiff and uncomfortable.

The Brigadier pointed at a clock on the mantelpiece. 'In a few moments, you will retire to bed. When it turns midnight, you will take on the identities you have been given for your mission. You will speak only in French. You will address one another by the names given in your French identity documents. You could be tested on your back story at any time and if you make a slip-up there will be consequences. Goodnight, and sleep well.'

Boo, Rufus and Henderson stayed in the house, while the six youngsters went out the back door and found their way across the lawn. They kept quiet until they were all under the curved metal roof of the Nissen hut, sitting on their narrow bunks pulling off shoes and unbuttoning shirts. Rosie was the only girl, but after more than six months of living together on campus, nobody thought about modesty.

'Brigadier whatsisname seems weird,' Marc said, as he burrowed through his suitcase looking for pyjama bottoms.

'Drunk as a skunk,' Joel said. 'Him and Henderson practically emptied that bottle between them.'

'Did you see Henderson eyeing up Boo?' Rosie said. 'He's got *such* a dirty mind.'

Troy cocked his leg and cracked a huge fart.

'Better than a dirty arse,' Marc said, as he gave Troy a dead arm.

'Henderson just has appetites, like all men do,' PT said. 'Most of you are too young to understand.'

'I know how to fertilise a girl,' Paul said, always anxious not to be seen as the baby of the group.

'A man either gets what he wants, or goes somewhere else for it,' PT said. 'That's the way of the world.'

'Not if you're a married man it isn't,' Rosie said furiously.

Joel laughed. 'Well, well: the two lovebirds are speaking to each other again.'

'Believe me,' PT said. 'I spent over a year crewing boats around the Mediterranean and when men go ashore, the ones who are married act no different to the ones who ain't.'

'Lots of men behave decently,' Rosie said. 'They're not all animals like *you*.'

'Can you two bicker tomorrow?' Joel asked. 'I've been up since half four, I'm getting the light. Is everyone ready?'

Everyone was either under the covers or ready to get in, so he popped the light off. Troy did another noisy fart as Joel walked back to his bed.

'Aww you stink,' Paul complained, as Troy laughed under his sheets.

CHAPTER THIRTEEN

Marc's eyes shot open as a hand clamped across his mouth. He thought it was Troy getting revenge for the dead arm, but Troy wasn't strong enough to pull him off his bunk and throw him over his shoulder. It was pitch black, but he could hear men dragging the others out of bed. Ironically, out of the six it was Paul – the smallest – who gave the most trouble by jumping up, swinging from a roof beam and giving his assailant a two-footed kick in the teeth.

'Name and age?' the man screamed in English.

Marc remembered what the Brigadier had told them before bedtime. 'Marc Hortefeux, thirteen years old.'

'So you speak English?' the man said, as he pinched Marc's cheek.

The pinch hurt, but the realisation that he'd fallen for

a simple interrogator's trick by answering a question in the language it was asked hurt more. The light in the room came on, and he glimpsed Paul wriggling through a window as PT was dragged outside with his hands cuffed behind his back.

Marc had a canvas bag thrust over his head. It smelled like mildew and its drawstring handle was pulled around his neck, not strangling him but enough to make breathing hard.

'Walkies!' the man said. His accent sounded slightly American, so Marc guessed that he was Canadian, like the Brigadier.

Marc couldn't see, but he felt mud under his soles as two men frogmarched him across a field at jogging pace. His breath and the dank smell made it stifling inside the mask. After a minute his feet moved on to tarmac. He heard a large door open, like a barn door. His feet were swept off the ground and suddenly he was plunged into a freezing bath filled with slabs of ice.

He kicked and slapped his arms in the water as his head was held under for a minute. Shivering uncontrollably, he was forced to kneel with his forehead resting against something hard, then his hood was ripped off. Marc saw that he was knelt against the front of a car and a second later the headlamps were switched on, shining directly into his eyes.

'Welcome to Gestapo headquarters,' one of the Canadians said.

Marc heard a groan to his right, and saw that Troy was in an identical position, knelt against the other headlight.

'Don't think we're going easy because you're kids,' another Canadian said.

Marc couldn't tell if there were three or four of them.

'How can kids go undercover? You'll break in two seconds flat.'

'Go screw your mothers,' Troy shouted.

Marc heard Troy get slapped.

'Now I know which one to electrocute first,' someone said.

'You can call me God,' the biggest man said. 'I'm setting an alarm clock to go off in twenty minutes. Every time you make an admission, the other boy gets an electric shock. If either of you wants to quit before the twenty minutes are up, you can beg for mercy. But if you can't stand this for twenty minutes, you're not gonna be tough enough to face the real Gestapo, are you?'

'No, sir,' Marc said.

'No, God,' Troy said.

God grabbed Marc's muddy foot and twisted his big toe. 'What do you call me?'

'God,' Marc said, gasping.

'OK, boy. You're going to admit that yellow is your favourite colour.'

'Am I bollocks,' Marc said.

'Give him something to drink,' God ordered.

Two men grabbed Marc. As one ripped his head back by pulling his hair, the other forced a rubber hose into his mouth and turned a wall-mounted tap, firing a powerful jet of water down his throat. The water triggered his gag reflex, but the vomit shooting up his throat was blocked by the water flooding his mouth and nose. He was drowning and vomiting at the same time. As he fought to break loose he could feel water splashing down his chest and a sense of dread, worse than anything he'd ever felt before.

The voice of God counted out the seconds, each one feeling like a month. 'Twenty-eight, twenty-nine, thirty.'

The hose was ripped out and Marc crashed forwards. He spat the water and thrashed about, coughing up chunks of vomit lodged in the back of his mouth.

'What's your favourite colour?' God demanded.

Marc remembered what Henderson had taught them: if you're being tortured, do everything you can to slow the process down. Cough for twice as long as you need to. Clear your throat three times. Look as if you want to speak, but make rasping noises and beg for a drink.

'I know what you're doing,' God shouted. 'Tell me that your favourite colour is yellow, or the pipe goes back in, this time for a full minute.'

Marc tried not to think about it. Once the pipe went in, you couldn't move or speak. He'd have to take the full minute. But he didn't want to look weak. What kind of sign was he giving if he gave in after one attempt?

Marc was hauled up off the dirt floor.

'Well?' God asked. 'Is yellow your favourite colour?'

Marc gritted his teeth. 'Always preferred red.'

'Right,' God shouted.

The other two grabbed Marc and tipped his head back. This time his fear made him fight much harder, refusing to open his mouth even when they pinched his nose. But Marc realised he'd only made it worse for himself, because he was already short of breath when the pipe went in. He managed to push his tongue back to stop the jet making him vomit, but the water seemed colder this time and after the struggle his neck was bent back painfully.

'Twenty-three . . . twenty-four . . .'

Marc tried telling himself that this was part of his training, they weren't really going to let him die, but that wasn't how he felt as the water choked him.

'Fifty-seven . . . fifty-eight . . .'

The tube came out and he slumped on to his chest, sobbing with pain and gasping for air.

'No delaying tactics,' God told him, as he placed his boot on Marc's back. 'Tell me in three seconds or the tube goes down for a minute and a half.'

'Yellow,' Marc sobbed. 'I love yellow.'

Troy yelped as one of the other Canadians delivered his electric shock.

'OK, Troy,' God said, as the other men positioned Marc back on his knees with the headlamp blazing in his eyes. 'You once owned a pet rabbit called Fluffles.'

One of the Canadians clipped a wire linked to the shock apparatus to the waist of Marc's sodden pyjamas, and another to the bottom of the leg.

Troy had watched Marc's suffering. He fought as the men pulled his head back, but chickened out when he saw the pipe, which still had chunks of Marc's puke stuck to it.

'I once owned a rabbit called Fluffles,' Troy shouted.

Marc went into spasm as the electric shock fizzed through his wet pyjamas. It wasn't too painful, but he turned angrily towards Troy. 'You can't even hold out for one little squirt?' he shouted. 'You useless wimp!'

'That's what they want you to say,' Troy shouted back. 'They're trying to set us against each other.'

'Don't give me that,' Marc shouted.

'Well isn't this fun?' God said. 'This time it'll just be electric shocks, but we'll up the current from fifty amps to four hundred. Marc, tell me that your favourite actress is Vivien Leigh.'

'Yeah she is,' Marc said, pointing at Troy. 'I love her.

Adore her. She's my favourite, now zap him.'

There was a fizz of electricity and the much more powerful shock made Troy howl with pain. The Canadians had backed off so that they didn't catch the shock and Troy – who also remembered what he'd been taught about delaying the interrogation process – jumped up and made a run for it.

He only got about three steps before one of the Canadians got him around the neck, swept his legs away and slammed him to the floor.

God was distracted and Marc saw his opportunity, standing up and jumping on to the bonnet of the car. He slid over the polished metal and jumped down beside the passenger door. The headlights were on, so Marc figured that the key was in the ignition. He went to get in the driver's seat, planning a daring charge through the wooden doors, but was gutted to see piles of bricks where the front wheels were supposed to be.

Instead he turned to the apparatus used for giving electric shocks. The device was on wheels and had been adapted from a rack used for charging car batteries. As a Canadian who'd run around the back of the car closed in, Marc gave it an almighty shove.

The apparatus toppled forwards, making the lead that was connecting it to the mains electricity pull tight, before lashing forwards with such force that the plug ripped the socket out of the wall. The bulbs on the ceiling flickered, then went out, plunging the barn into darkness, apart from the two narrow headlight beams which were powered by the car battery.

'That's the main fuse,' someone shouted.

Marc's path to the exit was blocked by God, but there was nowhere else to go so he made a run for it. Within three steps, he was sandwiched between God and the man who'd run behind the car. Marc's backward kick didn't connect, and he was soon flat on his chest with a knee pressed against his back and Troy's face close enough for the boys to feel each other's breath.

'Little shits,' God shouted, as he leaned over the shock apparatus. 'This is wrecked. You two are dead, you hear me, dead?'

'I'm not scared of you,' Marc shouted. 'Do your worst, I reckon you've got eight minutes left before you have to let me go, and you can't zap us because I broke your toy.'

'What do you want me to do, sir?' the man pinning Troy to the floor asked.

Troy whispered to Marc. 'Sorry I wimped out.'

'You bloody should be,' Marc replied bitterly.

'We've still got the hose and the ice bath, sir,' said the man holding Marc down. 'Or we could cuff 'em and hang 'em on the wall by their wrists.'

Marc saw someone new come through the door, and recognised his voice.

'And what exactly will that prove?' Brigadier Ouellet

asked. 'You're not here to torture them. You're here to see whether these boys have got what it takes to stand up to an interrogator, and I think they've made their case, don't you? Give 'em both a kick up the arse and send them back to bed.'

*

Henderson decided to let his team lie in until nine. When they came along to the house for breakfast, he sat at a long dining table, dipping bread soldiers into a soft-boiled egg and enjoying the act rather more than anyone older than ten was supposed to.

'Sleep well?' Henderson asked, stifling a smile.

'What do you think?' Marc said bitterly. 'You could have warned us.'

'Where would the fun have been in that?' Henderson asked.

The room filled with the sound of grating chairs as the kids took their places. The cook brought over two bowls of eggs and a steaming pot of tea.

'Soft-boiled, hard-boiled,' she explained. 'Go easy on the milk, we're almost out.'

'Where's Boo?' Rosie asked. 'She seemed shaken up by it all.'

Marc hadn't realised Boo had been dragged out of bed with the kids, though she was less experienced at undercover work than he was, so it made sense.

'I think she withstood the unpleasantness as well as

can be expected,' Henderson said. 'But she's mortified that the ice bath ruined her hairdo.'

'Of course, some of us didn't let ourselves get captured in the first place,' Paul said.

'You're *so* smug,' Rosie howled. 'You only got out because your bed was right next to the window.'

'And nobody except a skinny beanpole like you could have got through that gap,' Joel added.

Henderson spoke gravely. 'Actually, Paul, you've got to report to barn C after breakfast for a twenty-minute interrogation session with the Canadians.'

Paul looked aghast and dropped the egg off his teaspoon. A weak, 'Oh . . .' was all he could manage.

'Gotcha!' Henderson said.

Paul gasped with relief as the others cracked up laughing.

'Paul, you looked like you were gonna lay a brick in your pants,' Marc said.

'In complete seriousness, I'd steer clear of the chap you kicked in the mouth,' Henderson said. 'He got driven off to see an emergency dentist in Falmouth, so I don't think he's your biggest fan.'

Rosie leaned across and gave Paul a peck on the cheek. 'My baby brother,' she said proudly. 'I never knew he had it in him.'

'Morning,' Brigadier Ouellet said brightly, as he came in from the hallway. Boo was directly behind, and everyone looked shocked because her hair was combed flat, she was bare-legged and she wore a short summer dress instead of her smart Wren's uniform.

'I'm drooling,' Joel whispered to PT, who nodded in agreement once he was sure that Rosie wasn't looking his way.

'Your lot put up a jolly good fight last night,' the Brigadier told Henderson, before glancing at his watch. 'Remember to keep in character at all times. Our tailors are getting ready down in the garden, you need to be ready in the lounge with everything you're planning to take over to France.'

CHAPTER FOURTEEN

Marc and Troy left the house by the back door and walked the length of the garden with their suitcases. They were heading to a Nissen hut in a field several hundred metres from the house, but were struck by their own bare footprints in the mud leading towards the barns.

'I'm really sorry about last night,' Troy said. 'I should have stuck it out with the hose. I want you to even the score.'

Marc looked curious. 'How exactly?'

Troy put his case on the grass and stood still with his arms behind his back. 'Take a free shot at me.'

Marc shrugged. 'Just forget it.'

'I feel really bad,' Troy said.

Marc shook his head and grinned. 'You really want me

to thump you?'

Troy pushed out his stomach. Marc was pissed off that he'd suffered so badly from the hose, but he liked Troy and didn't blame him. Nobody is really in control of themselves when faced with that level of fear.

'I'm stronger than you,' Marc said, as he bunched his fist. 'You'd better not run back to the house bawling.'

'I won't,' Troy said. 'Hit me.'

Marc threw his first, but as Troy flinched Marc pulled his punch and went for Troy's nipple, giving it an almighty twist. This was painful, but there was no risk of causing an injury serious enough to jeopardise the mission.

'Bugger me!' Troy howled, as he stumbled backwards clutching his chest.

Marc tripped Troy up, but grabbed his arm so that he didn't hit the ground hard. Then he gave him a two-fingered jab in the ribs.

'You half killed me, you little bastard,' Troy said, in pain but laughing too.

'Good,' Marc said, as he picked his case back up. 'Now we're even.'

As Troy and Marc headed towards the hut in good spirits, PT and Paul started walking the other way with their luggage.

'Everything OK?' Troy asked.

'It's so bad,' Paul said gravely.

'Yeah,' PT said. 'Especially the bit where you have to

bend over and they shove a red-hot poker up your bum.'

Marc tutted. 'Yeah, I'm really falling for that. Are you gonna tell us or what?'

'*What*,' Paul said, as PT made a whiplash sound followed by a scream.

All Nissen huts were made from curved metal sections, but this one comprised twelve sections, making it twice as long as the one they'd slept in. Just inside the door were two large tables, designed for cutting fabric, with a pedal-powered sewing machine at the end of each one. Beyond this area was storage: rails of old clothes and shoes, shelves stacked with suitcases and boxes of personal items such as toothpaste, cigarettes and shaving foam. All were French brands in French packaging.

There were two Jewish Frenchwomen inside. One was elderly with shrunken mole-like eyes; she took Troy's case while a younger lady with witchlike tangles of black hair and a tape measure around her neck grabbed Marc.

'My name is Lael,' she began. 'Are you Hortefeux or Jarre?'

'Hortefeux,' Marc said.

'You're a handsome boy,' Lael said, then shouted across to her colleague. 'Yetta, look at this beautiful thing.'

Yetta laughed as she put Troy's suitcase on her tabletop. 'I think *mine* is more handsome,' she laughed.

'Now I need you to strip,' Lael said, as she opened

Marc's case and threw everything out. 'Have you got everything here that you're taking to France? Not a pyjama top still in your bedroom, or a picture of your mother on your bedside table?'

Marc shook his head as he unbuttoned his shirt.

'No point being modest,' Lael said, as Marc slowly unbuttoned his shirt. 'I've got to check every single piece of clothing, and this suitcase is no good for a start, it's got *Made in Derby* printed inside the lid.'

Lael and Yetta were mirror images, taking the boys' clothes and belongings and carefully inspecting the seams and labels. Very few passed muster.

'What are you looking for?' Marc asked.

Lael seemed happy to answer as she held up one of Marc's shirts. 'This came from France. You can tell by the soft collar and the feel of the fabric. But this one is different. The collar is stiffer, the cuffs are square rather than rounded and it's a fine Indian cotton that you wouldn't often see in mainland Europe. Even though it has no label, I can tell that it was made in Britain. And if I can tell that almost all of your clothes are British, the Gestapo can tell too.'

Marc was impressed as Lael accurately selected the few items in his wardrobe that came from France, and rejected the much greater number that he'd picked up after arriving in Britain. She let him keep his British army boots after he explained where he'd got them.

'Give me your undershorts,' she said finally. 'Unless you want me to stick your hand down the back and inspect them in situ.'

Marc reluctantly stepped out of his boxers, then to his horror saw that the back was completely brown.

'They made me walk through the field barefoot last night,' Marc explained, as Lael inspected them with a look of complete disgust. 'Then they made me kneel and the mud on my heels must have soaked into the back.'

Troy laughed. 'Don't believe him, miss, he's shat himself.'

'Such language,' Yetta said, reaching across her tabletop and giving Troy a hard slap across the face.

'Jesus,' Troy moaned, as Marc laughed at his expense.

Lael looked disgusted as she pinched Marc's shorts between thumb and forefinger, lifted the lid on a metal dustbin and shuddered as she dropped them in. 'Right, let's sort you out,' she said.

Marc and Troy glanced at each other as the two women disappeared into the storage area. They'd emerge periodically with armfuls of clothes to try on. An all-new wardrobe would be suspicious, so most were either second-hand garments sourced from refugees or new items made in the French style and then bashed about to look worn.

Items that fitted were packed in genuine French suitcases. Others were marked up with chalk for alterations. Toothbrushes and toothpaste were added, along with French comic books, a few basic first aid items such as iodine and gauze, and French-made alarm clocks. To finish off each boy also got a few packets of cigarettes and chocolate bars.

'Save the treats for bribes and winning favour,' Lael said. 'Don't scoff them.'

'You took my soap,' Troy said. 'Do I get a French one to replace it?'

'Our agents report that there is no soap available in France,' Yetta replied. 'If you're caught with soap, it's highly suspicious.'

Lael scowled at Marc, 'Not that you'll miss it much, will you?'

'I just had a shower three days ago,' Marc said. 'It's not our fault we got dragged across a muddy field in the middle of the night.'

'Special items,' Lael explained, as she reached into a shelf under her table and took out a long velvet-lined box, divided into dozens of individual compartments.

The first thing she pulled out was a tatty-looking belt. She held the buckle up to Marc's face. 'It's tarnished to look like brass, but it's twenty-two-carat gold. If you find yourself on the run you can sell the metal, or give it to someone as a bribe. You can tell it's genuine by the weight.'

Next she pulled out a large button. 'This pops

apart like so, and you can hide a standard L tablet inside. I'll sew one on to all your trousers.'

'Which one's the L tablet?' Troy asked.

'A is air-sickness,' Marc said. 'B Benzedrine to keep you awake, E knocks you out for thirty minutes if you need to buy time, K is the sleeping draught, though enough of it will kill you, L is the suicide pill.'

Troy shook his head. 'I'm not taking a suicide pill with me. Those things are creepy.'

'Finally there's a pencil for each of you,' Lael said, as she pulled out two stubby, chewed-up pencils. 'Twist and pull.'

Lael separated the pencil around a near-invisible line where the colour of the paint changed, revealing a sharpened silver spike in the hole where the lead would usually run.

'Agents in the field report excellent results with these. The blade is toughened steel, so put a little oil on it once in a while to stop it from rusting. Whatever you do, don't sharpen the pencil.'

Marc tapped the point against the tip of his finger. 'Sharp,' he said.

Troy laughed. 'Who would have thought that, genius?'

As the boys spoke, Lael and Yetta scooped their English clothes into canvas sacks and passed them over.

'Don't even think about taking any of them,' Lael warned. 'I'll bring your cases up to your hut later when we've done all the alterations. Now you two need to go back to the house for the Brigadier to sort out your money and identity documents.'

'Oooh money,' Marc said, as he headed out in one of his new shirts. 'I wonder how much we're getting.'

'Good luck,' Yetta shouted after them. 'And tell the next pair to get down here.'

CHAPTER FIFTEEN

Madeline II cruised out of Porth Navas Creek at ten the next morning, with Lieutenant Commander Finch at the helm. It was a fine day, but Henderson ordered the kids to stay below in the rear crew compartment. The locals had got used to seeing the German boat on test runs, but a bunch of kids standing on deck would be sure to set tongues wagging in the villages along the shore.

The boat was designed for sixteen, so the crew of eleven had been crammed into the nine bunks in the bow, Henderson and the boys had the six bunks in the rear compartment, while Rosie and Boo shared the captain's quarters, thanks to the addition of an upper bunk.

The boys squatted on beds in the cramped compartment, playing cards with the morning sun shining through the rear deck hatch above their heads. The boat's three prop shafts ran beneath their feet and the third engine was only separated from them by a couple of metres and a wooden bulkhead.

It was calm as they cruised out of the creek and down the Helford River, with Finch keeping their speed low to avoid upsetting the oyster boats fishing in shallows over the mudflats. But once they reached the ocean, Finch opened the triple throttle and put *Madeline II* up to twenty-two knots. The vibration from the prop shaft rattled the metal bed frames as the speeding boat bounced violently off the waves.

It was funny for about five minutes – laughing as the cards jiggled in their hands and their mattress springs squealed – but the voyage would last fifty hours and they'd be stuck in here for most of that time.

PT said he wasn't putting up with it and went up on deck. The Royal Navy ensign fluttered on the rear flagpole as he stood with his hands on the deck rail watching the three water jets thrown up by the propellers.

Behind the small bridge the deck was dominated by six fuel tanks which had been custom-built to fit in the bays where the Germans stored their torpedoes. The extra diesel would enable them to cruise at high speed for lengthy periods, but the trade-off was the danger of an explosion if they were shot at.

To minimise *Madeline II*'s chances of being attacked by friendly fire, she would travel south with a Flower Class corvette, HMS *Columbine*. She was twice the length of *Madeline II*, with a crew of eighty and six deck guns to *Madeeline II*'s two. Although *Columbine* offered protection, her class had been designed for escorting slow merchant ships and she couldn't steam above twelve knots over long periods.

Only the light through the deck hatch gave the boys any clue about the passage of time, but this was closed when the water got choppy. Even when conditions were good they had to stay below deck because Henderson didn't want the crew of *Columbine* asking awkward questions about a boatload of kids.

Meals came and went in rectangular metal trays. The only escape was when they walked the length of the boat to use the toilet in the bow, stopping off to say hello to Boo and Rosie. Joel and Paul threw up a couple of times and everyone got headaches from the diesel fumes. They invented games to eat up time: who can balance a playing card on their nose for longest, who can hook their foot behind their neck, who would dare to eat all the greasy pink bits everyone had picked out of their lunch?

When they got within eighty nautical miles of Lorient, *Columbine* peeled off to join two sister ships in a U-boat hunt. The boys were allowed up on deck for some air, and found the White Ensign swapped for a Swastika and the deck crew in German uniform.

It was four on a Saturday afternoon. *Madeline II*'s communication officer received a message via London to say that they were expected. Shortly afterwards radar picked up a fishing boat in the right spot.

Rather than risk canoes, or take *Madeline II* into a French port, where her mysterious arrival and crew's lack of German would raise suspicions, Henderson had arranged a liaison at sea. E-boats such as *Madeline II* routinely stopped and inspected fishing vessels, so even if they were spotted from the coast there would be nothing suspicious about it.

Nicolas' boat was called *Istanbul*. Built in the last century, the sail-powered fishing boat had been laid up for more than a decade, but was now back in service because the fishermen had no fuel. Her sails were brown and heavily patched, the hull was rotten and coated with barnacles and the old hulk creaked eerily with every wave, as if she was breathing.

'Did I ever mention that I hate boats?' Paul said, as *Madeline II* came alongside in mercifully calm water.

Istanbul's crew comprised Nicolas and his teenaged grandsons Michel and Olivier.

The Royal Navy crew didn't waste time, swinging a wooden gangway between the two ships to slide heavier items, while suitcases and provisions were simply thrown. Once the goods were over, it was time for the people.

Henderson saluted Finch and led the way, crossing the gangplank with a safety rope hitched under his arms.

'How are you?' a woman shouted in English, from the trawler.

Paul, Marc, Rosie and PT were delighted to see Maxine Clere, who they'd first met the previous summer.

'How have you been?' Rosie asked. 'I didn't realise you were the radio operator.'

'I've been living in Paris,' Maxine explained. 'I've been giving the Gestapo the runaround for a year, but it was getting too dangerous so they moved me here for a couple of weeks and booked me a ride home.'

As the kids took turns on the violently swaying gangplank over to *Istanbul*, Henderson tried to give Maxine a kiss. She only allowed him a peck before she began handing over detailed notes.

'I've not had long in the area,' Maxine began, 'but I have drilled security into them at every opportunity. Alois is a good man. Madame Mercier is extremely valuable to us, but she doesn't like being told what to do.'

'Tell me something I don't know,' Henderson said as he slipped the notes into his jacket. 'I'll read these through and burn them before we reach shore.'

Directly behind, two British airmen were crossing the gangplank over to *Madeline II*.

'I'm holding up the show,' Maxine said. 'Time to go.'

'Let's have lunch some time,' Henderson said. 'Somewhere expensive, my treat.'

Maxine gave Henderson a nod, then quickly hugged Paul, Marc, Rosie and PT in turn and told them to be safe before crossing over to *Madeline II* for her voyage home.

Life aboard the German boat had been pretty miserable, but she was a luxury liner compared to *Istanbul*. As Lieutenant Commander Finch opened *Madeline II*'s throttles and turned for home, Nicolas herded the new arrivals towards a large hold under deck, which was designed for storing fish.

'All below,' Nicolas ordered.

Henderson jumped first and helped carry their luggage down. The stench of fish was unbelievable, and there wasn't much space once Henderson, Boo, six kids and luggage were jammed in. When they thought it couldn't get worse, Nicolas told them to sit down before his well-built teenage grandsons fitted a slatted wooden frame to a shelf above their heads.

A net filled with the morning catch was then emptied out over the slats and the deck hatch closed above them. As a result they were in darkness, stifling hot, with the boat pitching and the layer of dead fish dripping its juices into their hair and down their collars.

'Germans often search us when we return to port,' Nicolas explained, 'but they never delve into anything fishy so you'll be OK.'

The journey back to port took until six. The fish were taken out of *Istanbul*'s hold, but the human cargo had to wait until dark, which at this time of year was after ten o'clock. They peered up anxiously as boots creaked across the deck, and were relieved to see Nicolas' seventeen-year-old grandson Michel rather than a German guard.

'There's a patrol, but they're up by the harbour mouth,' Michel explained. 'Take what you can carry, but nothing that slows you down. We can get the rest of your luggage tomorrow.'

They swiftly passed suitcases and equipment out on to deck. Michel's younger cousin Olivier stood on the shore keeping lookout. As they made dry land, Olivier pointed them up the alleyway towards Alois's workshop. Their joints were stiff after being caged for so long and a queue formed for the toilet in the courtyard, with two boys peeing at a time.

'Keep the noise down and don't flush until we're all done,' Henderson warned.

Back inside Nicolas had a bowl of hot water and they took turns washing hands and faces before tucking into bread, cheese and cold chicken. They all stank of fish, but after six hours they hardly knew it.

'PT, Joel and Troy will stay at my brother's house,' Nicolas said. 'They can rest tomorrow. On Monday we'll sort out jobs for the older two. I know a man who may be able to get one of them a job in the U-boat maintenance yard instead of the construction site. Troy will work on *Istanbul* with me.

'Mr Henderson, it's late, so you and Marc can sleep here tonight. Tomorrow, Madame Mercier will send a car and you will meet her for lunch in Lorient. She has lodgings arranged for you and jobs at Mamba Noir – that's her swankiest club.'

'Time to smooth-talk some Krauts,' Marc said.

'Which leaves us three,' Boo said, pointing at Paul and Rosie.

'Yes, the communications team,' Alois said. 'If you aren't too tired, I suggest you cycle out tonight. Maxine's transmitter is all set up at the cottage. She suggested that you spend a couple of nights there before finding a new location known only to yourselves.'

'Will we get there before the curfew?' Paul asked.

'It's a half-hour ride and curfew is eleven,' Alois said. 'But even if you don't make it, you'll be a few kilometres away from anything the Germans are interested in.'

It took a while to sort out the luggage and adjust the saddle on one of the bikes to fit Paul. Then it was time to split up. Joel, PT and Troy were already being led out by Olivier when Henderson called them back.

'Keep safe,' he told everyone. 'The next few days will be tricky. People are wary of new arrivals, so keep a low profile. Keep contact to a minimum. I'll work out a discreet communication system and get you word on how to use it. Don't take risks. Don't rush to make friends with everyone or go asking stupid questions until you know who you're dealing with. Remember your training. Good hunting and good luck.'

Part Three

Four and a half weeks later

Part Three

CHAPTER SIXTEEN

Sunday 22 June 1941

German army uniform wasn't ideal for police work. Edith squatted in a doorway on the wharf at Kerneval, and heard the patrol's hobnail boots on the cobbles half a minute before they saw her.

'Heil Hitler,' she said cheekily, as they came around the corner.

The Germans seemed to be getting older. These two could have been twins with their bald heads and fat bellies.

'Got any sweets, boss? Chocolate, bon-bons?'

But neither German spoke French. Edith asked for chocolate in German, but this only irritated them, and one shook his fist at her. When the boots faded out, Edith ran up the side street to Alois's workshop. She was surprised to see only Troy there.

'Patrol's just gone by. Where are the others?'

'Joel and PT aren't back from work,' Troy explained. 'Nicolas is flat out on the floor with his back but we can still do it if you keep lookout.'

'I guess,' Edith said. 'We really ought to have two though.'

'We'll have to risk it,' Troy said, as he threw Edith a ragged grey scarf. 'Don't let the agent see your face and only speak if you really have to.'

They headed down a back street, parallel with the dockside. It was past ten, but still too light for comfort.

Troy took a padlock off the side door of a small warehouse, as Edith walked on and checked for signs of life amidst the boats.

Troy moved quickly on Edith's thumbs-up. The tide was out, so he had to go down slippery rungs fitted to the dockside before stepping on to *Istanbul*'s deck. He cut into the bridge to pick up a sack filled with clothes, then covered his face with a balaclava before opening the doors of the fish hold as quietly as rotten wood and rusty hinges allowed.

'I'm suffocating down here,' the new arrival protested. 'I've been sick twice. I've had nothing to drink.'

When Troy had arrived with Henderson's team four weeks earlier they'd had a nightmare getting the stench of fish out of their clothes. So the new system was for agents in the hold to strip down to their underwear before jumping in.

'Where's my equipment?' the agent asked. 'I had three large cases, one with over sixty thousand francs.'

Troy cut him dead. 'Stop yapping. I don't care what you're up to, who you are, or where you're going.'

Running around in your pants covered in fish juice is as suspicious as it gets, so Troy went back up the ladder, and waited for a nod from Edith before leading the new arrival across the dockside. They shepherded the agent up the side street and into the warehouse.

It was dark, except for a few cracks of light coming through gaps in the tin roof. Troy threw down the bag of clothes and felt inside to find a bar of soap, as Edith switched on a hose and passed it to the agent. He gulped several mouthfuls before using the cold water to scrub off the stench of fish.

'When does the rest of the welcoming committee get here?' the agent asked.

'Nobody gets here,' Troy said. 'Clean and scrub, *quickly*. When you're dressed, go outside and turn right. Pass two streets, turn left, use the key inside this envelope to open the door of number twenty-five. There's food in the house, along with all your equipment. Tomorrow morning you need to leave the house by six. It's too risky going through the station at Lorient, so walk to Queven and catch the bus. They brought in a new dark-green ration card on Thursday. There's one for you in the house. Make sure you destroy your white one because the Krauts will arrest you if you're found with two. Is that all clear?'

'How old are you?' the man asked.

Troy was exasperated. 'Did you pay any attention at all during your training? The less we know about each other, the less the Gestapo can find out if they get their hooks into us. Now hurry the hell up.'

Edith threw the agent a grubby towel, as Troy laid out his clothes.

'Throw that soap away when you're done,' Troy said. 'Hitler himself couldn't get a bar of soap around here.'

'What about these?' the agent asked, as he held up his fishy underpants.

'Leave it here,' Troy said. 'We'll take it out with the boat tomorrow and dump it in the sea.'

'I was told there might be a fall-back,' the agent said, as he pulled on his vest. 'If the bus doesn't turn up, for instance.'

'If things are desperate, come back here to the harbour.'

'But I haven't got any names. The men on the trawler hid their faces when we boarded. The crew on *Madeline II* didn't even let me take a proper look at the fishing boat as we approached.'

'We'll spot you, provided the Krauts don't spot you first,' Troy said.

Once the agent was dressed, Troy passed over the envelope containing his house key and bus ticket. Edith checked that the street was clear before pointing him in the right direction.

'Good luck,' Troy said.

'Thank you,' the agent replied, though you could tell from his tone that he was put out at the way he'd been treated.

Troy peeled the balaclava off his head, as Edith turned the hose back on to wash the soap suds down the drain hole.

'What was he expecting?' Edith asked. 'Brass bands and banners in the street?'

'Probably scared out of his wits,' Troy said. 'He wanted his hand held, but unfortunately that's not how it works.'

*

The Anchor was a small café-bar. It served cheap meals to Organisation Todt workmen with their special high-calorie ration cards. The men preferred stews and soups that could be eaten fast so they could get on with the important business of drinking, fighting and gambling.

PT sat at a small table, holding court with twenty men packed around. His overalls were stiffened with dried-out concrete and he stank of twelve-hour shifts. For the first couple of weeks, the work had nearly killed him. He'd lost ten pounds, gained a dark tan and calluses on his hands. His body was young enough to adapt quickly, but the monotony of manual work crushed his spirit.

'I'm not taking your money,' PT told an elderly fellow, as he stacked up three cups and clutched them to his chest. 'You're going to lose, I'm too good for you.'

The crowd roared with laughter. His grizzled opponent pounded on the table, red face, red beard, chewing on a cigar stub.

'I know your game inside out, boy!' red beard shouted. 'I've seen this con played all over the world and you ain't even very good at it.'

'He's doing you a favour,' a monster called Gilles shouted. 'Piss off out, old-timer.'

Gilles was vast. He was the leader of PT's five-man gang, which poured concrete on the U-boat bunkers twelve hours a day, six days a week. Gilles covered PT's back. In return PT shared the spoils when his con tricks paid off.

'OK, granddad,' PT said, acting like he was doing a big favour. 'If you're going to be nasty about it, I'll give you *one* chance to outsmart me.'

Another member of PT's work gang pushed through the bodies with a tray of beers. PT took his and downed half in three big gulps. Red beard put a five-franc note on the table as he spat his cigar stub on to the wooden floorboards. PT raised his index finger.

'One franc,' he said. 'You work hard for your money,

old man. Keep hold of it.'

'One franc then,' red beard said. 'I guess you know when the game's up.'

PT spread the three cups on the tabletop, placed a ball in the central one before turning them upside down. He then repeatedly swapped the position of the cups, starting slowly but speeding up. The trick was to go fast, but if you made tracking the cups too hard nobody would place bets.

'Take your pick,' PT said.

The old man tapped the cup on the right. PT lifted it up and the little rubber ball bobbled out towards the edge of the table.

'You won a franc,' PT said. 'Congratulations.'

'Told you so,' red beard smiled. 'It's the oldest trick in the book. He palms the ball while you're not looking and puts it under another cup. That's why he'll only take one franc off me.'

'You think I'm a con man?' PT laughed. 'Everyone has a chance of winning, even if you guess it's one in three. I'm trying to be friendly, but if you *really* want me to prove my point I'll take any bet you'd care to place.'

'Thirty-two francs,' red beard said, slamming down everything in his wallet.

PT had learned the three cup trick from his father. The sleight of hand – switching the ball as you turned the cups over – only took a few days' practice, but working the crowd was the real art. If a bunch of drunks turned nasty you'd take a beating, so your attitude was everything: keep the crowd on your side, be humble, tell people you don't want to take their money so it doesn't seem like your fault when they lose.

'I'm only an apprentice,' PT said warily, eyeing the thiry-two francs. 'This is two weeks' wages for me. How about fifteen?'

'All or nothing,' red beard growled. 'Or admit you're ripping these working men off.'

Gilles put a reassuring hand on PT's shoulder. 'Pride's at stake boy. Go for it!'

A flurry of small side bets went on between the onlookers. With a crowd this lively a two-man team passing signals could make more money from side bets than at the table itself. PT wished that his dad or older brother was alive to join the fray.

'OK, here goes,' PT said, as he made the sign of a cross on his chest. 'Cups, one . . . two . . . three. One ball in the middle. Are you happy with that, old man? I'll give you one *final* chance to back out before I turn 'em upside down.'

'Stop dragging it out, you little turd,' red beard roared.

The old man's cigar drooped as PT turned the cups over and started switching them around. He'd been looking for PT to switch the ball when he turned the three cups over, but he hadn't. With no switch, PT genuinely had to lose the ball so he shuffled at his usual speed, but held two cups at a time and twisted his hand so that the cups could switch two places in one effortless move. If you were used to this, it wasn't that hard to follow, but introducing the technique suddenly could throw off a tense opponent.

'Clickety-click, take your pick,' PT said confidently.

Red beard looked rattled. 'You cheating little shit!'

'I did the same as always,' PT said.

The crowd wasn't so sure. Some tried to mimic the flicks of the wrist.

'Pick one,' Gilles shouted.

The old man tapped the centre cup. PT looked appropriately nerve-wracked as he raised the cup with a trembling hand. There was no ball.

'Can't say I didn't warn you,' PT smiled.

Red beard exploded, kicking PT, then swinging his fist. PT's combat training wasn't much use because he was pinned behind the table, but Gilles intercepted red beard's fist with one hand, grabbed his collar with the other and smacked his head down hard against the table.

'Start on him, you start on me,' Gilles warned. 'You lost fair and square.'

'He all but begged you not to play,' another of PT's workmates shouted. 'Piss off, you crazy old fool!'

PT eyed the crowd as red beard stormed off. PT's workmates were on side, but most of the rest thought there was something fishy about the business with his wrists. But he'd won a nice pile and figured he could afford to win the crowd back.

'Waitress,' he shouted. 'Let's share the wealth. Get me two bottles of whisky and enough glasses for any of these fine gentlemen that want some!'

Cheers went up, and were only slightly muted when the waitress said there was no whisky and offered Russian vodka instead.

'I propose a toast,' PT said, standing up as the vodka bottles got passed around. 'A toast to getting even drunker than we are already!'

CHAPTER SEVENTEEN

Fourteen-year-old Joel had landed an apprentice job in a dockside maintenance facility through a friend of Alois named Canard. He sat on an upturned crate, dressed in a cloth cap and greasy overall, while holding an enamel mug filled with tea.

'I have no idea what the Brits see in this filth,' Canard said, as he poked his nose suspiciously into his beverage. Canard was the French word for duck and he'd earned the nickname courtesy of a streamlined bald head and oversized lips that rolled out like a duck's bill when he closed his mouth.

Joel had developed a taste for tea while training in Britain, but couldn't admit this without blowing his cover. 'It's not *too* bad,' he said. 'Just a shame we haven't got any milk.'

Canard laughed. 'Well, King George's army left seven hundred crates behind. So tea's the one thing we'll never run out of. I even took some home to burn last winter.'

'Do tea leaves burn?'

'Go up in a flash,' Canard said. 'No good for keeping warm and I lost half an eyebrow.'

Joel's laugh tailed off abruptly as he heard footsteps on the concrete floor and looked behind. But it was only their workmate, André. He was in his forties, good with his hands, but not too bright.

The shed around them had been hastily constructed by the Germans. Ten metres high and twenty-five square, with a concrete floor and all the latest machine tools. It was one of three temporary workshops built for U-boat repairs within weeks of the German invasion.

'I told you,' André said, smiling like a five-year-old as he passed two large cans to Canard. 'Tinned bread. They have it on the U-boats.'

Canard punched a hole in one tin with a screwdriver, peeled back the lid and tore out a doughy clump.

'What's it like?' Joel asked.

Canard shrugged as he offered the tin. 'Another scientific miracle by our German masters.'

Joel grabbed a piece. 'Better than bread full of maggots, I guess,' he said. 'So is it OK for me to knock off now? It's nearly eleven.'

Canard nodded. 'I'm not starting on anything.'

As Joel headed across the deserted space to pick up his lunchbox, a Kriegsmarine engineer came through the door. Joel veered left and stopped at a workbench, pretending to examine part of a battery.

'Canard, over here!' the German shouted. 'Are the U-108 cells ready for deployment?'

'Not a chance,' Canard said, laughing.

The Kriegsmarine used its own engineers for the advanced U-boat equipment, but menial or unpleasant jobs – such as stripping down and refurbishing the batteries that powered the submarines underwater – got left to the French.

'Did you take this can from outside?' the German shouted, as he spotted the silver tins on the floor. 'These are German military supplies. I could have you *executed* for stealing them.'

'Then who'll fix your bloody batteries?' Canard asked, giving a relaxed shrug. 'The battery casings are cracked. There's no gas for the welding gear. What can I do?'

The German violently kicked one of the bread cans. It spun in the air and hit the wall with a clank.

'I have a boat due to sail on the tide tomorrow morning. It's already delayed more than three days.'

'I had a dozen men, but you sent them all up to Brest,' Canard said. 'I've got one man who thinks that two and three makes seven and a boy who's been on the job for less than a month. I'm not Jesus Christ, I can't perform miracles.'

'Everyone is short-handed,' the German said. 'I see very little effort here. That's your real problem.'

Joel had seen dozens of propaganda films while he was in Britain. They always portrayed the Germans as tough, well-equipped and efficient, but nothing he'd seen on the Keroman peninsula reinforced this view.

The U-boats constantly broke down, the crews were teenagers, even the officers were barely in their twenties. They were so short of lubricant that spills were scraped up and filtered through gauze. Screws were taken out of bed frames to repair torpedoes and replacement parts were made by taking office chairs apart and bending the metal legs.

But the labour shortage was worst of all. The British feared U-boats sinking their Atlantic convoys more than anything, but the Kriegsmarine was diverting the resources of the U-boat arm into repairing *Scharnhorst* and *Gneisenau*, two damaged battleships docked at Brest a hundred and forty kilometres north.

This policy meant U-boats spent weeks in port waiting for simple repairs, and left the door open for potential saboteurs like Joel to get jobs in sensitive areas a couple of hundred metres from the boats themselves.

Canard pointed another set of giant batteries out to

the German. 'Those cells came in with U-63 two days ago. They're in good shape.'

'U-63 is a new boat,' the chief engineer said, before pausing deep in thought. 'Her captain won't like being landed with a set of old batteries, but I suppose it gets the boats moving. I'll send two crewmen from U-108 with a trolley.'

The German looked pleased as he went out; Canard was happy too because he'd saved himself an overhaul job by getting rid of the batteries from U-63. Joel wondered if he could damage the batteries and stop U-108 from sailing, but Henderson had warned him against petty acts of sabotage. It was better to bide his time, keep his head down and use his access to the repair yards for a carefully planned operation that would do lasting damage.

'You still here?' Canard asked Joel, as he held out the unopened bread can. 'Better scram before the Krauts get back with their trolley, and take this home for your mother.'

*

Curfew was eleven p.m., but that didn't make much difference in Lorient's entertainment district. The curfew didn't apply to Germans, and civilians who worked on the bunker construction site or around the docks had exemption passes.

Madame Mercier had sorted Henderson out with a

bar job at Mamba Noir. It wasn't up to the standards of the best clubs in Paris, but it was the closest thing in Lorient. Every other late-night establishment was reserved either for locals or Germans and their female guests, but Mamba Noir was open to anyone who could pay the exorbitant prices.

The ground-floor restaurant served excellent food and didn't bother asking for ration coupons. Upstairs, the powerful and beautiful sat in a restrained interior, listening to an all-black Chicago jazz trio while drinking champagne cocktails. They even had soap in the bathrooms, though the attendant sprinkled tiny slivers into customers' palms so that they couldn't walk off with it.

While Henderson worked behind the bar, Marc was a cigarette boy, walking between tables with a tray of cigarettes and cigars hung around his neck. He didn't get wages, but the small tips mounted up and occasional big ones made it worthwhile. Best of all, nobody knew he spoke German, so the high-ups kept talking as he bent over to light their smokes.

Sundays were always quiet. It was the band's night off and people only stayed for a couple of drinks after their meal. Marc had been up until three the night before and he strode past empty tables towards the bar.

'I'm gonna take this off and go across the street,' Marc told Henderson. 'Is that OK?'

Henderson, dressed in a silk waistcoat and bow tie, furrowed his brow. 'What's this, a half-day?'

Marc could tell he wasn't serious. He rested the cigarette tray on the bar and scooped his tips out of a glass ashtray.

'If anyone wants cigarettes I'll send one of the girls over,' Henderson said. 'You get your beauty sleep.'

Marc said goodnight to a couple of people and unbuttoned his waistcoat as he walked downstairs. A few diners were eating dessert in the restaurant and the kitchen was dead, except for a couple of pot washers and a single waiter willing his final customers out of the door.

'Goodnight, Marc,' Madame Mercier shouted from behind the downstairs bar. 'Don't forget, bright and early at the stables tomorrow.'

As he pulled shut the back door of the restaurant Marc noticed a rusty can on the ground between the dustbins and the wall. He crouched as if tying his shoelace, then fished a screwed-up piece of paper from the can.

It was cool out, and a chill went down Marc's spine as the breeze hit his sweaty back. The fresh air was a relief after the heat and smoke inside the club and he wished he had more than thirty metres to walk.

The rooms he shared with Henderson were on the first floor of a dilapidated house that – along with almost everything else in this part of town – belonged to

Madame Mercier. The elderly sisters on the ground floor went bananas if you woke them up, so he took his shoes off before creeping upstairs.

Henderson had the small bedroom, while Marc slept in the living room. His single bed shared the space with a sink, cooker, kitchen dresser and small dining table. The curtains were open and they were in blackout so he pulled them together before reaching up to the hanging light bulb and screwing it in tight to make it come on.

A drunk retched outside as Marc unravelled the paper. The note was written on a sheet from a Mamba Noir waiter's pad, in Joel's handwriting: *Celery Coulis 10fr 80*.

This was crossed through as if the bill had been cancelled and some numbers scrawled on the back. Celery Coulis was a starter, which meant that a boat was sailing at the start of the day. 10fr 80 meant U-108. The coded scribbles on the back also told him that U-212 had docked that morning, while U-9 had not arrived as expected.

Marc pondered the fate of U-9 as he switched on the radio. Had she been sunk on the approach to Lorient, delayed by mechanical problems, or just diverted to a different port? He'd probably never know, but he'd pass the message on to Paul in the morning, and Rosie or Boo would transmit the information to London later in the day.

As the valves warmed and the radio crackled to life, he

took off his tie and shirt then ran a flannel under the cold tap. His feet ached and he could smell his own socks as he slumped on to his bed and slapped the flannel over his face. The icy water trickled down his chest as the solemn voice of the BBC French Service kicked in.

'. . . *high command issued a statement saying that the invasion was unavoidable as a result of a sustained and unacceptable build-up of Russian forces along the border . . .*'

Marc shot up off the bed in shock.

'. . . *With the German attack on Russia just a few hours old it is difficult to speculate on the success or failure of the endeavour. However, it is clear that the Reich has launched an unprecedented surprise operation against its former ally, involving thousands of aircraft and up to two million men.*

'*In Berlin, Adolf Hitler predicted that Russia's back would be broken within three months. Prime Minister Churchill stated that Britain would do everything it could to assist Marshal Stalin and the people of Russia. The French service will be interrupting regular programs with special bulletins as the situation develops.*'

CHAPTER EIGHTEEN

Drunks staggered and pissed in alleyways as Joel headed through moonlight into the entertainment district. After dropping the message off behind Mamba Noir, he walked a few hundred metres along the main drag to one of the all-night cafes where he could use his worker's ration card.

He'd made friends with the elderly waitress, who always made sure there were recognisable chunks of meat in his soup and double the cheese that the other men got. But there was nothing she could do about the black bread, which was made from rough rye flour and widely believed to be adulterated with sawdust. Joel had no idea if that was true, but he would have died for a fresh-cooked baguette with butter melting inside.

It was a twenty-five-minute walk back to Alois' place in

Kerneval. Before setting off Joel decided to check out a couple of likely spots to see if PT was around and wanted to come home with him. He found him easily enough, slumped at the back of Le Petit Prince with too much drink under his skin.

Le Petit Prince was the roughest joint in a rough town. Floor awash in spit, cigarette ends and dried blood, windows boarded, mirrors smashed. It sold the cheapest beer, and the prostitutes lined up on the first-floor balcony were either too old or too young for Madame Mercier's establishments.

'Sit down, mate,' PT said, then shouted towards a friend at the bar. 'Get an extra beer in for my pal here.'

'It's midnight,' Joel said. 'You wanna walk home with me? You've gotta start work at seven tomorrow.'

'Tomorrow can kiss my arse,' PT said. 'Sit down, my feathered friend.'

Joel half smiled. He wouldn't have minded if PT had wanted to walk home with him, but he really wanted to join in. At fourteen, staying out late and drinking seemed exciting, even in a dive like Le Petit Prince.

He settled in beside PT, who flicked off Joel's attempt to pay for his own beer. A cheer went up as Gilles emerged from one of the rooms upstairs.

'Ten francs well spent,' he roared.

Joel looked up at the girls on the balcony. He'd never even kissed a girl, so the idea that he could have sex with any of them aroused, scared and disgusted him all at once.

'Who have you got your eye on?' Gilles shouted.

Joel pretended like he didn't hear, but this wasn't a good idea because Gilles was a mean drunk.

He leaned forwards and boomed in Joel's ear. 'I'm speaking to you, sonny.'

'Nobody,' Joel said nervously, as he looked down at his beer.

Gilles looked at PT. 'Think your little brother's ever done it with a girl?'

'Not that I've seen,' PT said.

Joel blushed as PT's workmates jeered.

'Little virgin,' Gilles mocked. 'You're a working man now. Why not go up there and grab some fanny?'

'One from the end,' PT said, as he pointed up. 'Reckon she's only my age. Good tits, nice legs. You could do a lot worse.'

Joel blushed even more as he buried his face in his beer glass. He'd hoped PT would bail him out, not dig him in deeper.

Gilles shouted up. 'Oi, one from the end, will you do us a good price on the young lad?'

When Joel looked up from his glass, the girl blew him a kiss. His face burned like the surface of the sun.

'What's the matter with you?' Gilles shouted, giving Joel a tug. 'Go on up, she won't bite you.'

'She might if you pay extra,' another of PT's workmates shouted, to roars of laughter.

Joel half smiled, but saw a way out. 'I've only got a couple of francs.'

PT peeled out two fives. 'Take it if you want to.'

Joel reluctantly stood up and took PT's money. The girl was making *come on up* gestures and gently cupping one of her breasts.

'Go on, my son,' Gilles shouted.

The place wasn't packed, but it was busy. A few men at surrounding tables had also worked out what was going on and cheered Joel on as he walked towards the staircase. Sweat poured down his face as watching eyes bored into him.

Then he was at the bottom of the stairs. The girl was waiting at the top, but a greasy-looking man blocked his path. Joel hoped he was going to send him away for being too young or something, but he was there to take money.

'Three francs for the room. Then you pay the girl for whatever you want her to do.'

Joel's hands were tense and he'd scrunched PT's five-franc notes into sweaty little balls. He flattened one out and was about to hand it over when he looked up at the girl again and wondered what he was supposed to do when he got up to the room.

Thinking he was going to spew, Joel spun around and made a run for the door, almost knocking over a barman with a tray of glasses. Bursting into fresh air he doubled over and retched, but nothing came out. As he straightened up, he could hear laughter and shouts of *Get back here*, and *Chicken*.

Joel had never felt so embarrassed. He took three quick steps before realising he was going the wrong way, then turned and headed towards the main bridge out of town.

He'd only gone thirty paces when PT shouted after him. 'Wait up, mate. I'll walk home with you.'

Joel didn't slow down, so PT had to jog to catch up.

'You forgot your tin,' PT said.

Joel stuck the can of bread under his arm, but scowled down at the cobbles and kept quiet.

'They're just messing,' PT said. 'Don't let it get to you.'

'Well *you* could have stood up for me,' Joel finally said, stopping as they turned into an alleyway. 'Here's your ten francs. Now go back to your mates.'

PT refused to take the money. 'I feel bad. I saw your eyes going up her skirt. I wasn't being shitty. I thought you *wanted* to go up there.'

'I kind of did,' Joel admitted. 'But with all those guys pressuring me . . . And that Gilles is a dick.'

'He's all right, covers my back at work,' PT said. 'But he's been drinking since half seven.'

'I feel like such a prat,' Joel said, as he started walking again.

PT tried thinking of something to make Joel feel better. 'Probably for the best, anyway. Guy I know slept with a bunch of whores in Morocco when I was a cabin boy. He got all these sores. His dick looked like a corn on the cob.'

Joel laughed half-heartedly. 'Really?'

'The toilet was right next to our bunks. Whenever he took a piss he'd be screaming blue murder.'

'So did you ever pay for sex?'

'Me?' PT scoffed, as they turned a corner. 'Look at this beautiful face. I don't have to pay for it.'

'I'll tell Rosie that,' Joel said, starting to relax a little.

But he didn't get much of a chance before two men cut off their route out of the alleyway. PT recognised the red-bearded man he'd won thirty-two francs from earlier on. This part of Lorient was a warren of little alleyways and it wouldn't have been hard to spot PT leaving the Le Petit Prince and run on ahead.

'Where's your big mate now?' red beard laughed, as he brandished a stuck. 'Don't think baby brother's gonna be much help.'

'Get out of my face, old man,' PT said. 'I told you not to bet. It's your own fault.'

Red beard's companion was heavily built. 'Give us your money and there's no need for anyone to get hurt.'

'What are you, hired muscle?' PT laughed. 'Tell you

what, why don't you give me your money and then you won't get hurt?'

'Can't talk your way out of this one, con merchant,' red beard said. He then made a loud *OOOF* as PT kicked him in the balls.

While the old man staggered about clutching his nuts, PT swung a punch at the big thug. The thug staggered back, surprised by strength that came from combat training as much as raw physical power. But it was no knockout blow.

When the shock wore off, the big man lunged and got an arm around PT's neck. Joel saved him by smashing the can of bread down on the thug's head. PT's next punch hit his temple and knocked him cold.

As the big man tripped backwards and crashed into a doorway, PT expertly launched a roundhouse kick, knocking the old man to the ground as his false teeth spun out across the cobbles.

'Here's your money,' PT said, peeling notes from a fat money clip. 'Thirty-two, minus one franc you won on the first bet makes thirty-one.'

He bent forwards and stuffed the notes in red beard's shirt pocket, then cheekily flicked the end of his nose.

'Happy now, you old shit?' PT said.

He looked back as he strolled off, pumped with bravado. Joel inspected the can of bread and saw that it had a big dent. He realised PT was drunk, but still didn't understand the mixture of generosity and nastiness.

'Are you OK?' Joel asked. 'We'd better get out of here sharpish. If the patrol turns up they'll give us a week in the cells, minimum.'

'Nobody calls me a con merchant,' PT said bitterly, as they walked briskly away from the scene. 'Con merchants rob old ladies and water down booze. What I do is an art. I'm a con *artist*.'

CHAPTER NINETEEN

Henderson stood by the apartment window in vest and underpants stirring his morning coffee. He'd switched the radio on and opened the curtains to let the sun in but Marc was still fast asleep. He always slept the same way, sprawled in all directions with limbs hanging over the sides. Henderson took the hot metal spoon out of his mug, crept up to the bed and dabbed it mischievously against the top of Marc's hand.

The thirteen-year-old sprang up like a cat, rolling over, sheets flying about.

'Morning, sweet pea,' Henderson said, smiling at Marc's sulking face.

'You burned me,' Marc complained, though an examination of his skin showed nothing but a tiny egg-shaped blotch. 'I'm so knackered. What time is it?'

'Quarter to seven,' Henderson said.

Marc walked barefoot into Henderson's room and took a long piss into his chamberpot.

'Coffee?' Henderson asked. 'It's from Mamba Noir.'

'Yeah, seeing as it's decent,' Marc said.

Henderson handed Marc a mug as he came through the doorway rubbing his eyes. 'You can get some sleep this afternoon, but the chef needs his grub and Boo needs her messages to encode.'

'I know,' Marc said. 'I've got a message to pass on from Joel as well.'

'I'm hoping plenty of equipment came in via *Madeline II* yesterday,' Henderson said. 'I asked for a good quantity of plastic explosives. All the U-boat supplies come in by train. If we can hit the main engine yard outside of town I think we could slow things right down.'

'Sounds like a plan,' Marc said, as he looked along the open front of the kitchen dresser for some breakfast options.

Mamba Noir's nightly leftovers were fought over by the staff, but Henderson had pulled off a coup. Marc took a plate and filled it with a piece of fresh river salmon, slightly stale chunks of baguette, butter, tomatoes and a slice of cream gateau topped with tinned orange segments. It was only as he sat on his bed eating that his mind tuned in to the voice on the radio.

'What are they saying about Russia?' Marc asked.

Henderson shrugged as he used his teaspoon to attack the other half of the salmon. 'Germany says it's going well, Russia says they're defending bravely and advancing into German territory in some areas. But it's all propaganda. It'll take days for anything like the truth to emerge.'

'Do you think it'll be a German walkover, like France last summer?'

'Russia's a big old lump to bite off,' Henderson said. 'It's thirty times bigger than France, so it won't be quick, but the Russian military is a real mess. We had a defector two years ago when I was with the Espionage Research Unit . . .'

'What's a defector?' Marc asked.

'Someone who comes over to your side,' Henderson explained. 'Usually someone important. He was a military attaché, Red Navy admiral. Stalin had launched massive purges against his top commanders. Sending them off to camps in Siberia or putting a bullet through their heads.'

'Why?'

'Paranoia mostly,' Henderson said. 'Mixed with a healthy dose of communist dogma about privileged elites. The point was, the admiral was terrified that his head was next on the chopping block. I met him at a conference, smuggled him back to Britain. He gave us a lot of useful intelligence, he'd even brought plans for

Russian torpedoes. The designs were top-notch, but he said the service was a shambles. The most experienced units had been gutted of all the best commanders. Nobody was doing their jobs because it only took one wrong move to get a bullet through the head. The Red Army and Soviet Air Force are apparently just the same.'

'So the Germans are gonna win?' Marc said.

'I'd lay my shilling on it,' Henderson said.

'What does that mean for Britain?'

Henderson considered this for a few moments. 'In the short term the invasion is a good thing because Hitler can't wage large-scale wars against Britain and Russia at the same time. But in the long term, assuming Hitler wins, he'll have Russian territory and manpower to draw on.'

'And we'll be screwed,' Marc said.

Henderson rocked his head from side to side uncertainly. 'If Hitler deals with Russia, he can turn all his forces around and focus on a full-scale invasion of Britain. It's probably too late for this year, but by spring '42 he could be ready to crush us.'

'What about the Yanks?' Marc asked.

'Don't hold your breath expecting them to come to our rescue,' Henderson scoffed. 'But there's no point getting depressed about it. We're talking about maybes stacked up on a hundred more maybes. All we can do is keep calm and focus on *our* jobs.'

Marc sat on a cart, catching the sunlight as the hazelnut-brown horse pulled him along Lorient's main shopping street. Dot was an old nag who'd been walking the same route for years. She knew the way and only needed a tap to get her moving between stops.

Forty women and a couple of men queued outside the butcher's. The window display was bare and their choice was between gristly sausages and minced lamb. Marc cut to the front of the queue and walked behind the counter to collect two huge sacks filled with joints of roasting pork, lamb cutlets and veal medallions.

He peeled off several hundred francs as a couple of shoppers tutted with disgust.

'Mind your business or piss off,' the butcher warned them, as his boy helped Marc carry the sacks out to the cart.

The next stop was a fishmonger. Fish wasn't rationed, but the prices put it beyond the wallets of the people queuing for meat. Marc carefully stacked boxes of fish and crates of snapping lobsters into the cart, alongside the sacks of meat, two churns of milk and crates of fruit and vegetables.

He passed a sad-looking woman with two little kids and gave them each an apple. The Germans stopped the cart at a snap checkpoint. One man inspected Marc's identity card while the other helped himself to a handful of strawberries. They didn't dare take more, because Madame Mercier had half the town's senior officers in her pocket.

The final stop before turning for home was a drinking trough at the end of the street. Dot always took a ten-minute break here and wouldn't move on until she was ready. After a long drink, Marc gave her a strawberry as a treat before she dipped her head into a bucket filled with oats and apple cores.

'You'll rot her teeth,' Paul said cheerfully.

The school on the opposite side of the street hadn't been open in months, but local kids still congregated in the area, making it the perfect spot for the two boys to pass messages.

'That's information on movements from Joel and some stuff me and Henderson picked up at the club,' Marc told Paul as he handed over some papers. 'How have you been?'

'Boo picked up that stinking cold I had last week. Old girl on the next farm sticks her nose in more than we'd like but we reckon she's lonely. And the transmitter's working fine since I repaired it.'

Marc handed over a small bag of meat. 'Nice lamb chops,' he explained. '*Madeline II* came in OK, so I expect your new radio will have arrived.'

Paul nodded. 'Rosie got a message. She's heading down to Kerneval to buy fish later and she'll pick it up then if there are no Krauts around. Oh, and this came through for Henderson. It's in his personal code.'

'Oh he'll love that,' Marc smiled as he took the sheet of squared paper. 'He *hates* decoding his own messages.'

*

'Shit, shit, shit!' Henderson roared furiously, then stamped on the floor before remembering the two women in the apartment downstairs and lowering his voice. 'What the buggery am I supposed to do with itching powder?'

Marc had been dozing, but sat up on his bed, rubbing one eye as Henderson waggled the sheet of squared paper in front of his face.

'Read it,' Henderson growled. 'Just read what these deskbound morons have sent us.'

Marc took the paper. It was tissue thin, written in block capitals and full of crossings out and transcription errors where Henderson had decoded the message he'd been given by Paul.

Explosives in short supply, 1.5kg delivered. More next voyage, we hope. 18kg of itching powder, best used through local laundry. Has proved effective in Holland and brings German troops out in a severe rash when impregnated in clothes. Have discussed your access to U-boat repair facilities with experts. Please send all available information on U-boat batteries, including detailed drawings, via Madeline II *if possible.*

Marc tried to sound upbeat. 'Mamba Noir sends tablecloths and staff uniforms out to the laundry. We could easily find out where the Germans have their clothes washed and get that powder put in.'

Marc recoiled as Henderson reared up. 'I want explosives to blow stuff up with,' he said furiously. 'We're not going to defeat Hitler by making people itchy.'

'Do you want me ask a few questions about the laundry or not?'

'I suppose,' Henderson said.

'And is 1.5 kilos of explosive enough to do what you want at the train depot?'

'No,' Henderson said. 'But we've got 2kg that I brought over. We can make up a dozen or so medium-sized charges. If we get them in the right spots we can do some damage, but we won't have a stick of explosive left over for emergencies or special targets.'

'When would we do it?' Marc asked.

'Tonight's as good as any other night,' Henderson said. 'A small but successful raid would boost morale amongst good men like Nicolas and Alois, and I want the pen-pushers in London to see what units like ours are capable of achieving if we're properly resourced.'

'How many on the raid?'

'Four or five,' Henderson said. 'You and me, maybe Edith as a scout and one or two others.'

'Joel and PT?' Marc suggested.

Henderson shook his head. 'You'd have to take those two out of work, which would raise suspicion. Better to use fishermen, who'll be in port at that time of night. Alois and Nicolas are a bit old, but those two lads who work on the boat with Troy have been a big help with smuggling operations.'

'Nicolas' grandsons, Michel and Olivier,' Marc said. 'But isn't it a risk bringing them in on something like this?'

'It is,' Henderson said. 'But there's an old expression: give a man a fish and he'll eat, teach a man to fish and he'll eat for ever. The locals seem to have learned what we taught them about security well enough. The next step is teaching them to stand on their own two feet.'

'But how will we get a team together by tonight?' Marc asked. 'Won't we be better off with more preparation?'

'It's swings and roundabouts,' Henderson explained. 'The more you scout the area, the greater the chance of being seen. The more notice you give your operatives, the more chance there is for tongues to flap or people to get a dose of nerves.

'I took a walk up to the engine yard on my day off last week. There's a chain-link fence that's easily cut and a French watchman who never leaves his shed. The nearest

German presence is at the roadblocks on the edge of town and in the next station down the line over a kilometre in the other direction. By the time they hear the explosions and come running, we'll be long gone.'

CHAPTER TWENTY

It was a twenty-minute bike ride from the peasant cottage Rosie shared with Paul and Boo to the fishing wharf at Kerneval. The groups knew as little about one another's activities as they could get away with, so as Rosie stood under a dilapidated roof watching her fish being wrapped in newspaper, she had no idea that an agent had hosed down in this exact spot the night before.

With the parcel of fish in the basket between the handlebars, Rosie pedalled uphill, passing two streets before turning right. The sun was hot, but the breeze made it bearable. She'd spent so much of the last month cooped up in the little cottage sending radio messages back and forth that it was good to feel her heart pumping.

When she reached number twenty-five she took a

quick glance around before raising the latch on the side gate, leaning her bike next to a couple of metal dustbins and walking into the back yard.

There was a woman pegging out washing a couple of gardens down, so Rosie dipped her head below the level of the fence as she headed towards the outhouse. The stench made her gag as she opened the creaking door. The facilities comprised a broad plank with a hole in, directly over an open sewer pipe that ran downhill to the harbour.

She sent a dozen bluebottles into the air as she grabbed a key hanging from a rusty water pipe. After using it in the back door, Rosie was surprised to find herself in a bright open space, lit through large skylights. There were stacks of blank and unfinished canvases resting against the walls, most depicting the same woman in a variety of nude poses as she rested on the purple chaise at the far end of the room.

The radio she'd come for was in a leather case, stacked alongside bags and boxes of equipment that had been delivered by *Madeline II* and the trawler *Istanbul* the day before. The case was smaller than expected and a tug on the handle revealed that it was only half the weight of their current set.

Rosie should have picked it up and left immediately, but she was fascinated by the canvases and began flipping through.

'The artist was an Austrian Jew,' PT said. 'Fled here, then went off to America.'

Rosie spun around with her hands clutched to her chest. 'Bloody hell, you scared the daylights out of me!'

'He didn't get time to pick up any of his paintings,' PT explained. 'But he left a key with Alois' daughter and we're pretty sure he won't be back any time soon.'

'Oh yes!' Rosie gasped. 'I only saw her for a few minutes the night we arrived, but I thought the girl in the paintings looked familiar. Paul would absolutely love it in here, with the easel and the blank canvases.'

'So do I get a hug or what?' PT asked.

Rosie laughed, then they hugged tightly and started to kiss. They hadn't seen each other for almost a month.

'God I've *missed* you,' PT said, as he grabbed Rosie's bum and pushed her against the back of the chaise. 'Thinking about you is the only thing that's keeping me sane.'

Rosie opened her mouth to let PT's tongue in, but she wasn't keen on his stubbly beard and the whiff of alcohol in his sweat.

'Shouldn't you be working?' Rosie asked, as she pushed PT back gently.

PT looked thin and his eyes seemed desperate. 'I can't get you out of my head,' he said, as he wiped the slobber off his cheek on to the cuff of his shirt. 'I knew you were coming here to pick up the radio today. I *had* to see you.'

'You've lost weight,' Rosie said.

'It's the job,' PT said. 'Twelve-hour shifts on the roof of that bunker in the sun. It's so boring. After an hour your legs and your back hurt from shovelling concrete and you've still got eleven more to go. One day we were working near the edge. All the skin on my back was blistered up with sunburn and I just thought, *if I jump off and go head first into the dockside I'll never have to do this again.* It may sound crazy, but I was really considering it.'

'Poor you,' Rosie said sympathetically. 'It's boring working the transmitter all day with Boo, but it's not as bad as all that.'

'I'll have to speak to Henderson about it, or something,' PT said, but he cheered up when Rosie moved in close and started kissing him again.

As they snogged, Rosie backed on to the chaise. She grabbed PT's bum, as he squeezed her breast.

'I really love you, Rosie,' PT said.

Rosie was touched by the emotion in PT's voice. 'I love you too,' she said. 'It's maddening, knowing you're so near but not being allowed to see you.'

PT started pushing his hand up Rosie's skirt. She let him get away with it because the kiss was amazing and she didn't want it to stop, but she pulled him back when he tugged on her knickers.

'Don't spoil this,' she begged, but he pushed her hand

away and started dragging the knickers down her thighs. 'Stop it, now!'

'Come on,' PT said softly as he nuzzled Rosie's earlobe. 'I'll be really gentle. I know you didn't like it last time, but if you relax it'll be a hundred times better than any kiss.'

As Rosie pushed PT's head away, he made another lunge at her knickers. She pushed his arm back, but this time he kept tugging.

'I need to have you,' PT said.

He still had the emotion in his voice, but now there was anger too. The stretched elastic dug painfully into Rosie's thigh. She brought her free leg around and pushed PT gently, but when he still didn't take the hint she gave him a shove.

PT put his hand out to save himself, but his palm missed the edge of the chaise and he rolled off, banging his elbow on the paint-spattered floorboards. Rosie shot to her feet and pulled up her underwear.

'Why did you have ruin it?' she said, with a slight sob in her voice.

PT clutched his elbow as he sat up. 'It's what men and women do.'

'I'm not ready for that,' Rosie said. 'It *really* hurt when you tried before and you *swore* that you wouldn't try and make me again.'

'How can you not be ready?' PT said, dismissing the

idea with his hand. 'You're a *beautiful* young woman. You think God would have given you that sweet little body if you weren't ready?'

'It's not up for debate,' Rosie said. 'I'm fourteen and you're just dirty.'

'You're acting like a little girl,' PT shouted, as he stamped the floor and pointed accusingly at Rosie. 'Well I'm sixteen, OK? Girls are no good. I need a *woman*.'

'A woman is someone you cherish,' Rosie shouted back. 'What you're after is a whore.'

'There's a war on. For all we know a bomb will come out of the sky tomorrow and kill us both,' PT said. 'You'll be dead, and you won't even have lived.'

'AAARGH!' Rosie screamed, as she put her hands over her ears in frustration. 'I can't believe I said I loved you. You treat me like one of your con tricks: tell me what you think I want to hear and try scoring a jackpot.'

'Screw you,' PT said. 'Find yourself another boy when you've grown up.'

As PT charged down the hallway and slammed the front door, Rosie slumped on the chaise. She thought she was going to cry, but then realised that she was far too angry.

'Selfish, big-headed moron,' she mumbled, as she tilted her head back and looked at the clouds through a skylight.

After a few deep breaths she stormed outside with the

transmitter and started tying it to the rear end of her bike.

*

Instead of the afternoon nap he'd hoped for, Marc had to ride across to Kerneval. Troy, Olivier and Michel were at sea, so he left a message with Nicolas who was still laid up with a bad back. They were to meet before dark at the abandoned house where Marc and Henderson had stayed on the night of their first scouting mission.

He then walked to the artist's house, where he was surprised to find the back door left open.

'Hello?' he shouted.

There was nobody home, but he decided it wasn't suspicious: if the Germans had found the house and laid a trap they wouldn't do something as obvious as leave the back door open. Whoever had been here last had been clumsy though, and as there was no sign of a radio he correctly guessed that it was Rosie.

Marc found the plastic explosive. It came in waxed paper and had been dyed a creamy yellow colour so that it resembled butter, but its strong almondy smell meant it wouldn't fool anyone for long. The itching powder was in one-kilo cloth bags of the kind you got when you bought grains or flour.

He unknotted the drawstring and sniffed the powder suspiciously, while being careful not to actually inhale any of it. He then pulled up his shirt and sprinkled a few sticky flakes over his stomach, to no immediate effect.

Fifteen minutes later he rode over the bridge back into Lorient. It was always the same five or six guards who worked there. They knew he worked for Madame Mercier, and as they turned a blind eye when he came through with cartloads of black market food he wasn't worried about his little satchel.

'No strawberries?' the guard asked, as he waved Marc through.

'Maybe tomorrow,' Marc said cheerfully, as he pedalled off. 'I'll save you some.'

He'd forgotten about testing the itching powder, but as the checkpoint disappeared his skin started to burn. The compound was designed to be activated by the acidity in sweat and the exertion of the bike ride had done the trick.

Marc stopped by a drinking fountain and washed the powder off, but while the coolness soothed it, washing the powder away didn't stop the itching. It felt like hot pins digging into his flesh.

Still scratching, Marc sailed past Mamba Noir and the rest of the entertainment district, then cut down a side street and freewheeled into a stable block. Before the war, horses were popular for local deliveries in small towns like Lorient, but with the fuel shortages they were the only choice.

Part of Edith's fragrance came from the amount of

time she spent mucking out and grooming Madame Mercier's horses. For Marc straw, piss and manure reminded him of his hated rural upbringing, but Edith loved it here. She'd fixed up a little den at the back of the hay store, complete with books, blankets and a gas lamp. She often slept here if one of the horses was sick, or just because she liked being on her own.

'Why are you walking like that?' Edith said, as she imitated the way Marc stepped around the worst of the manure. 'You're such a pansy. It's only poop.'

Marc shuddered. 'I saw this boy's comic once. They had a drawing of what houses will look like in 1960. It was big block, twenty storeys high. That's where I want to live when I'm grown up. Right on the top floor, with no dirt or grime. Indoor toilet, electric heating, whitewashed walls.'

'That's so dirty having a toilet inside your house,' Edith said. 'It must stink.'

'The toilets in Mamba Noir don't stink,' Marc noted.

'You should try the ladies after Madame Mercier's been in there for half an hour,' Edith said. 'So did you want something, or are you here to admire my beauty?'

Marc looked around. There was nobody about right now, but people brought horses and carts in and out all the time and he didn't want anyone to overhear. 'Can we talk inside?'

Marc laughed when he stepped past the hay bales and

saw that Edith had pinned magazine pictures of good-looking movie stars to the wall of her den.

'I always thought you preferred horses to humans,' Marc said.

'Get on with it,' Edith said, as she blushed. 'I've got stuff to do.'

'It's two things,' Marc said. 'First, Henderson wants you to go up into the woods around the engine sheds on the edge of town at eight tonight.'

'Why do you keep scratching?' Edith interrupted. 'Have you got fleas?'

'I'll get to that in a minute,' Marc said. 'Can you go up there?'

Edith nodded. 'What for?'

'Just to look around. There's usually only one guard, but we want you to count the engines and make sure there's nothing unusual going on.'

'What are you up to?' Edith asked.

'Better you don't know,' Marc said. 'Can you do it or not?'

'Yeah,' Edith agreed. 'If they stop me I'll say I'm picking berries or something.'

'Great,' Marc said, as he pulled the bag of itching powder out of his satchel. 'This is why I'm scratching.'

'Itching powder?'

Marc nodded. 'A kid at my old school bought some from a joke shop in Paris one time, but you just shook it out of your shirt and you were fine. This stuff is like the industrial-strength super version. I only put a couple of little grains on my skin. It's driving me nuts and washing it off didn't make any difference.'

'So it's not the sort of substance you want in your long johns if you're stuck inside a U-boat for a month,' Edith said.

'That's exactly what I'm thinking,' Marc said, wagging his finger. 'But Henderson's not interested. He's angry that they didn't send more explosives to blow up the trains.'

'Ahem,' Edith said.

Marc looked awkward. 'Well it wasn't going to stay secret once half the town's heard them blow up, anyway.'

Edith sat on a bale of hay and acted thoughtful. 'You'd have to find out where the Germans have their clothes washed. Then you'd have to do it with the laundry for a boat that's about to sail.'

'Do you think the laundry is done separately for each boat?' Marc asked. 'Or do the sailors put their laundry in as and when they need it?'

'How should I know?' Edith asked. 'But I take the bed-sheets and tablecloths to the laundry up by the station for Madame Mercier. I bet one of the washerwomen would know how the Germans get their laundry done.'

'Don't ask too many obvious questions,' Marc said. 'It only takes one snitch and you'll be in a Gestapo cell.'

'And you don't want the poor washerwomen getting in trouble either,' Edith said. 'But there has to be a way.'

'There's a lot of working out to do,' Marc said. 'But I definitely think this powder could make more difference than Henderson seems to believe.'

CHAPTER TWENTY-ONE

Marc and Henderson arrived at the farmhouse at a quarter past eight. Since the single night when they'd slept here two months earlier, they'd repaired the front door and tidied up downstairs. A couple of airmen had used it as a hideout before their voyage home, but it was mainly set up as a bolthole.

If things went bad and any of Henderson's team had to leave Lorient in a hurry, they could stop off here and find a radio transmitter hidden in the loft. There were clothes, high-energy foods, a few first aid supplies, plus knives, guns and ammunition. There was also a gap in the garden wall where a fleeing agent could leave a message to say what had happened.

They always wound a piece of cotton between two tacks on opposite sides of the door frame when they left the house, which would snap if anyone opened the door. After turning the key, Marc pushed the door in a few centimetres and made sure the cotton was intact before stepping inside.

He kicked a garden rake out of the way and checked that the spade was still wedged under the back door handle, while Henderson inspected the windows for signs that they'd been forced.

'Looks safe,' Henderson said. 'Let's get to work.'

The plastic explosive – commonly just called plastic – was a recent innovation. Until its invention by a British chemist a few years earlier, all known high-explosive compounds degraded rapidly in open air and could detonate if dropped or handled roughly. Plastic was safe to handle, could be moulded into any shape and wouldn't blow your head off if you fell over carrying a backpack full of the stuff.

Henderson set all five pats of explosive out on the kitchen cabinet, along with two packets of detonating fuses. The first pack contained time pencils. Once activated these would go off when acid corroded through a metal wire, triggering the detonation. The corrosion time depended on the strength of the acid and the packet contained a selection of pencils designed to explode in anything between ten minutes and six hours. The second pack contained sympathetic fuses which were triggered by the shock wave from another explosion, enabling an agent to set off dozens of small explosions simultaneously.

It felt like cookery, as Henderson used the kitchen drainer to cut the sticks into fifteen evenly sized pieces. He put sixty-minute time pencils in the first two and sympathetic fuses in all the others, before passing them across to Marc.

The plastic was naturally sticky enough to mould on to a porous surface like wood, but steam trains were made of metal which was usually painted or polished. To ensure the plastic stayed where it was put, Marc dipped his hand into a large jar of Vaseline and smeared it liberally over each bomblet.

The results looked like iced cakes, with the fuses like birthday candles sticking out of the top. This unintentional effect was completed by dropping each bomb into an actual paper cake casing so that it could be handled without covering yourself in the greasy Vaseline.

'Perfect timing,' Henderson said enthusiastically when Michel and Olivier arrived. 'I know you've been out at sea all day, so thanks for coming at short notice.'

Michel was seventeen, though working as a fisherman had weathered his skin, making him look older. Olivier was two years younger and although they were only cousins the two lads were near identical in build and appearance.

Troy had also come along to show them the way to the

house. He was narked by the fact that two untrained French boys had been picked for the operation instead of him, until Marc discreetly called him into the front yard and explained that Henderson wanted the locals to feel like they were more than just couriers and lookouts.

'Steam engines are heavy, brutal machines,' Henderson explained, as he picked up one of the explosive cakes. 'I could stick all fifteen of these babies next to the main boiler of a big locomotive and they wouldn't make a dent. Train wheels are toughened steel and a cake exploding might buckle one, but you could jack the train up and have it running again within three or four hours. You can throw this in the firebox and blow a big hole, but that's an even simpler repair. Fortunately for us, all steam engines *do* have a vulnerable spot.'

Marc nodded knowingly, but hoped that Henderson wouldn't test him because he'd learned all this during his training and forgotten every word.

Henderson stopped speaking and used his fingertip to draw a childlike steam engine in the dust on the dining table. 'Down here by the wheels is the cylinder head. Steam pressure pushes the cylinder, which in turn pushes the coupling rods that make the wheels turn round. The cylinder is made from cast iron, which is brittle. Even a small explosion will shatter it.

'Cylinder ends never break in normal usage so nobody keeps spares and to replace it you have to dismantle half the locomotive. In peacetime, you might be able to get a new cylinder head cast and fitted within a few weeks, but with the current shortages of materials and mechanics there's a real chance that we could put every train in that depot out of action for a long time.'

Michel and Olivier looked at each other. 'We're up for that,' Olivier said.

'I hoped you'd feel that way,' Henderson said, with a smile.

'This is the Gestapo, you are completely surrounded!' Edith shouted, as she ran into the kitchen accompanied by her usual whiff of manure. Her voice was too childish to fool anyone, but she still raised a laugh.

'How's it looking up there?' Henderson asked. 'Did anybody see you?'

'I had a wander around,' Edith said. 'All I could see was one little old guard. I even got inside the fence and climbed up into a train.'

'That wasn't what I asked you to do,' Henderson said firmly. '*Never* take unnecessary risks.'

'What risk?' Edith said. 'I could outrun that old fart any day.'

'How many engines did you count?'

'Eleven,' Edith said. 'Three of the big ones that go up and down the main line. The rest were the titchy ones that take the cargo backwards and forwards to the docks.'

'Perfect!' Henderson said. 'We've got fifteen charges.

That's one each on the small trains. To maximise damage on the three big trains, we'll put a charge on the cylinder end on each side, and we'll still have one left over for luck.'

*

PT was angry at Rosie, or angry about how he'd behaved towards Rosie. He couldn't decide which, but either way he was wound tight and couldn't stand being in the house, with Nicolas in the next room moaning about his back and constantly shouting for someone to fetch a hot flannel, or help find his glasses.

'You can't take a day sick and then go into town,' Nicolas' long-suffering wife warned. 'You signed a contract with OT. Do you want to end up in a labour camp in Germany?'

But PT was sixteen and didn't let old ladies tell him what to do. He grabbed his jacket, crossed the bridge into town and went into Le Petit Prince. He recognised a few faces from the building site, but none of his gang were around, which seemed like a good thing because they reminded him of work.

He sat at the bar, ordered a beer and two large shots of vodka. The men sitting next to him were talking about Russia. One said the invasion was the end of communism and Hitler's final masterstroke.

'I hate old Adolf, but you can't deny he's a military genius,' he said.

The guy he was talking to was a quiet sort who just kept nodding, so the loudmouth turned to PT.

'What do you think about Russia, young fella?'

'I think I want to drink in peace,' PT said.

He didn't say it in a nasty way, but the man was cocky and a little drunk. He put his hand on PT's shoulder.

'You want to watch your mouth,' he said. 'That's why the Germans piss all over us. Their kids have discipline. Ours have smart mouths.'

As the man spouted opinions to nobody in particular, PT sneakily fed his hand inside the man's jacket and pulled out his wallet. Unnecessary risks like this were contrary to his espionage training, but turning such an easy haul down was like asking a hungry baby to turn down its mother's tit.

'Would you think more of the younger generation if it bought you a drink?' PT asked.

The man laughed warmly as PT put money on the bar, not realising it was his own. As the barman got more beers, PT stripped out all the banknotes before dropping the wallet back in the loudmouth's jacket.

'What a decent young fellow,' the man said, as he held up his glass. 'Thank you.'

'No, thank *you*,' PT said, smirking slightly. 'Now if you'll excuse me, I just saw a good friend of mine.'

He gulped the beer and dropped the empty glass on the bar. Two shots and two beers in ten minutes made him pretty drunk as he walked across the floor towards the bottom of the staircase. He paid the man three francs for a room, headed up and gave a sleazy smile to the little honey he'd caught Joel eying up the night before.

'You're what I need,' PT said, groping the girl's bum as she led him down a dingy hallway. 'Girlfriends are too complicated.'

CHAPTER TWENTY-TWO

Edith had done her job and headed home, while Troy walked back to Kerneval. The others – Henderson, Marc, Michel and Olivier – played cards until it was dark enough to head out. The yard was perfect territory for a raid: the sidings were surrounded by woodland on three sides and there was only a single-track gravel road.

In peacetime the adjoining goods yard would have been hectic as wagons shunted up from the docks were pushed together to make cargo trains up to half a mile long. But no civilian cargo had been unloaded at Lorient in a year and some tracks in the loading area were already disappearing under weeds.

Henderson dished out balaclavas and scanned the moonlit dockyard through a small pair of binoculars. He pointed out the guard's shed and looked at Michel.

'Can't have the guard finding the explosives, or taking a walk and getting himself blown up,' Henderson said, as he pulled a bottle of K tablets out of his jacket. 'Edith said he was a little fellow, so a couple of these should knock him out for a few hours. Do you want to give that a go?'

Michel and Olivier smiled, proud and scared at the same time. Marc now understood why Henderson had invited them along. Young men like these had many reasons to hate the Germans. Their fathers and older brothers had been imprisoned or killed. The Germans told them what jobs to do and when they could leave their homes. They kept food and fuel on tight ration, and most galling of all, money and smart uniforms made German soldiers magnets for the prettiest French girls.

'For sure,' Olivier said. 'What's the best way?'

'Take a guess,' Henderson said. 'If we're going to beat the Germans, you have to start thinking for yourself.'

'We could scout around the hut, peer through the window,' Michel said. 'Once we know he's in there, we burst in and grab him.'

Olivier nodded keenly. 'Maybe we should cut off the phone line, in case he calls out?'

Marc stifled a smile as Henderson spoke. 'You could do that,' he said. 'But the guard has no reason to be suspicious yet. Why not make him come to you?'

'How do we do that?' Michel asked.

'I'd suggest going up to the hut and knocking on the door. When he opens up, you point the gun at him. Or if he doesn't open it, you know he's not in there.'

'Right,' Olivier said. 'I guess that is simpler.'

Michel shook his head. 'We're no good at this,' he confessed.

'Espionage is ninety per cent common sense and ten per cent luck,' Henderson said warmly. 'A bit of experience is all you boys need.'

Michel and Olivier were eating up the praise.

'Pull your masks down and take this. It's loaded and ready to shoot. And *don't* call anyone by name.'

Michel pocketed the gun and led the way towards the guard's wooden hut. Marc moved to follow them, but Henderson pulled him back.

'Let them do it,' he said, then began a slow walk out of the trees.

Olivier knocked and the guard moaned as he opened the door.

'There's no work out here,' the guard said. He was a rotund little man in an oily French railways uniform.

'Inside, sit down,' Olivier ordered, as his older cousin aimed the gun at the guard's head.

The guard clutched his chest, like he was having a heart attack.

'We're not here to hurt you,' Michel said, as the shuddering guard backed up into a well-padded armchair. 'You need to swallow these pills. You'll wake up in the woods in a couple of hours.'

'There's nothing here to steal, boys,' the guard said nervously. 'If you want a couple of buckets of coal, go and grab it.'

Michel shoved the gun right up to the guard's head. 'Take the pills or take a bullet. Decide *right* now.'

The guard looked across at a hip flask. 'Can I take something to swallow them with?'

He put the two pills on his tongue and crunched them up a little before chasing them down with a shot of whatever was in his little flask. By this time Henderson stood in the doorway.

'Takes about three minutes before he gets woozy,' Henderson said. 'We want him well away from here, so walk him into the woods and make sure he is laid out somewhere comfortable.'

Marc stayed back on the edge of the woods, keeping lookout with Henderson's binoculars, while occasionally scratching the rash that had come up on his stomach. The little man weighed less than a net full of fish, so Michel and Olivier had no problems carrying him into the woods and laying him out with his back up against a tree.

Henderson spoke to Marc. 'You stay as lookout, OK? I want these boys to enjoy themselves.'

Marc understood why Henderson was letting the new

boys do all the exciting stuff, but he was used to being Henderson's favourite and felt jealous as he led the pair through the gate into the train depot.

Henderson surveyed the layout of the yard. The engines were spread over six sidings stretching back two hundred metres. He picked a large engine parked halfway down the second nearest siding as a starting point.

'I'll put one time pencil on this train,' Henderson said, as he showed the boys where to position the explosive. 'And a reserve with a time pencil a couple of sidings over. Always put the timed explosive at a central point, with your sympathetic fuses radiating out. Now check your watches.'

'We haven't got watches,' Olivier said.

Henderson smiled. 'Well, that's something we'll have to sort out. To activate the time pencil, you snap it like so, then you push it back into the explosive. In theory that explosive won't go off for an hour, but it's not an exact science. For safety, always aim to be well out of the blast zone in half the pencil time. So in our case that's thirty minutes for a sixty-minute pencil.'

Michel and Olivier smiled eagerly as Henderson gave each of them a drawstring bag containing five sticky explosive cakes.

'Move quickly but quietly,' Henderson said. 'Keep your ears open for a shout from Marc or any other noise.

If something happens and we get split up, go back to the safe house. But if you wait more than half an hour and I don't arrive, head for home. Is all that clear?'

'Completely, sir,' Olivier nodded.

Henderson laughed. 'You don't need to call me sir. Now let's get on with it.'

*

'Here,' PT said, throwing over an extra five-franc note as he grabbed his trousers off the floor.

The girl stood by a grotty sink in her stockings, shamelessly washing between her legs with a flannel before squirting herself all over with perfume. Her body was beautiful, but it was the least sexy, and possibly saddest, sight PT had ever seen.

'So what time do you get off?' PT asked.

'After your bedtime,' she said, as she grabbed her bra and the five francs in a single sweep. 'I don't want a boyfriend.'

PT noticed scratches down her back and fingertip-shaped bruises where men had groped her breasts. He'd come here expecting relief, but now felt disgusted with himself. How many labourers, scaffolders and dock workers had had sex in this room? What made a beautiful young girl so desperate that she had to lie on a bed and let men screw her for money?

PT wanted the girl to know that he was better than all the others, but how could he do that? Besides, it was probably standard to go in full of lust and come out feeling ashamed and hoping that you hadn't caught something nasty.

The girl kicked his boots across the floor. 'I'll get yelled at if you hang around any longer,' she said as she clicked her fingers. 'Snap out of the daydream, eh?'

PT looked back as he headed out of the room towards the balcony. Sex had sobered him up a little and he wondered what to do. Stay here and drink? Go to another bar? Go home and sulk? Try and find where Rosie was staying and tell her he was sorry? Or maybe just get a big knife and slash his wrists.

He saw Gilles's head above the crowd along with a couple of his other workmates. They would have had a tough day with one man down and might not be happy to see him cavorting, so he moved downstairs quickly, hiding his face.

'Get your money's worth from Mona?' the man at the bottom asked cheerfully.

'Great,' PT said, raising a false smile before cutting outside into what was now moonlight.

He tried to cheer himself up as he started the walk home. He made a plan: he'd apologise to Rosie and try persuading Henderson to help him find a less physical job. Maybe he could complain about a bad back or something. Though he had to be careful with that little game because people who signed OT contracts and didn't pull their weight had a habit of getting sent to chemical plants in deepest Bavaria.

'Coincidence or what?' a man shouted. 'How you doing, mate?'

PT turned, expecting someone he'd met in a bar or someone from the bunker site, but it was red beard's hired muscle from the night before and this time he'd decided to spice matters up with a dirty great bread knife. It was clearly no coincidence and PT realised that if he'd been thinking with his brain instead of his dick he would have given Le Petit Prince a wide berth for at least a week.

But here he was, with a saw-edged blade catching moonlight as it lunged towards PT's chest.

CHAPTER TWENTY-THREE

Marc watched the three figures jog across the gravel. Michel and Olivier grinned like kids who'd posted dog crap through an old lady's letterbox.

'All good?' Marc asked.

'So far,' Henderson nodded. 'We should have at least half an hour until the blast, but I don't trust time pencils so let's not hang about.'

They hurried through the trees, halting briefly to check that the guard was still unconscious. At the farmhouse they dropped off weapons, balaclavas and binoculars before washing the Vaseline off their hands. Henderson found four mugs and poured a shot of whisky in each.

'Quick shot to calm your nerves, boys. Cheers!'

Only Henderson enjoyed the taste, but they all liked

the drinking ritual and the sense of accomplishing something together.

'Remember what I've told you about security,' Henderson warned. 'When that guard wakes up he'll mention two boys, so walk home separately. One of you set off now, one of you give it a few minutes. If you can think up slightly different routes that's even better.

'Be proud of what you've done, but don't mention it. Not even to your uncle or grandfather. And especially not when you've had a few beers and you're trying to impress some girl, or one of the other lads at the harbour.'

'Can we do something like this again?' Olivier asked.

'Let's see if the explosives go off on this one first,' Henderson said. 'But there should be other chances. Now, which one of you is going to leave first?'

*

PT dodged the main thrust at his stomach, but somehow the bread knife snagged him between the knuckles.

'Slippery bastard,' the man roared.

PT yelped from the pain as he stumbled sideways into a man who had no idea what had just happened. They were on Lorient's main drag, with a crowd outside a café less than twenty metres away.

'Look where you're going,' he said, giving PT an angry two-handed shove back towards his attacker. This time the blade whistled across PT's chest, opening up his shirt and making a twenty-centimetre gash across his belly.

Most passers-by kept walking in the dark, but a few noticed the fight and people in the café stood up to get a look. With two knife wounds PT's plan was to run as fast as he could but as he turned away in a disorientated state his foot landed awkwardly, half in the road and half on a raised pavement. His ankle twisted painfully and he fell down hard, banging his hip on the cobbles.

As PT rolled on to his back one of the passers-by grabbed the big man's arm.

'He's a kid, you'll kill him.'

'That's the plan,' the big man roared, shrugging his anchor off with his elbow before charging back towards PT.

The crowd was growing. Someone tried to give PT a hand up, but he didn't think he could stand on his twisted ankle and shoved it away. As the big man lunged, PT kicked explosively with both legs, hitting his opponent so hard that he lifted clean off the ground.

PT's ankle was excruciating and the hand over his stomach glistened with blood, but he still felt satisfied as the big man doubled up and crashed to on his knees, badly winded. Onlookers gasped as a two-man German patrol ran towards the scene.

The smaller of the two soldiers got there first. 'Put the knife down.'

It was risky to stand around now that Germans were

involved. Onlookers moved off as PT finally accepted the friendly hand and found himself propped against an unlit lamppost, feeling faint.

'I know a doctor,' the man helping him said. 'Come with me.'

'Put the knife *down*,' the soldier repeated.

As the German unholstered his gun, the big man stood up explosively and charged with the bread knife. A woman screamed as the huge blade tore the German's throat open. The other soldier fired, shattering the big man's knee. His body pirouetted and his skull whacked the cobbles, while the knifed German staggered about, fighting for breath as blood flooded his lungs.

A dead soldier meant certain German retribution. People who'd been walking started to run. Men sitting outside the café drained glasses and started walking.

PT's vision was blurring. He looked around for the man who'd offered a doctor, but he'd disappeared along with everyone else. He staggered across from the lamppost, almost falling as he took three steps and hit a doorway.

The German who'd taken the shot blasted a whistle, as PT felt his way along the wall. His head was light and he desperately wanted to pass out, but if the Germans found him here with a knife wound they'd surely pin some of the blame for the dead soldier on him.

A couple of soldiers were running one way and a

gendarme[4] was coming the other. The pavement was clear and PT felt conspicuous, but the news that a German soldier had been murdered had now spread inside the bars and clubs.

Notices all over occupied France promised brutal reprisals if any German was harmed, so nobody wanted to be in the vicinity when the Gestapo turned up to investigate. As word spread through bars and cafés, bodies poured into the streets. In the dark it was hard to see PT's injury. People either didn't care or assumed that the young lad dragging himself along the wall was hopelessly drunk.

*

Marc and Henderson came back into Lorient through the northern checkpoint a little after ten p.m. When the guard asked why they'd been out of town, Henderson explained that he'd been collecting ledgers for Mamba Noir from Madame Mercier's accountant near her home in Queven. He had the ledgers in his briefcase, but the German didn't bother to look.

As they neared Lorient station in the centre of town there was a deep rumble, followed by an orange glow in the sky a few kilometres out of town. Henderson checked his watch and smiled at Marc.

'Fifty-six minutes since I broke the time pencil,' he said.

---

[4] Gendarme – a French civilian police officer.

'Hope they did the job,' Marc replied.

The metal engines wouldn't burn, so after the initial flash there was no smoke, or flames to light the sky. Beyond the station something seemed wrong. The pavements were crowded with revellers, pouring out of the entertainment district in a major hurry.

'Another power cut, I'd bet,' Marc said.

'I wouldn't be so sure,' Henderson said. 'When we had the power cut they just milled about in the street. This lot look worried.'

They grew more suspicious as two black Citroëns and an open-topped Mercedes packed with senior officers shot by, with the lead driver glued to his horn. Henderson spotted a regular from Mamba Noir and asked him what was going on.

'All sorts of rumours,' the bespectacled gent said, as his smartly dressed girlfriend pulled on his arm. 'Some kind of bomb by the harbour front, we heard. Quite a few Germans killed. Three, eight, ten, it depends who you ask.'

'Thank you,' Henderson said, as the couple hurried off.

'Who could have done that?' Marc said. 'Are you sure we should go back home?'

'Where else?' Henderson asked. 'It's safer in our rooms than hanging about on the street.'

'We could go back to the safe house,' Marc said. 'If

eight Germans are dead, they'll be tearing everything apart, making arrests, kicking down doors.'

'If they kick our door down, I want to be in my bed doing absolutely nothing suspicious. We'll be home in ten minutes. If they do stop us, we'll stick to our cover story about the accountant. The guards on the checkpoint will confirm our story.'

'I guess,' Marc said.

'It's your natural herd instinct,' Henderson explained. 'You're seeing hundreds of people going one way and your subconscious is telling you to do the same.'

Marc grew calmer as they neared home. The revellers were gone and all they saw were a few bar and café staff heading home. Henderson stopped a bar manager from the place opposite Mamba Noir.

'It wasn't a bomb,' she explained. 'German patrol officer had his throat cut. Everywhere has been shut. Drunken Germans have smashed a few places up. I wouldn't hang around on the street because they're taking people away in vans.'

'Thanks,' Henderson said. 'You keep safe.'

Usually the streets behind the main drag were full of puking and yelling, but tonight they were eerie. It was a relief to reach home. As Henderson took his key out, Marc looked around the corner towards Mamba Noir.

'I'd better check and see if Joel left a message.'

'Wait until morning,' Henderson said.

Marc shook his head. 'What if they collect the rubbish?'

Henderson realised it was less than thirty metres away and there was nobody about. 'OK, go and check but don't hang around. Do you want some hot milk before bed?'

'Great,' Marc said.

'I'll put the pan on.'

Marc jumped down off the doorstep and hurried across the road. It was unusual to see the bins behind Mamba Noir so empty. The staff had clearly left in a hurry without throwing out the rubbish.

As he crouched down and reached between the bins Marc heard German boots coming up the alleyway that led from the main drag. He slid himself between the two tall bins, knocking into one and making a rat scramble about inside. As Marc felt inside the tin and found a balled-up note from Joel, the German pulled down the front of his trousers and started pissing against the wall barely a metre away.

Marc strained his neck, trying to get a look behind. The heavily built German wore the sinister black uniform of the Gestapo, with leather gloves tucked into his pocket and a cigarette end between his lips.

The urine was splashing off the wall, but some made a drumming sound as it ricocheted against the empty bin. The Gestapo officer enjoyed the novelty of this and turned ninety degrees so that urine pelted the bins.

Marc buried his head and kept absolutely still, but his blond hair was a giveaway: clearly visible in the moonlight. As the stream of urine slowed to a drip, Marc heard the click of a pistol right behind his head.

'And why does a boy hide amongst the bins?' the heavily accented German asked, as he tugged on Marc's collar. 'Let's take a walk.'

CHAPTER TWENTY-FOUR

There was no light on the staircase and Henderson jumped with fright as he stumbled into a trailing leg on the top landing. He crouched quickly, thinking it might be Joel because he came down this street every night, but the shadowy outline was too bulky.

Henderson's heel dipped into blood as he unlocked his apartment. He ran to the window and pulled the curtains before screwing in the light bulb.

'PT,' he gasped. 'Shit, shit, shit!'

He'd passed out holding his stomach. There was blood smeared along the wallpaper up the stairs. Henderson crouched down and felt PT's cheek. It was cold, but at least he was breathing.

'Can you hear me?'

PT's eyelids flickered as Henderson cradled his head.

'What happened?'

PT could only groan. Henderson's first priority was to help him, but with the possibility of door-to-door searches he also had to avoid spreading too much blood around. He ripped the bedspread from the double bed in his room and laid it out flat just inside the apartment. He then dragged PT through doorway and on to the bedspread. As soon as Marc came back, he'd get him to mop up the blood outside and scrub the wallpaper along the staircase.

Henderson had done basic first aid training when he'd joined the Royal Navy and a more advanced course after joining Espionage Research. He filled a saucepan with water and put it on the stove to boil, then took off his jacket, rolled his shirt-sleeves and quickly washed his hands before unbuttoning PT's bloody shirt.

'What's it like?' PT moaned.

'Just keep calm,' Henderson said. 'Take deep breaths and try not to pass out again.'

The wound was an hour old and Henderson's first task was to see how serious it was. PT's abdomen was slick with blood, with a darker semi-clotted layer stuck to the skin beneath.

'This is going to hurt,' Henderson said, as he explored the sides of the wound with his fingertips, then pulled the edges of the deepest part of the wound apart.

Henderson had seen some horrible things in his life,

but he wasn't comfortable with blood and guts up close and took a deep breath before looking down. His nightmare had been spurting blood, or the sight of intestines, but as far as he could tell the slashing wound had penetrated no deeper than the abdominal muscle.

'Am I gonna die?' PT asked.

'I'm no doctor, but I think you've had a lucky scrape.'

Henderson peeked between the curtains as he walked to the kitchen dresser. It was hard to see because the street was in blackout, but there was no sign of Marc and he should have taken less than a minute to collect the message.

Henderson covered his bloody hand with a dishcloth as he opened the cabinet and grabbed a sewing kit and half-drunk bottle of vodka. He took out a needle, snapped off a metre of strong silk thread and dropped both into the saucepan which was now close to boiling

There was no obvious sign of dirt in the wound, but who knew where the knife had been? The cap of the vodka bottle slipped out of Henderson's grasp as he unscrewed it, and rolled under Marc's bed.

'Remember what Mr Takada taught you,' Henderson said. 'Pain is all in your mind. Go to your special place and stay there. OK?'

What are you gonna do?' PT asked. He raised his head anxiously, then groaned as he saw the bottle. 'Oh shit!'

'I know, I know,' Henderson said soothingly, as he

threw PT a handkerchief. 'I've got to sterilise the wound, then I'll put a few stitches in. Stuff that in your mouth and bite down hard. We can't wake up the old biddies downstairs. Ready?'

PT's movements were shaky, but he managed to push the handkerchief into his mouth and raised his thumb. Henderson opened the wound a fraction with one hand before filling it with vodka. PT reacted explosively to the pain. His legs shot up, kneeing Henderson in the side.

'Don't move, you'll make it worse,' Henderson said, as he crawled forwards and pinned PT's shoulders. 'Deep breaths. You're gonna get through this.'

*

Marc jumped down from a canvas-sided German army truck.

'Inside,' a black-uniformed officer ordered, before kicking out at a young waitress. 'Faster or I'll crack your heads.'

Most of the men and women who'd driven in with Marc were staff from the bars and cafés whose only crime was emerging on to the streets several minutes after their customers. There were drunks, and passers-by who needed to cross the main drag on their way to or from a night job, but Marc also realised that all the important bar and restaurant owners had been rounded up, including Madame Mercier.

Gestapo headquarters was in an opulent Roman-style

villa that had been requisitioned from Lorient's richest family. Fifty prisoners were made to sit cross-legged and hands-on-heads in a paved courtyard, surrounded on all sides by double-height columns. Marc knew Madame Mercier had friends in high places. If she spotted him she might be able to help, so he squeezed between a couple of bodies and sat down next to her.

They waited in silence for more than an hour as people were singled out and taken away for questioning.

'Hands stay on your head,' a Gestapo guard shouted, as he grabbed Madame Mercier's wrist.

'I have arthritis in my neck,' Madame Mercier said. 'I can't sit like this any longer.'

'You'll have a mouthful of teeth if you don't,' the guard said, as he forced Madame Mercier's hand back up on to her head.

'How dare you,' she cried.

The German swung his rifle butt downwards, smashing Madame Mercier across the top of the head and making her wig slip down over her face. Marc looked around instinctively and the German motioned towards him with the rifle, threatening the same treatment.

'Face front or you'll get some too.'

'Trouble here, Gefreiter[5]?' another officer said, as he stepped between rows of prisoners towards them. Marc

[5] Gefreiter – the lowest rank of officer in the Gestapo.

didn't dare look round, but knew the voice of the man who'd found him hiding between the bins.

'No problem, Oberst Bauer. Just a lady who doesn't follow instructions.'

Bauer laughed. 'I expect that this lady thinks she's much too important to sit on a stone floor. Isn't that right, Madame Mercier?'

She didn't answer.

'She has many friends in high places, but none of them within these walls. Up now, both of you. Walk with me.'

As Marc stood up, the junior Gestapo officer had to help Madame Mercier to her feet. She clutched her wig to her bosom like a little pet as Bauer marched them down a marble corridor and up to a narrow first-floor room.

The space was austere, with light patches where paintings had been taken off the walls. The only original furniture was two finely sculpted chairs and an antique desk with the drawers ripped out, but the Gestapo had added its own distinctive brand of decoration. There was a tin bathtub, lengths of rubber hose, chains, restraining bracelets and a rack of spiked and barbed instruments.

'Sit,' Bauer said, pointing at the chairs as a female Gestapo officer stepped up behind and clicked her heels.

'Do you need any equipment prepared, Herr Oberst?' she asked.

Bauer gave a chilling laugh. 'Well, that rather depends on whether I like the answers they give me.'

Marc took his first proper look at Bauer in the light. Like all elite military groups Gestapo officers were picked for strength and intelligence, but Nazi ideology also dictated that they have specific racial characteristics such as upright posture, fair hair and blue eyes. Tall, blond and powerfully built, Bauer made a perfect Nazi.

'Let's see if you told me the truth when I picked you up earlier,' Bauer said to Marc, while cracking his knuckles.

Marc was trembling. The last time he'd been this close to a Gestapo officer he'd ended up getting his front tooth yanked out. And while they'd probably just been brought in together because of the incident out in the courtyard, if Bauer did know anything about their undercover operations then things were about to turn nasty.

'This boy said he works for you, Madame Mercier. Is that true?'

'He's a cigarette boy at Mamba Noir,' she replied. 'He also takes a cart out for me in the morning, collecting supplies.'

'I see,' Bauer nodded. 'Has he worked for you long?'

'Two or three months.'

'And he's honest?'

Madame Mercier shrugged. 'I employ more than two

hundred people, Herr Oberst. I can only say that I've no cause to believe that he is dishonest.'

'So why would I find young Marc hiding in the bins behind Mamba Noir?'

'I don't know,' Madame Mercier shrugged. 'We throw out food sometimes. Or maybe he left something behind at the club.'

'But why would he hide?' Bauer asked fiercely.

Madame Mercier laughed. 'Because a great hulk like you thundered towards him in a black uniform, I should imagine.'

Marc's breathing eased. She'd confirmed everything he'd told the Gestapo officer as he'd walked to the truck.

Bauer scratched his chin thoughtfully, then spoke to his female assistant in German. 'Ursula, please escort Marc to a holding cell. I don't think there's any reason to question him further.'

Madame Mercier looked up at Bauer as Marc walked towards the door. 'I don't know why I'm even here,' she said indignantly. 'I was working in my office all night. It looks out on to the main drag, but I have to pull the curtains when the lights are on, so how could I have seen anything?'

'You're here because it's your responsibility to ensure that your customers behave,' Bauer shouted angrily. 'The man we arrested was drunk. He killed a German solider. Who sold him that drink? Was it one of your bars?'

'Oh don't be ridiculous,' Madame Mercier said, as she rose out of her chair. 'I am not responsible for the death of that soldier.'

'Don't you *dare* speak to a Gestapo officer in that tone,' Bauer roared.

'I speak to you like a fool, sir, because you are a fool.'

Bauer grabbed Madame Mercier by the neck and throttled her. The chairs flew out of the way as she slammed the back wall, then Bauer dragged her sideways and plunged her head first into the icy bath.

'You think you're important,' Bauer shouted, as Ursula led Marc out. 'But before this night is out I shall teach you to be humble, Madame Mercier.'

CHAPTER TWENTY-FIVE

After being stitched, PT managed to stand long enough to get on to Marc's bed. While he dozed Henderson scrubbed the landing floor and the wallpaper on the staircase. He thought about venturing out with a torch to look for Marc, but it seemed certain he'd been picked up by the Germans. What other explanation was there?

Henderson couldn't get Marc out of his mind as he sat hunched over the little dining table, watching PT's troubled sleep. He was used to dealing with complex situations, used to people getting hurt and killed in his line of work, but it was different with Marc.

Henderson had often heard the other kids teasing Marc, calling him *Henderson's pet*, but he'd never admitted this favouritism to himself until now. The fact was, he saw a younger version of himself in Marc and cared about him more than anyone except his newborn son. Henderson found this truth uncomfortable. If he favoured Marc, did that mean all the other kids resented him for it? Did it make him look weak? And had it caused him to make bad decisions?

Curfew ended at sunrise. At the first chink of light Henderson went down with a bucket of water. He wiped bloody finger marks from around the keyhole in the front door and was impressed that PT had managed to pick the lock while on the verge of passing out. He poured the water over the doorstep and used a stiff broom to wipe dots of dried blood from the doorstep.

'You're cleaning up,' a woman said frostily. 'To what do we owe this miracle?'

Henderson turned back down the hallway and saw the two elderly sisters who lived on the ground floor. They worked as cleaners in one of Madame Mercier's bars.

'Good morning, my dears,' Henderson said mockingly. 'Absolutely lovely to see you again.'

As the two women stepped out he considered warning them about what had happened the night before, but didn't feel the miserable old bats deserved it. Once they were out of sight, he strolled along to the back door of Mamba Noir and checked for any sign of a struggle. The exit had been unlocked by kitchen staff but he didn't bother going inside.

Back in the apartment, PT had sat himself up. He

looked white and his voice wavered, but at least he was conscious.

'Morning,' Henderson said, keeping deliberately upbeat. 'How's our wounded soldier?'

'Shaking like a leaf,' PT said.

'Hungry?'

'I'll try something,' PT answered warily. 'God knows if it'll stay down.'

Henderson usually relied on Mamba Noir leftovers for breakfast, but he made some coffee, found some stale bread and cut the last few pieces off a small joint of ham.

'You've lost a pint of blood, maybe two,' Henderson said as PT sat on the edge of Marc's bed, biting the end off a piece of ham. 'You could do with a transfusion, but I daren't take you near a hospital.'

'Is that serious?' PT asked.

'You're young and fit. You'll survive, provided we keep infection out of that wound. Your blood pressure will be very low, so you're going to feel weak for some time. Most likely sick and giddy if you move about too much.'

'I think I worked that much out for myself.'

'So how did the German die?' Henderson asked. 'I stayed awake all night with my gun on the table. I'm surprised we haven't had house-to-house searches.'

'It wasn't me that killed him,' PT said, shaking his head. 'This madman started on me with a bread knife for no reason. They shot him in the leg after he cut the German's throat. So they're probably not looking for a killer.'

Henderson knew PT's reputation for con tricks and doubted that someone had simply stabbed him for no reason. But he didn't push the point, this wasn't the time for an interrogation.

'Was the killer shot dead?' Henderson asked.

'He was knocked out for sure. I didn't stick around to see if he was dead.'

'If he isn't and they question him he'll be begging for his life,' Henderson said. 'He could blame you for starting the fight. The Germans have rounded a lot of people up, including Marc by the looks of it. It's possible they'll be looking for someone with a stab wound fitting your description.'

PT felt guilty. 'How did Marc get picked up?'

'Behind the club, looking for Joel's message. Do you think you can make it downstairs?'

'Probably,' PT said. 'But I won't be walking far.'

Henderson nodded. 'I've got to go to the stable and tell Edith that Marc's not around to do his delivery route. I'll try and get a cart to take you out to stay in the country with Paul, Boo and Rosie.'

'I don't even know where they're living,' PT said.

'Even I don't know their exact location,' Henderson said. 'But I know it's somewhere well out of the way and

I know where Marc meets Paul to pass on messages every morning.'

*

Gestapo HQ had less than a dozen proper cells. With more than fifty people rounded up for interrogation most prisoners had spent the night in the dank wine cellar beneath the villa's kitchens. Marc nestled under an archway and kept his eyes half open.

There was clearly no method behind the Gestapo's round-up. Some people took being locked up in their stride, while others shook with terror. One of the drunks set a barmaid off in hysterics when he said they were all waiting for a firing squad. Two women who hadn't seen each other in years caught up, talking husbands, kids, jobs and scandals.

There was daylight coming through the barred slots up by the ceiling when Madame Mercier came into the room with smeared make-up, torn dress and a large bloody welt down her right arm. She was probably the best-known and definitely the most controversial woman in Lorient. Many admired her skill as a businesswoman and the comparative decency with which she treated her staff. Others reviled her as a corrupt brothel keeper and a German collaborator.

People seemed frightened of her as she limped into the room, but all Marc saw was an old lady who'd taken a beating. He gave her an arm and led her back to his spot under the arch.

'What are you all gawping at?' Madame Mercier shouted. 'I'm not a bloody circus.'

When she settled on the stone floor, Marc caught a whiff of urine off her dress. He was disgusted, partly by the smell but also by the idea that Oberst Bauer had frightened her so much that she'd pissed herself.

'You OK?' Marc asked, as he stroked the back of her trembling hand.

She spoke extremely quietly because sound carried easily around the stone cellar. 'There's nothing you or your father need to worry about. It's politics.'

Marc didn't reply, but Madame Mercier felt the need to talk.

'I have good relations with the army and the navy,' she explained. 'Oberst Bauer doesn't like the influence I have over certain people, and wants me to know that he can drag me back to his little torture chamber any time I do something that displeases him.'

Madame Mercier's dealings were largely a mystery to Marc, so all he could do was squeeze her hand tighter and whisper, 'You'll be all right.'

'I overheard Bauer saying that *someone* blew up nine trains,' she said, as she gave Marc's hand a small but triumphant squeeze.

Marc was elated, but his smile didn't last long.

'The Gestapo rounded up dozens of suspected

communists after the invasion of Russia,' she continued. 'They're going to shoot one communist prisoner for each engine that was damaged.'

*

After helping PT to use the chamberpot, Henderson left the house and cut through Mamba Noir. The cleaning staff had been in for an hour already, but some of the restaurant tables still bore half-eaten meals abandoned the previous night.

Going through the revolving door on to the main drag was an even bigger shock. After the soldier was killed, groups of off-duty Germans had gone on a brief but highly destructive rampage, avenging the death of their colleague by kicking in doors, throwing café tables through windows and beating up anyone unfortunate enough to be in their way.

Across the street a four-strong German patrol had a young man pinned against the wall. Henderson wondered what questions they were asking, but the man was getting slapped about so it wasn't a good idea to stick around.

A big cart pulled by two horses was coming out of the narrow stable entrance as Henderson approached. He found Edith in an empty stall, shovelling manure into a wheelbarrow.

'Did you get back into town OK?' Henderson asked.

'Lucky I was indoors before any trouble started,'

Edith said. 'Have you heard anything?'

Once Henderson had explained the situation with Marc and PT, Edith gave her news.

'The driver who just went out to the brewery said the Krauts have already started putting notices up. There's gonna be a nine p.m. curfew. All clubs, bars and restaurants for French people in the centre of town are shut until further notice.'

Henderson sucked air between his teeth. 'Madame Mercier will have a few things to say to her German friends about that.'

'Gestapo have got her,' Edith said.

Henderson gulped. Marc being in custody was unfortunate, but Madame Mercier as well could mean that the Gestapo had suspicions about their operations.

'How do you know?' he asked.

'I stayed in my room above Café Mercier last night. The girls were all talking about it. The owners of the big clubs and bars were rounded up.'

Henderson sounded relieved. 'So not just Madame Mercier?'

'No,' Edith said. 'What about the trains? I *think* I heard the explosion.'

'Something went bang for sure,' Henderson said. 'But I've got no idea how effective it was.'

'I could go up there later and take a peek,' Edith said.

Henderson shook his head. 'Too risky. What matters

right now is finding a way of getting PT out of town. Can I borrow a cart?'

'Of course,' Edith said. 'But it's probably better if I drive him. I'll have to do Marc's delivery route if he's not around. The dairy is outside of town, so I can see if there's extra security when I pick the milk up. Then I can go back a bit later with PT.'

'That sounds ideal.'

'No problem,' Edith said, before breaking into a grin. 'Of course if I'm out for most of the day, I'll need someone here to muck out and feed the horses.'

Henderson clearly didn't fancy doing this himself. 'They'll need me at Mamba Noir if Madame Mercier isn't around. I'll speak to the cleaners. I'm sure one of them will be happy to do it for a few extra francs.'

CHAPTER TWENTY-SIX

The food collection route took an hour longer than usual because the Germans had put up snap checkpoints all over town. But if the Gestapo had it in for Madame Mercier, the message hadn't been passed down to regular soldiers yet: Edith drove the cartload of black market foods past every checkpoint unscathed, apart from the usual petty thefts of fruit and a senior officer helping himself to a nice bottle of wine.

When she got back to Mamba Noir, Henderson came out of the rear entrance followed by a pair of kitchen porters who began unloading the cart.

'I met Paul by the trough and explained what's going on,' Edith told Henderson in a whisper, as the porters took a milk churn off the cart behind her. 'He's going to wait for me at the dairy and take me to their place. Says it's a half-hour ride each way. There's also a doctor in their village who they think they can trust.'

'Where would I be without you, Edith?' Henderson asked. 'Do you want to go inside for a spot of lunch while I help PT get down the stairs? The irony is, you've brought all this food and we're not even sure if we'll be allowed to open.'

Edith thought about Mamba Noir's eccentric status. Every other bar and club in town was either for French people and had been ordered to close, or for Germans and was allowed to stay open. Mamba Noir was uniquely open to both.

'I'd bet they'll let you open but just allow Germans in.'

'You could be right,' Henderson said. 'But I'm the bar manager and I'm not making waves. We're staying shut until I get clear instructions from the Krauts.'

'Have you heard anything about Marc?'

'A friend of Madame Mercier's has been up to Gestapo headquarters,' Henderson said. 'They didn't let her in, but they've pinned a list of prisoners on the gate. Marc's name was there, so at least I'm certain where he is.'

As Edith headed inside to grab a quick lunch, Henderson jogged down the street and upstairs to his apartment. PT had some of his colour back, but still looked weak as he lay on Marc's bed.

'How's it going, champ?'

'Hurts like hell,' PT said. 'I get really woozy if I try going more than a few paces.'

'That's the blood loss. Is it still oozing?'

'A bit,' PT said, as Henderson walked into his bedroom. 'At least the stitches you put in are holding up OK.'

Henderson re-emerged with a shirt, two vests and a necktie. He folded one vest into a square pad and told PT to knot it over his wound using the tie. He then gave him the other vest to pull over the top, before helping with the buttons.

'That should be enough layers to stop the blood soaking to the outside,' Henderson said. 'We've got a few minutes while Edith eats her lunch. Put your arms around my neck. I'll try a piggyback.'

Henderson crouched down. He wasn't a huge man, but he was strong and carried PT without straining.

'Duck,' Henderson said, as he went through the doorway and on to the landing.

PT's gut tore painfully on every step, but he took the pain and tilted his head sideways so that he didn't scrape the ceiling as they went down. Four steps from the bottom there was a knock at the door.

'Coming,' Henderson shouted, thinking it was Edith and taking his time.

But the blur through the frosted panes in the front door was too big for Edith. A Germanic shout sent

Henderson into a panic. He dumped PT against the wall of the downstairs hallway and ran for the door.

'Mr Hortefeux?' the German shouted, as he pounded again.

Henderson opened up to a bulky, black-uniformed Gestapo officer.

'Good afternoon,' Henderson said, uncomfortably aware that he'd have a lot of explaining to do if the officer wanted to come inside and found PT propped against the wall.

'I am Oberst Bauer,' the German said importantly. 'I've been informed that you have the keys to Madame Mercier's safe?'

'I do,' Henderson said. 'But I don't have access to her office, I'm afraid.'

'Not a problem,' Bauer said. 'Come at once.'

Bauer led Henderson on the short walk to Mamba Noir and upstairs to Madame Mercier's first-floor office. The office door had been broken down with a fire axe. Two junior Gestapo officers stood inside turning out desk drawers and throwing about the contents of her filing cabinet. There was no method to their search, it was all about intimidation.

'If there's something you're looking for, I'm sure . . .'

Bauer shook his head as he snatched the safe key. He looked disappointed as the door swung open revealing several thousand francs and four cash register drawers filled with loose change.

'Step into the corridor with me,' Bauer said to Henderson in a friendly tone. 'The name *Hortefeux*. I questioned a boy with that name last night.'

'My son,' Henderson said. 'Unfortunately he was picked up when he came back here to fetch something. He's a good boy. Can I assume he'll be released soon?'

Bauer shrugged.

'I see *very* many signs of black market activity in this club,' Bauer said. 'Madame Mercier must have many connections to get away with these flagrant breaches of regulations, don't you agree?'

'I work behind the bar, sir,' Henderson said. 'I don't involve myself in Madame Mercier's business, and I don't think I'd be working here for much longer if I did.'

'But a man in your position must see and hear interesting things,' Bauer said, as a filing cabinet was toppled inside the office. 'People who've had too much to drink and say things they don't mean to? These things could be of interest to the Gestapo.'

'Discretion comes with the job in a place like this,' Henderson said. 'And you're always on the move. It's not like you get to stand still for half an hour listening to a conversation.'

'How do you feel about us Germans occupying your country?' Bauer asked.

This was a tricky question. If Henderson fawned,

Bauer might feel that he was saying what he wanted to hear, but saying he wanted the Germans booted out would hardly go down well either.

'Well . . .' Henderson began, before a pause to think. 'I'm a patriotic Frenchman, but I don't see things ever going back the way they were. We've got to move forwards and learn to get along.'

Bauer laughed. 'That's a very diplomatic answer, Mr Hortefeux. I take it you'd like to see your son released soon?'

'Naturally,' Henderson said, deeply uneasy as he sensed that Marc had become a pawn.

'If I see to it that your son is looked after, can I have your assurance that I'll be the first to hear of anything untoward involving Madame Mercier, or anything else you might hear that is of interest to the Gestapo?'

Henderson pretended to be shocked. 'Sir, my son hasn't done anything wrong except be in the wrong place at the wrong time.'

'Oh, I wouldn't be sure,' Bauer said teasingly. 'I believe he may have been involved in trafficking black market foodstuffs around town and offering items to German soldiers to get through checkpoints. I wonder how well your son would withstand a lengthy and *uncomfortable* interrogation.'

'I see what you're getting at,' Henderson nodded, fighting to keep nerves out of his voice as he fished for information. 'I'm sure we can come to some arrangement. Is there anything in particular that you'd like me to look out for?'

'You seem like a smart man, Mr Hortefeux,' Bauer said, as he smiled conceitedly. 'I'm sure you can work out what I'm likely to find interesting.'

With that, Bauer leaned into Madame Mercier's ravaged office and shouted to his two goons in German. 'Come on, let's go to the old bag's house. We can strangle her cat and break a few ornaments.'

*

When Edith saw the Gestapo officer leading Henderson upstairs she put down her lunch, ran up the street to Henderson's house and shouted through the letterbox.

'Are you PT?'

PT couldn't bend forwards because of his stomach wound, so he shuffled along the wall and opened the front door.

'You must be Edith. What's going on with Henderson?'

'They're upstairs searching, so they'll be a few minutes. If I bring the cart along, can you climb up on your own?'

'I'll manage,' PT said.

So Edith brought the cart up, and gave PT as much support as her skinny frame allowed as he stepped on to the cart. After closing Henderson's front door she looked behind for any sign of Gestapo before setting off.

First stop was the stables, where she swapped strong-but-stubborn Dot for a younger horse and made sure that her stand-in was feeding the animals properly.

There were back streets with fewer checkpoints, but Germans tended to treat you with extreme suspicion if they did stop you there, so Edith took the main road through the shopping district. They faced a twenty-minute wait at a snap checkpoint, during which PT clutched the side of the cart and looked ominously like he was going to pass out. Edith jumped down and fetched a mug of cold water from a friendly greengrocer.

'OT,' the German at the checkpoint said, when he saw PT's zone pass. 'Shouldn't you be working?'

PT faked a cough and gave an answer straight out of spy school. 'They sent me into town for a chest X-ray.'

PT's sickly pallor helped convince the guard that he might have a case of highly contagious tuberculosis. The guard flung back the documents and waved them on without even asking Edith for her ID card.

'Nice move,' Edith said when they were a few hundred metres past the checkpoint, 'I'll have to remember that one. How are you feeling?'

'Mind's a blur,' PT said. 'Keep talking to me. It really helps.'

'Hopefully the checkpoint out of town won't be as slow as that one. Once we're through, maybe you can lie down in the back.'

The cart now turned into the courtyard outside Lorient station.

'Oh *Jesus*,' Edith said, as she looked into the middle of the square.

A dilapidated Citroën truck had been parked by the station's main entrance. A wooden frame was mounted on the cargo platform and two bodies dangled from it. Each man had been choked to death using piano wire, which was fine enough to cut deep into their necks.

Their shirts were blood-soaked and they had painted signs hung around their necks. The first man was a giant, with *MURDERER* written on his board. He wasn't a pretty sight, but PT drew a certain amount of pleasure from seeing the man who'd tried to kill him.

The other man was smaller and wore a dark-blue overall. His board read *INCOMPETENT* and Edith felt a lump in her throat as she recognised him as the guard from the train depot.

PT was pretty out of it, but he reacted instinctively to the tear that streaked down Edith's face.

'Hey, what's the matter?' he asked.

'You feel so proud to be part of something,' Edith said, wiping her grubby face with her even grubbier hand. 'And then . . .'

Her thought hung in the air as the cart trundled out of the square.

*

The Gestapo's wine cellar cleared out as the day wore on. The drunks were the first to get kicked out, then all of the women apart from Madame Mercier and another lady who owned a restaurant. Marc's name was called in a list of all the remaining men, again except for those who owned bars, clubs and restaurants. Most of the owners had rips in their well-made clothes and minor injuries, similar to Madame Mercier's.

'You'll be OK,' Marc told her, as he headed for the door. 'I expect I'll see you at work this evening.'

'You're a sweetheart,' Madame Mercier said. 'I'll see you get a few extra francs in your wages this week.'

'I didn't do it for that,' Marc said.

He wound up at the back of a long queue in the courtyard, as men were given back their documents, rings and watches. An argument over a missing cane held things up but there was only one man in front when a stocky young officer tapped Marc on the arm.

'Hortefeux?' he asked. 'Back to the cellar.'

Marc assumed it was a mistake and his tone was sarcastic. 'Do I look like I own a nightclub to you, boss?'

The officer's hand swung across, making a sharp crack as it hit Marc's face. His chunky ring left a small cut as the boy stumbled backwards.

'Insolent dog,' the officer shouted, as he grabbed Marc by the back of his neck. Marc eyed up a backwards kick in the balls, but doubted he'd come off best if he started a fight in the Gestapo's back yard.

The officer sitting at the desk seemed surprised and stood up to ask what was going on.

'What's with the boy?'

'Oberst Bauer telephoned. Thinks he might be useful for some reason.'

CHAPTER TWENTY-SEVEN

Paul met the cart when it reached the dairy outside of town. Edith helped PT swing his legs around and slide into the back of the cart where he could lie down. It was a bumpy ride, but his heart had an easier time when it didn't have to pump his limited blood supply up to his head.

Edith rarely ventured this far out of Lorient and there was a strange feeling of isolation as the horse trotted along dirt roads, past overgrown fields and empty farmhouses. Paul had only met Edith a couple of times, but saw that she was troubled and tried to console her.

'Before he died, my dad said that the only thing worse than fighting the Germans is not fighting the Germans,' Paul said.

Edith nodded. She understood the reality of war, but

it didn't make thinking about the railway guard any easier. She didn't know him, but she'd imagined a wife, kids, a house. How were they all feeling with their dearly beloved attracting bluebottles in the centre of town?

'I'd like to live up in a mountain or something,' Edith said, as she looked up at the sky. 'Hours away from everyone else. I get so sick of *everything*.'

'I know what you mean,' Paul said. 'The war's like a trap with no way out.'

The last stretch of the journey was a steep hill dotted with the odd sheep. The height meant Boo and Rosie could get a good radio signal, along with a view of anyone approaching from the road below. Their home was a single-storey cottage, which had started small then sprouted two badly matched extensions and stable block converted into a garage.

Boo and Rosie helped PT down off the cart and laid him out in the living room. Edith and Paul fetched a bucket of water and pulled up a few handfuls of long grass for the horse. Rosie found herself alone with PT and he reached out to touch her skirt.

'I'm really sorry about the other day,' PT said.

He looked pale and weak, but Rosie felt no warmth towards him as she undid his shirt buttons and the necktie holding the makeshift dressing in place. She unfurled the vest and held it up to the light.

'You're not bleeding much, but it's better to get some

air to the wound. You're sweating, would you like a flannel to wipe down with?'

PT lifted his head, 'Rosie,' he began softly. 'I'm—'

She cut him dead. 'PT, it's not a nice time to have to say this, but I can't leave it hanging. What you did the other day and the way you spoke to me afterwards were unacceptable.'

'I'm *really* sorry,' PT said. 'I acted stupid. I should have shown you more respect.'

'Apology accepted,' Rosie said. 'But it's over between us. I'll look after you while you're sick, I'll work with you on the missions but I don't feel I can trust you.'

PT made a long sigh. 'How can you be so cold? There's something special between us. You can't flick it off like a switch and pretend it's not there.'

Rosie ignored PT's pleas and turned abruptly towards the kitchen. 'I'll get you the cold flannel.'

*

Two hours after Marc heard his name called, the roles were reversed. It was Madame Mercier's time to leave, along with the rest of the restaurant and club owners.

'Don't get upset,' she told Marc. 'I have connections. There's no good reason for them to hold you here.'

Marc had spent long enough in the cellar to think a few chilling thoughts, but on balance he still suspected his being held back was part of some administrative cock-up. After giving Madame Mercier an arm up, he burrowed into his trouser pocket and pulled out a scrunched-up page from a Mamba Noir waiter's pad. 'Give that to my dad as soon as you see him,' Marc whispered. 'Joel has some documents he needs to collect.'

Madame Mercier nodded as she pushed the paper inside her blouse. When the door of the cellar slammed, Marc found himself alone with only spots of dry blood and two overflowing buckets of urine to remind him of the former occupants.

With the cellar silent, he overheard Madame Mercier and the other owners getting lectured in the courtyard.

'All places that sell alcohol to French people will remain closed for one week. The curfew will remain at nine p.m. in the centre of town. It is the responsibility of bar and club owners to ensure that French workmen do not become violent or excessively drunk. If there are any more attacks on Germans by people under the influence, the owner of the bar where the attacker was drinking and the people who served them the alcohol will be held responsible. However, staff and owners who provide information that is useful to the Gestapo will be looked upon favourably.'

Marc understood what this meant: none of the owners could guarantee how their customers would behave. Every waitress and bar worker in Lorient would have to start snitching for the Gestapo or risk getting locked up the next time one of their customers got into trouble.

'We are all working towards peace and civility in the Lorient zone,' the Gestapo officer concluded. 'We shall be visiting your premises regularly to collect reports on all signs of suspicious or anti-German activity.'

*

It was nearly six p.m. by the time Edith had the cart back in the stable, made sure all the horses had enough food and water and walked across to Mamba Noir. They'd been allowed to open up for German customers only, but dinner service didn't begin until seven and there wasn't a single customer in the upstairs bar. She found Henderson and Madame Mercier clearing up the mess the Gestapo had left in the office.

'Your delicate package was safely delivered,' Edith told Henderson. 'Did Marc get out?'

Henderson looked crestfallen at the mention of his name. 'I phoned Gestapo HQ to ask if I could bring him some things or visit him, but they told me to stay away. Oberst Bauer was here earlier. He more or less threatened to have Marc locked up for black market trading if I didn't provide him with information.'

Edith looked alarmed. 'Do you think they know something about the trains?'

'I did wonder, when Madame Mercier and Marc both ended up in custody,' Henderson said. 'But it seems they're using the murder as an excuse for a general clampdown. Marc and I took jobs at Mamba Noir because it's where we have the best chance of hearing what important people have to say. Now the Gestapo are targeting me for exactly the same reason.'

'They ransacked my house and killed Persil,' Madame Mercier said.

It took Edith half a second to remember that Persil was Madame Mercier's slightly scary black cat.

'I haven't been home,' Madame Mercier continued, breaking into sobs. 'My neighbour said he'll find her and bury her in the garden, but I can't face going back there.'

Edith felt awkward as she stood in the office doorway. She'd didn't go in to comfort Madame Mercier because even in her current state she'd probably still throw a fit if Edith put her manure-crusted boots on the antique rug. Instead, Henderson sent her to the bar to get a glass of red wine.

When Edith got back, Madame Mercier had settled into her office chair. Henderson passed over the glass of wine and a bundle of papers to take her mind off things.

'I think I've got them back in order, but if you'll just check through.'

As Henderson turned away, he saw Edith making a discreet *come here* gesture. He followed her out to the empty bar, where she spoke in a whisper.

'I spoke with my friend who works at the laundry. She said that Germans are expected to do their own laundry in the barracks, or pay to have it done individually.'

Henderson looked baffled. 'Why am I talking to you about laundry?'

'The itching powder,' Edith said. 'You saw Marc last night, scratching like crazy after he rubbed two little grains on to his skin.'

'He should have gone through me before asking you to make contact with outsiders.'

Edith looked hurt and didn't mention that Marc had deliberately gone behind Henderson's back because he'd been so dismissive about the itching powder.

'I've known Natasha for *ever*,' Edith said. 'She was one of Madame Mercier's girls until she had a bad abortion.'

'Just because you know someone doesn't necessarily mean you can trust them,' Henderson said.

'Natasha hates the Boche,' Edith said. 'Her husband's a prisoner in Austria somewhere and her little boy got knocked down and killed by a drunken Kriegsmarine officer in his Mercedes. Ask Madame Mercier if you don't believe we can trust her. And I'm not stupid you know: I may only be twelve, but I understand how important security is. I talked everything through with Marc before doing anything.'

Henderson was impressed with Edith's clear thinking, even if he didn't agree with everything she said. 'So what did this Natasha say?'

'It actually looks quite easy to do. Apparently, when a

U-boat comes into port they send a big load of sheets, towels, foul-weather gear and stuff like that to the laundry. After the main wash, they have to add this special green de-lousing powder that the Kriegsmarine gives them. All Natasha has to do is go into the store room and mix our itching powder in with the German powder.'

'How many people have access to the store room? Could the sabotage easily be traced back to Natasha?'

Edith looked uncertain. 'I don't know, but I'm sure we can work something out.'

'I've got a lot on my mind right now,' Henderson said. 'But I suppose the powder did bring Marc out in one heck of a rash. Give me until tomorrow to think about it, OK?'

*

A Gestapo guard made Marc carry the overflowing urine buckets out of the cellar, and it was impossible not to get splashes over his boots and the bottom of his trousers. After that he got pushed into a tiny windowless cell on the first floor. He'd had nothing to eat or drink since the night before so he eagerly drank a mouthful of the watery broth they brought an hour later, only to find that it had been heavily seasoned with pepper and so much salt that it burned his lips.

Afternoon turned to evening as he sat in the unlit cell, desperate for water, listening to boots in the corridor outside. He started feeling nervous, imagining that they'd forgotten about him. After several hours he felt like he was going to pass out and banged on the door.

'*Please* get me a drink,' he begged, when a woman opened a flap in his door.

'Look up above your head,' the woman said.

For a moment Marc thought he'd missed some kind of tap. But all he saw was a pair of metal clasps.

'If you bang on that door again I'll have them come by and hook you up there by your wrists,' the woman said, before slamming the flap.

It was seven at night before the door finally opened. A guard took him to the same room where he'd been with Madame Mercier the night before. Oberst Bauer sat at the desk, with a clear jug of water in front of him. There were chunks of ice and an orange hue where the surface caught the sunlight. It was the most beautiful thing Marc had ever seen.

'Sorry to keep you waiting,' Bauer said, as he fiddled with his slim black tie. 'I've only just come back on duty. But boy, isn't it *hot* today? I've been drinking buckets!'

Bauer slid a piece of paper across the desk.

'Can you read?'

The statement was typewritten on a single sheet of paper. There was only one paragraph:

I, Marc Hortefeux, confess to trafficking black market produce in the Lorient Secure Zone on behalf of Brigitte Mercier, the owner of Mamba Noir and other establishments in the area.

Signed ....

Date ....

'Sign and you shall be released,' Bauer said, before chinking the glass jug with the end of his fountain pen. 'And, of course, you can drink all you like.'

'What will happen to Madame Mercier?' Marc asked.

Bauer raised one eyebrow. 'You need to be a good deal more concerned about what will happen to you. Do you know what my favourite part of an interrogation is?'

'What?' Marc asked sourly.

'It's when someone is so badly broken that you have to do *nothing*,' Bauer said. 'People become so scared of you that they go down on their knees and beg. They see my face and soil themselves in pure terror. Try to imagine that, Marc. Try to imagine being so scared of me, that I just have to walk into a room to utterly humiliate you.'

Marc was scared, but tried to think straight. The weird thing was, the Gestapo had absolute power. They didn't hold trials, there were no appeals. If they wanted to arrest Madame Mercier, torture her, shoot her, the only thing stopping them was her connections with powerful men in other branches of the German military. A slip of paper signed by a thirteen-year-old boy didn't change any of that.

'Why do you need me to sign anything?' Marc asked. 'What difference does my word make?'

Bauer shot up from the desk. 'Do not question me,' he shouted. 'The only reason you ever need for a question I ask is, *because I said so.*'

He effortlessly shoved Marc back against the wall, kneed him in the stomach then swung him around. After bending Marc over, Bauer squeezed his head against the desktop with one hand, pulled a thick bracelet out of his suit pocket and slid it over Marc's wrist.

When Bauer released a metal pin from the top of the bracelet, jagged metal jaws clamped Marc's wrist with bone-crushing force. His fingers tensed and the excruciating pain went up to his shoulder.

'Get it off,' Marc screamed. 'Please.'

'If I leave it on until morning you'll lose your hand,' Bauer explained. 'It's a wonderful device. Made hundreds of years ago. Quite rare, but still effective, don't you think?'

'Oh god,' Marc wailed, as Bauer backed away. 'Get it off me. Please, I'll sign it. I'll sign anything you want.'

Now that Bauer had let go, Marc was free to move. He tried pulling off the clamp, but moving it just made the jaws sink deeper into his wrist.

'Take it off,' Marc bawled. 'Please take it off.'

Bauer smiled as he pulled a clockwork key out off his jacket pocket. 'One word of defiance when I take it off and I'll put it back on for an hour.'

'Anything,' Marc sobbed. 'Please.'

Bauer inserted the large key into the bracelet. It took several turns to pull back the powerful spring that clamped the jaws.

'Sign it,' Bauer shouted.

Blood poured down Marc's hand as he grabbed the fountain pen and scratched his name on the confession.

'Nice job,' Bauer said, as he swept the confession away before Marc dripped blood on it. 'Take a drink if you'd like one.'

Marc tipped up the jug, smearing blood all over the glass as he guzzled half a litre of water in six massive gulps. He felt ashamed that he'd given in so quickly, but he tried to rationalise it. His confession did little real harm to Madame Mercier and he'd bought himself a ticket home.

'Theiss, get in here now,' Bauer shouted, as he leaned out into the hallway.

A slim and rather nervous Gestapo officer raced into the room and saluted before Bauer addressed him in German, unaware that Marc understood every word.

'Get the boy a bandage, we don't want him dripping on our nice polished floors. Clear up the mess. Take special care with my pen and put oil on the bracelet. When you're done, take the boy downstairs and process his paperwork. I want him on the first train to Rennes in the morning.'

'Yes, Herr Oberst,' Theiss nodded.

Rennes was the regional capital more than a hundred kilometres away. Marc's head whirled, but he couldn't say anything without giving away the fact that he spoke German.

'It's important that none of the locals see where he is going,' Bauer told his colleague. 'Madame Mercier seems to be fond of the boy, and I think his father might also be a useful source of information. So it's good to keep him under our thumb, but we're chronically short of cells here.'

Thiess took Marc's signed confession, along with a couple of printed forms. He noticed that one box hadn't been filled in.

'You haven't put the length of his sentence, Herr Oberst.'

'Six months,' Bauer said, but changed his mind, turning back as he headed out of the room. 'Actually, scrub that, Theiss. Make it a year to be on the safe side.'

Part Four

Twelve days later

Part Four

CHAPTER TWENTY-EIGHT

Friday 4 July 1941

Lieutenant Commander Finch was taking *Madeline II* on her fifth round trip between Porth Navas and the Brittany coast near Lorient. Luck had held for the first four runs, but the fifth seemed cursed.

The right engine blew while they were still in British waters, and the corvette sent to escort them on the voyage south had been called away to pick up survivors from a downed merchant ship. Sailing unescorted, they'd been spotted by Swordfish biplanes from a Royal Navy aircraft-carrier and watched its torpedo miss the bow by less than five metres.

This sense that everything that could go wrong would go wrong came to a peak when a storm brewed up an hour before they were due to liaise with *Istanbul*. It was mid-afternoon, but the sky was the colour of slate. The rain was almost vertical as the narrow craft bucked on two-and-a-half-metre waves.

Radar could detect only the large boats in stormy weather and they found *Istanbul* more by luck than skill. In calm seas the two ships could come alongside, in moderate weather they could use ropes and pulleys to swap passengers and cargo, but in a storm there was no way to bring the boats together.

Visibility was less than two hundred metres, which at least meant the two boats could stay in touch without the risk of being spotted from the coast four kilometres away. Three hours passed before Alois flashed a message across saying that he thought it was calm enough to swap cargoes using ropes and pulleys.

The first rope was fired from *Madeline II* to *Istanbul* using a compressed-air gun. Further ropes and pulley wheels were fed across until a block and tackle system linked the two craft.

Luc threw his suitcase on deck before coming up through *Madeline II*'s rear hatch, dressed only in boots and underpants. The burly thirteen-year-old clutched the deck rail to stay upright as men in waterproofs transferred the first load of cargo.

The ropes between the boats couldn't be tight, because if a wave pulled the boats apart it could snap and do serious damage. Luc stood beside a young female agent in a swimming costume as the wooden chest hanging precariously between the two boats was hit full force by a wave.

'My god!' she blurted in heavily accented English. 'How can I do this?'

'No point losing your nerve,' Luc said. 'It's got to be done, that's all there is to it.'

'I want to be out of here in five minutes,' Finch shouted from the bridge. 'Get this show moving.'

The race was on because while German boats identical to *Madeline II* regularly came alongside to do inspections in calm weather, transferring cargo in this way in daylight was highly suspicious.

As the second chest zipped across on the pulley, a sailor grabbed Luc by the arm.

'You wanna go first and show the young lady how it's done?'

Luc was scared, though he wasn't the kind who'd let it show. As one sailor pushed Luc's suitcase into a rubberised pouch, another helped him into a bulky harness-cum-life jacket and buckled its leather straps tightly across his chest.

The pulley rope between the two boats had loops every two or three metres. The pouch containing Luc's suitcase was hooked over one loop, then a short chain was run between the harness and the next loop.

A wave caught *Madeline II*, slamming Luc backwards

into one of the spare fuel cylinders. The weight of the harness knocked him down, but a sailor hauled him up before knotting an extra safety rope to the harness and pointing at a steel collar near the top of the chain.

'Can you remember how to work the quick release if you get into trouble?'

'Yank it down and turn to free the bolt,' Luc said, shouting over a gust of wind.

'Exactly,' the sailor said.

He gave Luc a thumbs-up, then guided him to the edge of the deck. Luc hesitated for a second before swinging his legs over the deck rail.

'Heave-ho,' a deckhand shouted.

As three sailors tugged the rope, Luc flew off the side of the boat and dangled from his harness with his knees in the water. The next pull plunged him into the icy wash as he inhaled. Salty ocean water stung his eyes and shot up his nostrils. His body jerked as the rope dragged him rapidly through churning sea towards *Istanbul*.

When the rotten hull was in sight, Michel and Olivier reached into the water with long deck poles and used the hooked ends to grab Luc's harness. One knee slammed the hull painfully, and he came aboard, shuddering and hacking water out of his lungs.

As Luc coughed, Michel unfastened the buckles on his harness. Within seconds, it was off and being buckled on to PT who was going the other way.

Luc stopped coughing long enough to acknowledge his former training partner. 'Feeling healthy now?'

'Pretty much,' PT said, as Michel buckled the lifejacket. 'But my goose is cooked, cos I missed two weeks' work. If I show my face around Lorient the OT will stick me on the first train to a labour camp in Germany.'

By this time the chain was attached. Olivier flashed a lantern three times, the men on *Madeline II* pulled the rope and PT zipped forwards and plunged into the sea.

It was chaos on *Istanbul*'s rear deck as the four wooden crates were lowered into the fish hold. There was a net of fish rolling about the swaying deck, an RAF pilot and a British agent who'd been working in Brest nervously awaiting their transfer by rope, while Nicolas did all he could with *Istanbul*'s manual rudder to keep close to *Madeline II* on the choppy sea.

Luc was extremely strong for his age. When he saw Troy struggling with the cargo he jumped down into the stinking hold and helped him lower the equipment chests.

'This is a lot more equipment than we've had before,' Troy said. 'Henderson's gonna be chuffed.'

Luc looked up at Troy with a grin. 'I bet he'll be chuffed to see me, too.'

By the time the fourth chest was in the hold, the female agent and a French army officer who worked for the London-based Free French Government had joined Luc on the deck of *Istanbul*. As soon as the agent was aboard *Madeline II*, a sailor flashed three times with a lantern then waved his arms to signify that the operation was complete.

Michel unhooked the pulley ropes and threw them back into the sea.

'Mainsail going up,' Alois shouted. 'Olivier, get on the rudder.'

Luc found himself crammed in the fish hold in his pants; his only consolation was having the pretty French girl squeezed up alongside. His world turned dark as Troy fitted the shelf into the hold above their heads and began tipping fish out of the net into the space above so that they wouldn't be detected by a German inspection when they returned to port.

Istanbul tilted violently to starboard as a storm force gust caught the mainsail, while *Madeline II*'s two surviving diesels sent her blasting away towards a liaison with an escort destroyer and what would hopefully be a less eventful return to Porth Navas.

*

Rennes prison was built for four hundred, but now housed two thousand inmates. Marc's cell was on the top floor. The long hall had once been a machine shop where prisoners sewed French army uniforms, but now it was jammed with more than eighty men. Fitting bars was a skilled job, so the windows had simply been bricked up. Air and light only came in through small ventilation holes drilled in the brickwork.

There were a dozen bunks, most of which were used in shifts by the stronger men. Marc only had a spot on the floor up against the wall, and not even enough space to fully unravel his flea-infested sleeping mat. The only sense of time passing came from the condensation running down the brickwork and the clumps of mushrooms growing up by the ceiling joists.

He'd arrived ten days earlier. His boots and knife had been taken away and the pockets cut out of his shirt and trousers to prevent him hiding things. A food trough was wheeled in morning and evening: black bread, vegetable scraps, fish heads or stringy meat all in a greasy soup. You had to scoop it out into your enamel mug. Most men had a spoon, but they'd run out on the day Marc arrived.

There were fights, usually the alpha males in the bunks picking on a new arrival. Marc had his spot by the wall furthest from the beds and kept himself out of trouble. He'd had the odd conversation with the men packed around him, but in such cramped conditions the space in your head was the only space you had and everyone seemed reluctant to share what was in there.

For the first few days Marc expected some miraculous release every time the cell door opened. When the initial burst of hope wore off, he concentrated on looking after himself by stretching, washing his body and clothes as well as he could and trying to stay away from the men with the horrible coughs, and the mental cases in the middle of the cell who lay in their own filth, too sick or deranged to care.

Bad food, damp and overcrowding were good company for disease and Marc lasted only three days before coming down with stomach cramps and diarrhoea. He still had a job keeping the awful food down and got feverish sometimes, but it was nothing like at first when he'd barely been able to walk to the filthy drain hole that passed for a toilet.

Gil was the closest thing Marc had to a friend. He was fifteen, sentenced to five years for stealing a tray of meat while working as cook at a German barracks. Like everyone who'd been in for a few months, he had shaggy lice-infested hair. Gil had the corner space next to Marc and they looked after each other's cups and bed roll at mealtimes, or if they went to the toilet.

Marc had been thirsty for some time, but Gil had fallen asleep with his head resting against his shoulder, and rather than wake his neighbour he waited until he stirred. Getting to the tap at the opposite end of the cell required finesse, stepping over bodies, and placing feet carefully to avoid the most visible examples of human filth.

As Marc turned on the tap a thickset Spaniard named

Carlos squatted over the drain hole less than two metres away. Marc tried not to think about this as he rinsed a few dregs of soup out of his cup, then filled it with the tepid water and drank it down quickly.

The men who lived nearest the tap didn't like you leaving it on for too long because of the sound of water trickling down into the drain. Marc quickly splashed water over his face, hands and chest, before filling a second cup to take back with him and shutting the water off.

There was no toilet paper, so Carlos wiped with his bare hand and swaggered towards the tap to wash the shit off. He was olive-skinned, mid-twenties, with straight dark hair and the kind of physique that came from heavy work, like mining or construction.

'I've had my eye on you, pretty boy,' Carlos said, crouching down to mouth the words in Marc's ear as he turned on the tap.

Marc backed off instinctively and stepped on an ankle.

'Watch out, you oaf!'

'Sorry,' Marc said, as some of the water in his cup splashed the floor.

'I could look after you,' the Spaniard said.

He blocked Marc's path, before reaching around and groping his bum.

'Hands off, you dirty bastard,' Marc shouted, backing up to the wall and trying to wrench off the fingers clamped to his buttock. A few bodies shifted around to watch the action.

'Now that's not polite,' Carlos said. 'I might have to learn you some manners.'

He was much heavier than Marc and every inch the confident bully as he pressed the boy against the wall beside the tap. Carlos moved his hand down and slid two fingers between Marc's legs, touching his balls.

A couple of the Spaniard's friends were laughing. 'Carlos has himself a new girlfriend.'

Carlos turned back towards them. 'I'm a generous man, we can all share.'

The glance away provided Marc's opening. He dropped his mug and threw his arm up, jamming his thumb into Carlos' eye socket. The Spaniard stumbled backwards, swinging a wild punch. Marc ducked under it, then exploded up with his fists leading, hitting Carlos in the solar plexus and stomach. With his opponent doubled over, Marc brought his knee up, smashing Carlos' nose and leaving him on the edge of consciousness. Marc grabbed his opponent's shirt collar and shoved him head first into the metal tap.

Carlos slid down the wall and rolled on to his back, gasping for air and bleeding from a deep gash above his eye. Marc knew he'd never be able to get more than five metres from the big Spaniard in this cell. If he was to have any peace, there could be no possibility of revenge.

Marc glanced behind to make sure none of Carlos's cronies were closing in before kneeling on the Spaniard's chest, using his bodyweight to stop him breathing. As Carlos tried to throw Marc off, the boy dug his thumbnail into a small ridge in the button on the waistband of his trousers. A slight twist dislodged the button's brass cap and as the metal pinged against the wall, the deadly white L-pill dropped into Marc's palm. He crushed it between thumb and forefinger to release the cyanide then took his weight off Carlos' chest.

With Marc off his chest, Carlos opened wide to draw a great breath. Marc dropped the pill on the Spaniard's tongue, then clamped his hand across his mouth to stop him spitting it out. Marc groaned in agony as Carlos' teeth sank into his fingers, but within seconds the L-tablet had paralysed Carlos' lungs.

Marc's hand dripped with blood as he rolled off his opponent. Carlos clutched his chest and caught Marc hard with his boot. Until now the Spaniard's bunkmates hadn't reacted because they thought Carlos could easily handle Marc, but now one of them yelled and men rolled over and pulled in their legs to clear a path.

Carlos' legs spasmed, but he hadn't drawn breath in over a minute and these movements were just random pulses sent out by a dying brain. Charged with adrenaline and dripping blood, Marc pulled himself to his feet as Carlos' mates arrived.

'What have you done to him?' one of them roared.

Marc wasn't confident about taking on two grown men, but he acted cocky because bravado was all he had.

'Back off,' Marc shouted. 'I've done nothing to you. Nor will I if you keep your hands off.'

The two men looked at each other. Everyone had been looking, but nobody had seen the tiny L-pill through the gloom and they had no idea what Marc had done.

'Carlos is married to my sister, you piece of shit. He's got a wife and five kids.'

'He must have had a weak heart or something,' Marc said. 'Besides, I didn't start it.'

'You ain't gonna finish it either,' the bloke said, as the other man crouched down and looked at Carlos.

'He's not breathing.'

The heavy cell door slid open. It led in from an open balcony and after so much time in the dark the July sunlight felt like needles spearing Marc's eyes. Two French prison guards entered, with rags tied over their faces to mask the stench. The prisoners grabbed their bedding and huddled towards the far end of the cell, but an old man caught a swinging club in the face for being too slow.

As the two guards charged in, a German soldier stood in the open doorway with his machine gun ready to deal with any trouble. Carlos' brother-in-law had vanished back into the mass of bodies, but Marc and the guy who'd been crouching down were cut off by the guards.

As Marc grew used to the light, a guard shoved him hard against the wall. He opened his eyes a little, seeing the streaks of blood running from the bite wound in his hand.

'Where's your weapon?' the guard shouted, punching Marc hard in the back before turning to the crowd. 'No food comes into this cell until it's in my hand.'

'There's no weapon,' Marc said.

'Sod the investigation,' the other guard shouted to his colleague. 'I'm gonna puke if I stand in here any longer. If they wanna kill each other, let 'em.'

The guard gave Marc an almighty shove towards the door, then ordered Carlos' friend to drag his body out of the cell. Marc looked up at the gun-toting German, expecting a boot or a shove, but saw surprising kindness in his teenaged face. Even though he was scared, Marc enjoyed his first breath of outdoor air in over a week.

The French guard jabbed Marc between the shoulder blades with the end of his baton. 'Start walking, you dumb turd. You'd better have a good story for the commandant if you don't want a bullet through the back of your head.'

CHAPTER TWENTY-NINE

After hosing off in the warehouse, Troy gave the two newly arrived adult agents their travel documents. Henderson had ordered them to stop using the artist's house for a while, in case neighbours got suspicious, so the agents would spend the night lying low in the dockside café, while the newly arrived explosives and equipment were taken to an unlet shop a few doors from Alois' workshop.

Luc spent his first night undercover in Nicolas' house. After a fish supper, he went upstairs, sat on the end of Joel's bed and produced a screw-top aluminium can, with the label of an upmarket brand of French coffee beans.

Joel inspected the tin and nodded with approval. The label was faded and the tin itself battered and scratched, exactly like the old coffee tins they used to store things in the workshop at Keroman. He felt extremely tense as he unscrewed the lid.

He'd taken a risk, photographing the inside of the U-boat batteries with Henderson's miniature camera. There hadn't been time to send pictures back to Britain aboard *Madeline II* so Henderson had developed them using supplies scrounged from a local newspaper reporter, then the girls – Boo and Rosie – had transmitted as many details as they could back to Britain.

Joel delved into the can and took out one of the metal washers, then reached under his bed for an example of the original.

Luc leaned forward anxiously. 'Is it good?'

'Well I can't tell the difference,' Joel said, as he held it up to the flickering bulb on the ceiling. 'I still don't understand how these washers can make so much difference. And it's so secret, they wouldn't tell us over the radio even though everything we send is in code.'

Luc had never been undercover before, so he was eager to impress, instead of being his usual arrogant self.

'I went down to London to pick the tin up and met the professor who designed them,' Luc explained. 'He calls it a platinum pill. The normal washers are made from hardened steel. The ones in that can are made from an alloy of steel and platinum. When the platinum touches the acid inside the battery it reacts, producing a toxic chemical which stops the battery from producing energy.

'Apparently, the biggest problem was getting the platinum to release slowly enough. If you just made the washer from solid platinum it would kill the battery before the U-boat left port. But he's found a way to get the platinum to react very slowly so that the U-boat's battery doesn't die until it's been used for about a hundred hours, by which time it'll hopefully be stuck in the middle of the Atlantic.'

Joel finished the story, 'So the boat has no battery to move underwater. The Royal Navy closes in, drops a few depth charges, blows the Krauts to smithereens and everyone celebrates with tea and crumpets.'

'Sounds right,' Luc said, smiling. 'So do you think you'll have problems getting the washers inside the batteries?'

'Nah,' Joel said. 'Every time a battery comes in for servicing you have to unscrew the electrodes and clean all the furry muck off. You switch the regular washer for one of these when you put it back together. There must be a hundred washers in the tin and there's six battery units in each boat. That makes enough for sixteen or seventeen boats.'

Luc nodded. 'That's what the professor said. He reckons it's easy enough to make another batch if they work well.'

'I'm just glad we've found a way to sabotage the boats,'

Joel said. 'Otherwise I'd have spent the last two months wasting my time. So what's it been like on campus lately?'

Luc shrugged. 'Henderson's wife's as nutty as ever. McAfferty's looking after the baby more than she is and they're trying to find a nanny. Khinde and Takada have started training the group C recruits.'

'And what are people saying about the war?'

Luc put his hands over his head. 'It's *too* depressing,' he said. 'They've had more big bombing raids all over the country. More boats than ever are going down in the Atlantic and they reckon the Germans are advancing east into Russia by up to thirty kilometres a day.'

Joel nodded. 'Sounds about the same as what we've been hearing from Radio France. They reckon the Germans could be in Moscow by November. If that happens we'll be up the creek without a paddle.'

Luc pulled off one of his boots and lay down on what had been PT's bed until he got stabbed. 'Well I don't care what the odds are,' he said, as he interlocked his fingers behind his head. 'The Germans killed the only person in the world I ever cared about, so I'd get blown to bits sooner than surrender to any of those Nazi shitbags.'

*

Rennes prison had rows of tiny solitary cells in the basement that made the converted workshop on the second floor seem like paradise. Fortunately for Marc they were full up and he found himself sitting cross-legged with both wrists manacled to the outer wall of the prison's administrative building.

Fresh air and sunlight were welcome, but the view over a small courtyard to the opposite wall pitted with bullet holes where men had faced firing squads was depressing. Marc envied the birds circling overhead as he wondered if all he had left was a short walk across the dried-out grass and a bullet through the chest. But was death really so bad compared to a year crammed in the cell upstairs, getting weaker and sicker by the day?

'Left or right?' a German asked, as he placed a metal can on the floor. It was the same guard who'd stood in the cell doorway. Chubby and no older than nineteen, he'd grown several centimetres in all directions since he'd been fitted for his uniform.

After freeing Marc's right hand, the German gave him the freshly opened tin of fruit.

The chubby soldier struggled with his French. 'From a Red Cross parcel.'

Marc looked down at the brightly coloured chunks of fruit. He was too nervous to feel hungry, but he forced them down because he wanted the German to see that he was grateful. And with his life balanced so precariously, it hardly seemed to matter if he spoke in German.

Marc knew that civilians didn't get Red Cross parcels. 'So you have prisoners of war here?'

The soldier smiled at hearing Marc speak his own language. 'About eighty,' he replied. 'They get treated better than the civilians. You looked hungry.'

'So they're definitely gonna shoot me?' Marc asked, as he tipped up the can and drained the syrup in the bottom.

The soldier didn't know how to answer this and looked down at the ground. 'You'll have to give me your hand now you're finished.'

Marc let the German lock his wrist back inside the manacle.

'What's so great about being alive anyway?' Marc said, half smiling.

'Commandant's gone home for the day,' the guard replied. 'So they won't be shooting you at dawn tomorrow and nobody gets shot on a Sunday, so you've got until Monday at least.'

*

Henderson prided himself on his mental strength. He focused on his job at Mamba Noir and his burgeoning espionage network, and felt ashamed when he caught himself in a private moment worrying about Marc. He worked harder and pretended to be happier, but angst gnawed at his insides.

Saturday was a few minutes old. Mamba Noir heaved with Germans and their female guests, with the jazz trio in full swing. With her wealthy French customers banned, Madame Mercier's business brain had gone into overdrive to keep Mamba Noir profitable.

She'd put German dishes on the restaurant menu, lowered the price and quality of the cocktails and shipped in a dozen beautiful girls to keep lonely German officers company until their wallets ran dry.

'Where's that blasted cigarette boy?' a German captain asked, as Henderson stepped behind the bar carrying a tray of dirty glasses.

He took a moment to recognise him, because one eye was half closed and his neck was swollen.

'Captain Hartt,' Henderson said warmly. 'Good to see you. Hopefully we'll have a new boy in tomorrow night, sir. Have you come up from the restaurant? You're a whisky man, aren't you? We've actually got hold of some American bourbon if you'd like to try.'

'American?' the German said curiously. 'What harm can it do?'

Henderson grabbed a shot glass. 'This one is on the house. See what you think.'

Hartt knocked it back and sloshed it around his mouth a few times before slamming his glass down. 'Smooth, different to Scotch but I can't taste much wrong with it.'

'It's not bad, is it? Would you like another?'

'Absolutely,' Hartt said. 'I have enough sorrows to drown the crew of a battleship.'

As a barman, you never pried into people's business unless they gave you an opening. 'Nothing too serious I hope, sir.'

Hartt lifted his chin and pulled down his shirt collar, revealing blotchy red skin. Henderson was tired and a little drunk, and it was only now that he recognised the distinctive rash that Marc had on his stomach after testing the itching powder.

'The men started getting it almost as soon as we were out of port,' Hartt explained. 'Thought it was odd, but we kept sailing. By the following morning, half the crew was coming up with red welts and peeling skin. Couple of fellows started getting breathing problems. I had no choice but to turn around.'

Henderson was delighted, but couldn't show it. 'Any idea what caused it?'

'The lord alone knows,' Hartt said. 'Some kind of infection, or a parasite I suppose. Probably some dirty bugger on my crew picked it up from a French whore. When you've got forty-eight men crammed together like that, disease spreads like wildfire. And it's not just us. U-53 was headed down to the Mediterranean. She had to pull in for emergency medical assistance at Vigo.'

'Christ,' Henderson said. 'So when can you sail?'

'Days, weeks, who knows?' Hartt said, giving a shrug. 'Until we work out the cause of this we're crippled.'

CHAPTER THIRTY

Marc couldn't get comfortable with his wrists chained to the wall, but somehow managed fitful sleep under the stars, with the shouts of caged men coming from cells along three sides of the courtyard. At first light a metal door crashed open. A three-man firing squad and two cuffed and hooded prisoners clanked up a basement staircase.

There was no great drama as the first man knelt down facing a wall, barely twenty metres from where Marc sat. The instructions were shouted in German: *take aim, fire.* His body crumpled, but they didn't bother moving him.

The second man gave more of a fight, jabbering in Russian and begging for someone called Anna. He got himself clubbed a couple of times and had to be manacled to the wall, but he died just the same. The

Germans disappeared and a few minutes passed before two prisoners came along with a handcart and took the bodies away.

As ways of dying went, the firing squad didn't seem so bad. Marc decided he'd go like the first man: strong and silent, don't give the Krauts any satisfaction. Though when he thought about Henderson and McAfferty and his mates, he wasn't so sure. He wanted to hear them all talking and eating, the sound of footsteps on the stairs at campus and waking up in his own bed, all snug on a frosty morning.

He imagined the prison wall blowing up and Henderson charging through, though it seemed unlikely. They'd used every stick of plastic blowing the trains and Henderson probably didn't even know where he was.

Prisoners and guards walked past as the sun came up and he got a tin cup filled with water and chunks of bread so hard that he had to soak them to bite through. It was past nine when an elderly French prison guard took his manacles off.

'Where am I going?' Marc asked.

'Where I tell you,' the guard said grumpily, before leading Marc down to a basement room with a puddled floor.

Marc was ordered to strip, abandoning his clothes to a huge metal basket. The guard threw de-lousing powder at him before following up with two buckets of cold water over the head. There was nothing to dry off with and he got dressed in a freshly laundered singlet and baggy cotton trousers with a length of rope for a belt. Once his trousers were fixed, his hands got cuffed behind his back.

The clothes were ragged, but it was Marc's first proper wash or change of clothes in two weeks and he felt wonderfully fresh as he was marched barefoot across the prison yard, past the spot where he'd spent the night. He ended up in a corridor, behind a queue of a dozen similarly dressed men waiting to see the commandant. A sign hanging from the ceiling read *Absolute Silence*.

At the head of the corridor were the double doors to the commandant's office. The first prisoner out was frogmarched into a side room by two guards. The door closed and the prisoner screamed as he was brutally flogged.

'They pickle the whip in brine,' one of the men in front whispered. 'So it burns like hell itself when it cuts you. Then they sterilise by rubbing salt into your wound.'

Some men were escorted out of the commandant's office unscathed, but most would return to their cells with blood and sea salt on their backs. The pain made every victim scream, so Marc was quaking when the double doors opened in front of him.

'Face forward,' a fierce-looking prison officer named Verne shouted from the back of the room. 'State your name and number for the commandant. Any smart-mouthing and I'll flog you till you pass out.'

The prison commandant – who much to Marc's surprise was also a Frenchman – sat behind an antique desk. To Marc's partial relief, the chubby German soldier who'd given him canned fruit the evening before stood alongside him.

'Name and number, what are you waiting for?' Verne repeated, giving Marc a shove towards the desk. 'And stand straight when you address the commandant.'

'Marc Hortefeux,' Marc said, as he stood bolt upright. '6060452.'

The commandant looked down through half-rimmed glasses as he picked up a set of papers which Marc had last seen at the Gestapo HQ in Lorient.

'Verne, what's the charge against this young man?' the commandant asked, in a surprisingly soft voice.

'Murder of inmate 6059738.'

The commandant looked at Marc, raising one eyebrow suspiciously. 'What do you have to say for yourself?'

Marc took a deep breath, knowing that the commandant only had to squiggle a signature to sentence him to death.

'It was self-defence, sir. It was dark. He was very much larger than me.'

The commandant looked up at Verne, 'Any idea what sort of age and build 6059738 was?'

Verne nodded. 'Big Spanish fellow, sir. Nasty piece of

work, raped and murdered a fifteen-year-old girl.'

'But the boy came off best in this altercation?' the commandant said, frowning at the apparent unlikeliness of this. 'How old are you, Hortefeux?'

'Thirteen,' Marc said.

'Are you sure it wasn't another man in your cell that killed him?' the commandant asked. 'It's no good covering up for someone in this situation, is it?'

Marc shook his head. 'I don't know how it happened, sir. I've always been strong for my age. I must have caught him with a lucky punch in the dark and then I think his heart gave out.'

'I could put him over the bench and flog the truth out of him,' Verne suggested.

The commandant shook his head as he looked at Marc's file. 'Black market trading, one-year sentence,' he said irritably. 'How does a boy caught smuggling a few bits of illegal food end up in a place like this?'

The commandant's obvious frustration hung in the air for a few moments, until he spoke again.

'I'll ask you one final time, Hortefeux. Did another man in your cell kill the Spaniard and force you to take the blame?'

Marc thought about lying, but knew that the next question would be about the identity of this alleged killer, and as the commandant seemed sympathetic, honesty seemed the best policy.

'It was me, sir,' Marc said.

'Shall I flog him, sir?' Verne asked eagerly.

The commandant stood up from his desk. 'We are *not* going to flog him, Monsieur Verne. He's a thirteen-year-old boy, for Christ's sake. He shouldn't even be in here.'

Now the young German spoke for the first time. 'Commandant, the Spaniard has a brother-in-law inside the prison and several good friends. If you put Hortefeux back in the cells after this incident, it's very likely he'll end up dead.'

'Tell me something I don't know,' the commandant said with a sigh. 'So my options are to flog the boy, have him put before a firing squad, or send him back to an overcrowded cell where he'll most likely wind up dead within a week.'

The young German leaned across the desk and spoke quietly, as if he was taking the commandant into his confidence. 'Can I suggest we use him to help fill the quota?'

'He's too young,' the commandant said.

The German looked at Marc. 'Do you have any experience of agricultural work?'

'A bit,' Marc said warily.

'He's obviously a tough little lad,' the German said. 'Change his year of birth from twenty-eight to twenty-six on his papers and he'll be old enough for agricultural work. It's no picnic, but even if he doesn't get murdered in a cell, how long before he picks up TB, or a group of men tries to take advantage of him? We'd at least be giving him a fighting chance.'

The commandant nodded reluctantly before looking up at Marc. 'How would you feel about agricultural work, Hortefeux?'

Marc hated everything about farms, but compared to the filthy cell and the threat of getting murdered, manure and hard graft seemed attractive.

'If you think that's best, sir,' he said, trying to hide a smile.

The commandant took Marc's Gestapo paperwork, tore out several sheets and threw them in his waste basket.

'Monsieur Verne,' the commandant said, 'it appears that the paperwork for 6060452 is incomplete. See to it that he gets new documents, with a suitable date of birth. Then enter him against our quota for the agricultural labour programme.'

'Yes, sir,' Verne said, sounding as if he'd much rather have given Marc a flogging. 'I'll get one of the girls to type it up immediately. I believe that Organisation Todt's next train leaves for Frankfurt on Tuesday. I'd suggest leaving Hortefeux manacled in the courtyard for his own safety until then.'

'Frankfurt,' Marc said, as his jaw dropped. 'That's in Germany, isn't it?'

The commandant nodded. 'It was the last time I looked. Is that a problem for you?'

Marc had to make a split-second decision. But with no realistic prospect of escape or rescue and the strong possibility of being murdered back in the cell, there was really no decision to make.

*

Henderson was up on a set of steps dusting the rarely used bottles high above the bar when he heard German army boots on the stairs.

'The bar doesn't open until twelve,' Henderson shouted, hoping to save the German the bother of coming all the way up.

'This isn't a social call,' Oberst Bauer said, as he came around the top of the stairs and sat on a bar stool.

'How's my son?' Henderson asked, struggling to contain his anger.

'He's doing fine,' Bauer said. 'I went by his cell when he was eating breakfast this morning. He seemed rather bored, but that's to be expected.'

Henderson reached behind the bar and pulled out a paper bag. 'I thought you might come by today,' he said. 'There's a clean shirt and underwear for Marc. Plus some chocolate, a peach and apple pie from the restaurant and a couple of books to read.'

'It's most irregular for Gestapo prisoners to receive these things,' Bauer said.

Henderson took one of the bottles of American bourbon up from behind the bar. 'Perhaps . . .' he began.

'I don't drink,' Bauer said. 'I'm not here for idle chat and if I want any of Madame Mercier's black market goods I'm perfectly entitled to seize them. I'm here because I want to know if you've heard anything that might be of interest to me.'

Henderson shook his head. 'I'm trying but it's difficult, Herr Oberst. Our French clients are still not allowed in the bar and the German guests speak in German, which I can't understand.'

'I'm more interested in Madame Mercier,' Bauer said. 'Any information you have on her black market dealings could be valuable in securing the release of your son.'

'I understand,' Henderson said. 'I'd very much like to visit Marc. Other Gestapo prisoners are allowed visitors, I believe.'

Bauer rose up from his stool and thumped on the bar. 'Mr Hortefeux,' he shouted. 'You do not make demands of me. So far your son has been well treated at Gestapo headquarters, but you've given me *nothing* of value. Things could become a good deal less pleasant for Marc if I do not start receiving more cooperation from you.'

'I understand, Herr Oberst,' Henderson said, raising his hands meekly. 'I'll try my best.'

'For your son's sake I hope your best is good enough,' Bauer said. 'Good afternoon, Mr Hortefeux.'

As Bauer walked down the stairs, Luc – who'd arrived in town a couple of hours earlier – came out of a storage room behind the bar. The plan was for him to replace Marc as Mamba Noir's cigarette boy and he'd been trying to find a waistcoat that buttoned over his broad chest without hanging halfway down to his knees.

'Have you got any evidence that Marc is even still alive?' Luc asked bluntly.

Henderson didn't like this line of reasoning, especially coming from Luc who he found irritating. But it was a perfectly valid point.

'I've had no evidence that Marc is still alive,' Henderson replied. 'On the other hand, they've had no particular reason to kill him.'

'Have you tried getting someone inside Gestapo headquarters?' Luc asked. 'Maybe a cleaner or something, who could verify that he's still alive?'

'We've looked into some options but the Gestapo runs a tight ship,' Henderson said. 'As far as we can tell they don't employ any local staff, but I'm keeping my ear to the ground all the same.'

CHAPTER THIRTY-ONE

Dot hadn't been out of her stable for several days because of an excruciating foot abscess. A vet had drilled a small hole in her infected hoof to enable the pus to drain off, but it was Edith's job to keep the wound clean.

She stroked the old horse's side to settle her down before squatting on a three-legged milking stool. Getting Dot to raise her front left hoof was easy, because she wasn't keeping any of her weight on it.

'Good girl,' Edith said, before splashing a piece of rag with vinegar and using it to clean off a mixture of manure and dried pus. She then used an awl to unblock the drainage hole.

Younger horses got cranky or put up a fight when they were sick, but Dot was never a problem and Edith rewarded her with a carrot.

'You're on the mend, old girl,' Edith said. 'We'll have you galloping in no time.'

This was a joke, because Dot was a carthorse and hadn't galloped anywhere in years. Truth told, if it wasn't for the shortage of horses caused by the Germans commandeering all the trucks, Madame Mercier probably would have sent Dot to the butcher rather than pay a vet's bill when she got sick.

As Edith stepped out of the stable a hand clamped her mouth shut. She sank her teeth into a young man's little finger as he picked her off the ground and threw her against the wall.

'Bitch,' the youth shouted, as he pulled his bleeding finger out of Edith's mouth.

She turned around and got a look at her attacker. He had a scarf tied over his mouth and a wide-brimmed hat putting his face in shadow. His arms were well muscled, but his voice and skin seemed young. No more than sixteen, she guessed.

'We've got nothing here worth stealing,' Edith said urgently. 'There's some fruit we give to the horses, but it's mostly rotten.'

'I'm not a thief, I need information,' the young man said nervously.

'What would I know about anything?' Edith asked.

'The powder you delivered to the laundry,' the man said. 'Who did you get it from?'

'Powder? What powder? I don't know what you're talking about.'

The man took Edith's slender hand and gently squeezed her knuckles. 'I don't want to hurt you,' he said. 'But whoever gave you that powder has links to something important. If you give me a name I'll let you go.'

'You're off your rocker,' Edith said. 'I have no idea what this powder you're talking about is.'

The man swung Edith around and bent her over the side of a cart.

'I don't want to hurt a little girl,' he said. 'But I know there's a guerrilla movement in town. The powder you brought to the laundry and the train yard getting blown up. You can see I'm no German. I just need to get in touch with these people.'

'Get stuffed,' Edith said, as she stamped on the youth's foot and broke free. But he was much bigger than Edith and she was cornered. The youth grabbed Edith's blouse, thumped her back against the wall and throttled her.

'Please don't make me hurt you,' he said.

Edith gasped and coughed as the pressure came off her throat. 'You'll have to kill me,' she spat. 'But I'm waiting for two carts to come back soon and the drivers will make mincemeat out of you. So I wouldn't stick around.'

The youth looked round, unsure what to do. A girl walked down the sloping path from the main stable gate. She was fifteen or so. She'd covered her head with a knitted shawl, but her gait and the shape of her body were enough for Edith to recognise her from the laundry.

'You're *completely* useless,' the laundress told the youth, as she bent down and picked up the pointed metal awl that Edith had used on Dot's hoof.

Dot was extremely trusting and her head swung around over the stable doors, expecting a treat from the stranger.

'Edith, listen to me,' the girl said ferociously, as she stroked Dot's cheek. 'If you don't tell me who you got the powder from, I'll jam this point in the horse's eye.'

Edith had known Dot all her life and if the girl blinded her, she'd be put down for sure.

'It's Madame Mercier's horse,' Edith said fiercely. 'She'll hunt you down.'

'Do you think I'm scared of that old bag?' the girl said. 'I'll give you three seconds to save the horse's eye. Three, two . . .'

'OK,' Edith said desperately, as the girl held the point of the awl centimetres from Dot's cloudy brown eye. 'I can't tell you the man's name, but I can probably help you find him.'

'I don't believe you,' the girl said.

'It's true,' Edith said. 'That's how they work. It means

nobody can give too much away if they're caught.'

'So where can we find this man?' the girl asked.

'I don't know where he works,' Edith lied. 'But I'm pretty sure where he lives. If I meet you back here at about eight o'clock I'll take you.'

'OK,' the youth said.

But the girl wasn't having it. 'Do you think I'm an idiot?' she hissed. 'How will we know you're not setting us up? You'll stay with us until the meeting, and if turns out you're trying to trick us it won't be a horse that loses an eye.'

*

With Marc gone, Henderson now passed the radio messages to Paul. On most days, Henderson dropped a coded message into a mailbox behind a tobacconist's shop and Paul would collect it a couple of hours later. But once a week he'd meet Boo at a café near the edge of town.

'We've moved again now that PT's gone,' Boo said, as she sat in the afternoon sun sipping her coffee. 'The other place seemed perfect, but that old girl kept sticking her nose in and she was half off her rocker. You never knew what she'd say to whom.'

'Do you think she had any clue what you were up to?' Henderson asked.

'No,' Boo said. 'I won't tell you where we've moved to.'

Henderson nodded. 'Absolutely not. We've got

drop boxes, fall-backs and the safe house if there's a real emergency.'

'According to this morning's signal, *Madeline II*'s making good progress. PT should be back at Porth Navas tomorrow.'

'The latest load of equipment was well above expectations,' Henderson said. 'According to Luc, the biggest problem they're having at Kerneval is finding where to hide everything. We've got explosives, mines, silenced pistols, plus money and plenty of chocolate and cigarettes to keep our friends happy.'

'Will Luc stay with you like Marc did?'

'No,' Henderson said. 'It might seem odd if I took another boy in, especially with Bauer keeping an eye on me. Madame Mercier has found him his own room a couple of doors from my place. Once Luc knows his way around I'll arrange for him to collect Joel's messages and drop them for Paul. The less direct contact I have with people at the moment, the better.'

'I could use some money,' Boo said.

'No problem,' Henderson said, as he drained his coffee and threw a few francs into his saucer. 'I'll give the OK to Joel. Rosie can collect a couple of thousand francs from the café at Kerneval tomorrow.'

'And I suppose I'd better get home,' Boo said. 'Always good catching up.'

They exchanged a friendly kiss before walking off in

opposite directions. If either Boo or Henderson was being tailed by the Germans, the meeting provided an opportunity for them to begin following the other party, so Henderson took unnecessary turns and doubled back a couple of times to ensure that he wasn't being followed.

It was on the last of these diversions that Henderson spotted a black Mercedes convertible parked illegally on the pavement in a narrow alleyway. Oberst Bauer was taking a break, sitting in the front passenger seat, drinking milk, with a half-eaten peach and some Mamba Noir apple pie sitting on the glove box flap in front of him.

Henderson didn't turn back because it would seem suspicious. He kept walking, passing less than two metres from Bauer, who remained cheerfully engrossed in the pie he'd been given for Marc. If Henderson had a gun he would have happily shot Bauer, but instead he quickened his pace and walked home, ashamed to find himself close to tears.

Before heading to his own rooms to get changed ready for his Saturday night shift, Henderson stopped by Luc's place. The house was similar to the one where Henderson was staying, but the loft had been converted into living space and Luc had a cramped but well-furnished room under the eaves.

'Looks like you've landed on your feet,' Henderson said.

Luc eyed Henderson suspiciously. 'Have you been crying?'

'Spot of hay fever,' Henderson lied. 'Paul, Rosie and Boo all said to welcome you to France. Do you think you'll be OK on the job tonight?'

'I hang the tray round my neck and sell cigarettes,' Luc said. 'How hard can it be?'

'It's Saturday,' Henderson said. 'So expect to work hard and *always* be polite, even when some Nazi arsehole thinks it's a big lark to strike his match off your trouser leg.'

'Gotcha,' Luc said. 'I'll start getting changed and I'll meet you over there?'

'Sounds about right,' Henderson said. 'But I've got another job for you. I'm more certain than ever that Bauer is lying to me about Marc. The only way we'll know for sure is to take the bull by the horns.'

'Getting something on Bauer?' Luc asked.

Henderson nodded. 'I need to know everything about him. In particular, where he lives and what he does when he's off duty. Do you think you can manage that?'

'I'll figure something out,' Luc said.

CHAPTER THIRTY-TWO

Henderson heard footsteps coming up behind as he turned the key in his front door. By the time he'd looked back, a burly lad with a scarf tied over his face had bundled him into the hallway. As Henderson slipped on polished floorboards and stumbled towards the staircase, the lad was followed inside by Edith and the pair who'd abducted her two hours earlier.

'Mouth shut,' the big lad ordered. 'We're just here to talk.'

One of the women who lived on the ground floor stuck her head out of her doorway. 'What's all this racket?'

'Mind your business,' the big lad shouted, before shutting the door in her face.

Henderson had ended up spread-eagled over the

bottom of the stairs. He used the distraction to deliver a two-footed kick. As the bulky teenager doubled over clutching his guts, Henderson sprang up and gave him a two-handed punch to the back of the head, which left the lad sprawled out, unmasked and flat on his face.

As Henderson stepped around his body, ready to deal with the other pair, the girl pulled an ancient flintlock pistol out of a bag and pointed it at Henderson's chest.

'I'll kill you,' she shouted.

The girl was all nerves and, with their leader flat out on the floor, she had no clear idea what to do. It was the kind of situation where triggers get pulled for no good reason.

'Easy,' Henderson said, as he backed up to the stairs with his hands raised. 'You be careful with that gun. I'm moving away, so why don't you point it up at the ceiling? Then there won't be any accidents.'

Down on the floorboards, the big fellow rolled over clutching his side. He was older than the other two, but still spawned teenage acne.

'Help him up,' the girl ordered.

The lad shook his head as he sat up. 'Let me get my breath first.'

'I'm sorry, Mr Hortefeux,' Edith shouted from down the hall. 'They threatened to blind the horses.'

'Shut *up*,' the younger boy said, shoving Edith against the front door.

'Edith, don't worry,' Henderson said, keeping a nervous eye on the gun still pointing at him from less than two metres. 'Done is done. Now tell me what you people want?'

'Up in your room,' the big lad said, leaning on the wall as he found his feet. 'We need to talk.'

Henderson led the way upstairs, with the girl holding the gun to his back and the others behind.

'Edith,' Henderson said, 'knock on Madame LeBras's door and apologise for the disturbance. Tell her everything is OK now.'

'You're not in charge,' the girl said angrily.

Henderson stopped walking and looked back at her. 'Do you want the old ladies to run out into the street and shout for a gendarme?'

The girl looked back and nodded to the younger boy. 'Let her.'

Henderson stepped into his apartment, which soon felt cramped with five bodies inside.

'Sit on the bed,' the girl ordered.

The big lad peered into the bedroom to make sure nobody was in there, as the younger boy told Edith to sit at the table.

'So, here we are,' Henderson said. 'What's all this about?'

'You got hold of the powder that Edith brought to the laundry,' the big lad began. 'And my people

314

think your group was involved in the train explosions too.'

Henderson didn't know how much Edith had given away. If they saw that the first answer he gave was a lie, he'd have problems getting them to believe anything he said afterwards, so he sidestepped the question.

'And who are *your people*?' he asked.

The big lad smiled. He was good-looking in a wholesome sort of way, but the zits ruined it. 'I ask the questions, Mr Hortefeux.'

Again, Henderson avoided a direct answer. 'I work behind the bar at Mamba Noir. A gentleman approached me about the matter.'

Henderson left this hanging in the air. When the big lad didn't react violently to his fabrication, he elaborated.

'He asked me if I knew of anyone who worked in the laundries. I told him that I didn't, but I mentioned Edith because she takes the table linens from Mamba Noir to the laundry.'

'I told you,' Edith shouted. 'Nobody knows anyone else. That's how they keep secure.'

Henderson felt more confident as he sensed that Edith hadn't given much away.

'When do you see this man?' the big lad asked forcefully.

'Not any more,' Henderson said. 'Mamba Noir is no

longer open to French people.'

'Shit!' the girl shouted. 'He's just a barman. It's a dead end.'

'Shut your mouth and let me think,' the big lad told her, before turning back to Henderson. 'You must have known this man well to have trusted him. Is there no way you'd be able to get back in touch?'

'Why would you want to?' Henderson asked.

'Since the invasion of the Soviet Union it's the duty of every member of the proletariat to assist in her righteous struggle against Hitler.'

Henderson smiled a little. 'So you're communists. Do you have a particular target in mind?'

The big lad thought he'd caught Henderson out. 'Aren't you a humble barman?'

'I obviously have certain anti-German sympathies,' Henderson said. 'My job at Mamba Noir means I occasionally meet others who feel the same way.'

'So you can contact these people?'

'Not easily, but it's possible,' Henderson said. 'People in our situation must fight the occupiers, not each other. Kidnapping little girls, waving guns around and threatening to kill horses! What kind of people are you? Why is this aggression even necessary?'

'I didn't threaten to kill the horse,' the girl said angrily. 'Just stab its eye.'

Edith rose up from her seat angrily. 'Dot's an old

horse. If you blinded her, you'd as good as sentence her to death.'

'Everyone needs to stay calm and keep their voices *down*,' Henderson said firmly. 'Why don't we let Edith make us some coffee while we have a sensible discussion.'

'Agreed,' the big lad said, as he motioned for the girl to put the gun away.

'Do you people have names?' Henderson asked.

The lad shook his head, and sounded aggressive again. 'You don't need our names.'

'Fine, fine,' Henderson said, pleased that they were making some attempts at security even if it was half-arsed. 'What is it you want, more of the itching powder?'

'We want explosives,' the younger lad said.

Henderson looked shocked. 'That might be a lot harder.'

'He knows more than he's letting on,' the girl blurted angrily.

Henderson sensed that his façade of lies about a mysterious man he'd met while working in the bar was crumbling, but kept the strain out of his voice.

'Look,' he said. 'If you give me some details of what you want, I *may* be able to help. You say you want explosives, what for?'

The big lad gave the younger one a nod.

'Quarantine,' the younger lad began. 'The night before any U-boat sails, the crews have to report to a new crew bunker inside the base at Keroman.'

Henderson had learned about this system from Joel. It had been implemented because several U-boats had missed departures after vital crew members turned up late or went AWOL.

'One of our comrades knows the facility well.'

Henderson laughed. 'You'd need truckloads of explosive to blow up a reinforced bunker. They're designed to take a direct hit from RAF bombs.'

The big lad smiled. 'We're not talking about blowing up the bunker, just the men inside it. Our contact thinks we'll be able to sneak into the secure compound and drop explosives through the ventilation shafts.'

Henderson found this concept fascinating, but couldn't let on. 'I see,' he said coldly. 'You'd need to know when the U-boats were sailing to inflict a decent number of casualties.'

The big lad nodded. 'We'd pick a night when several boats were leaving port on one tide. Then you could kill the crew of several boats.'

'We got talking to a young sailor when he was drunk,' the younger lad said. 'Apparently the Germans have got a few new U-boats up in the Baltic Sea, but training crews takes months. So if we blow up a boat, they'll send another. But if we blow up men, training replacements will take months.'

'I understand, but have you considered the

consequences?' Henderson asked. 'If the crews of several U-boats were killed, you could expect revenge attacks on an unprecedented scale. The Krauts would execute hundreds – if not *thousands* – of people. Others would be rounded up and tortured. Women and children.'

The girl smiled. 'Conflict and violence are inevitable in a capitalistic society. Long-term harmony will only be achieved after the communist revolution has reached every country on earth.'

Henderson resisted the urge to laugh, knowing that it wouldn't go down well with the young communists.

'Well, thank you for the lesson in political theory, young lady,' he said. 'But the reality is, if you kill that many Germans there *will* be savage reprisals. The local population will be terrorised, you'll have no popular support, someone will snitch or break under interrogation and your people will end up being tortured to an agonising death in a Gestapo cell.'

'Suddenly you're an expert,' the girl said.

'Not really,' Henderson said. 'It's common sense. I'm all for fighting the Germans, but there's no point getting yourselves and a whole bunch of innocent people butchered, is there?'

'So we just sit back and let Hitler take over the world?' the girl asked.

'What would you suggest we do?' the big lad asked simultaneously.

'First of all, take a step back and don't rush into anything,' Henderson said. 'I'll put out some feelers. I can probably get back in touch with the people who supplied the powder. They're the real experts.'

'How long will that take?' the big lad asked.

'Hard to be certain,' Henderson said. 'A few days, maybe a week. I'll need a way of getting in touch with you.'

The girl shook her head. 'You don't need to know who we are. We'll contact you, and if you're lying to us, or messing us around, we *will* kill you.'

Henderson smiled as the younger lad opened the door. 'I'll consider myself suitably threatened.'

The girl led the trio of teenaged communists downstairs, just as the water boiled for the coffee.

'I'm so sorry,' Edith said, scared of how Henderson would react now they were alone. 'I know Dot is only a horse, but—'

Henderson didn't pay much attention because he'd rushed to the window to see which way the trio walked as they left the house. He turned back to Edith once they were out of sight.

'I'm really sorry,' she sniffled.

Henderson pulled Edith close and tried to ignore her distinctive aroma as he rubbed her back and spoke soothingly. 'Did you mention anyone's name apart from mine?'

Edith shook her head. 'I did like you said when you taught us security: just say it was one person that you hardly knew. I probably should have made a person up, but I was really frightened.'

'I'm not upset with you,' Henderson said soothingly. 'But this shows why we've always got to be so careful. Every time we bring someone into the network, there's a risk that other people will find out, and it only takes one bad egg for the Gestapo to sink their teeth into the whole lot of us.'

'I know the girl,' Edith said. 'Not her name, but she used to work at the laundry, so I can probably find out.'

'You do that as soon as you can,' Henderson said. 'Did they take you anywhere?'

Edith nodded. 'But they had me blindfolded. It wasn't far from here, two or three streets at most.'

'Probably even nearer than that,' Henderson said. 'Unless they're stupid enough to walk around town with a gun in a bag.'

'So if we find them, will you have them killed?' Edith asked.

'Not unless we have to,' Henderson said. 'Their idea of attacking the U-boat crews in the bunker is actually pretty sound, provided you could find a way to prevent revenge attacks. Joel actually mentioned that four U-boats are sailing on a joint operation at the end of next week.'

'So you actually think the communists might be useful to us?' Edith asked.

'Maybe,' Henderson said. 'But they can't run the show. Our first job is to track them down and show them who's boss.'

CHAPTER THIRTY-THREE

Joel started work at eight on Monday morning. With five U-boats in Keroman dock, the workshop floor was covered in giant batteries mounted on wheeled platforms. His lumbering colleague André had already started work, replacing one of the rubber shock absorbers designed to prevent batteries getting damaged in heavy seas. There was no sign of his boss, Canard, but that was no surprise.

'Coffee?' Joel shouted.

André raised his head and gave a thumbs-up. 'Cream and five sugars.'

Joel laughed. The only coffee they had was vile-tasting muck which was actually made from acorns, not coffee beans. There was no fresh milk and sugar was hard to get hold of, even on the black market.

'You wish, mate,' Joel said. 'Has Canard dragged his lazy arse in?'

'On a Monday?' André said. 'Be lucky to see him before nine.'

Joel picked up a clipboard with the order of work on it. After six weeks in the job he could drain, strip, clean and repair batteries as well as anyone. It was boring and the ten-hour shifts were a grind, but he never had to work particularly hard and he was happier working with his hands and earning money than he'd ever been sitting in a classroom learning something useless.

According to the clipboard, the batteries for U-17 and U-23 were being given top priority because both would sail within the next three days. Two other boats were part of the four-boat flotilla that would sail next week, while U-93 had suffered severe damage on its last voyage. She was being used as a floating spare parts bin and her crew had been sent to Germany to work up a new boat.

After taking André's coffee across, Joel opened his toolbox and dropped a handful of the platinum-infused washers into a compartment. He moved to his workbench and donned a pair of elbow-length rubber gloves before dipping his hands into a milky alkaline bath and lifting out a thin lead plate. This heavy lump was a battery electrode. It had soaked overnight to loosen the chemical deposits that built up when the battery was charged and discharged, seriously impeding its performance.

With a mask over his mouth and eyes slightly stinging from the fumes, Joel held the electrode over a metal tray and used a wooden scraper to peel off chalky deposits. After five minutes' scraping and brushing, he was sweating from the effort, but the plate was clean.

The empty cell casing was half a metre square and one metre long – designed to be lowered through a type VII U-boat's main hatch with millimetres to spare. The battery was well past its best. The outer casing had been dented and hammered flat, and the inside had chemical scars where seawater had leaked inside and reacted violently with battery acid.

The plate was the first of 120 that slotted into ridges in the cell casing. It would take Joel the whole of today's shift and most of tomorrow's to scrub and insert all the plates. When this job was complete the cell would be taken aboard the U-boat and its crew would flood the cell with sulphuric acid and seal it shut.

Joel took a nut, a bolt and one of the platinum pill washers. He'd got used to working in the thick gloves and handled the small pieces deftly as he leaned inside the battery and bolted the plate into position. If the boffins in London were right, the platinum in this single washer would react with the sulphuric acid and destroy the battery.

'Joel, André,' a German shouted fiercely. 'Get over here.'

The uniformed chief mechanic couldn't have timed his arrival more perfectly in terms of making Joel paranoid about getting caught.

'Quickly,' the German barked, as the two overalled workers stopped walking in front of him. 'Canard will not be joining you today.'

'Is he sick again?' André asked in his distinctive slurred voice.

'I've grown tired of his attitude,' the mechanic said, smiling. 'I've long suspected that he has communist sympathies. His home was searched, illegal materials discovered and we've found him a *delightful* new assignment at a labour camp in Poland. I'm trying to get more skilled mechanics brought back from Brest, but in the meantime you two must take up the slack.'

Joel was slightly flustered. 'Canard knew more than us. Me and André can do the basics, but if something goes awry, Canard's the man to sort it out.'

'A three-legged dog would be more bloody use around here than Canard,' the engineer said dismissively. 'Canard only knows what I and other German mechanics have taught him. If you need help, report the problem to me. I'm also bringing in new rules. From now on, you must get my approval before you take a break or leave at the end of your shift. If your work isn't on schedule, you will stay here until it is.'

With that, the chief mechanic turned sharply and headed for the door.

Joel was torn. On a human level Canard had made a good boss, but he only cared about getting through the day with as little effort as possible and his absence created an opportunity.

'Sir,' Joel shouted, making the engineer turn back. 'I have a mate who might be interested in working here. Even if he just learns to scrape electrodes and clean out the cells when they first come in it'll still be a big help.'

The German pushed his lips into a circle as if he was thinking about this. 'Yes, another boy would be good. Tell this friend to come and meet me for an interview.'

*

Luc didn't like Henderson and Henderson didn't like Luc, but they were both making a rather strained effort to get along as they walked up Lorient's main shopping street.

'You did well in the bar the last two nights,' Henderson told Luc.

'Thanks,' Luc said. 'That bloody cigarette tray kills your neck though.'

'Madame Mercier believes they'll be opening the bars and restaurants up to French people again soon,' Henderson said. 'That should earn you some extra tips.

One chap used to give Marc two francs every time he lit his cigar.'

'Nice,' Luc said, but his attention was caught by a small shop: *Enzo Maillard Watch Repair*. 'Is that the one you were talking about?'

Henderson nodded. 'I just couldn't remember the exact name. You can use the telephones at the train station. Just be careful who's standing nearby.'

'I know,' Luc said irritably. 'Where are you off to?'

'The library. I've got a little research project.'

Luc had to pass through a security checkpoint to enter Lorient station, then had to queue fifteen minutes for the phone box, slamming the sliding doors for privacy.

'Operator. What number please?'

'Gestapo headquarters.'

'One moment . . . Please insert one franc to connect your call.'

After a few crackling sounds and three sharp rings, a German-accented receptionist answered the phone.

'Good morning,' Luc began politely. 'I'd like to speak with Oberst Karl Bauer if that's possible.'

'I'm afraid the Oberst is out at the moment, can I take a message?'

Luc was relieved. His plan relied on Bauer being out, but Henderson only had a rough idea of his working hours.

'It's a personal matter,' Luc began. 'I work at Maillard

Watch Repair. Oberst Bauer left a pocket watch with us for a service. He was most insistent that I deliver it back to his apartment this afternoon, but we've lost the docket with his address and we're most anxious not to cause him any upset.'

The receptionist laughed. 'Upsetting Oberst Bauer is never a good idea, but I'm sure I'll be able to find the address of his quarters. Could you wait for one moment?'

'Of course,' Luc said, smiling to himself. 'Thank you so much.'

*

The skies were dark grey as Paul pedalled home, carrying the messages Henderson had deposited in the mailbox less than an hour earlier. The hammerhead clouds looked ominously like a thunderstorm heading in, but the single track pathway was heavily pitted so he couldn't ride any faster.

Their latest home was the third in under two months, because bitter experience had shown that undercover radio teams couldn't stay in one location for long periods. German military intelligence had monitoring stations all over France. These picked up radio transmissions made by undercover agents and could calculate a two-by-two-kilometre area from which the transmission was sent. This location was relayed to specially trained Gestapo squads that used radio detection equipment to track down and arrest radio operators.

The shabby cottage was on a dead-end road, at the edge of a lively village seven kilometres from Lorient. Paul was pleased to reach the front door as the first large raindrops pelted his cap.

'How much have we got?' Boo asked. 'We're on a tight sked.'

Rosie snatched Henderson's papers from her brother. The sked – or schedule – gave them a transmission time each day when the monitoring stations in southern England would be listening out for their signal. Today's sked was half past twelve. It was already gone eleven so they had a little over an hour to convert Henderson's message into code.

'Submarine movements from Joel,' Rosie said, as she flipped through the four sheets of paper. 'Information about the arrival of a U-boat supply vessel at Keroman. Continuing difficulties shunting supplies into the dockyard due to shortage of small locomotives and blah, blah, blah. It's about a hundred and fifty words plus a short message that's already been put into Henderson's personal code.'

As Rosie spoke, Boo started a small fire in the kitchen range so that they could burn all their notes as soon as the transmission was over. She then tore several sheets from a pad of squared paper. Rosie's first step was to condense all of the information on the four sheets into the smallest number of words. When she'd done this, she gave it to Paul to make sure that it made sense and had left nothing out.

A lightning bolt lit up the whitewashed wall behind them.

'Static electricity will play havoc with our signal,' Boo said.

Boo and Rosie halved the shortened message, and sat at a table with pencils and squared paper converting it into code. This was done using a specially prepared book of Dutch poems. On each day, they'd pick a different poem based upon a prearranged schedule. The first line of today's poem was:

Myn Ideeën zyn de times van myn ziel.

And the first line of the message was:

Sailing four subs Thur next week. Atlantic.

To convert the message into code, they added the numeric values of the letters together, or took them away, depending on which day of the week it was. Monday was a subtraction day.

M from myn was the 13th letter of the alphabet, S from sailing was the 19th letter of the alphabet. So Rosie had to calculate 13 minus 19 to give –6. She would then have to transmit the 6th letter from the end of the alphabet, which is U.

This calculation was repeated for every letter in the message and would have to be reversed at the receiving end to decode what they were saying. The only way for the Germans to decipher this message would be if they got hold of the poetry book.

'Paul,' Boo said, as she glanced up from her squared paper. 'Turn the radio on to warm up, then unroll the aerial and head uphill to your lookout position.'

Paul looked pretty miserable at the prospect as Rosie stuck her tongue out. 'You're gonna get soaked, baby face.'

'Oh get stuffed,' Paul moaned, as he headed out the front door.

CHAPTER THIRTY-FOUR

Boo and Rosie could transmit Morse code at around thirty words per minute. Their message was less than two hundred words, but the actual transmission took much longer than the six minutes this raw speed implied.

To avoid detection, their suitcase-sized radio could only transmit a weak signal. Even in ideal conditions, Rosie or Boo would be delayed by three-letter Q code instructions sent by their receiving station in England. QTC was a request to confirm the number of letters sent. QRS meant slow down the speed of transmission. Worst of all was QSM, which was a request to repeat the last section of the message.

The thunderstorm caused interference with the radio signal and Rosie had to send some chunks of the message seven or eight times before hearing confirmation of safe receipt in her earpiece.

Paul was utterly miserable, hunched on a hillside a couple of hundred metres from the cottage. He was under a tree, but the breeze was whipping up the rain so it gave him little protection. He had his arms folded and it felt like such a long time that he was half convinced the girls were playing a joke on him.

Then he spotted a car.

One of the reasons they'd rented this cottage was its location at the end of a long gravel track that nobody else had any business using. Paul grabbed a small pair of binoculars from his coat pocket and wiped beads of rain off the lenses before taking a look.

There was no doubt it was trouble. The car moved fast and a fellow leaned out of the front passenger-side window aiming a long direction-finding aerial.

'Rosie,' Paul screamed, the binoculars swinging from his neck as he broke into a sprint.

The route downhill was precarious, with loose rocks and prickly bushes, but he kept focused on the house as water spattered his trouser legs.

'We've get to out,' he shouted, as he heard car tyres splash through a puddle less than fifty metres from the front of the cottage. There was a second car and a motorbike behind and he looked over his shoulder half expecting to find Gestapo officers stalking in the bushes.

As Paul reached the cottage's back door, Boo burst out

and almost knocked him flying. She didn't need Paul to explain because she'd heard the motorbike and the squealing brakes on the other side of the house.

Rosie was still hunched over the Morse key as she heard Boo shout. As she stood up, she transmitted QXX, to indicate an emergency, while her other hand freed a grenade taped into the lid of the leather radio case.

As two Gestapo officers got out of the car, Rosie pulled the pin and lobbed the grenade underarm through the open window above the kitchen sink. She then grabbed papers and the poetry book off the table and ran barefoot towards the back door, as the motorbike rolled around the side of the house and stopped in the back yard.

Paul and Boo dived into bushes behind the house as the grenade exploded around the front, taking out every window and blowing a Gestapo officer out of his boots as he was about to shoulder-charge the front door.

'Get moving,' Boo shouted to Rosie, as Paul turned over a heavy stone and pulled up a metal box buried in the sodden earth.

Rosie took one step towards the bushes, but the German motorcyclist was less than ten metres away. He'd recovered from the shock of the grenade blast and was pulling a pistol from its holster. There was no way she'd make it into the bushes before he fired so she dived back into the house.

Paul opened the metal box, took out an automatic pistol and loaded the ammunition clip while Boo grabbed a net with six grenades inside.

'Where are you going?' Boo shouted, as Paul swung back towards the house.

'My sister's in there,' Paul said.

'You'll get shot,' Boo said.

Paul didn't argue further because two armed Germans were running around the near side of the cottage towards them. The leading German took aim with his machine gun as Boo yanked Paul out of the firing line and broke into a run.

Inside, Rosie charged down a short hallway, reaching the kitchen in three steps. The grenade blast had pulled down a section of the front wall, making it impossible to get through the front door.

'Halt!' the motorbike rider shouted as he followed her inside.

He took a wild shot as Rosie spun around and started up the narrow staircase. She was dead if he fired at her from this range and she moaned with relief as she reached the top of the stairs and charged into the bedroom she shared with Boo.

She reached under her bed to grab a kitchen knife stashed there for emergencies, but in her panicked state she misjudged and knocked it back under the far side of the bed, out of reach. As the motorbike rider burst in, the only thing that came to hand was a china piss-pot.

Rosie lobbed it, more in hope than expectation. It rotated as it flew, hitting the German in the head as he took aim, then shattering against the wall. Another wild shot hit Boo's mattress with a muffled thud as Rosie charged forwards and kicked the German in the balls. As he went down hard on his knees she grabbed the biggest shard of the chamberpot and speared his throat with the jagged end.

As the German gurgled blood, Rosie grabbed his gun and a shout came up the stairs in German. She only knew about fifty words of German that she'd learned on campus, but she put on her deepest voice and a corny German accent and took a shot. 'Girl dead. Two ran off.'

She froze in terror as the voice shouted a long stream of words up the stairs. The only bit she understood was that someone was dead.

'Yes, sir,' Rosie said.

By some miracle – possibly because the grenade blast had set the soldiers' ears ringing – Rosie's terrible German had held them off. She crawled to the door and listened as the two sets of hobhailed boots moved outside and broke into a run.

Rosie stepped on to her bed and peered through the shattered window at two regular German soldiers and two Gestapo officers chasing across the fields behind the house. There was no sign of Boo or her brother.

She tried to work out if there were more Germans in or near the house. She'd seen a motorbike and two cars and calculated that four men in each car and one on the bike made a likely maximum of nine men. She'd killed one man, another had been blown up on the doorstep and four were chasing after Paul and Boo. So there were up to three men waiting to machine-gun her at the front or sides of the house.

The only certainties were that Rosie could see nobody in the back yard, and that she'd get caught for sure if she stayed in the house. Rosie quickly grabbed the knife from under her bed and stuffed it into a canvas bag, along with her identity documents, a dress and some underwear. She slid her feet into a pair of canvas plimsolls before opening the little window, knocking away a few triangles of broken glass and swinging herself out on to the cottage roof.

She shuffled down the sloping thatch on her bum, then jolted with fright as a grenade exploded a couple of hundred metres away. It set a large tree ablaze and sent a cloud of birds into the sky. One of the Germans wildly blazed his machine gun until a Gestapo officer furiously ordered him to calm down.

The explosion and gunfire gave Rosie a good moment to jump down off the roof, clattering into wet bushes. She glanced through the back door of the cottage and to her annoyance saw that there were no Germans inside, meaning she could have walked down the stairs.

Almost a minute had passed since she'd last heard a German, but she still crept around the front with the pistol poised. The grenade blast had concertinaed the roof of the Gestapo Mercedes. The officer who'd caught the full force of the grenade was breathing, but his face was bloody and his right arm was wedged between two fence posts several metres away.

Henderson probably would have told Rosie to shoot the injured man to prevent him identifying her later on, but she didn't have the heart and her attention turned towards the machine gun lying halfway between the body and the road. It would give her a lot more firepower than the pistol if she got into a scrap.

She picked it up and made a quick visual inspection. It seemed OK, though the only sure test would be to fire the weapon, and she didn't want to do that because the noise might attract the other Germans back in her direction. She slung the gun strap over her shoulder and walked around the back of the Mercedes, whose trunk had been blown open by the blast.

Inside was a wooden box containing ammunition clips and grenades. Rosie didn't want to slow herself down with too much weight, so she threw three of each into her bag, along with what looked like instruction manuals for the German radio detection equipment.

Rosie planned to walk up the hill, going in the

opposite direction to Paul, Boo and the four chasing Germans, but she saw the motorbike resting on its kickstand with the engine still running. She was no expert rider, but she'd driven cars, trucks and bikes around campus during training and realised it was the most effective way to quickly put several kilometres between herself and the Germans.

After glancing over into the scrubland beyond the cottage to make sure none of the Germans had turned back, Rosie buckled her bag, hitched up her skirt and swung her leg over the saddle. She hoped Paul and Boo were OK as she opened the throttle and drove the bike precariously up the rutted hill.

CHAPTER THIRTY-FIVE

'How was the library?' Luc asked.

'I struck gold,' Henderson said coyly.

They sat in a garden square in one of Lorient's better neighbourhoods. The blazing sun was evaporating the aftermath of heavy rain. The four-storey houses set around the square had large windows and elaborate wrought-iron balconies across the first and second floors.

'Bauer lives at number seven,' Luc said, as he pointed discreetly with his little finger.

'Is he home?' Henderson asked.

'The car parked outside matched the number plate you gave me. He took lunch on the first-floor balcony, served by an elderly woman. Housekeeper, I guess.'

'Live in?'

'No, she left an hour ago. You can't be totally certain

he's alone but I've not seen anyone else go in or out.'

'I suppose an Oberst isn't quite important enough to have his own bodyguard,' Henderson said.

'Quite a few Gestapo officers and other senior Germans seem to live in this square,' Luc said. 'And a patrol comes by at least once per hour.'

'I'd assumed that from the number of German cars,' Henderson said. 'Did anyone pay much attention to you?'

'Not unless they're watching from a distance with binoculars, or something,' Luc said. 'So when do we make a move?'

'Right now,' Henderson said, as he stood up from the bench.

'What are you going to do?'

'Bauer's the main reason Marc is in custody,' Henderson said. 'Once he's dead, I'll have a much better chance of securing his release.'

*

Paul and Boo ran along a pre-planned escape route with the four Germans about fifty metres behind. The first stretch was heavily wooded, then they vaulted a crumbling wall and sprinted down a steep valley to the edge of a stream.

It was usually only a few centimetres deep, but after the heavy rain it was a half-metre torrent of thrashing muddy water. One of the Germans took aim as they waded through, hitting a tree trunk and sending a cloud of splinters into the air.

Paul saw a ten-centimetre piece of wood sticking out of his arm, but his adrenaline was pumping and he was only aware of a vague stinging sensation as they stumbled up the muddy embankment on the other side.

'Get the bikes out,' Boo said, as she snatched the pistol. 'I'll hold them back.'

Paul splashed across a single-track dirt road, ran around the side of an abandoned cottage and pulled down a sheet of mouldy timber covering the entrance of a tool shed. They'd left three bikes inside, along with a small cache of food and weapons.

Boo took a couple of pistol shots at the Germans as they came over the top of the embankment. She missed her first target, but hit a Gestapo officer in the chest and knocked him head over heels down the embankment. But with a pistol versus the Germans' sub-machine guns she couldn't stand her ground.

As Paul wheeled two bikes out of the shed, Boo cut behind him and dived inside. She grabbed a Sten machine gun and slotted in a stick of ammunition. By this time, the three surviving Germans had reached the front of the house, but seeing their comrade shot had made them cautious and they made no attempt to come down the near side of the house towards the shed.

'Take these,' Boo told Paul, as she walked out of the

shed. 'They'll split up and try to flank us.'

Boo handed Paul the pistol and a grenade, and grabbed a pair of grenades for herself.

'I'll throw one forwards to the road, you throw yours to the side. We'll get on our bikes as soon as they go bang and ride as hard and fast as we can. If we do it right, we'll be out of shooting range by the time the dust clears.'

'Gotcha,' Paul said, pulling the pin out with his teeth because he had the pistol ready to shoot.

'On three,' Boo said, before giving a quick count. 'One, two, three.'

Paul lobbed his grenade on a low trajectory so that it landed in a low hedge at the far side of the house twenty metres away. Boo threw one grenade up towards the road, before quickly tugging the pin from the second and lobbing it through a frameless window into the house.

'Grenade,' one of the Germans on the road shouted, as Paul and Boo grabbed their stuff and straddled the bicycles.

A Gestapo officer poked his head around the back of the house. Boo couldn't shoot straight because she was straddling the bike, with a bag of heavy equipment on her back, but the blast of the Sten gun was enough to send the German into retreat.

Two seconds later the first two grenades exploded.

'Ride,' Boo shouted, though she barely heard her

own words because her ears rang from the explosive shock wave.

Paul pedalled towards the road, fighting for breath and balance as he charged blind and half deaf into smoke and rubble. Boo's starting position was only a couple of metres behind, but this difference was enough for her to catch the secondary blast inside the house. The shock wave knocked her bike sideways and chunks of rubble pelted her back.

As he turned on to the road, Paul looked behind where a dusty German was running back from the house, afraid of more explosions. He got fifty metres up the road before realising that Boo wasn't following. He thought about stopping, but the dust was clearing and he was still easily within shooting range of German machine guns.

The secondary explosion inside the house was meant to go off after they'd pedalled away, further distracting the Germans, but Boo had mistimed. The blast had knocked her off her bike and she'd badly grazed her arm.

Her back wheel had buckled and she'd kicked the bike away furiously. Her leg was hurting and she wasn't sure if she could stand, so she pulled out the Sten trapped awkwardly under her body and crawled forwards until she had a clear sight of the German in the road who was targeting Paul.

Paul heard the gunshot and glanced back, seeing a

vague outline of the German writhing in the road. He was now beyond the range where machine-gun fire was accurate so he swerved off and threw the bike into a ditch. Then, abandoning everything except the pistol and a couple of grenades, he ran back towards the house.

He kept close to the bushes along the roadside, with his head low. The ringing in his ears made him feel detached, like it was a dream. The air had the freshness that you only get after a big storm, his eyes were gritty and his shirt sleeve was soaked in blood with the wooden splinter still sticking out of his arm.

He kept focused on the German in the road. He was writhing around, but he wasn't dead and it was impossible to tell if he was capable of shooting. Paul was a decent shot and wished he'd had a rifle to finish him off from long range.

Paul knew they'd been chased by four Germans. Boo had shot one as he came out of the valley, one was lying in the road, the one who'd peeked around the side of the house seconds before the grenades blew had to be dead or seriously injured. That left one man unaccounted for.

Realising that he was vulnerable approaching the house from the road, Paul cut through the bushes behind and moved stealthily towards the back of the shed where they'd stored the bikes. He jolted with fright as something touched his hand, but he spun around and after a moment's panic saw that it was nothing but a red drip from the cuff of his blood-soaked shirt.

He peered around the side of the shed and saw a classic stand-off: Boo had her Sten gun pointed at a perspiring bald-headed Gestapo officer, and the officer had his MP-40 pointing at her. With his hearing screwed, it felt like a scene in a silent movie that was about to cut to a title card that said *No way! Why don't YOU put YOUR gun down?*

Paul couldn't afford to miss, but the German was less than four metres away. You normally aimed for the chest because it was the biggest target, but the Gestapo officer was sideways on so he aimed for the ear.

He felt a little sick. Nerves and blood loss caused part of it, but mainly it was the sense of taking another life. Paul was a sensitive soul and knew he'd remember that sweat-streaked head if he lived to a hundred. But he had to pull the trigger and he did.

The Gestapo officer's head exploded. His body stayed upright for several seconds, during which Boo rolled over on to her belly and pumped out a couple of shots to finish off the German lying in the road.

'Are you OK?' Paul asked, as he gave Boo a hand up.

The back of Boo's dress was bloody and torn where the debris had pelted her. Her right arm and leg were badly grazed.

'I'll survive,' Boo said, as she looked at the buckled wheel of her bike. 'Can't hear a damned thing though.'

'Me neither,' Paul shouted, as he staggered into the shed and pulled out the third bike. 'Someone will have heard the explosions. We need to ride out of here fast.'

CHAPTER THIRTY-SIX

Oberst Bauer was due on duty in less than an hour. He came to his front door dressed in his trousers and freshly polished boots, but with only the straps of his braces over his muscular chest.

'I have a message for Oberst Krauss,' Luc said, trying to sound official, although he was far too scruffy to be a messenger boy.

Bauer looked contemptuously at the folded sheet of paper in Luc's hand. 'There is no Krauss here. You either have the wrong name or the wrong address.'

'Are you sure there's nobody else in there?' Luc asked.

'Give me that,' Bauer said impatiently, as he snatched the piece of paper.

His eyebrows shot up as he read the message: *Oberst Bauer wears lady's knickers.*

'Who put you up to this?' Bauer shouted, as Luc backed away. 'Do you know how powerful I am? I could make you disappear like that.'

To make his point, Bauer clicked his fingers. The click coincided with Henderson jumping out of a bush. He grabbed the much larger Bauer around the neck and held a pad soaked in chloroform across his nose and mouth.

Luc caught a powerful kick in the thigh, but Henderson won his battle to keep the mask in place. As the Gestapo officer struggled, he grabbed him under the arms and dragged him into the hallway.

'Door,' Henderson shouted.

Luc looked back into the square to make sure nobody had seen what had happened before limping inside and slamming the front door.

'Grab his ankles, he weighs a bloody ton.'

Henderson walked backwards into a large living room and they threw the semiconscious body on to a sofa.

'You didn't give him enough,' Luc said.

'I want him to come round as quickly as possible,' Henderson explained. 'Check every room, make sure we're alone.'

As Luc rushed out, Henderson pulled the curtains in the bay window overlooking the street. The house was tastefully decorated and Henderson saw a gold menorah candlestick over the mantelpiece, indicating that the original owners had been Jewish.

'Nothing,' Luc said, as he came back through the arched doorway. 'There are four bedrooms upstairs. One looks like Bauer's, one seems to be a guest room. The other two are kids' rooms, but they're dusty. Nobody's been in there in months.'

'Perfect,' Henderson said, as he rested his leather document case on a compact piano, pulled out a false bottom and removed a separate zipped pouch containing syringes and pill bottles. 'Help me turn Bauer on to his back. Then I want you to search the house for documents or anything else that looks useful. Don't make a mess, his death has to look natural.'

'Loud and clear, boss,' Luc said.

As he waited for Bauer to regain consciousness, Henderson saw a decanter on a side table. Being careful not to leave fingerprints, he put a handkerchief over his hand before removing the stopper and getting a sniff of expensive brandy. He poured a large measure into a cognac glass and knocked it back in two gulps. 'I'm sure you won't mind, Herr Oberst.'

Bauer made a low groan as Henderson walked back towards him. Henderson pulled the German's eye open. His pupil shrank rapidly in response to the bright sunlight, which meant he'd almost regained consciousness. Within a minute or two, he'd be capable of getting up and starting a fight.

Henderson sat on the low table in front of the sofa and pulled a large needle out of the medical case. It was about the length of a pen, made from stainless steel, with a hook at the blunt end so that you could get hold to pull it out.

After feeling along Bauer's spine to find the gap between two vertebrae, Henderson marked the spot with his thumbnail, carefully aligned the needle and then punched it into the gap between the bones with a hard slap. Bauer's eyes shot open and he screamed out in pain. The resulting adrenaline rush more than cancelled the lingering effects of chloroform.

'Welcome back,' Henderson said in German, as he crouched down near the arm of the couch so that Bauer could see him. He then gave the needle the gentlest of nudges to make Bauer scream again. 'You have a needle wedged between two vertebrae in close proximity to your spinal column. I assume you're familiar with this technique?'

'You shit,' Bauer said, trying to move but finding that even the tiniest movement shifted the needle and caused excruciating pain.

'You certainly *ought* to be familiar,' Henderson said, ignoring Bauer. 'German intelligence invented the technique during the last war. It's not effective for lengthy interrogations because there's a serious risk of blackout or instant paralysis, but it leaves no obvious marks and there's only one question that I need answered.'

Luc came back into the room and laughed at Bauer's suffering. 'Nice! Can I give the needle a wiggle?'

For the first time that day, Henderson found Luc irritating. 'What did you find upstairs?' he asked tersely.

'I looked through his papers, there's a bit of stuff in his desk.'

'We've got time. Take the camera and photograph anything that looks interesting.'

'I'll try, but I can't read much German,' Luc said.

'Keep an eye out for any names you recognise. Especially Brigitte Mercier or Marc Hortefeux.'

As Luc headed back upstairs, Henderson turned to Bauer.

'We're both professionals,' Henderson said, trying to sound friendly. 'You understand how this works. I'm undercover in occupied territory and you know my identity, so I'll have no option but to kill you when this interrogation is over. The only question is whether you choose to spend hours or minutes in agonising pain before you die. So, where is Marc?'

Bauer looked determined and smiled slightly. 'You won't find him, Mr Hortefeux.'

Henderson gave the needle sticking out of Bauer's back a slight upwards push. The big German's legs jerked involuntarily as Henderson pushed Bauer's face down into the sofa cushions to muffle his scream.

'And why won't I find him?'

'His heart gave out,' Bauer said. 'I had your son impaled on a hot spike. He died, moaning like a little bitch.'

Henderson flashed with anger, but tried not to lose his cool. There was a strong possibility that Bauer was lying.

'What did Marc tell you?'

Bauer smiled. 'He told me that his father was a Jew-loving, homosexual communist. You should have heard his boyish screams when I broke his arms, Hortefeux.'

'You'd better be lying,' Henderson said angrily. 'Because if you're not, I'll hunt down your family. Wife, kids, whatever.'

Bauer shook his head by as much as he dared do without moving the needle wedged into his spine.

'The war is almost over, Hortefeux. Russia's practically finished, Britain won't hold out for long and scum like you will be captured and killed.'

Henderson swept his hand across angrily, knocking the needle. Bauer wailed, and Henderson had to stand and force Bauer's head down into the cushions for almost a minute before he calmed down.

'I can do that again *so* easily,' Henderson warned.

'Do it then,' Bauer said. 'Your brat will still be dead.'

Luc came into the room holding a sheath of papers.

'I've no idea what it says, but it's Marc's picture at the top.'

Henderson snatched the papers eagerly. He felt sad as he saw the blurry black and white photo of a tired-looking Marc. Was that the last picture ever taken of him?

The papers didn't give much away except times and dates. The time of Marc's arrest and his first interrogation. His intended release the following morning was written on the paper, but crossed through. Then there was the time of Marc's second interrogation and the words, *confession on file, 12-month sentence*. The final entry was a single word: *Rennes*.

Henderson turned towards Bauer. 'Is Marc being held in Rennes?'

'He's dead,' Bauer said firmly. 'I already told you what happened.'

Henderson waggled the paper. 'It doesn't say that here.'

'I didn't mean to kill Marc,' Bauer explained. 'At least not until I'd got a lot more out of him, and some of my superiors are surprisingly squeamish. They don't like it when someone dies accidentally, especially a kid, so I covered my tracks.

'I didn't want Marc buried in Lorient, in case word somehow got back to you, so we sent his body to Rennes prison. The paperwork says he was alive when he left

Lorient. At Rennes you'll find another set of papers saying he was transferred to Germany for labour duty, but that's just to cover my tracks. The fact is, Mr Hortefeux, I tortured your precious son to death and enjoyed doing it.'

'Bastard,' Henderson shouted, giving in to emotion as he grabbed the needle and yanked it sideways.

Bauer screamed for about two seconds before his entire body locked stiff.

'Is he dead?' Luc asked.

'Blacked out,' Henderson said, as he took a vial of smelling-salts from the pouch and held them under Bauer's nostrils.

'He could be lying about Marc just to piss you off,' Luc said, as Bauer's eyes flickered open. 'If Marc was tortured he can't have given much away or he would have had you arrested, or followed at the very least.'

'Call the commandant at Rennes prison if you don't believe me,' Bauer said, springing back to life as suddenly as he'd blacked out. 'There's a phone in my hallway. Tell him you're from the Gestapo at Lorient. Say that you want to bring Marc back for further interrogation and see what he tells you.'

Henderson picked up the phone by the front door and was surprised to hear the operator speaking in German. He hadn't realised that military lines were connected to a separate desk at the telephone exchange.

'Rennes, the prison commandant please.'

'I'll have to look that number up,' the operator said.

She took a couple of minutes to find the number. Henderson got the commandant's secretary, then the commandant himself.

'This is Oberlieutenant Schmidt at Lorient Gestapo HQ,' Henderson said in German-accented French. 'I'm enquiring about a prisoner named Marc Hortefeux. We may need to bring him back to Lorient to speak with him in the next day or two.'

The phone connection was crackly, but Henderson thought the commandant sounded nervous.

'Hortefeux is in transit to a labour camp in Germany,' the commandant said.

'Why would that be?' Henderson asked. 'He's too young for labour service, isn't he?'

Now the commandant sounded upset. 'I stand by my actions and if you wish to place me under formal investigation, so be it. Good day to you, sir.'

With that, the commandant slammed down his phone.

Henderson had no way of knowing that the commandant had sent Marc to Germany because he thought it would be better for him, or that the commandant was frightened because Bauer had gone bananas and threatened to arrest him when he'd discovered that Marc had been shipped off to Germany without his permission. Henderson simply assumed that Bauer's story was true and the commandant was complicit in covering up Marc's death.

'So, was I lying?' Bauer asked, sounding remarkably chipper for a man facing death.

Henderson didn't answer because he was choking back tears.

Luc gawped. 'Marc's really dead?'

'It seems so,' Henderson sniffed, as he took a small glass vial and a syringe from his leather pouch. His hands trembled as he pushed the needle through the bottle's foil cap and drew the liquid into the syringe.

'What's that?' Luc asked.

'I'm not sure exactly,' Henderson said. 'They extract it from some Indian frog. It stops the heart dead and looks like a heart attack when you do an autopsy.'

'Can I do it?' Luc asked. 'I want to get one Nazi in the bag to avenge my brother.'

'If you wish,' Henderson said coldly. 'Put it somewhere hairy so you can't see the injection site.'

'One more thing,' Bauer said, as Luc leaned over to deliver the fatal injection.

'What?' Henderson asked.

'When your son was dying,' Bauer said, 'I held his face against a hotplate, just because I could.'

'Kill him now,' Henderson said angrily as he stepped back in disgust.

Bauer was pretty hairy all over, but Luc found a good spot near the Gestapo officer's armpit and pushed the needle through his skin.

CHAPTER THIRTY-SEVEN

A girl riding in broad daylight with a machine gun slung over her shoulder was suspicious, so Rosie abandoned the motorbike after three kilometres and began a nervy walk towards the safe house, avoiding villages by sticking to the back country and taking cover whenever she saw anyone.

She'd last seen Paul and Boo heading into scrubland pursued by four Germans. She spent most of the walk wondering if they'd got away, while torturing herself over whether she should have gone in the same direction and tried to help them.

It was nearly six when Rosie approached the safe house. Her skin was glazed with sweat and it felt like every insect in France had taken a bite at her arms and legs. If Paul and Boo had been captured there was a chance they'd have given away the location of the safe house under interrogation, so she crouched in the bushes for several minutes looking for signs of life, then crept up to the kitchen window with the German machine gun poised.

When Rosie bobbed up, she saw Paul sitting shirtless on the kitchen floor, with a bandage around his upper arm and the huge scars across his back where he'd been hit by debris when their boat went down the previous year.

Rather than shout, Rosie rapped one knuckle on the glass to attract Paul's attention. This way he could signal if something was wrong.

'Hey!' Paul said, jumping to his feet and smiling.

They met on the front doorstep and pulled each other into a relieved hug. The death of their parents and the stresses of war had forged an exceptionally close bond between the two siblings and they both began to well up.

'I was so scared they'd got you,' Rosie said, as Boo came around the bottom of the stairs and joined the hugs.

They swapped their escape stories as Rosie took off her dress and washed down with cold water and a flannel. But they'd killed five Germans, including three Gestapo officers, between them so it was no time for chitchat.

'We have to split up,' Boo began. 'All the Germans who saw us are dead, but when they question the villagers they'll get a good enough description of us.'

'Agreed,' Rosie said. 'They'll be hunting for two girls and a boy. Did either of you leave your identity documents, or anything else around?'

'My ration card was in the house,' Paul said. 'I didn't have it on me because I only went up the hill as a lookout.'

'You should have kept it with you, really,' Boo said. 'But it doesn't have your photo so it's not all that important.

'I've had a look at the supplies and equipment in the rooms upstairs,' Boo went on. 'There's a lot of options for us, in terms of clothing, documentation and suchlike. I'd suggest that two of us make up the fake American passports and head south. It'll be hairy until we get out of the Lorient zone, but the Germans treat all Yanks with kid-gloves. The third person needs to go into town and warn Henderson.'

'Getting into town might be risky,' Paul said. 'But I've never seen a checkpoint between here and Kerneval. It's probably better to warn someone at the fishing village, and they can pass the message on indirectly.'

Boo considered this for a couple of seconds. 'Yes,' she said finally. 'That does make more sense. Joel will be able to pass the message on to Henderson on his way to work in the morning. There's a spare radio set here if they need to send an emergency signal.'

Paul laughed, 'Though if they're relying on Troy's or Luc's Morse code skills for transmission, God help them.'

'Wait a minute,' Rosie said, tapping a thoughtful finger on her cheek. 'Why are we so sure that the Germans weren't tipped off? For all we know, Henderson and the others were arrested before us and gave our position away.'

'No,' Paul said, shaking his head. 'First off, Henderson only knew our approximate location and he'd be the last person to break under interrogation. Second, I watched the Germans driving towards us like lunatics, with the aerial sticking out the side of the car tracking our signal. If they'd been tipped off, they would have waited until we were off guard and encircled the house.'

'Actually, you're right,' Rosie nodded, 'because I grabbed a bunch of documents out of the car and it was all about their tracking equipment. It must have been a signal detection squad, because they never would have sent three cars thundering down that road if they'd known it was a dead-end leading to their target.'

'So which one of us should go to Kerneval?' Boo asked. 'We really need to get cracking on making up these passports and getting out of the area.'

'I'll go,' Paul said. 'The guards never hassle kids.'

'But you've left your ration card in the house, stupid,'

Rosie said. 'They'll have your name, and probably a description.'

'Oh,' Paul said.

'I reckon it's best if I go and meet Joel,' Rosie said. 'I go there to buy fish, so I'm known around there. And besides, I'm only fourteen. Paul and I will get grilled at every checkpoint if we travel long-distance without an adult. Boo, you can say you're Paul's nanny or something. Shuttling him between his French divorcee mother and his wealthy American father.'

Paul would rather have stayed with his sister, but he could see Rosie's logic and didn't make a fuss. 'I'll have to practise my American accent,' he said.

'And you're the artistic one,' Boo told Paul. 'I'll fetch the box with the blank passports and stamps out of the loft and you can get cracking on filling in everyone's new documents.'

'Get the camera and developing fluids too,' Paul said. 'We'll need photographs.'

As Boo headed off upstairs, Paul turned towards Rosie who looked sad. 'I hope you get through OK. I bet there's gonna be snap checkpoints everywhere after what happened.'

'Seems a shame to break up our little trio,' Rosie said. 'But if it all goes OK, I guess I'll see you back on campus in a few weeks' time.'

*

Henderson and Luc crouched in a dilapidated stable which was currently home to a bunch of scrawny chickens. They'd been in position for more than an hour and were starting to get cramp.

'I still think Bauer might have been lying about Marc,' Luc whispered.

Henderson's head swung around furiously. 'The commandant at Rennes corroborated Bauer's story. And Luc, *please* stop going on about this. There's a job to do here, and we've got to keep our heads clear.'

Luc thought he heard Henderson sniffling in the dark and felt resentful, because he doubted he'd be shedding any tears if it was him that got killed.

'Why was Marc so special?' Luc asked. 'I mean, he was an OK guy, but all of us know the risks when we sign up for this.'

Henderson's hand shot up. He grabbed Luc's throat and shoved his head back against the cobwebbed bricks behind them.

'Keep your damned mouth shut,' Henderson growled, as the fading light caught a tear trickling down his cheek. 'I don't want to hear one more word out of your bastard mouth, you piece of—'

He released Luc's throat as two pairs of footsteps sounded in the alleyway in front of the stable. Henderson peeked out and saw two young men, one much bigger than the other.

'Is that the two from your apartment?' Luc whispered.

Henderson nodded. 'Take the smaller one, but don't move until there's a key in the front door.'

They crept closer to the stable doors, as the larger of the two youths unlocked a small terraced house less than three metres away. Luc accidentally clattered the wire over the chicken cages, setting off the birds, and they ducked down as the pair at the door looked back.

'Shut up, dumb birds,' the bigger lad said. 'I'd wring your necks if you had any meat on you.'

Luc and Henderson burst out of the stable as the youth opened his front door. Before either lad knew what was going on they'd been coshed over the head. The smaller lad was out cold, but the bigger one struggled until Henderson got an arm around his neck and choked him out.

As Luc dragged the younger lad into the house, small boots splashed down in the cobbles behind them. Henderson turned around in a state of alarm, only to see Edith walking towards him.

'Have you been up on that roof the whole time?' he asked in a furious whisper.

'They threatened Dot,' Edith said. 'I want to see these pricks suffer.'

Henderson pointed at Edith and spoke angrily. 'Following me around is not acceptable. We'll have words later, but for now *get* inside.'

The doorstep of the small house led straight into the kitchen. Once the two young communists were dragged in, Edith closed the front door as Luc pulled the curtain and turned on a flickering electric light. They already knew there was nobody else inside, because they'd watched the boys' mother switch all the lights off before she left an hour earlier. But she'd left something in the oven for her sons.

Luc pulled a length of thick cord from his pocket and expertly wound it around the younger lad's wrists and ankles until all four limbs were trussed together behind his back. Henderson's stomach rumbled as he did the same with the larger victim.

'Dinner smells half reasonable,' Henderson said, as he looked around for a cloth to protect his hand before opening the oven door. 'Edith, find some plates.'

As the two young communists came around they found themselves helplessly trussed on the terracotta floor while Edith, Luc and Henderson sat calmly at the kitchen table eating the carrot and potato stew their mother had left them for dinner.

'You'll pay for this,' the big one shouted, as his eyes rolled. 'I know people.'

Henderson swung his leg away from the table and pushed his shoe gently between the young man's legs.

'I don't like to be disturbed while I'm eating, so be a

good boy and pipe down, or I might have to stand on your testicles.'

Edith laughed as she tucked in, making a point of keeping her manure-crusted boots right under the younger lad's nose.

'It's a little bland, don't you think?' Edith said. 'She should have used some red wine, or a sprinkle of pepper at least.'

'Yeah, this food is shit,' Luc grunted, as he flicked his victim's ear. 'Tell your mummy to make something decent next time we come here to smack you around.'

Henderson let the trussed-up victims sweat as they finished eating, then he casually took the three bowls and the cutlery to the sink.

'So, it's Antoine, isn't it?' Henderson said, as he began washing up. 'And baby brother is Étienne. Would you like to know how I found you?'

'How?' Antoine asked.

'I took a trip to the library this morning,' Henderson explained, as he placed a clean bowl on the wooden draining board. 'They have an archive of local newspapers. It took me about twenty minutes to track down a few stories relating to the local communist party. I thought I might have to visit a former party member or two and twist their arms in order to find you two, but then I found a match report for the Young Communist Group football team. There was a nice photo of you when the under-eighteens won the cup two years back.'

'Shit,' Antoine said.

'Shit indeed,' Henderson said. 'Because if I can find you, then the Gestapo can too. I bet if I chased up the names on those football team sheets and newspaper articles, I'd unearth most of the rest of your organisation. The only reason it hasn't happened already is that the Germans didn't want to upset their Russian allies by being too aggressive with communists in France. But the Soviet Union and Germany are at war now. So if you start killing Germans, the Gestapo will hunt you down, torture and execute you. Probably your families and friends too.'

Antoine and Étienne both looked dejected.

'So we surrender?' Étienne asked bitterly. 'Maybe it's *better* to die than to live like this.'

'I'm not telling you to surrender,' Henderson said. 'But you can't take the bull by the horns either. I'm willing to help, but if you want to survive long enough to see your glorious communist revolution, you'll have to learn some smarts. Now, do you promise to be good boys if we untie you?'

Antoine and Étienne both nodded. They'd been bound for twenty minutes and moved stiffly as they stood up and sat at the dining table.

'So what sort of equipment can you get for us?' Antoine asked. 'Guns? Explosives?'

Henderson smiled. 'You'll get equipment as and when you need it for operations that my people approve. Now, the other night you said you were planning to target the new crew bunker at Keroman. Do you have good information on the bunker?'

'We know the layout,' Antoine said. 'We get information on when the U-boats are going to sail from a friend who works in the docks. But *you* were the one who said there would be terrible retribution if this number of German sailors get killed.'

'Undoubtedly,' Henderson said. 'But the opportunity to kill so many U-boat crewmen while they're all in one place is irresistible. And there won't be any retribution against locals, provided the Krauts think that it's a British commando raid.'

Part Five

Eleven days later

CHAPTER THIRTY-EIGHT

WARNING NOTICE TO ALL CIVILIANS IN THE LORIENT MILITARY ZONE

On the day of 7 July 1941 five members of the German military were murdered by British spies based in the village of La Trinité. After interrogation, twenty-three villagers were executed for collaboration with these spies. The remaining population of the village has been removed to Germany for compulsory labour service. All buildings in La Trinité were subsequently destroyed by controlled explosions.

Any communities harbouring spies or other anti-German activity will face identical measures.

BY ORDER
The Gestapo

Warning poster put up around Lorient, July 1941

Monday 21 July 1941

A month after the invasion of Russia, Lorient's small German army garrison had seen its youngest and fittest men sent to fight on the eastern front. Security was now in the hands of gendarmes and middle-aged German soldiers.

The French police were recruiting and Madame Mercier had worked with Henderson to ensure that some of these hastily trained new officers would be loyal to their burgeoning resistance group rather than the occupiers.

The shortage of German manpower meant that soldiers worked long shifts and only got one day off per fortnight. Checkpoints had become erratic. At some, bored and tired Germans did little more than glance at paperwork; others took the opposite course and vented their frustrations on the locals.

Joel encountered one of the vengeful ones as he headed to work that Monday. It was seven a.m., with a breeze coming off the nearby sea and the U-boat maintenance sheds where he worked in plain view beyond the checkpoint. He was fifth in line and had already been waiting more than twenty minutes.

At the queue's head, a fat German guard and a cocky French police officer were hassling a young woman, on the grounds that the signature on her identity card was smeared. The policeman groped her breasts as he searched her and then made her lift her dress up to her waist in front of twenty queuing workmen. Joel thought her legs were sexy, but felt guilty about his lustful thoughts as she grabbed her basket and hurried off in tears.

'Was it as good for you as it was for me?' the Frenchman shouted after her, as he grinned at his German workmate seeking approval. 'Next.'

Joel had been in France for two months now. The checkpoints, queues and petty rules wound him up, but he'd also come to realise that they were the key to the long-term success of their resistance operations.

Ordinary workers didn't much care if their leader was elected French, German fascist or Russian communist, but they cared a great deal if their loved one was in a labour camp, that the schools were still closed and that you had to queue for three hours to buy a small ration of cheese.

Joel eventually got to work twenty minutes late and the chief mechanic was straight on his back. He usually kept his boss sweet, but this would be his last day on the job so he snapped back.

'It's not my fault if it suddenly takes an hour to get through a German checkpoint that usually takes ten minutes, is it?'

'You should always leave extra time for unforeseen circumstances,' the mechanic said.

Joel cast his arm out at the almost empty workshop. 'We got everything finished a day early anyway. This place never worked at this pace when Canard was in charge.'

The chief grunted. 'You worked hard over the weekend and the new boy is doing well, but don't make the mistake of thinking you're indispensable. Canard was also under that illusion, and look where he ended up.'

With that, the chief stormed out. Joel gave André a good morning wave before finding the seventeen-year-old communist sympathiser Étienne pretending to work at the far end of the room.

'How's your brother this morning?' Joel asked.

'Antoine packed his bag last night,' Étienne said. 'Had to hide it up in the loft so that our mum doesn't find it. She'll cry her eyes out this evening when she finds out he's left home.'

'What time does he finish work at the bakery?' Joel asked.

'Early. Threeish or something like that,' Étienne said.

'And you're OK with everything here?' Joel said.

Étienne nodded. 'I'm not trying to be big-headed or anything, but our dad ran a garage before he died. I grew up fixing cars. A battery isn't tricky compared to a car engine.'

'You've done well,' Joel said. 'You've got enough of the

platinum pill washers to last for a while, but don't put them in every battery you do or they'll trace the problem back to this workshop. I'm told we're trying to infiltrate some of the other U-boat bases along the coast, but I expect Hortefeux's replacement will tell you all about that.'

'Has the new boss arrived yet?' Étienne asked.

'Not that I know of,' Joel said. 'And no offence, but with this stuff the less you know the better. Mr Hortefeux's replacement will be in touch within a few days.'

*

After *Madeline II*'s previous stormy trip, Commander Finch was pleased to pull her alongside *Istanbul* on a perfect glinting sea. The deck of the wooden fishing boat was overpopulated, and Troy had to fight his way around to say emotional goodbyes to Nicolas, Olivier and Michel, who he'd lived and worked with for more than two months.

'Be safe, guys,' Troy said, as he ran across the gangplank.

Henderson had already crossed over to *Madeline II* and stood in the radio room below the bridge with Commander Finch and Captain Warburton, a New Zealander who captained a small torpedo boat named HMS *Gulliver*. The three senior naval officers leaned over a coastal chart as they quickly discussed that evening's operation to destroy the U-boat crew bunker at Keroman.

Up on deck Finch's crew formed a human chain, loading guns, explosives, uniforms and other weapons into Istanbul's fishy deck hold.

Henderson shook Warburton's hand when it was time to leave. 'Hope to see your crewmates on time this evening.'

'They'll be there, Captain Henderson,' Warburton said confidently, as he glanced at his watch. 'Eleven hours, fifteen minutes and counting.'

Henderson said a quick goodbye to Troy before crossing the gangplank back on to Istanbul.

'All clear,' one of the navy men shouted.

Madeline II was already blasting away as Henderson lowered himself into the deck hold. As well as the boxed supplies, he found himself squeezed in with Lavender – a twenty-two-year-old who would replace Boo as their group's chief radio operator – along with a muscular nineteen-year-old called Eugene.

Eugene was a former German prisoner who'd escaped the country with Henderson the previous summer. After reaching Britain he'd enlisted in the Free French Army and undergone espionage training. Now he was returning to France to take over from Henderson in charge of the burgeoning Lorient resistance circuit.

Henderson shook both their hands as the wire mesh

was fitted over their head, followed by a layer of freshly caught fish.

'I feel like I have big shoes to fill, Captain Henderson,' Eugene said.

Henderson was concerned about Eugene taking over the operation he'd built up so carefully. He was young and had no field experience, but Britain was rapidly expanding its espionage network in France. Experienced agents like Henderson were being used to establish new intelligence circuits, rather than run existing ones.

'I think you'll do absolutely fine,' Henderson said. 'Provided you can survive three hours trapped down here.'

*

Time was tight, so rather than the usual procedure of keeping the new arrivals in *Istanbul*'s hold until dark, Edith, Rosie and Alois kept watch as the equipment was unloaded, while Lavender, Eugene and Henderson dashed across the dockside to hose down and put on fresh clothes in the warehouse.

As Rosie walked Lavender and a radio set to a prearranged safe house close to Kerneval, the new radio operator confirmed that Boo and Paul had successfully made it to Vichy in the unoccupied southern portion of France. A sympathetic official at the American embassy there had sorted out their exit visas and they were now in Lisbon waiting for seats on a passenger plane bound for London.

Henderson, Alois and Eugene walked into Lorient and had a long lunch with Madame Mercier in a private room at Mamba Noir.

It was risky bringing the most senior figures in the circuit together in one place, but Henderson was going home after the operation that evening and it was vital that Eugene met everyone and understood what was going on.

Over lobster, steak and English trifle – made because it was Henderson's favourite – they discussed the challenges that lay ahead. On the positive side, the Germans' brutal retaliation at La Trinité, along with increasingly strict curfews and regulations, meant that the average French civilian was much more hostile towards the Germans than they'd been a few months earlier. But the extra security regulations also made operations more difficult.

The group was growing, with tentacles spreading into the police and tentative links with local communists. *Madeline II* was regularly delivering supplies and agents, as well as smuggling out the occasional refugee or downed airman. But more operatives meant more chance of being caught and more equipment meant more chance of the Germans finding it.

'At some point things will go horribly wrong,'

Henderson warned. 'But the key to the group's survival is security, because nobody can tell the Gestapo what they don't know.'

Eugene felt overawed as he began to grasp the complexities of his new job.

'I feel like you've built me a tower of cards,' Eugene told Henderson. 'And my job is to stop them from getting blown away.'

The four diners laughed, as they finished their meal with bitter chocolate and small cups of espresso coffee.

Henderson took a glance at his watch. 'And now it's goodbye,' he said, as he went around kissing everyone's cheeks. 'Alois, we didn't get off to the best of starts what with you trying to kill me and all, but you're a good man and we'd be nowhere without you and your brother's work at the harbour. Madame Mercier, you are a true French heroine. Finally, Eugene, there's no need to look so bloody scared because these two will look after you.'

Madame Mercier stood up and gave Henderson a hug. 'Promise you'll come back and see us all after we've won the war.'

Henderson laughed. 'You want me back as soon as that?'

'Nicolas will bring the cart with your equipment to Edith at the stables,' Alois said.

The rugged old fisherman had tears in his eyes as Henderson headed out of the private room and left

Mamba Noir for the last time. He crossed the street to his apartment. He'd already packed most of his things and left them aboard *Madeline II* that morning, but he had a final soapless shave and then packed his few remaining items in a leather bag.

His last act was to check the two rooms thoroughly for anything left behind. He didn't bother pulling out the used handkerchief down the back of his bedside table, but he was surprised to find one of Marc's undershirts trapped between his mattress and the rusty bed frame. It smelled vaguely of sweat, and Marc's smell triggered a thousand memories.

Henderson looked around and saw Marc washing at the sink, Marc in bed, Marc pulling the curtains. He blamed himself for Marc's death as he slammed the apartment door and bolted off down the stairs.

CHAPTER THIRTY-NINE

The U-boat crew bunker was at the heart of the huge construction site on the Keroman peninsula. Attacking it successfully meant carrying large quantities of weapons and explosives into the most secure part of the Lorient military zone. Henderson had planned meticulously, using information gathered by PT when he worked on the construction site, Edith's local knowledge and, most valuably, information on the design and layout of the crew bunker which came from an exiled Spanish communist who was a friend of Antoine's.

The guards on the main bridge going west out of Lorient knew Edith well and she had no trouble bringing the open-backed cart into town. After stopping to unload milk churns and fruit at a workmen's canteen close to the docks, Edith turned the empty cart into the depopulated streets on the western side of the main U-boat dock.

She hadn't been this way since the day she'd brought Marc over to take photographs of the bunkers. Organisation Todt was concentrating its manpower on completing the bunkers on the opposite side of the dock, so little had changed except for the demolition of a row of terraced houses, opening up a rubble path that would enable easy access for trucks bringing cranes and other large-scale equipment to the dockside.

'Fleabag!' a young lad shouted from the kerb. 'Haven't seen you for ages. What you up to?'

Jean-Paul was eleven, the youngest member of a little gang that Edith used to mess around with but had grown out of now she was almost thirteen and busy working for Madame Mercier.

'Just came out to look around for old times' sake,' Edith said, stopping the cart out of politeness but hoping Jean-Paul would go away because she'd almost reached her destination. 'Seen many Germans around?'

'Not unless you go near the coal yards. No kid dares now. They got rid of Fat Adolf and the new guards bash your brains out if they catch you stealing coal. They got my brother one time. Mum had to come and fetch him and he was black and blue.'

'Well it was nice seeing you,' Edith said, as she gave the horse a tap. 'I'd better go.'

'You should come down and catch rats with us,' Jean-Paul said, as he jogged alongside the cart. 'We catch big massive ones with catapults and sell them to the butcher on Rue du Port. He pays us three francs per sack load.'

'I'll be sure to avoid his sausages in future,' Edith said.

Then, much to her alarm, Jean-Paul jumped up on the cart.

'Hey,' she shouted. 'This is Madame Mercier's cart. Get off.'

'Make me, Fleabag,' Jean-Paul said, poking out his tongue.

Jean-Paul was a tough little lad. Edith might have been two years older, but she was skinny and knew she couldn't make him do anything. Her only choice was to take him along and let Henderson deal with the situation.

Her destination was only a few hundred metres down the next street. Rosie and Henderson dashed out of a boarded-up shopfront as Jean-Paul sat up on the back of the cart.

'What are you up to here?' the boy asked suspiciously.

Edith didn't want Jean-Paul running off and flapping his big mouth.

'Come inside, if you want to see what we're up to,' she said.

Henderson wasn't pleased to see that Edith had bought company.

'He just jumped on the cart,' she whispered. 'He's a total brat. There was *nothing* I could do.'

'OK,' Henderson said, giving Edith a wink before looking up at Jean-Paul. 'I could do with an extra pair of hands actually. If I give you three francs, will you help me to unload the cart?'

Jean-Paul beamed like it was Christmas and his birthday in one, but then looked perplexed.

'The cart's empty.'

Rosie had already jumped into the back of the cart. After a quick glance to make sure that the street was deserted, she pushed a metal lever into a gap between the floor and side of the cart and pulled out a narrow plank. She then reached through the resulting slot and removed two wooden bolts. As Rosie jumped down, Edith stood behind the cart and slid the floor out revealing a large hidden compartment twenty centimetres deep.

Jean-Paul's eyes bulged as he saw the array of grenades, pistols, machine guns, ropes, detonators, dinner-plate-sized cakes of explosive and black British army commando uniforms.

'Start carrying,' Henderson ordered.

Rosie reached over the side of the cart and gave Jean-Paul a wooden box filled with grenades. 'Put it inside, quickly.'

They rushed back and forth, carrying the boxes of equipment into the house. Luc joined in, after apologising because he'd been out the back peeing. In two minutes the cart was empty and Rosie had the false floor bolted back into place. At this point Edith was supposed to have ridden off, but Jean-Paul had complicated matters.

'Everyone inside,' Henderson ordered, then pointed at Edith. 'Tell me about your little friend.'

'He's just a kid,' Edith said. 'He's always out on the street. His family's rough and he's got more siblings than toes.'

'I can keep my mouth shut,' Jean-Paul said. 'I swear.'

'He's seen all our faces,' Luc said, as he sneered at Jean-Paul. 'Safest thing is to wring his neck.'

'Luc, shut up,' Rosie said, as Jean-Paul started to look scared.

Everyone was looking to Henderson for answers, but none were popping into his head.

'We've got to kill him,' Luc insisted. '*We're* all leaving but Edith isn't and that brat will know she brought the cart here.'

'I'm not murdering a young boy, Luc,' Henderson yelled, then looked at Jean-Paul, who backed nervously up to a crumbling wall. 'Why do you stay out on the street so much?'

Jean-Paul shrugged. 'Dunno, there's never much to do.'

'Their mum's always drunk and the bloke she's with

knocks all the kids around,' Edith said.

'She's not *always* drunk,' Jean-Paul said defensively.

Jean-Paul flinched as Henderson moved closer and looked at finger-shaped bruises where someone had grabbed him around the neck, and scars down his arms where he'd been regularly thrashed with a branch or a length of wire. Trusting him was a risk, but Henderson thought a boy with a hard background would respond to kindness.

'OK, here's what you do,' Henderson said. 'Jean-Paul, are you listening?'

Jean-Paul nodded solemnly, as Henderson glanced at his watch.

'Rosie is going to take you back to the stables with Edith and the cart. When you get there, she'll give you two pills that will make you sleep until the morning. When you wake up tomorrow, Edith will give you ten francs. But if you *ever* mention what you just saw to anyone, I'll send Luc after you.'

'Ten francs!' Jean-Paul grinned.

Edith eyeballed him. 'Swear on your life, Jean-Paul.'

'I swear on a *stack* of bibles,' Jean-Paul said, still grinning at the thought of ten francs.

Henderson took Rosie to one side. 'You've got plenty of time. Those pills react differently with different people, so tie the boy up just in case.'

'Gotcha,' Rosie said.

'Take Jean-Paul out to the cart,' Henderson told Rosie, 'I need a private word with Edith.'

Edith expected a telling-off, but instead Henderson went down on one knee and put a hand on her shoulder.

'I wish you'd accepted my offer to come back to Britain and train with us,' he said, as he took his wallet out of his coat and passed over two ten-franc notes. 'The other one's for you.'

Edith shook her head determinedly. 'I'd never leave my horses,' she said. 'Whoever took over would probably send old Dot off to the knackers' yard within the week.'

Henderson smiled. 'Have a word with Madame Mercier and tell her to find Jean-Paul a little job. I'd rather he was kept busy than out on the street tempted to tell his little friends tall stories.'

'I think we're OK,' Edith said. 'Jean-Paul is a bullshitter. Even if he does announce that he saw a cartload of guns nobody will believe him.'

*

'I tied his wrists and ankles and laid him out on a couple of hay bales,' Rosie said when she got back. 'He's sleeping like a baby and Edith's going straight over to speak with Madame Mercier about fixing up a job.'

'Still say we should have wrung his neck to be on the safe side,' Luc teased.

'I'll wring *your* neck in a minute,' Henderson said.

Joel had arrived ten minutes earlier after finishing

work and meeting up with Antoine along the way. Henderson wanted Antoine to take part in the operation then travel back to Britain with them, where he could undergo full espionage training. If all went well, he'd return to Lorient in six to eight months' time as a fully trained agent.

For now though nineteen-year-old Antoine had to be shown the basics. As Henderson and Luc checked, assembled and prepared all the equipment, Rosie took Antoine through aiming, firing and reloading an automatic pistol and throwing a hand grenade. Most important for tonight, she showed him how to insert an explosive fuse into plastic and explained the differences between the three kinds of fuses they'd use in the operation.

When this was done they took a break to eat dinner. Luc and Henderson wolfed down bread, tomatoes, salad potatoes and sausage. Joel, Rosie and Antoine felt varying degrees of nerves and didn't have much appetite.

When they were done, Henderson got off the floorboards and looked at his watch for the two hundredth time that day. It was past eight, and just starting to get dark.

'Have you all memorised your tasks?' Henderson asked. 'Including secondary tasks you need to perform if one of us is killed during the operation?'

'What if more than one of us is killed?' Antoine asked.

'Cross your fingers and run like hell,' Joel suggested cheekily.

Henderson laughed. 'I always say the same thing: the only certainty in an undercover operation is that nothing will go as planned. But clear heads and common sense should get us through.'

'Unless we all get shot,' Rosie said cheerfully.

'It's time to say goodbye to our identities,' Henderson said. 'From this moment forwards, we're an Anglo-French commando unit. I hope you've all memorised your new identities and background stories. Luc, where did you train?'

'Gosport army barracks,' Luc said.

'What's your rank and date of birth?'

'Private second class, Jean-Marc Clemence, Free French Army, born 16 January 1924.'

Joel laughed. 'You'll never pass for seventeen. You haven't even got pubes yet.'

Luc responded by pulling down the front of his trousers, showing the mass of frizzy hair around his crotch. Rosie pretended to retch.

Joel and Antoine laughed, but Henderson's attempt at staying friendly with Luc hadn't lasted and he smacked him hard around the back of the head.

'Don't be disgusting,' Henderson said. 'There are ladies present.'

'You've seen my man meat before, haven't you, Rosie

pops?' Luc said, as he leered at her.

Rosie smiled mischievously. 'I had to squint pretty hard, but I believe there was a small worm-like object in there amidst the grime and lice.'

'OK, stop pissing about and start preparing,' Henderson said irritably. 'I need your old documents, *now*.'

They threw the identity cards, ration papers, zone passes and all the other paraphernalia that enabled them to move through German checkpoints on to a metal tray which had previously held their dinner. Henderson tore the documents into small squares and splashed them with lighter fuel. As he was about to light them everyone dived away from the windows as three boys belted past the front of the house, running at top speed down the deserted street, pursued by a Kriegsmarine police officer.

After a pause, Henderson set the documents on fire, stirring them with the end of a pen to ensure every piece was thoroughly burned. While he did this, Rosie handed out waterproof pouches and there was some excitement because each one contained items of significant value.

First off there were papers, British military documents, sets of dog tags and French paperwork.

'These papers are piss poor,' Luc said, as he studied his new French identity document. 'Why are we using this crap when there's a stack of blank originals at the safe house?'

Henderson gave a wry smile. 'Because we're likely to

be captured or killed with these documents on us and we don't want the Germans to know that we have access to originals.'

'But this won't do us a lot of good if we get stranded and need to go through a checkpoint,' Joel said.

Luc reacted with typical cynicism. 'We're five ordinary scumbags. If we pull this off they'll probably pin a medal on us, but if we all get killed who'll miss us?'

It was common for groups to turn on each other when they're nervous and Henderson wanted it nipped in the bud.

'That's enough doom and gloom,' he said firmly.

The other contents of the pouches were enough to raise spirits. Each one contained high-quality waterproof watches, waterproof lighters, several hundred francs and three gold ingots which could be used as bribes.

'I synchronised my watch with Captain Warburton aboard *Madeline II* this morning,' Henderson said. 'It's now 8.32 p.m. So wind your watches and set them now.'

The reminder of the time gave everyone a hurry-up, because the aim was to be out of the house by 8.50.

They swapped their French clothing for British army-issue underwear and black commando uniform, then they had a few tense laughs as everyone blackened faces, hands and necks with camouflage make-up.

The final stage was tooling up. They each had an identical backpack full of ammunition, a set of civilian clothes, plus food, water, compass, maps and a basic first aid kit. They wore holsters with silenced 9mm pistols, plus Sten machine guns fitted with bayonets, shoulder belts ringed with grenades, a multi-tool and a jagged-edged hunting-knife.

Luc looked as happy as anyone had ever seen him. 'I'm gonna kill!' he said as he thumped his chest proudly. 'Let me at those German sons of whores.'

He seemed slightly less enthusiastic when he realised that besides the weight of their personal equipment, they had two large equipment bags, each containing more than a hundred kilos of plastic explosives.

Their last act before leaving the house was to push a two-hour time pencil into a small slab of plastic and place it in the middle of the living room, with their clothes and everything else they'd left behind piled around it.

'We're two minutes behind,' Henderson said, as he opened the front door and looked up and down the street. 'Let's move out.'

CHAPTER FORTY

They jogged down the street, with Henderson leading and the others running in pairs taking one handle of an equipment bag. It wouldn't be completely dark for another forty minutes and they had little cover, but a nine o'clock shift change for the construction workers was the ideal opportunity to penetrate the bunker site.

They had no chance of getting through the strict security around the bunker complex on the eastern side of the dock, so the plan was to penetrate the lightly defended coal yards on the western side and then cross the fifty-metre-wide dock in one of the small motorboats used by harbour patrols.

They were dressed as soldiers now – although their youth and, in one case, sex stretched credibility a little. After months of sneaking around, Rosie felt weird brazenly approaching the security booth at the main entrance of the coal yard. She knocked on the door of a guard hut and tried sounding seductive as the door opened.

'Hi, I'm so sorry,' she said. 'I think I'm lost. I arrived in town this morning and I was trying to find . . .'

As she spoke, she reached behind her back and signalled with three fingers, indicating the number of men she could see inside.

'How'd you get that muck all over your face?' the soldier asked, as four silenced shots pulsed through the small window at the rear of the hut. As he looked back at two colleagues who'd been shot through the chest and head, Rosie snatched her pistol from its holster, took a backward step and shot him through the heart.

She saw Luc's smile and thumbs-up through the back window as she stepped into the hut.

'Clear,' she said.

She spotted the telephone and cut the cord with her multi-tool. Antoine dragged the dead soldier inside the hut and they closed the door as they left so that the attack wasn't obvious to anyone passing by.

Meanwhile Henderson had led Antoine and Joel through the main gate and moved across the dockside with his pistol ready. Edith's best guess was that somewhere between three and five men patrolled the coal yard.

The fourth man got taken unawares as he sat with his legs hanging over the dockside crunching into an apple. After slitting his throat, Henderson dragged him out of sight between two huge pyramids of coal.

The three small patrol boats were moored around a pontoon, accessed by a steep ramp. The first boat Henderson stepped aboard had a hole where the engine was supposed to be. The others came down the ramp with the two heavy bags as Henderson moved to a slightly smaller boat, studied its controls and checked the fuel gauge.

All the watches said 8.59, which meant they'd made up the two minutes they'd lost before leaving the house. As Antoine unwound the mooring ropes and stepped aboard the small patrol craft, a huge klaxon sounded in the bunker complex across the water, signalling a shift change.

Henderson gave the starter cord a good yank and the boat's engine thrummed to life. As he pulled off, the bow rose alarmingly out of the water.

'Move forwards,' he ordered, but there was already water pouring over the stern. They were still alongside the pontoon and Luc and Rosie saved the day by jumping out on to it.

The small craft were designed for three or four men. Henderson had assumed that they'd take five easily enough for the short ride across the dock, but hadn't properly accounted for heavy backpacks and two hundred kilos of explosive.

As Luc and Rosie grasped the slippery deck of the floating pontoon and found their feet, Antoine and Joel used their helmets to frantically bail out the small boat.

Luc's eye caught a man running on the dockside. It seemed he'd discovered his colleague with the slit throat and was running towards the security shed to warn his colleagues, not realising that they were all dead.

The dockside was littered with coal that crunched underfoot and the Kriegsmarine police officer turned back when he heard Luc. The boy commando was less than fifteen metres from his target and took a good aim at the chest, but heard nothing but the click of the gun's hammer when he squeezed the trigger.

The German swung around with his automatic rifle. Luc panicked, because even if he didn't get hit the German's unsilenced weapon would alert the much larger security teams on the other side of the dock.

Unlike Marc, Luc had never mastered knife throwing, but with no gun, the blade and a desperate dive towards the nearest coal heap was his only choice. A bullet whistled past his shoulder, but there was no gunshot, which meant it was silenced.

Confused, Luc looked behind and saw that Rosie had covered him. He'd almost stepped into her line of fire, but her hasty shot had missed him by centimetres and hit the German in the gut. As he stumbled backwards Rosie shot again. This bullet entered the neck and passed out the back of his skull. He plunged over the dockside and landed with a mighty splash.

If Luc had had time to think, his pride might have been dented at being saved by a girl, but for now he was just glad to be alive. The splash had seemed loud from where they stood, but it was nothing compared to the crack of a gunshot and it had caused no obvious commotion on the other side of the dock.

Luc cursed his jammed pistol as he jogged back down to the pontoon. Henderson had made it across. Joel and Antoine had climbed on to the eastern dockside using one of the rickety wooden ladders built into the wall and were now using a rope to pull up the second equipment bag.

To their right, the recently completed dockside bunker formed a menacing dark slab. There were U-boats inside three of its seven pens, while the others were still being fitted out with lights, winches and electrical gear.

Behind and to the left of the first bunker, the inland bunker where U-boats would be repaired out of the water was floodlit. Tired construction workers climbed down the massive scaffolds on all four sides as their replacements stood at ground level waiting to take over.

Luc began casting off the second boat, but neither he nor Rosie were sure how to start the engine or confident about steering a boat accurately into the wall across the dock, so they were pleased to see Henderson coming back for them. He'd been spooked by his uncharacteristic miscalculation and the near sinking of the boat, and had no idea about the drama with Luc's pistol except a vague notion that he'd heard a splash in the water.

'Let's hope the rest of your plan isn't as screwed up as this,' Luc said with a typical lack of tact.

As they crossed the water, Luc took the clip out of his pistol and saw that it was a simple jam caused by an improperly expelled cartridge casing. Tapping the gun against the side of the boat dislodged the casing and he pumped a shot into the water to make sure he was up and running.

'I thought it made a funny sound when I shot the German in the shed,' Luc told Rosie. 'At least I'll know what it means next time.'

The ladder on the dock wall was slimy and Antoine gave Rosie and Luc a hand up. Henderson switched the boat's engine off and came up last.

They'd elected to cross during the shift change because it offered the lowest chance of being spotted. The old shift would be tired and wanting to get home without making a fuss, the new shift would see them and assume that they were supposed to be down there and the Kriegsmarine police who guarded the area would be at full stretch checking identity papers of new arrivals and making sure the departing workers weren't pilfering tools or lumber.

The major downside was that Henderson's team now had to hide out inside the base, because it wouldn't be dark enough to attack the crew bunker for another thirty-five minutes.

The German master plan for Keroman involved building not only the three huge submarine bunkers, but subsidiary buildings of which the crew bunker was the first. There were to be workshops, torpedo storage bunkers and zones for crew training and leisure activities. This armoured complex would be linked by tunnels that would enable the base to function normally even during aerial bombing.

None of the main tunnels linking the bunkers together had been built yet, but sections had been put in place under the bunkers as they were constructed. After scrambling down a muddy embankment, the five set off through a hundred metres of partially flooded tunnel that took them directly underneath the inshore bunker and to within twenty-five metres of their target.

If their intelligence was correct, no less than five complete U-boat crews would be spending the night in the crew bunker, before sailing as a pack on a late morning tide the following day. The bunker itself consisted of eight dormitories filled with wooden bunks, each designed to hold the forty-eight-strong crew of a U-boat.

According to Antoine's source, the interior of the bunker comprised simple wooden partitions that could easily be reconfigured if the bunker was repurposed. At the northern end was the entrance and recreation building. This was built above ground with a canteen and a few basic facilities such as ping-pong tables and a postbox. The southern exit was below ground. Eventually it would be linked to the rest of the complex, but currently there was ten metres of bare concrete followed by a half-metre-deep mud pool.

By the time Henderson's team exited the long tunnel they were all panting from the weight of their packs and the bags of explosives. The final stretch to the exit tunnel from the crew bunker was through knee-deep mud and had to be traversed quickly because there was a chance they'd be spotted by workmen up in the scaffolds.

They made it to the temporary wooden exit door at the rear of the crew bunker, gasping and clutching their sides. Henderson shone his torch about the tunnel around them and was alarmed to see hundreds of cigarette butts, which suggested that some of the submarine crews escaped the noise and smell of their crewmates by sneaking into the tunnel for a smoke.

Henderson's team spoke in whispers as everyone downed their equipment packs, reloaded their weapons and took drinks from their water bottles. After a few minutes' respite, Rosie and Joel began unzipping the equipment bags, which were filthy after dragging through the mud.

Antoine lit the gloomy tunnel with the torch as the other four worked quickly, pushing fist-sized chunks of explosives against the tunnel walls and sticking sympathetic detonators into each one. As Joel worked near the back door, a pair of young Germans almost hit his head with the door as they stepped out.

Luc turned to shoot, but Henderson saw them off by shouting in German. 'This is a construction area. This exit is out of bounds.'

'Pardon me,' one of the men said, and they both shot back inside like little boys who'd been caught stealing from a cookie jar.

When there were more than thirty explosive charges rigged around the door and along the length of the tunnel, Henderson decided that they had enough explosive left over to leave a football-sized slab in the middle of the mud pool outside the tunnel.

When this was done he checked his watch and saw 9.27.

'We're on schedule,' Henderson said. 'Joel, it's time to go and put out the lights.'

CHAPTER FORTY-ONE

Workers on the inland bunker toiled twenty-four hours a day, in two twelve-hour shifts. To work through the night, the Germans trained huge lamps on the site. This light spilled on to the adjacent crew bunker, making it impossible for Henderson's team to rig the rest of their explosives without being seen.

PT had hated every moment working on the construction site – Henderson and Rosie even joked that he'd stabbed himself just to get out of the job – but before his safe return to Britain he'd passed on detailed information about the layout of the construction site. Most importantly he'd learned that when the air-raid sirens sounded the entire site was blacked out and the workmen climbed down from the scaffolds and sheltered in the U-boat pens.

The base received air-raid warnings by telephone from Luftwaffe radar stations along the coast. Henderson had considered raiding the command area, killing the base's senior staff and triggering an air-raid warning from the main communications room. But the command bunker was a secure facility twenty metres below the U-boat pens. So rather than tackle this head on, the plan was to set off the air-raid siren illicitly at a remote electrical junction box.

Joel had been picked because he was fast and a good climber. He left his heavy pack in the tunnel with Henderson and the others before cutting back across the mud, ending up at the mouth of the tunnel under the inland bunker.

The next part was trickiest. With muddy hands and boots he had to run up a steep embankment and clamber on to the tunnel roof using the reinforcing wires jutting out of the concrete as handholds.

As his head rose over the tunnel roof, Joel could see six storeys of brilliantly lit scaffold, with men and buckets hanging over the side. After waiting a few seconds for two men to pass, he bobbed up and walked over the bouncing scaffold boards until he reached a rectangular metal cabinet attached to the bunker's wall.

After unlocking the cabinet with a T-shaped key, Joel swung the metal cabinet door and cautiously glanced left and right before studying the rows of switches and knotted bundles of wire inside. They were all labelled in French and German and controlled the temporary supplies of light and power to the various sections of the six-storey scaffold.

In the top row was a yellow switch box marked *Sirens Test – Do not activate without clearance*. Two wires fed into the bottom of the switch. Flipping it would complete the circuit and set off the air-raid warning, but flipping it back again would instantly turn the sirens off. Joel needed them to stay on long enough to trigger a full-scale base-wide alert.

To begin he used a set of wire cutters to cut off the telephone handset in the bottom of the box. This would delay any attempts by staff in the command bunker to find out why the siren had sounded. He then pulled the first wire out of the siren test switch, peeled a two-metre length of insulated wire from his trouser pocket and twisted the bared ends together.

He looped this wire around several bundles of cables to hide its path before pulling the second wire out of the siren switch. This wire had plenty of slack and he used the same trick, winding it through several other cable bundles so that it would take a significant amount of time to track it down and disconnect it.

When the two wire ends were dangling out of the wiring loom a few centimetres apart, Joel took a golf-ball-sized lump of plastic explosive out of his trouser pocket, inserted a three-minute time pencil detonator and moulded it into a recessed corner of the cabinet.

'Mind your back, son,' someone shouted.

Joel pressed his body against the wall as two workmen passed behind carrying a cauldron of hot tar. As soon as they were past, Joel snapped the end of the time pencil to activate the three-minute countdown to the explosion. Then he joined the two bare pieces of wire together and looked up as the massive sirens on the bunker roof began warbling.

Within ten seconds about half the lights on the scaffold around the inland bunker were out. The rest stayed on a bit longer to allow men over the sides or moving heavy equipment to get to a safe position before everything went black.

Joel jumped off the tunnel roof, splashing down into half a metre of mud. After wading across to the crew bunker he grabbed his pack from the tunnel mouth and clambered up a slushy embankment where he found Henderson squatting on his haunches holding an electric hand detonator.

'Nice work,' Henderson said. 'You stay here to trigger this, I'll run along and catch up with Rosie. If possible, give it a good twenty seconds after the main explosions before blowing the tunnel, OK?'

'Gotcha,' Joel said, as he looked at the crew bunker's arched roof less than twenty metres away, and the shadowy hulk of the inland bunker, with workmen climbing down off the scaffold in the darkness behind him.

'See you at the railway siding,' Joel said.

The crew bunker was about sixty metres long. Henderson saw Luc and Antoine walking up the gently sloping roof as he ran along the side of the building. Rosie was struggling with seventy kilos of plastic and was grateful as Henderson grabbed one of the handles.

Their target was the overground building at the head of the crew bunker. The lights inside had gone out as soon as the siren sounded. Any U-boat crews who were above ground had descended into the bunker behind an armoured, blast-proof door. The only men above ground were two navy police officers standing in a gloomy lobby under a giant portrait of Hitler.

Henderson drew his silenced pistol as he walked through the main door. He clinically shot the two guards and an unexpected U-boat crewman who'd apparently failed to get into the bunker before the blast door was closed. He then turned back and held the door open, enabling Rosie to drag the bag of explosives inside.

The heavy door that led into the bunker would easily withstand a blast from a hundred kilos of explosive, so rather than attack the door, the plan was to bring the building down on top of it to prevent the Germans getting out.

As Rosie and Henderson linked four charges together with fast-burning detonator cord and placed them against the building's load-bearing walls, Luc and Antoine were at the top of the crew bunker's gently sloping roof.

This structure was made from two metres of concrete and thick steel plate, and was angled in such a way that the energy of a bomb blast would be deflected away. But with hundreds of men inside, the bunker needed a hefty ventilation system, which came in the form of four armour-plated vents fitted on the roof. These vents could be sealed in the event of a gas attack, but Henderson correctly guessed that they'd be left open on a warm summer night when there were two hundred and fifty men down below.

The two lads started at opposite ends. Luc hurriedly dropped six grapefruit-sized balls of explosive through the first ventilation shaft. Each was fitted with a sympathetic fuse, which would go off in reaction to the main explosion being set by Henderson and Rosie.

As he dropped six more balls through the second vent, the wailing air-raid siren faded out. Luc could hear German voices echo up the ventilation shafts, and while his German was rubbish he definitely got the impression that they'd heard the explosive balls dropping into the aluminium channels over their heads.

He looked anxious as he scrambled along to the

middle of the roof where he met Antoine.

'Done your two OK?' he asked. 'They've stopped the siren, so the lights could come back on at any second.'

'All good,' Antoine said, his voice crackling with excitement and fear.

Luc pulled a torch out of his pocket and flashed it three times, aiming towards the main entrance. After a couple of seconds he got an identical return signal from Henderson.

'We've got two minutes to get out of here,' Luc said, as he pulled the straps of his backpack up his shoulders in preparation for a slide down the roof and a sprint across open ground towards the railway sidings three hundred metres away.

And then all the floodlights came back on.

CHAPTER FORTY-TWO

Rosie and Henderson were largely hidden by the crew bunker's entrance building, Joel was exposed but he kept low and was so muddy that you'd have to look damned hard to spot him, but Luc and Antoine were up on the roof with the illuminated scaffold lighting them up.

A shout went up and Luc saw three Kriegsmarine guards charging out of a command post by the main gates a couple of hundred metres away. But the first shot came from the other direction, hitting the roof and spraying up concrete shrapnel. The next gunshot ended with a whoosh of air from Antoine's lungs and a squelching sound like a boot being swallowed by deep mud.

Luc was aware of a mist of blood on his face. The three guards were charging in from one side and there was a shooter up in the scaffold behind. One of the guards went down, though Luc had no idea if he'd been shot by Joel at one end or Henderson at the other.

Luc had an impossible choice, but marginally preferred his chances of going back the way he'd come, rather than risk running straight into the two surviving guards, who'd now taken cover behind a tin shed.

'Let's move,' Luc said, but his mind was racing and it was only now that he put the mist of blood and the squelch together and grasped that Antoine had been shot.

The black commando gear made it difficult to see blood, but there was a spike of bone sticking out of Antoine's leg. Luc grabbed him by the arm and gave him a push. As another bullet slammed the concrete less than a metre away, Antoine rolled helplessly down the roof into the broad gutter where the roof met the mud.

There was a loud bang as the explosive Joel had left in the junction box went off and the site plunged back into darkness. Another shot came, spattering the mud some distance away as Luc crouched over Antoine.

'It's agony,' Antoine said, with pleading eyes. 'Get Henderson.'

'Of course it's agony, you've been shot,' Luc said coldly, as he glanced back over his shoulder, acutely aware that Henderson would set off the first explosion within seconds.

Luc reached inside Antoine's jacket and removed the pin from one of his grenades. Then another, then another. They had ten-second fuses and Antoine realised what he'd done.

'Bastard,' he shouted.

'They'll kill you anyway,' Luc said, as he turned to run. 'See you in hell.'

Luc sprinted about eight paces then dived blindly off the edge of the steep, muddy embankment. He wasn't sure whether Antoine or the entrance building exploded first, but the oven blast of hot air toasted his bum, vented up his back and propelled him with enough force to double his normal jumping range.

He landed in the mud with such force that he made a huge bow wave and ploughed on for more than three metres, hitting his shoulder on something hard somewhere along the way. As he caught his head, the sky above was bright orange. Chunks of rubble fell like rain, and the six storeys of scaffolding around the inland bunker flexed dramatically, sending boards, tools and men over the edge.

*

Henderson knew a good deal about explosives. The quantity they'd carried into the base was less than one third the amount contained in a single RAF bomb, but positioning and tactics made it more effective than a whole planeload.

The first explosion comprised four eighteen-kilogram blocks in the crew bunker's entrance. Each was positioned close to a load-bearing wall and this had caused the entire structure to collapse in on itself, and more importantly on to the bunker's main entrance.

The twenty-four two-kilogram charges spread through the ventilation system were set off by the shock wave from the first explosion. The U-boat crews panicked as these blasts sent jets of flame and hot gas out of the vents into every room across the bunker's entire length. The force also knocked down or ignited the lightweight wooden partitions between rooms.

Less than a dozen men were killed by these explosions, but those that survived found themselves trapped. Most went for the main exit and wasted precious seconds trying to force it open. When they gave up, these men found themselves at the wrong end of a sixty-metre-long corridor, with choking smoke and men crawling along the floors trying not to breathe.

About twenty men made it out of the back of the bunker and into the tunnel. The men who came after that were crawling and panicking and soon there was a massive jam around the narrow doorway. Joel heard screams and coughs as the first few staggered out of the end of the tunnel and into the mud. He counted seconds in his head, *eighteen, nineteen, twenty.*

On twenty he wound a small lever to charge the handheld detonator, lifted a safety flap and pressed the red button. More than thirty small charges erupted inside the tunnel, blowing the men inside to pieces, bringing down the tunnel's roof and sealing the last remaining exit, with more than two hundred men choking to death inside.

A few seconds after this explosion, the sympathetic fuse in the football-sized slab went off, spouting a thirty-metre geyser of mud and engulfing the dozen or so men who'd made it out of the tunnel alive.

The sky was an orange fog as Joel heard desperate screams and German curses. He was already caked in mud, but the next layer that pelted him from above was hot. Not enough to burn, but hot like a bath when you need to run a drop more cold.

It fizzed and steamed as it slapped the ground and took the air out of Joel's lungs. He felt sick, as he began to run and the heat and smoke sapped his strength. They'd come here to kill five U-boat crews and it seemed they'd killed five U-boat crews, but the reality of the shouts and coughs was haunting and he wondered how many men he'd killed when he'd pressed that little red button.

Joel was staggering toward a pair of Germans. He was ready with his machine gun, but they didn't see his commando gear or his backpack, just a young man staggering out of a mud bath.

'Are you OK, boy?' one asked. 'Did you see what happened?'

'I . . .' Joel gasped in German. 'I don't know. I just ran.'

He clearly wasn't hurt, so the Germans carried on. The lights were still out and the smoke made it difficult to see more than a few metres.

Joel had lost all sense of time, his boots were slipping in the mud and he started getting paranoid that he was walking in the wrong direction. But within a couple of minutes he'd reached concrete and he saw the moonlit railway sidings up ahead.

Antoine's Spanish friend had promised to leave a railway handcart out in the sidings. This simple device comprised a small flat-bed railway truck with a two-sided pivot lever. Pushing down on the lever made the cart move. Rosie and Henderson bobbed up behind it as Joel got close.

'Enough mud for you?' Rosie asked, as Joel staggered towards her like some kind of swamp creature. But she saw that he looked upset and changed her tone. 'Is everything OK?'

'It all worked,' Joel said. 'But it was brutal down there, watching them escape and then pushing the button to blow them up.'

Henderson put a hand on his shoulder. 'When you stop feeling it you're not human any more,' he said. 'Did you see Antoine or Luc?'

'I saw them under fire when the lights came on,' Joel

replied. 'They went sliding down the roof, but I never saw anything after the bunker went up.'

Henderson spoke after his three hundredth glance at his watch. 'We're four minutes behind. The Germans will get the lights back up any minute, and their wits about them pretty soon after.'

'Shouldn't we wait a few more minutes?' Rosie asked.

Henderson shook his head. 'If Luc and Antoine are alive, they can still get away by running along the tracks. If they don't catch up in time to reach our boat, they can go to the safe house, but it's too dangerous to stick around here.'

*

Luc was on his feet by the time the third explosion went off, but the shock wave blew a wall of warm mud towards him, knocking him sideways until he slammed into an embankment. His nose and throat were clogged and he coughed for several seconds. He grasped blindly inside his pack, found his canteen and swished the choking combination of mud and smoke out of his mouth with water

When he peeled himself out he'd left an indentation, like a gingerbread man cut from a pastry sheet. He realised that he must have spent a minute or so in a daze because his head was thumping, he didn't remember seeing some of the lights come back on and several Kriegsmarine police were lined up on the undamaged roof of the crew bunker.

Luc tried to ignore the pounding in his skull and think straight. With men up on the roof he didn't fancy his chances of walking the full length of the bunker and then crossing three hundred metres of open ground to reach the railway sidings.

Then he remembered that he had a watch. It was 10.16, and that was the final nail in that idea. If Henderson hadn't left already, he definitely would have done by the time he reached the sidings. He considered going back the way they'd come along the tunnel beneath the inland bunker, but the entrance was close to the blown crew bunker tunnel and there were dozens of Germans around there searching the mud for signs of life.

So Luc's only chance of escape was over the partially collapsed scaffold around the inland bunker. Luc was terrified as he crept through the mud, aware that one of the men on the roof only had to glance down and he'd be killed, or captured. Several boards from the scaffold had toppled into the mud and one that rested against the embankment made his life easier.

He was now at ground level, with scaffold less than five metres away. The scaffold here looked OK, but the blast had shifted each level by more than a metre, and at the top several upright poles had buckled, leaving the entire structure close to collapse.

Luc was strong, and even with the weight of weapons,

backpack and ten kilos of mud he reached up and clambered effortlessly on to the first level. All but one board had been knocked down by the explosion and he held on to a pole with his hand and walked heel to toe. He was now at the corner where the scaffold along the rear of the building joined the scaffold down the side leading to the dock.

Down below, a French engineer was shining a torch beam across the face of the building, while loudly expressing his opinion that the whole scaffold would have to be torn down. Luc deduced that he'd feel safer if he climbed up another level. He reached up to grab a pole above his head, used an angled pole as a step and pulled himself up on to the next layer of boards.

He repeated this until he was four storeys up. There was a childlike thrill to being up high and the clear air helped his head. He wished he'd had a lump of plastic and a fifteen-minute time pencil, because it would have been great to bring the scaffold down into the hole and kill even more Germans.

Most boards along the side were intact and Luc moved easily towards the dockside. At one point he passed a vent and peered down on hundreds of workmen in a gloomy U-boat pen, smoking and talking excitedly about what had happened.

When Luc reached the front of the bunker he crouched down, planning his next step. He chose to drop down and run fifty metres to the spot on the dockside where they'd landed less than an hour earlier. There was a chance the boat would still be bobbing somewhere along the dockside, but more likely they'd have discovered the dead Germans in the coal yard and the whole place would be infested with soldiers.

The only certainty was that it wouldn't be easy and he'd almost certainly need to kill someone, so Luc pulled a dry cloth out of his backpack and made the best job he could of cleaning the mud out of his machine gun and pistol.

When he was reasonably satisfied, he walked to the edge of the boards and began climbing down. As he was about to drop from the second level a huge searchlight swung around and blinded him.

Someone shouted and he heard German boots running up the alleyway towards him as a shot ricocheted off the wall. He had no idea where it came from, but he was hemmed in and needed to escape before reinforcements arrived.

He ripped a grenade off his shoulder belt, pulled the pin, then lobbed it into the alleyway towards the advancing Germans. After swinging out over the edge of the scaffold he slid down a pole to the ground, fireman style. As his mud-caked boots touched down the grenade exploded, instantly killing one German and blowing the other one back more than ten metres, minus several fairly important body parts.

After a sprint, Luc glanced out on to the dockside and was surprised to find nobody nearby, but his relief didn't last. The coal yard on the opposite side of the docks was ablaze with light, and the searchlight that had picked him out in the scaffold soon traced him to the ground.

Bullets pinged across from the opposite side of the dock, as well as from some unseen position behind him. It would only be a matter of seconds before he got shot so he started a run, took a huge breath and launched himself over the dockside into the moonlit water.

The water was salty and contaminated with effluent flushed out from one of the U-boat pens. His eyes burned as the weight of the pack dragged him down. He kept sinking until he'd fought himself free of the pack. But he was still heavy and he abandoned his machine gun as he kicked up powerfully.

Random bullets punched the water as he gulped two huge breaths and dived down, trying to swim as far and as fast as he could underwater. After another dash he surfaced under the floating pontoon on the western side of the dock. His proximity to the high dock wall made it impossible for the Germans on this side to pick him out with their searchlight or shoot at him, but they'd spot him soon enough if he didn't find somewhere to go.

CHAPTER FORTY-THREE

Henderson worked the handle on one side of the handcart, while Joel and Rosie shared the other. It was a job getting it moving, but once they were underway it was exhilarating and exhausting, bobbing up and down with the wind in their hair and the wheels clattering on the iron rails.

The railway lines that led from the docks to the freight yard where they'd attacked the trains a few weeks earlier were only guarded by occasional foot patrols. They left the Lorient navy base unhindered and clattered on through the centre of town, passing the crummy warehouses and tenement blocks that backed on to the railway line.

They were keen to put distance between themselves and the navy base, but the lines were designed for slow-moving cargo trains and the handcart almost threw Henderson off as they juddered over an uneven join between two rails.

After this shock they kept the speed down to running pace, which also had the advantage of being quieter. There were bridges across the railway lines in central Lorient, but as they reached the outskirts they faced several ungated level crossings.

It was after curfew, so the only people on the streets were Germans and workers with special passes. As they approached one crossing they heard, but couldn't see, a speeding motorbike. Henderson had previously tried the brake lever when they'd picked up momentum on a slope, but it was simply a wooden lever with a brake shoe at the end that rubbed against the wheels. It caused a great deal of noise and sparks, but had little effect in terms of altering the cart's speed.

There was a collective gasp as the German motorbike blasted its horn and slammed on brakes. Joel and Rosie saw terror in the rider's eyes as he swerved around the back of the cart, missing it by less than a metre. He came off the bike, tumbling across the opposite track, and hit a tangle of bushes with enough force to uproot them.

The next and final crossing was less distressing. The track beyond it ran alongside the Lorient's northernmost entry point. This checkpoint had been beefed up following the raid, and they sped up as they passed within five metres of heavily armed guards and a roadblock comprising four parked Kübelwagens and a sign saying *All Checkpoints Closed*.

The trio pumped the handcar another few hundred metres.

'I reckon that's enough,' Henderson said, as he let the handle go.

They'd intended to cruise to a stop about a kilometre beyond the edge of the city, but there was a train stalled on the opposite track half a kilometre ahead. It had been kept from completing its journey because of the raid, and while it was hard to see in the dark, it looked enough like one of the heavily guarded trains that brought men and equipment from Germany for Henderson to yank the brake and pull with all his strength.

The lever shuddered violently, shaking his whole body and sending a sharp driving pain up both arms. As they slowed to jogging pace they were passing a level patch covered with gravel and weeds. Joel jumped off first and landed with a squelch from his muddy clothes, Rosie stifled a yell as her elbow hit a rock, while Henderson landed hard and needed a hand up because his arms were numb after fighting the brake.

As the cart trundled on, they scrambled up an embankment and emerged on to a stretch of country road. Henderson recognised it from the night when they'd blown up the trains.

'We're roughly three kilometres from the cliff at Lamor Plage,' he said. 'Be ready to shoot first and ask questions later: we've got no papers and the Krauts are on high alert.'

*

Luc was a powerful swimmer. The searchlights swept across the water as he swam out of the dock. After a brief tangle with a torpedo net, he squatted on a muddy embankment and prepared himself for a long swim across the river mouth.

Water and driftwood lapped against his legs as he stripped down. He'd ditched his machine gun, backpack and grenades already, now he removed his thick outer jacket and dumped the spare ammunition from his pockets. He knew he'd swim better without his heavy boots, but didn't fancy the idea of walking barefoot on the other side.

After pulling the boots off, he tied them together by the laces and knotted them around his waist. Besides his boots, trousers and T-shirt the only equipment he had left was his hunting-knife, watch, silenced pistol and compass.

'Did you hear that?' a German asked, as he peered over the end of the dock.

By the time he'd looked down, Luc had slid off the embankment and plunged underwater.

Lorient and the Keroman dock were on a peninsula

with rivers feeding into the ocean on either side. Luc now had to swim five hundred metres to reach the opposite shore. The distance would be no problem for him in a pool, but the water was bitterly cold and the tide pushed him downstream.

As he swam, he could hear the engines of patrol boats, and caught the odd glimpse of searchlight beams, but his bobbing head was a tiny object in a huge bay and his real battle was with himself.

After ten minutes he was halfway across and felt fine, but at two-thirds distance he hit the pain barrier. Every kick strained his thighs and the shoulder he'd injured earlier was screaming for mercy. The pain was so bad that he was tempted to scream for help or ball up and let his body sink.

Somehow he made it to the far embankment, but he found himself several metres below a flood defence wall. As he swam along the wall searching for a way up he started going cross-eyed and sensed that he was close to blacking out.

The wash from a fast-moving patrol boat slammed him against the wall and when he came to he was underwater with no strength in his arms or legs. It almost didn't seem worth making the effort to surface, but when he broke back into the moonlight and took a huge yawning breath he saw a set of stone steps reflecting the moonlight.

Half convinced that his mind was playing tricks, Luc swam the hardest ten metres of his life and only believed they were real when he'd propped himself on to the first stone step. His heart pounded at more than two hundred beats per minute and he gulped air as he shivered, and clutched his sides fighting a stitch.

When he'd caught some breath he moved shakily up a couple more steps, clearing the lapping water. He untied the boots around his waist and tipped out the water before pulling them back over his feet. Whatever had been in the water around the dock was making his skin itch like crazy and his eyes were on fire as he staggered up the steps.

He kept low as he reached the landing at the top and peered out on to a tatty wooden promenade spattered with gull droppings. At the limit of his blurred vision a German pill-box was built above the wall.

The Germans were short of manpower and the chances of it being occupied were only about one in three, but he still kept low as he raced across the promenade, vaulted a wall and collapsed in a shuddering heap.

It was after curfew so being outdoors was suspicious and being outdoors in soggy British commando gear doubly so. As he crept up the alleyway and peered out he recognised the outline of a plain little church. He didn't know the place well, but he was less than a kilometre from Kerneval and he'd been here three weeks earlier, stashing some of the equipment that *Madeline II* delivered in the home of a friendly blacksmith.

He thought about visiting the blacksmith, but he couldn't remember the exact street. He checked his watch and saw that it was twenty to eleven. The extraction point was less than two kilometres from here. He'd make it if he moved quickly and didn't encounter any Germans, but with the patrols likely to be on high alert and his body weakened after the swim it would be a close thing.

*

All the beaches were well defended, so Henderson had chosen a cliff for their extraction point. He arrived with fifteen minutes to spare and located a marine signalling lamp and some supplies that Olivier and Michel had hidden under bushes that afternoon.

They all drank copious amounts of water from a canteen and Joel washed the worst of the mud from his hands and face.

'There's a German pill-box fifty metres that way, and another eighty-five metres that way,' Henderson whispered. 'So keep your heads down and your guns ready.'

At three minutes to eleven, Henderson moved up to the cliff's edge. He flashed the signalling light for an instant as Rosie looked down fifteen metres of sheer cliff face into a choppy sea.

'How do we know it's deep enough?' she asked nervously.

'Trust me,' Henderson said. 'Put your hands on your shoulders, jump two-footed. You'll be fine.'

Henderson flashed the light again, and this time he got a little flash back, from an open motorboat about a hundred metres from the cliff.

'Get the life jackets out of the bush,' Henderson said. 'Fetch mine over, and tell Joel to start strapping his on. Best if you lose some of the heavier clothes too.'

As Rosie turned around, she bumped into Joel coming the other way.

He sounded anxious. 'Someone's riding a bike up the path.'

'OK,' Henderson said, as he processed the new information. 'I've got to stay here with the signal light. Put your life vests on so that you're ready to jump if needs be, then take flanking positions covering my back and be ready to shoot if you don't see a signal. Use your silenced weapons if you possibly can.'

Rosie crawled rapidly through the long cliff top grass behind Joel with her machine gun and pistol ready. Joel pulled on a life jacket, and threw one across to Henderson.

Henderson looked down and saw a double flash from the small motorboat at the base of the cliff.

'They're in position,' he said. 'Time to go.'

Joel's eyes were fixed on the meandering path. The cycle was a women's model with a basket on the front and it wavered as if it was being pedalled by an OAP. He aimed the gun sight at the rider's chest.

'I think it's Luc,' Rosie said.

Moments later a hand came off the handlebar and punched the air three times.

'It's Luc,' Rosie told Henderson.

'Alone?'

'No sign of Antoine,' she confirmed.

Joel ran twenty metres downhill to meet Luc as he clambered off the bike. He was pouring sweat and he could hardly stand up straight.

'You look beat,' Joel said.

'I'm completely buggered,' Luc said, as Joel took his arm to help him stay upright. 'I've already thrown up twice.'

'Where's Antoine?'

'Dead,' Luc said.

Joel grabbed the water and handed it to Luc as Rosie helped him into a life jacket.

'We're ready to jump,' Henderson said, as he gave three flashes to the boat below.

'Luc's exhausted,' Rosie said.

Henderson threw the signalling lamp aside and stood up to inspect Luc. He put a hand on the boy's forehead.

'You're close to passing out,' Henderson said, as he saw Luc's eyes drifting out of focus. 'We'll jump together, holding hands, OK?'

'Right,' Luc agreed.

Rosie thought she saw something move in the long grass about thirty metres away. As she backed up from the bushes for a better look she saw a German helmet bob up above the tall grass.

'Duck,' she shouted.

They all hit the ground as a rifle-shot cracked the air above their heads. Joel rolled over and started blasting through the bushes with his Sten gun, as two more soldiers revealed themselves. The shots were wild, but they were enough to send the Germans diving for cover.

'Rosie, Joel, jump now,' Henderson ordered.

Henderson covered them with his pistol as they crawled to the cliff edge. They had to stand to jump, but the threat of being shot in the back meant that they didn't fanny around on the edge worrying about the drop.

As Rosie and Joel hit the water, Henderson spotted one of the Germans making a charge. He shot with the pistol, knocking the man down, but at the same time a shot came at Henderson from the opposite direction. The plan had been to jump individually so that the crew inside the small motor launch could focus on picking one person at a time from the water, but there was now more chance of getting shot on the cliff top than of drowning in the sea.

Henderson quickly lobbed a couple of grenades in opposite directions, then grabbed Luc's hand.

'Ready?'

A bullet whizzed overhead as they stood up and ran for the cliff's edge.

The first grenade exploded as their feet left the ground. Luc gripped Henderson's hand so tightly that it hurt as the water came towards them. They speared the sea feet first, as a half-metre wave knocked them back towards the cliff.

Henderson felt his boot touch the bottom. As he surfaced he grasped at a life preserver attached to a rope. Two tough New Zealanders hauled the rope in and within moments they were alongside the open motor launch.

'Take him first, he's weak,' Henderson shouted.

As the sailors took care of Luc, Joel and Rosie grabbed Henderson's life jacket and helped him aboard.

'Is that everyone, Captain?' one of the New Zealanders asked, as Henderson lay gasping in the bottom of the boat. 'Can we head back to HMS *Gulliver*?'

'Better get a move on before the Germans find my lantern and spot us in the water,' Henderson said.

As the small launch turned towards the British torpedo boat anchored a few hundred metres off shore,

Rosie knelt over Henderson with a look of concern.

'Are you OK?' she asked.

'Got winded when I hit the water is all,' Henderson said as he managed a slight smile. 'That and the fact that I'm getting far too bloody old for this nonsense.'

EPILOGUE

Two weeks later

The mission control building on CHERUB campus was a prefabricated Nissen hut and new enough that you could still smell wood glue and paint when you walked in. The main internal feature was a bulky radio set, which would enable direct communication with agents in the field, instead of relying on MI6 for reception and decoding as had happened up to now.

But there were currently no agents in the field, so seventeen-year-old radio operator Joyce Slater was spending most of her time working on indecipherables: transmissions where the decoded signal made no sense. She was part of a highly skilled group of girls – radio operators were all girls – with a talent for unscrambling them.

Joyce usually received five or six each morning in the secure post, and regarded it as a good day if she managed to solve half of them. Today's envelope had arrived half an hour earlier. Her first step was always to eliminate the hopeless cases. These were usually ones where the message source was a long way away, which meant it was completely garbled, or ones where the notes indicated that an able colleague had already been given a chance to solve it.

As well as the usual typed messages and accompanying notes on the codes used by the operators, today's messages came with a handwritten note from the head of the MI6 radio section:

Dear Joyce,

Caroline had a go at this first one overnight, but I thought you might do better as you and Lavender were pals.

Lavender is on sked at two p.m. today, so please let me know if you crack it so that she avoids a tiresome and risky repeat transmission.

GLT

Joyce smiled at the thought of Lavender sending an indecipherable message. They'd trained together and

Lavender had always scraped through her examinations by one or two marks.

'Right, let's see what we've got,' Joyce told herself as she grabbed a clean sheet of squared paper and pulled her wheelchair up to her desk.

Almost immediately, Joyce realised that Lavender had missed the first line of the poem she'd used to encode the message. But Caroline had also worked that out and still got nowhere. Joyce tried a few other tricks such as guessing some of the words and looking for repeated phrases or patterns, but the whole thing was utterly garbled.

Joyce was close to giving up when she remembered that Lavender had an eccentric habit of sometimes writing left to right when she encoded her messages, and sometimes top to bottom. What if she'd encoded top to bottom and transmitted left to right?

This didn't work, but what if she'd encoded left to right and transmitted top to bottom.

'Eu-*bloody*-reka!' Joyce squealed, as the words started to make sense.

The first part of the message was routine information from the Lorient resistance circuit: movements of U-boats, requests for supplies and a report that Hitler had personally ordered the hanging of the German security chief at the Lorient base after the raid. But the final part of the message made Joyce excited:

Madame Mercier has received a brief letter from Marc. His location was cut out by a censor, but he appears to be in a German labour camp awaiting a work assignment. He says he is as well as can be expected and not to worry about him.

Joyce had never met Marc, but she'd attended his memorial service and the mood on campus had been subdued ever since. She decided to tell Captain Henderson immediately.

There was a telephone within reach, but unfortunately they were still on the waiting list for an army engineer to hook it up. Joyce spun her wheelchair around and pushed herself energetically towards the door at the far end of the hut.

Beyond this door was a fairly steep ramp and she got a thrill as she wheeled down it at speed, turned in a broad arc and pushed on across the concrete playground towards the main building. Her progress was halted by the single step at the main door, but she saw someone through the frosted glass inside and yelled.

'Excuse me.'

Unfortunately it was Luc. He came to the door in his PE kit, looking strong and healthy with sweat running down his face.

'What can I do for you, legless?' he said, grinning nastily, before adopting a squeaky voice. 'Oh the little cripple girl can't get up the step. How saaaaad.'

'Let me in now, you brainless moron,' Joyce shouted.

'Not if you're going to swear at me,' Luc said, pretending to be outraged.

'Learn manners, you scum!' Instructor Takada shouted, as he came out of the school hall behind Luc. He'd been demonstrating the use of a baton to some of the younger kids and gave Luc a brutal whack across the back of the knees, knocking him to the floor. 'Sometimes I wonder if you're even human.'

As Luc rolled around the floor howling, Mr Takada helped Joyce up the step and knocked on Henderson's door. As Joyce rolled in, she saw Henderson sitting at his desk looking like it was the last place on earth he wanted to be.

'I've cracked an indecipherable, sir,' Joyce said proudly as she handed over the paper. 'And I think you're going to like what it says.'

READ ON FOR AN EXCLUSIVE FIRST CHAPTER OF THE NEXT CHERUB BOOK, *PEOPLE'S REPUBLIC*.

1. LAPS

July 2011

Three women sat in the chairwoman's office on CHERUB campus. Blinds shut out low evening sun as the air conditioner battled high summer.

'Tell me about him,' Dr D said, speaking in a brash New York accent as she studied a photo of a twelve-year-old. 'He's a good-looking boy. Do I see a touch of Arab in him?'

Dr D was tiny and the wrong side of sixty. Despite the heat she wore a tartan cape, thick grey stockings and knee-high boots. She looked like someone's cranky old secretary, but was actually a senior officer with the American intelligence service – the CIA.

Zara Asker was another spy who didn't look the part. CHERUB's forty-year-old Chairwoman sat opposite Dr D, wearing a three-quid plastic watch and her youngest son's dinner down the front of her dress.

'Ryan joined CHERUB fourteen months ago,' Zara explained. 'His grandparents were a Syrian, a German, an Irishwoman and a Pakistani.'

Dr D raised one eyebrow. 'Sounds like the first line of a bad joke.'

'Ryan was mainly brought up in Saudi Arabia and Russia. His dad was a geologist in the oil industry, but drink and gambling problems led to debts and he turned up dead under some rubbish bags. Nobody knows if it was murder or suicide. Ryan reached Britain in 2009 with his mother and three younger brothers. She'd bluffed her way into a private treatment program for a rare form of cancer, but got kicked out when she hit the limit on her credit cards. Immigration tried sending the family back to Syria, but she was too sick. She died penniless in an NHS ward, with four boys under eleven and no known family.'

'Are they all here at CHERUB?' Dr D asked.

Zara nodded. 'We never split families. Ryan's the eldest, he's got twin brothers who are about to turn ten and Theo who's seven.'

'You said Ryan's not had much mission experience,' Dr D noted.

'Just a couple of one-day things,' Zara said. 'But he's champing at the bit, and the operation you're proposing should be well within his capabilities.'

Dr D nodded as she reached forward and dropped Ryan's photo on to a glass coffee table. 'So when do I get to meet him?'

*

Ryan didn't know he was being talked about as he strolled off the campus athletics track. It was baking hot and he had a six pack showing as he stretched up the bottom of his grey T-shirt and used it to mop sweat off his face.

The twelve-year-old was muscular but not bulky. He had brown eyes, straight dark hair in need of a trim and a silver stud in a recently pierced ear. After two mouthfuls from an underpowered drinking fountain, Ryan went up three paved steps towards a tatty shed used by the athletics staff.

It was gloomy inside because the frosted window was boarded following an encounter with a football. There was nobody home, but the coaches' smell lingered in tracksuits and musty all-weather gear on wall hooks.

A clipboard on the window ledge bulged with crumpled forms. You could flip back and read through four months of minor crimes paid off with punishment laps.

A bead of sweat pelted the A4 page as Ryan grabbed the Biro-on-a-string and started filling boxes on the first blank page: *Time, date, name, agent number, laps run, reason for punishment.*

This last box irritated Ryan and he was tempted to write *No good reason.*

He had no problem accepting the tough discipline faced by agents who broke CHERUB rules, but having to run five kilometres because he'd got a fit of the giggles was ridiculous. Especially when other kids doing the same had got off.

'You holding on to that all night?' someone asked irritably.

Ryan's heavy breathing meant he hadn't heard the girl in red CHERUB shirt and pink Nikes step up behind. He reluctantly scrawled *Laughing in class*, signed his name and passed the board over.

'All yours,' he said sourly.

Ryan jogged along a gravel path towards campus' eight-storey main building. Campus was dead because loads of kids were holidaying at the CHERUB summer hostel. A lift took him up to the seventh floor, but he broke off before reaching his bedroom to get a drink from a small kitchen.

'Ryan, you reek!' Grace complained, wafting in front of her nose as he squeezed by.

Grace was Ryan's age, but a full head shorter. Her best friend Chloe sat bare-legged on the worktop between a microwave and three dessert glasses, which were halfway to becoming trifles.

The vibe was awkward because Grace was the closest

Ryan had ever come to having a girlfriend and their weekend of holding hands and awkward silences had ended with Grace lobbing macaroni cheese at his head.

'Can't help stinking,' Ryan explained, as he grabbed a pint glass from a cupboard and quarter filled it with ice chips from the dispenser in the fridge door. 'Punishment laps. In this *bloody* heat.'

The girls seemed curious as Ryan took a bottle of Diet Pepsi from inside the fridge door and poured it over the ice. As he gulped fizz, Grace bashed up pink wafer biscuits before sprinkling the crumbs over custard in the dessert glasses.

'It's not like you, Ryan,' Chloe said, with a slight tease in her voice. 'You're usually a good boy.'

'Blame Max Black,' Ryan said, before ripping off a vast Pepsi-fuelled belch.

'Dirty pig!' Chloe protested, before Ryan began his story.

'We were in Mr Bartlett's maths class. Bartlett goes out of the room to fetch something. Max and Kaitlyn had been rowing all through morning break. Kaitlyn calls Max a *mongoloid*. And you know how oranges shrivel up when they're really old?'

The girls looked mystified by this turn in the story, but nodded anyway.

'Max has got untold crap in his backpack,' Ryan said. 'I mean, he's had the same school bag for years and

I don't think he's cleaned out once: snotty tissues, socks, leaky pens. It's basically a biohazard. So he reaches down his bag and comes up with this shrunken old orange, about the size of a ping-pong ball. He throws it really hard at Kaitlyn.

'She dives out of the way, tilts off her chair and bops her head on the desk behind her. The orange whizzes on. It hits the handle of the cup on Mr Bartlett's desk. Max's throw was so hard the dried-out orange explodes and the mug does this little pirouette before toppling over.

'Earl Grey tea, almost a full cup. It goes *everywhere*. All over Bartlett's paperwork, and the desk drawer's open, so it's running in there: hole punch, staple gun, calculators, whole pack of squared paper and exercise books. Bartlett comes back inside. Kaitlyn's bawling and waving her arms around and totally milking it. Bartlett starts screaming at Max.'

Chloe and Grace were both into the story, and Ryan felt more relaxed. It was the first time he'd spoken to either of them since the macaroni incident six weeks earlier.

'So Bartlett was venting steam, going ape,' Ryan said. 'He gives Max a hundred punishment laps and sends Kaitlyn off to first aid. Then he gets everyone to calm down, but I can't stop. Like, I'm swallowing and trying to keep a straight face, but me and Alfie are wetting ourselves laughing. So Bartlett kicks us both into the corridor and gives us five kilometres of laps.'

'Harsh,' Grace said, as she topped each trifle off with aerosol cream and Maltesers. 'Bartlett's usually mellow. I can't even remember him raising his voice.'

Ryan tipped more Pepsi on to the ice. Chloe put on a serious voice. 'Well *I* don't think it's funny. Kaitlyn needed three stitches in her head.'

Ryan looked shocked. 'Seriously? Max's an idiot. He never knows when to stop.'

Chloe raised one eyebrow and burst out laughing. 'Had you going there, Rybo.'

Ryan shook his head, then smiled with relief. 'I was gonna *say*. Her head barely glanced the table. Gimme some Maltesers. Who's the third trifle for?'

'Not you, that's for sure,' Grace said, tipping brown balls into Ryan's outstretched palm.

Ryan dropped six Maltesers in his gob and crunched as he grabbed his half-drunk Pepsi glass off the worktop and headed out.

'Oi,' Chloe shouted. 'Where do you think you're going?'

Ryan backed up to the kitchen doorway and saw Grace pointing at the Pepsi bottle.

'What did your last servant die of?' she asked. 'Put it back in the fridge.'

Ryan stepped back grumpily. He was knackered and

the girls had loads of stuff out on the worktop already.

'Putting one bottle back's hardly gonna kill you,' Ryan said.

'We might kill *you* if you don't,' Chloe said, as she jumped down off the cabinet. She was barefoot and Ryan's eyes fixed on her painted toenails as he opened the fridge door and bent forwards to slot the Pepsi back inside the door.

If he'd looked the other way he might have seen Grace before she yanked the elastic of his shorts and fired a long blast of cream towards his butt crack.

'Yuk, it's all sweaty down there,' Grace yelled, shielding her eyes as the aerosol whooshed.

Ryan tried backing out, but Chloe was pushing on the fridge door, wedging him in place until the can gave its last gasp.

'Cameraphone, cameraphone!' Grace said.

Chloe let go of the fridge as the empty can clanked against the floor tiles. As Ryan straightened up Grace smacked his bum, making the whipped cream explode out of his shorts. Then an iPhone camera flashed.

'Psychos,' Ryan shouted. 'What was for?'

'The hell of it,' Grace said.

The second photo was the best shot, showing Ryan's face halfway between laughter and fury, with cream streaking out the bottom of his running shorts and dribbling down his thighs. The third showed Ryan lunging towards the iPhone, while Grace leaned into the frame with a mad grin and a double thumbs-up.

'You wait,' Ryan yelled, as he waddled towards his room like he'd crapped himself. 'You'd both better watch your backs.'

'We're really scared, Rybo,' Grace shouted, between howls of laughter.

They both knew he hated being called Rybo.

'Rybo, Rybo, Ryboooooo!' Chloe said, making it sound like a football chant.

Ryan slammed the door of his room and turned the key so the girls couldn't get in.

If tough training and punishments were the downside of being a CHERUB agent, the bedrooms were the biggest perk. Ryan had a comfortable space, with a leather sofa and TV one side of the door and a mini fridge and microwave on the other. His bed was a double and a large desk with a laptop and schoolbooks on it stood by the window.

Not wanting the cream streaking down his legs to end up on his carpet, Ryan took three long strides and cut into his bathroom. Rather than mess up the floor, he stepped into his bath fully clothed: any gunk left in the tub would wash away when he turned the taps on.

Once his trainers were off, Ryan turned on the shower head. As the water got warm he stripped off, letting sweaty, cream-soaked clothes rinse in the swirling pool around the plughole.

His T-shirt was clingy and stuck halfway over his head when a phone started ringing.

'Tits!'

There was a handset mounted on the wall beside his toilet. Ryan was in two minds about answering. It was probably Grace and Chloe on a wind-up, but could also be something important. He almost slipped as he reached over and stretched the curly-corded handset across the room.

'Ryan, it's Zara.'

Ryan jolted. The chairwoman only called individual agents for serious business, like an important mission, or the kind of trouble that earned punishments far graver than laps. It was hard to hear so he used a soggy-socked foot to turn off the shower.

'What do you want?' Ryan asked nervously, as his brain flipped through possibilities.

'Just yourself,' Zara said. 'I've got two people down here who'd like to meet you.'

THE ESCAPE
Robert Muchamore

Hitler's army is advancing towards Paris, and amidst the chaos, two British children are being hunted by German agents. British spy Charles Henderson tries to reach them first, but he can only do it with the help of a twelve-year-old French orphan.

The British secret service is about to discover that kids working undercover will help to win the war.

Book 1 – OUT NOW

www.hendersonsboys.com

Hodder Children's Books

SECRET ARMY
Robert Muchamore

The government is building a secret army of intelligence agents to work undercover. Henderson's boys are part of that network: kids cut adrift by the war, training for the fight of their lives. They'll have to parachute into unknown territory, travel cross-country and outsmart a bunch of adults in a daredevil exercise.

In wartime Britain, anything goes.

Book 3 – OUT NOW

www.hendersonsboys.com

Hodder
Children's
Books

THE RECRUIT
Robert Muchamore

The Recruit tells James's story from the day his mother dies. Read about his transformation from a couch potato into a skilled CHERUB agent.

Meet Lauren, Kerry and the rest of the cherubs for the first time, and learn how James foiled the biggest terrorist massacre in British history.

The first explosive CHERUB mission.

THE RECRUIT
Robert Muchamore

Book 1 – OUT NOW

Also available as an ebook

www.cherubcampus.com

Hodder Children's Books

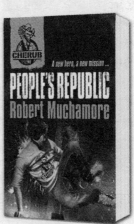